Worlds Apart

Joy Taylor

Published: 2026 by The Book Reality Experience,
Leschenault, Western Australia

ISBN: 9781923454354 - Paperback
ISBN: 9781923454361 - E-Book
****

Cover Design by Brittany Wilson | Brittwilsonart.com

For Susan

Prologue

About 18 years ago in Perfection

She got past the security guards with a smile. It was late at night, but Stuart recognised the young wife of the director of Advanced Laboratories.

He leant out of the window of the guardhouse. That smile — he'd always thought it lit up her face,

"Hi Anna, you've just missed Mr. Rochester. He left ten minutes ago."

"Yes, I know," she said, still smiling. "He phoned me. He's on his way to the airport, left his wallet in the office." She raised her eyes in a little exasperated signal. "I'm picking it up for him."

Stuart watched her fingers tapping the steering wheel. She was in a hurry — he could see that. He turned to the other guard beside him and nodded.

As the gates began to slide open, he kept watching her. She flicked her gaze away. Breathe, she told herself. You're doing ok. Her tongue ran across her dry lips. One hand moved to rest on her stomach. Stuart hadn't noticed before — it had started to show.

"How long now then?" he asked softly, his voice dropping as though afraid to startle the baby.

She didn't answer, just twisted her hands on the wheel. The slow steel gates kept rolling back. Stuart suddenly felt awkward. Maybe he shouldn't have asked. But it was obvious; everyone at "Advanced" knew that Rochester was going to be a father and they pitied any kid of his.

Stuart had a daughter her age. He wouldn't want her married to Victor Rochester for all the money in the world.

Anna was watching the gates, the engine purred as her foot tapped the accelerator; she didn't look back at him.

"Two months," she said, as the car lurched forward.

"Whoa, take it easy," Stuart called after her, but she wasn't listening. She was already thinking of escape.

CHAPTER ONE

6 weeks ago, in Perfection

Scott punched the air with his fist. "We're in, Lewis! We're in!" His voice rang with excitement.

Lewis didn't look up from the map he was studying. He didn't look surprised—he'd known they would pass. There had never been a doubt in his mind that he would make it through the two months of training. Scott, though… Scott had been a different matter. Impulsive. Unfocused. Lewis had spent most of the time pulling him into line, trying to get him to concentrate instead of chasing girls.

"Did you hear me?" Scott swivelled around in his chair, grinning wildly. "We're in!"

They were alone in the **Secured Documents** room of the **Perfect World Security Bureau—The Bureau,** as everyone called it.

Outside the reinforced, bulletproof, glass-lined room, the late-night librarian, Lilian, sat at her desk, reviewing the catalogue of incoming research material. She glanced over at Lewis and Scott. Scott was waving his arms around and pumping the air. She guessed he had just read the admission notice.

She had seen the results earlier and recognised their names. The selection training had ended three weeks ago—they had made it through.

Admission to the Bureau was no easy feat. Each year, thousands applied. Four hundred were chosen for provisional training. After two months of intense testing, only the best became cadets.

Lilian's gaze returned to the boys. The one with the curly hair—Scott— was clearly thrilled. She tapped her pen against her lips. Yes, Scott. He was the friendly one. The other, taller, dark-haired boy—Lewis—seemed bored, as always.

She narrowed her eyes. Too many students passed through the library to remember them all, but the friendly ones stayed with her. Scott had smiled at her that first week.

"How's your day so far, Lilian?" he'd asked.

He had bothered to learn her name. She remembered him. That dark-eyed boy with the springy curls. He'd smiled and added, "We'll try not to bother you for anything."

She liked his curls. Felt a quiet, ridiculous urge to run her fingers through them. She resisted.

Her expression flattened when she looked at Lewis. He was in here nearly every day, always needing documents. Not quite demanding, but never warm. He acted like access was his right—which, yes, it *was* a library—but it was the *way* he spoke. Aloof. As if addressing a filing cabinet.

She hadn't seen him smile. Not properly. Once, maybe—a half-smile, more like a twitch—but even then, it had felt off.

She remembered the moment. She'd been searching for the material Lewis wanted while he and Scott waited near the counter. A new student—Poppy— had walked into the library. Not walked—sauntered. Like she was being filmed. Lilian recognised her. Blonde. Blue-eyed. Pretty. Definitely not her favourite flower.

Poppy gave her hair a flick and blew a kiss in the boys' direction. Lewis didn't react. Just stared through her like she wasn't there. But Scott? He waved back with a grin and turned to Lewis.

"Did you see that, Lew? Poppy likes me. I'm taking her to the Enders' Farewell—no question."

Lilian had smiled. *Lucky girl,* she'd thought.

That was when she'd seen Lewis's version of a smile. A curl of the lip - dismissive. Not kind.

That's how **she** saw it.

What Lewis had actually been reacting to was the idea of a *farewell event* for those who hadn't made the cut. He couldn't imagine anything worse—losers trying to be upbeat, winners trying not to gloat. Everyone pretending to be the most witty, vivacious version of themselves.

Scott was nothing if not optimistic. "Can you believe it!" Scott leapt up from his chair, practically doing a war dance of excitement. He stopped, ran both hands through his curls, pushing them back until his hair stood on end.

"You know," he said, suddenly serious, "I couldn't have done it without you, Lewis. You know that, right? Can you believe it?" He grinned again.

Lewis did know. And yes, he could believe it. He'd worked hard to get selected—and dragged Scott with him. He'd coached him through the written and oral tests, all five Bureau manuals, and now he was buried in the history of DZ168. And truth be told, he wasn't surprised. He'd been told the results four days ago—by none other than Sampson Monk, the Director of the Bureau.

Lewis had received the summons late at night, a day after the final exam: a direct call from Monk.

Scott had been out partying with the intake girls. One of them was Poppy. Scott had been obsessed with her from day one—ever since their eyes locked at the first training session. But someone had to focus on the job of getting into the Bureau, and it clearly wasn't going to be Scott.

Monk had wanted to see *both* of them. Lewis tried to reach Scott, left a message, and then went on his own.

Monk's first words were a bark. "Where's Streathfield? Why isn't he here? We can't get him on the phone." He shot Lewis a look of irritation.

Lewis shrugged. Scott wasn't his responsibility.

"I'm here, sir. I can relay your message."

Monk rolled his eyes toward the ceiling. "No. That's not how we do things in the Bureau. You should know that. I'll speak to him personally. You won't."

He leaned back in his chair. "You and Streathfield have passed. You've both been selected for a mission."

Lewis raised an eyebrow. A *mission*? Before they'd even begun the full three-year training?

Monk gave a slow nod. "This is something of an exception," he said, choosing his words carefully. "A relatively straightforward operation. It's urgent. You'll receive intensive preparation beforehand. You'll both get a full briefing—later."

He steepled his fingers, studying them for a moment, then looked at Lewis from under his thick brows.

Lewis had already stood out. He was calm, analytical. He didn't speak unless he had something worth saying. He didn't ask asinine questions. Monk appreciated that. The Bureau needed agents who could think.

There was only one reason they had been selected thought Lewis. He gave a small nod, "Our age, sir. Essential criteria for the mission, I assume." *A mission. I'm going on a mission.*

Monk suppressed a smile. Any other student would have jumped out of their chair at the news. But not Lewis. He didn't show emotion. Monk approved.

"Yes," Monk said. "You'll need to infiltrate a college."

That was all he'd reveal for now. He wanted both boys present for the full briefing.

You didn't need to be a genius to figure it out. Lewis and Scott were both nineteen. They would blend in. Look the part.

Lewis absently touched his chin, feeling the rough stubble. He took after his father—could grow a beard in two weeks. Give him another year or two and he'd be the same.

Monk checked his watch. "I'll be away for a few days. I'll speak to Streathfield when I return. You—"

"—won't," said Lewis.

Monk nodded slightly. "Good. I'll see you both after the Enders Ball. Briefing will follow. Understood?"

"Security level?" Lewis asked casually. But Monk heard the faintest edge in his voice—maybe suppressed excitement.

Lewis crossed his fingers in his mind. *Please be five. Let it be five.*

The lamp on Monk's desk caught his eyes and made them glow like coals. He placed his hands flat on the surface of his desk. The meeting was over. He stood. Lewis stood at the same time.

"Five," Monk said, as if it meant nothing. He didn't meet Lewis's eyes.

"Location SHC7, Section DZ 168. I suggest you look into it—quietly." Lewis walked back to the student block. He wanted to run. Wanted to burst into the dorm and yell at Scott, "We're going on a mission! Security level five!" But he didn't. He walked slowly, hands in his pockets, mind buzzing.

Security level five. That meant one thing. The mission was *out of this world.*

He stopped under the night sky and looked up at the stars. Somewhere out there. He grinned. *I'm going there—to the parallel universe that bumps up against our world.*

Scott stopped dancing around the secure documents room and leaned back over his laptop.

"Dave Gilmore's in… Remmy Stewart…" He scanned the admission list, eyes flicking quickly down the names.

"Helen Barlow… Verona Stotsw—whatever her name is… knew she'd get in… the twins…"

He was really looking for one name. Poppy. She had to have made it. He smiled to himself when he saw it. Yep—she was there. He skipped over her quickly, pretending not to care, then continued reading aloud.

Lewis looked up from the map in front of him. He knew exactly who Scott was searching for.

"Soppy Poppy?" he said mildly. He still couldn't believe she had even made the first cut.

"Not that soppy," Scott grinned, turning to him. "She got in."

Lewis raised an eyebrow.

Scott flicked off the screen and wandered over to peer over Lewis's shoulder. "Stop studying, man. Let's celebrate! Campus bar's open—few drinks. The others will be there too."

Lewis gritted his teeth. He couldn't tell Scott the real reason he wasn't in the mood to celebrate—because something a hundred times bigger was four weeks away.

He'd already tried to steer Scott away from Poppy early on. "Maybe give the girls a break," he'd said. "Focus on passing the entrance exams."

"It's working great, isn't it?" Scott had replied. "You study, then teach me. Teamwork!"

That wasn't exactly how Lewis saw it. *He* did all the heavy lifting—figuring everything out, then handing Scott the answers. Right now, he was trying to locate SHC7—Southern Hemisphere, Location 7, Section 168. He didn't bother hiding his mild annoyance. Scott only had one thing on his mind.

Lewis still couldn't quite believe Poppy had passed. She'd been a latecomer, joining halfway through the selection phase. He didn't get it. She seemed… vacuous. All hair twirls and pouts. But apparently, looks could be deceiving.

"Who else will be there?" he asked, raising an eyebrow.

"Yeh, come on, man," said Scott. "She's gorgeous. You know it. I've seen you looking at her."

Lewis shrugged. He had glanced at her—who hadn't? Poppy was hard to ignore. *Mesmerising* in a way that annoyed him.

"You go ahead," said Lewis, leaning back in his chair and stretching. "I just want to check something first."

Scott didn't bother asking what—Lewis was always checking *something*.

"Okay," he said, grabbing his jacket. "See you in ten. You gotta chill, man. You'll blow a gasket with all that studying."

"Yeah, but look where all the studying got… *us*," Lewis said softly.

"And now it's time to celebrate." Scott punched Lewis on the arm and headed out.

He knew Lewis was right. Without all the hours Lewis had spent studying—for both of them—he wouldn't have even made it into the preliminary admissions round.

Scott recognised that. He was grateful. In return, he had made it his unofficial job to take charge of Lewis's social life. It wasn't easy. Lewis was a loner by nature. He liked girls but hated socialising, especially the small talk that came with it. Most students thought he was arrogant or just plain cold.

"Nah, he's not," Scott would say whenever he had to defend him. "He's just reserved."

Still… sometimes he wondered if that was all it was. He hadn't known Lewis that long—just a couple of years. They had first met at seventeen, competing at the interschool sports carnival.

It was the long-distance event—five kilometres. The two of them were leading the field, only a pace apart as they rounded the final bend. The roar of the crowd—eight schools' worth of spectators—was deafening.

Lewis never tired of that sound. He had won every race before—usually winning by a clear fifty metres. But the boy behind him, the one with the mop of bouncing curls, wasn't falling back.

Lewis pushed harder, trying to break away. But Scott didn't fall behind. Then, just ahead, Lewis spotted it out of the corner of his eye—a black-and-white dog, bolting toward the track. Lewis shortened his stride. The dog dashed past him. Scott wasn't so lucky Lewis saw him go down. Heard the sickening crack, the yell of pain.

He hesitated.

The boy, or the finish line?

The boy, or the win?

He saw the pack charging down the straight—and then his mother's voice in his head, sharp and familiar. *Keep going, Lewis. Don't stop. Keep going.*

He won. But it was a hollow victory. His mother was jubilant. "Your race, Lewis. You would have won anyway."

Later, his father came over, a worried look on his face. "It was a close race… that other boy, Scott something, he's okay." He glanced at his wife, the winner's cup in her hands. "They think he broke his arm."

"It wasn't Lewis's fault," his mother snapped. She could hear the sadness in her husband's voice. "He won. There's no time for sentiment in a race. No prizes for coming second." Her eyes burned into Lewis's father.

"It's not about winning," he said quietly. "It's about trying. It's about…" But he didn't finish the sentence.

Lewis never found out what his father would have said. He moved out not long after, taking a job on the far side of Perfection. They still talked—every week—but the calls were awkward. Lewis wasn't good at small talk.

After that, he lost interest in athletics. He told his mother he needed to focus on exams.

"Good idea, Lewis," she said. "Make sure you top the year again."

He did. And that year, Scott won the long-distance race—with a record-breaking time.

Lewis enrolled at Rochester Senior Academy for his final year. On the first day in the school canteen, the curly-haired boy from the race walked over to his table.

"Hey, you're Lewis—the guy who beat me last year. Might not have happened if this hadn't broken." He held up his left arm and grinned. "You just start here?"

"Yeah. First day. And—no doubt about it—you would've won. I saw your time. Faster than mine."

He wanted to say sorry. But he could still hear his mother's voice: Don't you dare.

Two girls wandered over. Scott gestured to the chairs. "Join us." Lewis didn't want company—but the girls were only inviting Scott to a party. Somehow, Lewis got roped in too. That's how they started hanging out.

His mother didn't like Scott. Too charming, too unserious. She worried he'd be a distraction. But she never said so directly—instead, she invited him to the house, where she could keep watch.

Lewis once told Scott he hoped to get into the Bureau. "Travel. That's what I want. Who knows… I might go through the looking glass."

"No kidding! That's what I want. Already put in my application. Gotta do it early," said Scott. That sealed the friendship.

Scott understood that going through the looking glass meant crossing into that other world—the one brushing up against theirs. A world on the edge of extinction, two hundred years left if it was lucky. That world didn't know they existed—and Perfection wanted it to stay that way.

Lewis soon realised 'focus' wasn't part of Scott's vocabulary. Girls were his biggest distraction. He was outgoing and social. Lewis preferred silence.

Still, Scott valued the friendship. Lewis might be cold, but he was solid. Dependable. He had Scott's back.

Scott often saw Lewis's mild irritation. That raised eyebrow. That faraway look. Most of the time, it felt like Lewis was doing everyone a favour just by being there. And yet, the girls still chased him.

"They're trying to break through that cold exterior," Scott teased once. "I think there's a bet going. Money's riding on it."

"You're kidding," said Lewis, horrified. "Tell them the heart's beating fine. Tell them… they're all… very… god… delightful."

"Delightful? Never say that to a girl!" Scott groaned. "Try 'gorgeous,' 'sexy,' 'irresistible'—"

"Stop. Got it. Charm school later. Right now, focus on the Bureau."

Lewis could prioritise. Girls could wait. The Bureau mattered more. He did the studying for both. Coached Scott through Senior College. Got them both into the PWSB Academy. Lewis topped the exam. His mother was thrilled.

After Scott left the library, Lewis went back to his map. Section 168. A vast landmass surrounded by ocean. Scattered islands. Dense coastal cities. A desert in the centre.

He zoomed in on the western coastline. Streets fanned inland from a road hugging the ocean. He studied the road network slowly, brushing his hair back from his forehead.

He grinned. It was going to be easy. A walk in the park. Might even be that park right there, he thought, placing a finger over a green square.

Then he headed off to join Scott.

CHAPTER TWO

The bar in the oak-lined dining hall was packed. Lewis paused at the entrance, scanning the room for Scott. Even some of the students who had failed the entrance exams were there, laughing and drinking, as if nothing had happened.

Students jostled for space at the bar, but Lewis looked past them, his eyes sweeping the shadowy booths along the perimeter. He spotted Scott with a group of students. Poppy was there too, sitting close—too close—her golden hair brushing Scott's cheek. Scott's head was bent towards her, his lips seeming to graze her skin. Lewis shook his head. Scott was making progress. He sighed. *Damn, he'll never concentrate now.*

"Lewis! Here!" Scott's voice rang out as he waved a hand high in the air. Lewis pointed to the bar, detouring to buy himself a drink before heading over.

Dave Gilmore sat next to Helen, one arm casually draped behind her chair. The moment she'd felt the pressure of his arm on her neck, Helen had leaned away. Now, she was angled across the small low table, talking to the twins—Rose and Daisy. She hoped Gilmore got the message: she wasn't interested.

Lewis reached the group's edge. There was one seat left—next to Poppy. She wore tiny white shorts and a red halter top, her tanned skin glowing under the amber lights. Lewis hesitated. He preferred standing. Or the floor. Something about Poppy put him on edge.

"Lew, you made it! Dragged yourself away, or did Lilian kick you out?" said Scott, grinning.

"Lilian kick me out. She adores me," Lewis replied.

Poppy leaned in closer to Scott, murmuring something Lewis didn't catch. Whatever it was, it made Scott laugh.

"Ha! Right," said Scott, gesturing toward the empty seat beside her. "Come, sit."

Poppy looked up at Lewis. Her long blonde hair spilled over bare shoulders, and she blinked at him slowly. She wasn't smiling.

Lewis turned his attention to his glass. *Poppy is dangerous*, he thought. She reminded him of Cleo, a cat they'd once had. Unpredictable—purring one minute, clawing the next. Though he'd never seen Poppy do either, the feeling was the same.

Poppy edged even closer to Scott, still watching Lewis. He had no choice now but to sit beside her. Her bare arm brushed Scott's, and Scott gave Lewis a raised-eyebrow grin.

"Grats," said Gilmore, raising his glass.

Lewis, perched stiffly on the seat, made sure no part of him touched Poppy. There wasn't enough space at the table. Helen looked uncomfortable, leaning forward to avoid Gilmore. The twins moved as one, shifting closer to Helen to make more room—but Scott wasn't budging from Poppy's side.

Lewis lifted his glass. "Congratulations." He winced at the abbreviation—*grats*—it grated on him like Daisy's laugh, which was building, building...and there it was: a top 'C' screech.

"Here's to us!" Gilmore shouted. "The next secret service agents!"

Lewis raised his eyebrows. *Well, not much of a secret now, is it?*

Helen had been watching Scott. Everyone knew he was keen on Poppy; he hadn't exactly kept it to himself. She bit her bottom lip. Poppy was smiling, laughing at Scott—while pressing her thigh against Lewis. *What are you doing?* Helen wondered.

She caught Lewis's eye across the table. He wasn't great at reading girls' faces. She widened her eyes slightly, glancing from Scott to Poppy and then back at him.

Lewis frowned. *Nope. No idea what that look means.* He could read maps, decode puzzles, solve complicated problems—but not girls. He liked them, sure. Just not now. Not when he was on the threshold of something bigger. Something *out of this world.*

***

Twenty-four hours later, they were stepping out of Monk's office. Scott had finally heard what Lewis already knew: they'd been selected for a mission. Scott hadn't stopped talking since.

"Quiet, Scott," Lewis hissed, glancing around. "Security, remember?"

"Chill," said Scott, punching Lewis's arm. "I forgot, okay? I'm just... this is huge! You can't tell me you're not excited."

Lewis didn't reply. He was still trying to process what Monk had said. A mission—under the radar, Monk had emphasized. Twice. What did that mean, exactly? And who was the seventeen—nearly eighteen—year-old girl they were meant to extract? And why? Hands shoved deep into his pockets, Lewis replayed the scene in his head.

"You don't need the details," Monk had said. "You just need to know it's a female."

Lewis remembered the way Monk had shut his laptop with a definitive snap, fixing him with a cold, flat stare. That look—*follow orders*—Lewis understood.

Then Monk's tone had shifted, just slightly. "The operation will run smoothly. Just follow instructions." He'd walked them to the door. "Training starts tomorrow. The lab. Eight a.m."

"Can you believe it?" Scott said again. He tugged at Lewis's sleeve. "What's up?"

"Nothing. I was just thinking. Something doesn't feel—"

"—Give it a break. You think too much, Lewis."

The next two weeks, Scott showed up on time for every lab session. Lewis was quietly grateful there was no Poppy to distract him. The rest of the students who'd passed the admission test were on break before the Academy term officially began.

The training focused mostly on undercover work, surveillance, and technical skills. But Monk had added an unexpected module: socialising.

Scott thought it was a waste of time. *He* didn't need help socialising, Lewis did. After their final session with Dr Frost on body language, she'd praised Scott for his near-perfect score.

"To be expected," said Lewis, pressing his fingers to his temples. His head was throbbing. "You've been practising since your voice broke."

He envied Scott. Lewis was struggling with this part of the training.

"Don't worry," Scott said as they left the lab and made their way to the canteen. "We make a good team—I'm good at this, and you're good at the rest!"

Lewis dismissed the idea of failure. He *was* confident. He *had* to be. In a real mission, with a clear objective, he could do it. He told himself that he'd never cared much about this before—he'd been too focused on his career. But now, socialising was part of the job.

I can do it, he thought. *Yes. I can do it.*

"What's next?" asked Scott.

"The implant," said Lewis, cutting across the lawn toward the lab. He wasn't looking forward to it.

Inside the pristine white laboratory, it was just Lewis, Scott, Monk, and two technicians. The room gleamed like the inside of a spaceship. Lewis felt the unease crawl higher in his chest.

The implant would be positioned just behind his left ear—a tiny transmitter designed to download assimilation data. It would help him blend into the teenage culture of DZ168 and keep him connected to Monk and the team.

"I'll go first," said Scott, straddling the operating chair and resting his forehead against the padded headrest. He knew Lewis was tense about this part—having a foreign object placed under your skin, near your brain.

"It's only on the surface," Scott said. "Smaller than a pinhead. You saw the video."

"I know," Lewis muttered. "Didn't say I liked the idea of getting my head drilled." *And I still don't,* he thought as the steel dome was lowered over Scott's head. One of the technicians spoke calmly from the screen behind them.

"Lowering now... then the clamp... and a sting, okay?"

"Great," Scott said cheerfully.

Did you really say great? Lewis didn't flinch, but he couldn't keep the tension from his posture. He shoved his hands deep into his pockets and watched.

The procedure took less than fifteen seconds. Scott didn't make a sound.

Monk observed silently, arms folded, then stepped forward, glancing at the data-filled screen beside the technician. The technician nodded. "It's good to go."

Monk tapped Scott on the shoulder. "You're done."

Scott swung his leg over the chair and turned to Lewis. "Nothing to it," he said.

He was right, Lewis thought moments later, as the dome was lifted from *his* head. It was nothing—just a sting. He touched the back of his ear, fingers brushing through his hair until he found the warm, almost imperceptible dot of metal.

Monk gestured to the wall of screens. Streams of coloured lights flowed across the displays.

"They're both working fine," the technician confirmed.

"The assimilation program will be downloaded just before you exit," said Monk, rubbing his hands together. "It will provide the essential data to help you transition smoothly into DZ168. It also lets us monitor your location." He turned to the technician. "Smith, activate the locator."

Lewis wasn't sure if he actually felt the buzz behind his ear or if it was just the idea of it, but two amber lights pulsed on the screen.

"Wow," said Scott, moving toward the display.

"It's not live until you pass through the exit," Monk said to Lewis, noting the flicker of discomfort in his eyes. "And when you return, it's removed. Painless. You could do it yourself with the right equipment."

He paused, then added, "Carry on as usual for the next four days. The rest of the students are returning today. You've got the admission dinner tomorrow night—you should both go. Then the weekend as normal. Monday, you will attend your first class and be assigned skydiving training at Settlefield Airbase. You leave that evening."

"Great! Sky dive training," Scott said brightly.

Monk turned to look at him. He hoped he hadn't misjudged Scott. The boy was impulsive. Thoughtless, sometimes. Monk's eyes drifted to Lewis. He saw the muscle jump in his jaw.

Lewis leaned toward Scott and murmured, "There is no sky dive training. It's our cover story—explains our absence."

Monk's mouth thinned. "Yes. Neither of you will be going to the air base, nor will any other students. It's a legitimate explanation, nothing more."

There was a sharpness in his tone that made Scott straighten, rolling his shoulders and offering a nod. A simple mistake. Anyone could have made it.

"I suggest now that you know the mission location, you use the library," Monk said. "Familiarise yourselves with the region's history. "He looked directly at Scott. "Any questions?"

Scott shook his head. He *did* have a question—why learn the history when the data was downloadable? But he wasn't about to ask Monk. He'd ask Lewis later. Lewis didn't look at him like he was a child the way Monk did.

Monk turned to Lewis. "Questions?"

"No," Lewis said. "Perfectly clear. Heading to the library now."

CHAPTER THREE

They had only been in the library for twenty minutes when Scott leaned back in his seat and yawned loudly. "That's it, Lew. I've had enough. My brain can't take in any more information. The download's going to provide everything we need." He stood up and faced Lewis across the table.

The library was empty. Lillian wasn't at her desk. Lewis lifted his head from the screen and glared at Scott. He lowered his voice and whispered furiously, "You do realise we've been selected out of all the graduates? We haven't even started training yet… we'll be the youngest ever to enter that world."

He still couldn't believe it—they were just days away from the biggest adventure of their lives. This opportunity would probably never come again. They'd been chosen to go to DZ168. Only a handful of people had ever been granted a pass into the universe that pressed against theirs. And no one got through without a damn good reason—and a security check that left nothing to chance.

It was both exhilarating and terrifying. He knew exactly why Scott wanted to leave—to go find Poppy. Lewis gritted his teeth. He wanted to call Scott out, tell him he was being a selfish idiot—but he wouldn't lose control. He took a breath and said, more quietly, "You heard Monk. He told us to research the history."

Scott could see Lewis wasn't backing down—his jaw was clenched, and he was giving him that familiar death stare with those ice-grey eyes.

"Okay, okay. Are you ever going to let your hair down? It's long enough," Scott muttered, slumping back into his seat.

"What do you want me to look at?" he added, clearly less than enthusiastic.

Lewis frowned. "I don't know—what might be useful in a world you've never been to? How about the history of DZ, a few hundred years back? I read that the place we're heading to was untouched for thousands of years.

The original Indigenous people had a connection to the land—until they got invaded or something. Might be important we know that."

He could see Scott wasn't convinced.

"Oh, come on, Lewis. That'll all be downloaded. We won't have to learn that stuff—the history will be embedded."

Lewis stifled a sigh. "No, not all of it. That's why Monk sent us to the library. Just do it, Scott. We need to have every thing covered in case something goes wrong."

Scott grumbled but began flicking through the databanks. He typed in the location and hit 'History,' scrolling through the years. He thought to ask Lewis how far back to go, but Lewis didn't look in the mood for questions. He opened a page headed '18th Century England' and hit the summary button.

Meanwhile, Lewis pushed his hair back and searched through world news from the other world. It was all disaster: global warming, rising sea levels, famine, pollution, wars, plagues. What kind of dangers were they walking into? It wasn't called DZ for nothing – danger zone.

"Hey," Scott said, his voice tight. Lewis looked up.

"Listen to this." Scott read aloud: "In 1788, the British First Fleet of eleven ships, carrying about 1,500 people, arrived at Botany Bay. Seven hundred and seventy-eight were convicts. About 160,000 convicts were brought to Australia between 1788 and 1868."

He looked at Lewis, eyes wide. "You know what that means, right? It's a place full of descendants of convicts. Criminals. Man... more dangerous than we knew."

Lewis couldn't tell if the look in Scott's eyes was fear or excitement.

"Could be," he said, not wanting to disappoint Scott's sense of drama.

"I didn't realise history could be this interesting," said Scott, clicking into '19th Century Regency England'.

***

Three Days Before the Exit

Lewis and Scott were in the Academy canteen when the message came: Monk wanted to see them. The meeting was brief. Monk told them they were to meet someone important—a generous benefactor of the Academy and the man who had funded the student recreation centre. A car would collect them in two hours.

Lewis wondered if they would finally learn more about the girl they had to locate. So far, the briefing had been sparse: find a missing person and bring her back to Perfection.

He'd asked Monk again for more detail, but the man had silenced him with a hard look. "You'll get everything you need—when you get there. We have a contact in DZ. His name is Cross. He'll meet you at the exit point—their exit point. He's arranged everything."

Lewis understood the mission was classified, but filling in the blanks this late made him uneasy. He liked to plan, to understand the objective. He said as much to Scott.

"Fuck, you worry too much," Scott replied. "Let someone else do the planning. We'll just go along for the ride."

"We're not soldiers being sent over the top." Lewis's jaw was tight. This surprise summons to a private residence was making him nervous.

"What top?" said Scott.

Lewis didn't answer. He knew Scott hadn't done the homework—hadn't read about the major wars in DZ, especially the first world war. He didn't know that "going over the top" meant climbing out of the trenches and charging toward near-certain death.

The car that came for them was sleek—a solar-powered limousine. It glided silently out of the city and onto the freeway. Scott spent the trip on his phone, talking to Poppy. Lewis tried to block it out.

Nauseating, Scott. Give it a rest.

They left the freeway, passed through small towns, and finally crested a hill overlooking the ocean. In the distance, a gleaming white building rose from a sea of green fields.

Scott whistled. "Wow. That's where we're going? Some kind of frigging palace."

"Manor," Lewis corrected. He recognised it—one of the few preserved stately homes. He also knew who owned it.

The car followed a winding road, disappearing behind a tall cream sandstone wall. At the ornate iron gates, the driver entered a code, and they slid open. Ahead stood the manor—three stories of white stone, set back along a perfectly trimmed avenue of trees. The sun caught the windows, throwing an orange flare that made the building look as though it was on fire.

A deep portico and broad steps led to a recessed entrance. Beside the steps, a dark blue car was parked.

The front door opened. Monk appeared, followed by a tall man with auburn hair. Monk said something to him, then hurried down the steps, glanced back once, and climbed into his car.

"That was Monk," Scott said.

"Yeah and that's Rochester."

Lewis had been right. The man standing on the steps was Victor Rochester—benefactor of the Bureau, owner of the house, and director of Advanced Laboratories, the research giant credited with eliminating all known disease in Perfection.

Rochester waited as they stepped from the car. He extended his hand but didn't introduce himself. Everyone already knew who he was.

"The two top students from the admissions programme," he said, shaking Scott's hand. "And you are?"

"Scott Streatham. Jeez, this place is amazing," Scott said, arms wide.

Rochester frowned at the gesture. He disliked dramatics.

"You must be Lewis," he said, turning to shake his hand.

"Come in," he gestured towards the open doors.

They followed Rochester along polished floorboards, beneath high vaulted ceilings and alongside a gallery of modern art and gilt-framed old masters.

"Here," said Rochester, pushing open a door, "my study, it has the best view in the house."

Some study, thought Lewis, bigger than the house he had lived in with his mother.

A marble-topped desk faced a wall of glass, so clear that you could have thought there was no barrier to the grassed area beyond and the view across the undulating blue ocean.

Rochester indicated two deep green velvet chairs either side of the desk. "Take a seat, I'll just ring for something to drink; juice for you boys?" He didn't wait for an answer, he pressed a button on his phone. "Three glasses of fresh-pressed orange juice, my study now." He leant back in his chair and rested his fingertips on the desk. He drew his brows together and looked steadily at Lewis. "I know that you are both undertaking a mission... but..." he waved his hand in the air.

Lewis kept his face still. *He knows about the mission?* Scott wasn't listening; he had just felt his phone buzz in his pocket and he wanted to look at it. Poppy was on his mind.

"I know nothing of its nature..." Rochester raised his eyebrows as if to say 'of course.'

That's a lie. Lewis stared back.

Lewis looked towards the door as a middle-aged woman entered carrying a tray of drinks. Rochester turned his head, moved two small black boxes on his desk to the side, and made room for the silver tray. The woman handed the glasses around. She looked at Rochester, a question in her eyes. He dismissed her with a flick of his hand and she turned and left the room.

Rochester held the orange juice under his nose. "I always think it smells nicer than it tastes," he said, taking a small sip. He made a face and put the glass on the table. He studied the orange juice as he spoke. "You probably aren't aware that I take a keen interest in the progress of the students." He raised his eyes to Lewis. "I understand that you topped the finals of the admission exam, with a near perfect score. I hope that your future with the Bureau continues as well as it has begun." He pressed his lips together and nodded at them both. It sounded like an order, thought Lewis.

"I told your director Monk that as a small incentive, I would like to give you both a bonus when the mission is completed." He looked from Lewis to Scott. He saw the flare in Scott's eyes but not the other one. He clenched his jaw and leaned across the table and spoke to Lewis, "It's something I've done from time to time with new cadets."

Lewis felt uneasy. He thought he felt a pulse behind his ear. He wanted to touch it. He gripped the glass of juice and downed it in one go.

They were supposed to be working for the Bureau, no salary, and now they'd just been told by Rochester that they'd receive a bonus…after.

Rochester turned his attention to Scott. "A generous bonus, boys. Enough to set you up for life." He pulled his lips wide in a smile, a rare smile; he didn't like to show his teeth, as perfect and white as they were.

Scott could barely conceal his excitement. "Wow, that's… wow."

Lewis showed no emotion. There was something about Rochester. His broad smile didn't match the cold calculating steel in his eyes. Rochester glanced at his watch. "That's all I wanted to say, I have a meeting now." He pushed his chair back.

"I wonder if I could use the bathroom before we leave?" asked Lewis.

"Of course, at the end of the gallery on the right."

Lewis wasn't looking for the bathroom. He didn't know what he was looking for, but he was looking. He took the first door on the left—a large sitting room with ice-white sofas and white carpet. He walked quickly and silently around the room, scanning the walls, the furniture, and then homed in on the silver gilt-framed photos on the sideboard.

Mostly photos of Rochester—as a boy, a student, receiving awards, next to a car (a green sports car with solar panels in gold across the roof), sailing a boat—and a wedding photo. Rochester grim, the sun glinting off his hair; it looked a deep red in the light, and his wife, younger, beautiful, her hair blonde. Lewis brought his head closer to her face. She looked as though she was staring straight at him… and she was afraid.

Just before they got in the car to take them back to the Academy, Rochester left them on the steps and went back inside the house. He returned carrying the two boxes that had been on his desk. "Almost forgot. These are the latest technology from our digital laboratory; the 'Sixty-Six Chronometer.' Not on the market yet."

Lewis saw the frown on Scott's face. "A watch, Scott."

"Yes, essentially a watch. It will tell the time. I'll leave you to work out the other features."

"Sixty-Six, I presume?" said Lewis, turning the box over in his hand.

Rochester gave an imperceptible lift of his eyebrows. Presume all you want.

"Do well… both of you. I…" He didn't finish the sentence. Lewis had lifted his head just as he was about to say, 'I expect results.'

Lewis was silent on the drive back to the Academy. The uneasy feeling was sliding its fingers up his spine. He looked across at Scott, absorbed in opening the gift from Rochester; he looked positively elated. Lewis closed his eyes and wondered what Rochester had been going to say.

When they got out of the car, Scott held up the watch to the light. "A bonus and this! I've worked out ten of the features—pretty standard. Look how thin the face is, and the strap… not just a strap… twenty features in it. That man's a genius."

Lewis didn't share Scott's assessment of Rochester. "He's got a team—a small army working for him—but he gets the credit. I want to know what his connection is to the mission. It's supposed to be level five security and he knows about it. Why?"

"Who cares," Scott shrugged his shoulders. "His money helps fund the Academy, probably funds the mission. I'm going to find a girl for you for the ball tonight and don't say no. You're coming." He slipped the watch over his wrist, and a small green light on the strap, no bigger than the head of a pin, began to pulse. He slapped Lewis on the shoulder. "Let the hair down, remember."

Lewis went straight to the library. Rochester—*what's the connection?* He sifted through Rochester's archived history. He found a news article from seventeen years ago and read that Rochester's wife and unborn child had died in a fire, in one of Advanced's laboratories, which also destroyed several of the medical research facilities.

"The heartbroken husband told reporters he blamed himself for the tragedy. The security guard, when questioned by the police, said Rochester's wife had told him that Mr Rochester had left his wallet in his office and she had gone to retrieve it."

The rest of the article was about Rochester's achievements, awards for advancements in medical research and technology. There was nothing about his social life; he hadn't remarried. Apparently, he led a quiet life, no pictures of him at any social events.

When Lewis left the library, he was thinking about Rochester, the bonus he was offering, and the watch still in its box back at his room.

***

The moon hung like a giant balloon above the trees. Lewis was late for the Academy's admission ball. He didn't have a partner; the thought of making small talk with a girl he didn't know filled him with dread. His mind was elsewhere.

Darkness had settled in. The lights from the Academy illuminated the winding paths through the trees. He passed the recreation room where the ball was underway. Through the glass doors, he caught flashes of coloured dresses and black suits moving in rhythm. The noise – laughter, music, chatter – spilled out into the night.

He wasn't thinking about the ball. He was thinking about Monk. Why had he breached security? How else would Rochester know? It didn't make sense. Not with the level of surveillance surrounding anyone exiting Perfection and entering DZ.

He turned off the main path, stepping into the deeper shadows, when a girl stepped in front of him. He hadn't seen her on the bench set back from the path. His hands were in his pockets, head down when they collided.

"Sorry," he said, stepping back.

She rubbed at her shoulder. "Ouch." She smiled - bright white teeth. He recognised her instantly.

Poppy.

She was dressed for the ball in a red satin dress that clung to her curves like it had been poured onto her body. Her blonde hair fell loose over her over bare shoulders. She stepped closer, eyes wide as if seeing him for the first time.

"Hi, Lewis. You're not dressed for the ball," she said her eyes sliding over his T-shirt and bare arms. She reached out, touched his bicep with one finger. "Nearly broke my shoulder with that," she smiled again. "just came out for a breath of air. It's stuffy in there." She tilted her head and didn't move.

Lewis rolled his shoulders uncomfortably. He wasn't an idiot—he knew when a girl was flirting.

"Where's Scott?" he asked, cutting through the moment.

"Scott?" She said his name like it was a foreign word.

"Yes, Scott. I thought he was taking you to the… dance thing… ball." He moved sideways.

"He is. He's inside. He's fine." She tapped her chest lightly with her fingers. "Why didn't you ask me?"

She pouted, her eyes full of a message Lewis didn't want to decipher.

"Well…" He hesitated. It felt like a trap and he was about to fall into it.

"Well? You like me, don't you?" Her hand landed on his chest. Cold. He thought it might stop his heart.

Like her? No way. "Well…" *Fuck. What did Scott say?* "You're… gorgeous," He scrambled for words. "Sexy. Irresistible." He forced a smile. "And now I'm leaving."

She laughed, a bubbling gurgle that made him want to run. He stepped back. She stepped forward.

"You're gorgeous too… and irresistible!" She whispered. Before he could move, her arm slid around his neck, pulling him down into a kiss.

He didn't pull away. Her lips found his, and she kissed him. She knew how to kiss a boy, and she showed him.

Heat flared low in his stomach. Her body pressed against his. Her perfume - spiced, heady – wrapped around him. he felt light-headed. His hand moved to her waist, fingers slipping across her bare back. She felt like silk. He was falling, free-falling off a cliff and for one brief moment it was exhilarating. The blood pounded in his ears, but a voice rose above the noise.

STOP. Over and over.

He pulled the ripcord. Dropped his hands. Stepped back.

But Poppy grabbed his wrist, tugging him deeper into the shadows. He stumbled after her. Her hands slid beneath his T-shirt, fingers grazing his stomach. She hooked a finger in the band of his trousers.

"No!"

The word tore out of him. He grabbed her wrists and pushed her away.

"Sorry… that shouldn't have happened." His voice was tight. He wasn't trying to be cruel, but he was angry—angry at himself.

She broke free, laughing like it was a game. "Don't you like me?" she pouted, bathed in the moonlight.

He stared at her. She was beautiful, yes. But did he like her?

"Poppy, I'm sorry, I… don't know what…" He stepped back. She grabbed at his shirt.

"You said I was irresistible, and yet here you are resisting me. You like me - I've seen how you look at me." Her fist tightened around his shirt.

Lewis froze. Had he looked at her that way? He didn't think so. He shook his head and gently unpeeled her fingers free. Her smile vanished.

"You're here at that event," he said, jerking his head toward the glowing hall of lights. "With Scott. My friend." He stepped back from her. "And right now, I don't like myself much." He hesitated. This would hurt. "And I don't like you much either."

He turned before she could respond. Didn't see her lips press into a thin line or the sharp glint in her eyes. He stepped onto the path and walked quickly away, cursing himself with every step.

I'll tell Scott one day. After the mission.

CHAPTER FOUR

One Week Later – Day One of the Mission

Lewis leaned against a basketball post in the middle of the schoolyard, one leg bent, his foot resting against the metal pole, his hands deep in the pockets of his grey school trousers.

Breathe. You can do this.

Scott should have been here. His best mate. *Yeah—the best mate you betrayed.*

If only he hadn't kissed that damned girl. If only he hadn't made her angry. If only she hadn't told Scott.

Forget it.

Focus.

But the image of Scott's face – jaw clenched, eyes blazing – refused to leave his mind. Lewis had never seen him like that. He hadn't even known Scott had a temper until he'd stormed into the briefing room, fury pulsing through every muscle. In front of everyone - the three-person support team, and Monk.

Scott hadn't thought it through. He was impulsive. Lewis knew that about him. He'd tried to calm him down with a whispered, "It's not what you think," Eyes flicking toward Monk, signalling Scott to calm down. "We'll talk later."

"Talk about it now!" Scott had hissed, fists clenched, pacing, "My best mate, huh?"

Lewis held his stare, warning him. Back off. We're too close to the mission to blow it now.

But Scott was boiling over. And then Monk looked up from speaking to Leena, the room fell silent and the fallout began. Lewis had turned away, moved to a screen to give Scott space – but Scott followed grabbed his shoulder, spun him around.

He shouldn't have said what he did. But Scott hadn't given him a chance. Hadn't trusted him. Believed Soppy Poppy over him. His best mate.

Too late now.

Monk had made the call. One of them would go. It wasn't Scott.

***

Now Lewis focused on his breathing, slowing the flutter in his chest. He wasn't calm – but he wasn't scared either. And if anyone had dared suggest it, he'd have fixed them with those icy grey eyes stare and raised a single brow.

He breathed in – slow deliberate – then again. He had to succeed. Had to make it right with Scott. Get the bonus. Split it down the middle.

He looked around the school. Different to the one he had attended, but the same undercurrent: bored students, restless energy. The smell of gum and wet grass. The hum of adolescence.

It felt strange being back. He shifted his shoulders and rolled against the pole, flicked his hair back. Maybe it should have been cut shorter – too late now.

He'd shaved that morning, The stubble would grow quickly – he always looked older by afternoon. That wasn't ideal. He had to blend in, look like a final-year student.

The mission still felt vague. He'd wanted more details. All he knew: he was searching for a seventeen-year-old girl. A student here.

"She belongs in Perfection," Monk had said as though that explained anything. "Just locate her. Get a photo. We'll verify it's her. Then bring her to the exit point. We'll handle the rest"

"And we're sure she's at this school?" Lewis had asked.

"As sure as we can be."

"And I'm meant to just convince her to follow me?"

"Yes." Monk had looked hard at him. "Think you can do that?"

Lewis had nodded without hesitation. "Of course." But privately, he had thought – Scott would have nailed this in a day. Make friends with a girl? Invite her somewhere? Easy.

As if reading his thoughts, Monk had added, "You've got three weeks. If you follow the plan, you'll find her on day one. You will be the new guy, asking questions-it won't raise suspicion. And as for the photo – don't worry, you won't need a reason, they take photos of themselves all the time.

From the moment he'd been briefed, Lewis hadn't been able to shake the feeling that this wasn't a rescue-it was a kidnapping. But he'd pushed that thought away. He couldn't let Monk see any hesitation.

The exit from Perfection had been disappointingly smooth. No heart-stopping drop. No stomach-lurching freefall. Scott had predicted a roller-coaster.

"Nah," Lewis had said, "more like a parachute jump. Stomach under your chin."

It was neither. One moment he was in Perfection, and the next – after a blast of blinding light-he was here. DZ. Earth. And now, twenty-four hours later, he was leaning against a basketball post, at a school that he didn't belong to, waiting to spot a girl he didn't know, on a mission he barely understood.

***

He looks like a poser. Violet pushed her bike past him. Quick glance. Then eyes down. *Scared probably. Trying to look cool. New guy.*

Lewis furrowed his brow, focusing. His memory was excellent – almost photographic. He had no name, no photo, just a vague description. He let the corners of his mouth twitch - a near smile.

If the intel was right, today would be the easy part. Infiltrate the school. Blend in. Take the pictures. And then wait. Three weeks. Twenty-one days. Then receive the coordinates. Make the extraction. And return—with the girl.

He imagined what success might bring. A new life. Redemption. He and Scott—set up for good. A penthouse. A beach house. A car.

Lewis stretched his back. *Stay alert. Stop dreaming.*

The schoolyard was mostly empty. Clusters of kids talking, scattered around. He'd walked instead of taking the train. It had taken longer than he thought but he wanted to get a feel for the town. The streets. The people. Feel the World.

A tingling buzz behind his ear. He flinched. *No. Not now. Monk?*

He heard the flap of wings. A brush across his hair. A crow landed on the basketball post above him. Ominous. He shivered. A shadow crossed the school yard. Storm clouds—plum-dark and heavy—rolled across the sky.

Idiot. Should've worn the rain jacket.

A whooping sound made him glance toward the school gates. Two girls were hugging like they hadn't seen each other in years. The yard was filling with students – talking, shouting, laughing.

His head throbbed. He winced. Glanced at his watch—sleek, black, with a soft green pulse. The Sixty-Six. He'd cracked half its functions already. Skimmed the brochure. Indestructible. Waterproof. Fireproof. Every kind of proof in the universe. If he was right, he could contact Scott. But not yet. Let things cool down. He tapped the screen. Five to nine.

He folded his arms. So cold. *Thought DZ was supposed to be warm.*

The sky was fully loaded now. One dark cloud twisted into the shape of a dog. He'd always wanted one. His mother hadn't. "You don't want unnecessary attachments, Lewis."

He adjusted his pose again—nonchalant -trying not to look like he'd been standing there twenty minutes. He brushed back his hair – black like his father. Same grey eyes too. His mother had once stared at him like he was a stranger. He often wished for siblings—someone to distract her.

The last bus pulled up. More students streamed in. A faint buzz in his ear again. Monk hadn't stopped checking on him. Longer this time. Lewis sighed. *C'mon, man. You're giving me a headache.*

Then—A familiar voice and not Monk.

"All systems go, my man. Assimilation's on and working."

Scott?

Lewis froze. "Scott? What are you doing? I thought you got—"

"—kicked out of the Academy?"

"Yeah."

"Reprieve. Mission's top secret. Monk's keeping me where he can see me. Just calling to wish you luck."

Scott sounded… cheerful. Too cheerful. Something felt off. Lewis's gut twisted. He looked across at the bike shed. A shadowy figure of a girl bent over her bike.

But then Scott said something else. It sounded like: "We're over." Or maybe just: "Over."

Lewis stared at his phone. What did he mean? No time to process. *Focus.*

The schoolyard was buzzing now. Kids were moving towards the covered area. Getting to the school early had given him time to scope out the perimeter. He stood opposite the bike shed. Only looked like one student had a bike. Across the road a steady stream of parents dropping off their kids.

He glanced at his backpack at his feet—laptop, notebooks, sports gear. Everything he needed. His shoulders still ached from carrying it. He rolled them.

A boy in glasses walked past. Lewis felt a flicker of pity. In Perfection no one had worn glasses for fifty years. Medical tech had taken care of that.

He reminded himself what he was here for: a girl, seventeen, maybe eighteen. Medium to tall. Blonde or brunette. That was it. She could be anyone. He took a breath squared his shoulders. The cold bit through his uniform.

Then he saw her. The girl in the bike shed. Alone. Huddled in the shadows. Smart enough to shelter from the rain, dumb enough to ride in it? Hard to tell.

She slipped off her helmet. Pale skin. Unusual hair – coppery red, tied in a ponytail. Not easy to forget. She moved into the shadows. Lewis squinted and raised his phone. First mission photo. He glanced at the screen. *Damn.* She was looking straight at him. Wide green-gold eyes. Mouth set in a firm line.

He snapped a few cover shots – clouds, roof tiles, his own feet – then slipped the phone into his pocket and folded his arms. She was still staring.

Lewis shivered as a dark shadow crept across the schoolyard. Clouds like bruised plums, heavy with rain, rolled in from nowhere. *Idiot, should have worn the rain jacket.*

A girl whooped near the school gates. She was hugging another girl like they hadn't seen each other in years. The yard was filling with students—talking, shouting, laughing. Lewis winced. His face was tight, the tension behind his eyes building to a dull pulse.

He glanced towards the girl, she was still staring. She had already decided he was a poser, *thinks he's a model or something, the way he's folded his arms and that look.*

He faced the gates, his face blank. The wind ruffled his hair and he pushed it back from his forehead.

Violet narrowed her eyes. He'd taken a photo of her without asking. She hated that.

He wasn't the first. She didn't want to remember that boy and that photo. Didn't he know how it felt? He was new. Year 12, probably. No one transfers this late – not unless something's wrong.

She locked her bike. She was going to make him delete that photo.

Lewis stayed still, waiting for her to make the first move. He shouldn't have taken it. He knew she'd confront him, and he'd have to speak. He hadn't said a word since arriving.

Hs mother's voice returned: *Shoulders back, head up. Don't frown. Look confident, Lewis. That's better. Don't let failure in.*

Lewis hunched his shoulders and tucked his hands under his armpits. The air was thrumming with energy. His scalp tingled. That sensation- he knew it. An electric storm. He shivered. Time to move.

He glanced at his watch, *severe thunderstorm.* No mention of lightening. He cursed himself. He hadn't checked the weather before leaving the apartment. The sky had been clear, the air warm. Like yesterday when he'd slipped into town unnoticed.

Any minute now, he thought, it was going to bucket down. He looked toward the bicycle shed and made a decision.

A crack of thunder split the air.

Lewis reached for his pristine school bag, one hand gripping the basketball post. That's when it hit.

A white-hot blade of lightening sliced through the sky. Pain tore through his left wrist. His hair lifted. His knees gave way.

He could vaguely hear screaming in the distance. And something was burning – a bitter, acrid smell, like scorched metal.

His hand clung to the post, welded there – but that was good. It kept him upright. His ears rang, a sharp insistent whine. He wanted it to stop. He couldn't think.

The ringing faded, replaced by a crackling hum — static. White noise.

I've been struck by lightning. Fuck.

The transmitter behind his ear throbbed like it was boring into his skull. That was bad. He shook his head. The noise, the pain — he gritted his teeth. It was driving him mad.

He wiped his arm across his forehead. His skin was burning. He couldn't feel his legs. Tried to stand. His legs buckled — jelly. Agony shot through his wrist. He couldn't move his fingers. With his other hand, he pried them loose from the pole and collapsed to his knees.

Across the yard, under the shelter of the bicycle shed, Violet watched in horror.

The boy with black hair lit up like a Christmas tree —his hair standing on end, one hand on the basketball post, the other reaching out. Toward her.

She didn't move. Not until he dropped to his knees. Then she ran — ignoring the rain, ignoring the screams of the kids dashing into the school.

He was frozen. Couldn't move.

Then — she was there. Right in front of him. White face. Trembling lips. Eyes wide with alarm.

Nice lips. Greenish eyes.

"Are you okay? Oh my god — here—" She slipped under his arm. His hand fell across her shoulder. Rested against her breast.

He's burning up.

She grasped his hot hand. Hers felt small inside it. His body vibrated beside hers, like a running motor.

Lewis stood, breathing hard. Just a minute — to regroup, clear his head. Drown out the rushing in his ear. Monk's voice in his skull.

Fuck off, Monk. He shouted it into the rain.

Violet caught a muffled voice — one ear pressed to his chest, the other beneath his heavy arm. She moved, trying to take his weight — but he was too tall, too heavy. She had to get help — but she couldn't leave him here, soaked and swaying.

"It's okay. I'll get help. Just—get to the shed. Out of the rain."

Help, she said. Get help. No! Don't want help. No attention. Get to the shed. Stop her. Fifty steps for me. She's small—at least 17 centimetres shorter. He focused on putting one foot in front of the other. Just get out of the rain. Get to the shed.

"Here—hold this," Violet said, guiding his hand to the bike rack. But he wouldn't let go.

Gotta stop her getting help.

He formed the words in his head, but they slid into each other.

His lips felt numb. Nothing came out. A low, mournful groan escaped — the mating call of a bear. He clamped his mouth shut. The horror hit — worse than lightning, worse than anything.

Don't draw attention. Monk's last words: *"Good luck. Keep a low profile."*

He couldn't speak. The words weren't there. He stared down. Black school shoes. Shiny. New. His heart pounded in his throat. *Get a grip.*

He lifted his head slightly. Her shoes — old, scuffed. Black tights — a hole in one knee. Pale skin. A dark green pleated skirt. He counted the pleats. Width. Number. Anything to calm his mind. Anything to make the assimilator work.

A flimsy scrap of calm drifted across his thoughts. He focused. Willing the assimilator to sync.

Please, 2025… please.

He spoke — the assimilator kicked in, translating his thoughts.

"Thank you, Clorinda. Your further assistance is not necessary. I am perfectly fine. A minor mishap."

Silence stretched between them.

A long, slow breath escaped him. Almost breathing normally now. *Thank the fuck for that.*

He kept hold of her hand. Not until he was sure she wouldn't run.

"I'll get help," Violet said. "You could be dead."

Do I look dead?

He met her eyes — green, wide with concern. *Got to reassure her.* He raised an eyebrow, trying to look unbothered.

"Not dead. I mean… you could… have died." Her face flushed pink. She stared into his eyes, then blinked — remembered to breathe.

"You need to get checked. See if you're okay." She pointed at his chest. "Your heart."

No. That couldn't happen. Stay under the radar. Get in. Get out. Mission accomplished. He shook his head. *Got to speak. Get it right.*

Violet tugged her hand. Lewis didn't let go. He'd thank her, grab his bag, and disappear across the wet tarmac. He felt confident. It felt right.

He brought her hand to his lips. "Thank you. I'm in your debt. I assure you, I'm perfectly alright. Heart beating—" he paused. "Fifty-two beats per minute. No evident damage." Hi lips brushed her knuckles as he gave a small, formal bow.

He squared his shoulders and strode toward his rain-soaked bag. It looked like the dog he never had—waiting for its master.

Not bad. He smiled, broke into a jog. No point being late for class. At the top of the steps, out of sight, he paused. His wrist was on fire.

The watch's steady green pulse was gone. Dead. It had saved him — absorbed the shock. He eased it off, sucking in a breath through clenched teeth. His skin blistered red — an angry imprint of the watch. He slipped the watch into his pocket. Maybe it would come back to life. He'd keep it forever. Frame it when he got home.

"Thanks, Rochester," he whispered.

Violet watched him cross the yard. His school bag hung from one shoulder, black as his hair. His grey sweater clung to him, soaked through. He moved lightly, feet barely touching the ground.

She rubbed the back of her hand across her eyes, frowning. *How did he survive that?* She touched her knuckles where his lips had brushed them and wrinkled her nose. *Idiot.* She pressed the back of her hand down her skirt. *He could be brain damaged.*

The thought flashed through her mind like the lightning that had struck him. She ignored the voice telling her not to care, grabbed her backpack, and ran after him — rain soaking her tights, filling her shoes.

She caught up to him in the school foyer. He was smoothing his long dark hair, studying his reflection in the glass-fronted trophy cabinet. She stopped behind him, watching as he ran his fingers through it again.

She curled her lip. *He's fine. Not my responsibility. Not my responsibility.*

She turned to leave — then froze. The image returned, vivid and sudden. His hand reaching for her, a blaze of light, hair lit with fire. She screwed her eyes shut. She'd never forget that. She stepped beside him.

His eyes flicked to her reflection in the glass — he caught the worry in her face. *Damn. She's still worried. Must reassure her.* He addressed her reflection, speaking quickly. "Apologies for rushing off and leaving you so abruptly. I merely wished to avoid tardiness on my first day." *And any further attention.*

She gave him a strange look. Violet studied his profile — the strong jaw, the shadow of a beard. *He looks older than seventeen.* Her eyes moved to his hair. Black, glossy to the roots. It looked fine now...*But I saw it on fire.*

Lewis watched her in silence. He shifted his bag to the other shoulder, then turned to face her. Her face was pale. Her eyes, wide. He closed his own, inhaling slowly. In her green eyes he read concern — and something else. Disapproval?

He tilted his head, studying the slight curl of her upper lip. What had he done to deserve that look? Concern, yes — but also thinly veiled contempt. *Freaking hell.* He raised his eyebrows. No smile.

She dropped her bag to the floor and glanced toward the school entrance. She didn't want to be seen with him.

He raised both brows now and leaned toward her, one hand braced on the trophy case. She took a sharp step back. *Who does he think he is?*

She bit her lip, frowning There was something wrong with him. She picked up her backpack and stared down at the strap.

"I'm perfectly fine," Lewis said, his voice a husky whisper.

Violet's eyes blazed. "Are you? I don't think so!"

Lewis swallowed. He had to get away from her. A dull throb pounded behind his eyes.

"You were struck by lightning! Your hair was on fire — I saw it!" Her voice was sharp, almost accusatory.

He frowned, puzzled.

"It looked on fire. I saw smoke," she added. Her tone softened, sounding almost apologetic — like she'd seen something too private.

Lewis's expression didn't change. His thoughts were. feverish *Mistaken. She's in shock. The rain. Shut her up.*

Pain pulsed through his wrist. He'd forgotten it — a band of fire encircling his skin. He wanted to check the watch, to see if it was working again. But not now — not while she examined him with that contemptuous look glued to her face.

"Your hair…" Violet said again.

He stared at her — as if reading her thoughts. Lewis raked his fingers through his black hair, then shook his head. He gave her a smile of such dazzling brilliance, it seemed to light the foyer. He leaned in, voice lowered to a whisper. His lips brushed her ear. "Hair's fine; see?" He shook his head again. "Black like the devil's heart."

Violet jerked back. "Are you a drama major?"

Some dawning realization smoothed the frown from her forehead. Lewis cursed inwardly. *Something's wrong. Or it could be the girl. Can't tell. Something I said — she's only okay with it if I'm a drama student.*

He glanced at the entrance. Empty. He was late. The classrooms would be filling. No time to question her now. He nodded. "Obvious, is it?" He had to know what he'd done wrong. He couldn't afford to make that mistake again.

Violet nodded. Of course it was obvious. "Do you know what class you're in? It'll be on the board." She pointed down the wide corridor.

She was leaving. Good. He could find his own way. But then she hesitated. She saw the arrogant look slip away as he pressed a hand to his head and squeezed his eyes shut. He shook his head, grimacing.

"I'll show you where it is," she said. She didn't know why she wasn't just walking away. *Brain damage — that's why I'm doing this.*

"Thank you. Obliged," Lewis said.

Violet shot him an exasperated look. It wasn't funny.

"So," he said, stepping into the corridor crowded with students. He turned to her, took her hand, and tucked it under his arm with a warm, unnecessary smile. He squeezed her arm gently with his elbow.

"What was it precisely," he said, "that led you to guess I was…"

Violet stared at her arm. She felt unreal. Mind fogged by what she'd just witnessed — this idiot boy nearly struck dead, and now… now he'd tucked her arm under his and smoothed her hand on his forearm. He was escorting her down the corridor. Like—

What the hell. Her face flamed. She swore under her breath and yanked her arm.

Lewis tried to stop her, trapping her elbow lightly against his chest. Violet tore her hand free like she'd just been bitten by a tiger snake.

Jenna was leaving the girls' cloakroom, phone pressed to her ear, when she looked up and saw Violet. She narrowed her eyes and smiled. This was too good.

"Talk later," she said, switching the phone to video. She filmed everything — Violet's hand on his arm. She'd edit out the part where Violet pulled away. As she passed them, Jenna lowered her head to hide her smile.

"Don't do that," Violet whispered as they passed. "It's not funny. You may enjoy being on stage — I don't."

Lewis swallowed. *What the freak? Note to self: don't escort girls.*

He touched the transmitter behind his ear. It was warm but not burning.

Something's wrong. Please not the assimilator. He needed a quiet place. Contact Monk. Sort this out. He didn't dare speak.

He glanced down at Violet — she was glaring at him, her cheeks even pinker now. Her eyes flashed. *Angry. And attractive. Bad combination. Don't speak.*

Violet's face was fading from beetroot to plain pink. *Of all the people to see me walking down the corridor on his arm — it had to be Jenna.*

The one girl at school who hated her. Violet had tried to explain. To fix things. But the memory came back — Jenna's tearful shout: *"You were supposed to be my friend, Violet. You did this. I'll never forgive you."*

Violet shook her head, pressed a hand to her cheek, and stopped walking. *He can find his own way. Freak.*

Lewis paused, turned — and saw Violet's glittering eyes. He swallowed. *She's going to cry.* Panic flared. *I did this. I don't even know what I did. Touching her arm? That's it? That brought her to tears. Note to self: kissing — out of the question. She'd probably kill herself.* He shook his head hard to chase the thought away.

Violet stared after Jenna's retreating back, her lips trembling. Lewis followed her gaze. It wasn't the arm thing. The girl who passed them… damn. *The phone.*

His bored, aloof mask vanished. His brow furrowed. *She filmed it.*

How do I fix this? I can't let her leave yet. Think. Say sorry? Say headache? No — she'll try to get help. Say…

Nothing came. Only an impulse to charm her. Distract her. It was overwhelming. He stepped in front of her, blocking her from view down the corridor.

She stared at his wet, polished shoes. He reached out, fingers brushing her chin — gentle pressure — lifting her gaze. Before she could react, she was looking into grey eyes that no longer looked like ice.

"Clorinda, look at me. I'm sorry." He gave her a wicked smile and raised both eyebrows.

Violet twisted away. Her cheeks flamed. God, she could feel it. She looked like a beetroot. Tears welled in her eyes. *Don't cry. Don't cry.* She bit her lip, wanting to run, but he seemed to surround her.

Lewis's smile vanished in a heartbeat. His pulse kicked too fast. *Wrong. Wrong. Wrong.* He took a slow breath. *Calm. Stay calm.* He ran a hand through his hair. "Sorry," he blurted, making a face — the kind his imaginary dog would make after chewing the furniture.

Violet stared at him. She didn't want to forgive him. But he looked pathetic. Afraid. That same look she'd seen in the school yard. She frowned and said quietly, "You're still doing it, you know — acting. And," her voice turned cold, "my name's Violet."

Lewis swallowed. He bowed slightly, suppressing the urge to offer his hand. "Pleased to make your acquaintance, Violet. Beautiful name. My friends call me Lewis. Please do."

"Shut up," she muttered, pushing past him.

She spotted the group gathered around the notice board and started walking. *Get away from him.* She glanced back. He was watching her, running frantic fingers through his hair.

She beckoned, pointing above the crowd. He stepped beside her and glanced at her face — fierce, jaw tight. Lewis noticed. His eyes narrowed, thoughtful. His mind working to steady itself. He touched the transmitter. It felt cooler. Relief spread through him.

Find a quiet place. Sort this out.

"That's it," Violet said, nodding toward the board. Then she turned and walked the other way. Lewis watched her go — her red ponytail swinging like a pendulum. He wanted to stop her. Ask what he'd done wrong. But fixing the glitch mattered more.

Get to Monk.

He scanned the board above the crowd. Subject lists, room numbers. One curly-haired boy stood directly in his way — wide shoulders, nearly his height. Lewis instinctively straightened his own. He leaned over the heads and tapped one of the shoulders blocking the view. His voice came out smooth, precise, just a touch commanding.

"As you were, old chap — might a fellow have a gander?"

Silence.

Curly Hair froze. Then turned — slowly. Menacingly, Lewis thought.

I've said something wrong. I don't need a genius chip to know that.

Now they were eye to eye. Lewis's face became a mask of bored indifference. Black eyes stared into his. The boy's jaw tightened.

Had Lewis looked down, he'd have seen fists. Instead, he casually flicked an imaginary speck from his damp sweater. Then finally registered: this was not working.

Wide Shoulders looked ready to punch him.

Hell. What now? What did I say? Idiot. Don't speak.

Lewis's eyes slid to the notice board. He prayed that Cross had enrolled him.

Three sheets — rows of names. Alphabetical? Yes.

His name jumped out: *Lewis Green. Homeroom 22. A Wing.*

He flicked his gaze to the top of the list. Scott's name was there — with the false surname: *Scott Brown. Green, Brown.* He frowned.

I miss him. Damn. Don't think about that. Focus!

Lewis turned abruptly and strode down the nearest corridor — away from Wide Shoulders, away from a fight.

Ahead, three girls huddled around a phone. He recognized the one holding it.

He needed direction. That couldn't be too hard. Just say a number. No need for words. He stopped beside them, voice raised just enough to interrupt.

"Twenty-two?" He was already poised to bolt.

The nearest girl replied without looking up.

"Down the corridor, out the far door, across the courtyard — A Wing."

Lewis turned to go — but froze at the words behind him.

"There. I'll pause it. See? She was holding his arm. She looks like an idiot. Did she go red?"

"Is it her boyfriend?"

"Freak. He's hot."

"Who is he?"

"Who cares. He's a dick."

Lewis stared over the girl's head — and saw the phone screen. There he was. And Violet. Her hand on his arm. Him looking down at her, smiling. Frozen in time. DZ mobile footage.

One of the girls turned. Met his gaze. He returned it — cold and contemptuous.

She could have been Poppy.

Without hesitation, he reached over and plucked the phone from Jenna's fingers. Held it high. Ignored the cries, the hands reaching for his.

He found the delete button.

Jenna's mouth was still open when Lewis handed the phone back. He gave a short bow. "Obliged for the directions." He hadn't meant to say anything.

So much for staying under the radar.

His mind reeled, teetering on overload. He had to get to the classroom. Get his name checked off. Leave. Fix the transmitter.

Or…Don't think about the alternative.

He tugged his sleeve down, covering the angry burn on his wrist. His hand slid into his pocket. The watch was pulsing — green again — but the time hadn't changed since the lightning strike. Still, it blinked. He took comfort in that small, steady light. Slipped the watch back into his pocket.

He found the classroom. It was packed. He slipped in through the door and stood at the back. Every seat was taken. At the front, a woman with hair like a grey bird's nest was speaking in a flat, buzzing voice. She sounded like a bee trapped in a jar. Droning. On and on.

Lewis folded his arms, leaned against the wall, crossed one leg over the other. He rested his chin on his chest. Closed his eyes. The bee-drone became oddly soothing. The white noise in his head had stopped. Relief.

He let his mind drift. Let it reset. He wasn't listening. He'd tuned out seconds after stepping through the door. Same old school crap. Final-year filler. *Some things never change, whatever the universe.*

He meditated on the swaying rhythm of a red ponytail. The oscillation angle. Calculations, numbers, formulae —

"You! Yes, you. With your eyes closed."

The room stilled. Rustling stopped. Bodies froze. He *felt* the attention more than heard it. He opened one eye. She was looking straight at him.

Hands on her narrow hips.

"Yes, you. Tired, are we?" Her voice dripped with sarcasm.

He caught it. And the mood shift in the room.

Ignore it. Stay invisible.

Then the screeching began. A dagger to his eardrum. He jack-knifed away from the wall —Blinding white noise screamed through his skull. His name, faint and urgent, repeated under the static.

He clamped his hands over his ears. *Shut up. Shut up. SHUT—*

. "SHUT—" He shouted into the silent room. The word hung in the air, unfinished. Floating, weightless, all the way to the front of the class. He stood up. Lowered his hands.

"Shutting the door. Frightful draft out there." He stepped toward it, pulled it closed with quiet finality. He turned and faced a sea of blank faces. Don't speak,

"Wrong room. Sorry." His voice sounded slow and thick. *Perfect. Sound like an idiot.* He pulled the door open, slung his bag over his shoulder, and left. *Now what? Find… Violet. Yes. Find her.*

Lewis retraced his steps back to the notice board. How many Violets could there be in one school? He scanned the pages. Stevens, Violet. Just one. Homeroom 6, Main.

He found the room two doors down. Through the small glass window, he searched for the familiar ponytail but couldn't see much. He pushed open the door and poked his head in. His eyes landed on a girl with a ponytail.

A short, podgy man with a shaved head was writing something on the board. He turned. "Any further suggestions? You, skulking in the doorway— come in or get out."

Lewis bristled. *You arse.* Not used to that tone—not where he came from. *Ignore him. Just find Violet.* He scanned the room. Ponytail girl not Violet.

"Are you in this class? Podgy man demanded. Lewis glanced at the whiteboard. "Classroom Rules." He skimmed. Something snapped. He straightened to his full height, raised an eyebrow, nostrils flared.

"You should add to that list, you, manners maketh man." He nodded once and shut the door behind him.

Pandemonium erupted inside. He'd drawn more attention to himself in ten minutes than he had in his entire life.

Back at the board, he looked again. One more: Violetta Mackenzie, Homeroom 22. Back to the same class.

He wiped his forehead. Moist. From the rain? Or panic? The screeching in his head was rising again. Nausea twisted in his stomach. He needed to lie down—but there was no time.

He stood by the classroom door. Dropped his bag. Arms crossed. Waited. Students poured out. One stopped in front of him—Jenna.

"You've got a bloody nerve. That was my phone. Who do you think you are?"

Lewis tilted his head, lips pursed like he'd never seen a girl before.

"I deleted it so you wouldn't regret it later," he said softly. "It would have hurt someone."

Jenna went pale. "Wanker," she spat.

Behind her, Violet appeared, pressed against the wall like she was about to be shot. Lewis stepped in front of her. "Found you. Need your help. Your servant.

"You deleted the video?"

He nodded. He tried not to speak. Glanced at his phone—next class, then break. Time to find somewhere quiet. "Class?" he asked.

"English Lit. You?"

He had Physics. But he nodded anyway and tried a grin. She frowned at it. It felt fake. He followed at a distance, resisting the urge to reach out. In the classroom, she glanced back—his face looked wild, unhinged. She found a seat at the back. He sat beside her. She unpacked her books second-hand not new, stacked them neatly. Two pens, blue and red. A pad labelled "Violetta Mackenzie – English Lit." Everything aligned.

Lewis watched from the corner of his eye. *Violetta, huh. Explained a lot*

The room buzzed. When the teacher arrived—blonde, messy bun—she stood silently until the class settled.

"That's better. Welcome back. Let's not waste time. Three books this term: 'Great Expectations'—yes, groan, I heard you—and two coming-of-age novels. Anyone read them before?"

Silence. Lewis studied his hands. Violet fidgeted. She's read them all, he thought.

The teacher sighed. "Start with Dickens. Read to Chapter ten. Questions are online."

Violet opened the battered copy and set it between them. Lewis read a page at a glance. She wasn't reading—just staring. He turned the page. "Careful, it's old," she whispered. He nodded and slowed. Miss French passed by.

"You're not on my list," she said to Lewis.

He started to rise—something in his head demanded it. Violet kicked him. Hard. Twice. He froze. *Got it. No standing. No bowing.*

He enrolled late," Violet said smoothly. "No classes yet. I figured… with the laryngitis, he should stick with me for now."

Miss French nodded. "Good thinking, Violet."

When the bell rang, Lewis exhaled deeply. His muscles ached. He grabbed his bag and made for the door. The white noise was rising again.

Violet saw him leave, hesitated, then reached for her bag – it vibrated. She didn't need to check. She knew who the message was from.

CHAPTER FIVE

Lewis could only think of one place — the bicycle sheds. Isolated. No one would be there now. He retraced his steps to the school entrance. It was still raining — a relentless rain. He needed an umbrella. He was damp anyway.

What the hell. He took the school steps two at a time. Head down, water dripping from his lashes, he rounded the building, past the basketball post — still standing, untouched by lightning. The bicycle shed was clear, the metal racks empty but for Violet's solitary bike.

He dropped his bag and sat on it, knees around his ears, hands clasping his head, trying to shut out the nerve-jangling whine vibrating in his skull. He stilled his mind, a smooth lake. It took longer than usual to cut through the noise. He didn't move. Eyes closed. Blocking out everything: the rain, the traffic, even the footsteps sloshing through puddles across the schoolyard.

And then, through the calm, he heard Monk. He sounded tense. He was talking to someone. "He's not responding. It's turned on — we've been keeping the channel open. Some catastrophic incident. Our data indicates massive electrical interference. We're not sure but—"

There was a pause. Lewis briefly wondered who Monk was talking to.

A deeper voice filled the gap. 'Lightning. He was struck by lightning?"

Lewis frowned. He'd heard that voice before.

Monk again. Lewis could almost hear him swallow.

"Yes. That's what the data is telling us."

"And nothing from Lewis?"

Rochester! He's talking to Rochester.

"No, nothing. The transmitter is on, but he's not responding."

"A fault on his end?" said Rochester.

Lewis gritted his teeth, waiting for Monk to reply.

"Yes… appears to be an intermittent fault."

There was concern in Monk's voice. It made a pulse throb in Lewis's temple.

"Do we know if the assimilation program is working?"

Lewis didn't like the way Rochester was asking the questions — as though he were in charge.

A long silence.

"It is… but—"

Lewis froze. Why was Monk hesitating?

"But what, Monk?" Rochester's voice was low, almost inaudible.

An ocean of static filled Lewis's head. He could hear nothing but white noise. He slapped his hand against his temple. *Come on, come on. Don't let me down now.*

"But what, Monk?"

Lewis could hear the contempt. He held his breath.

"I said. But. What. Monk?"

"A fault… we're working on it."

"Fault? What kind of fault?" Rochester sounded calm — but Lewis could hear the anger, tightly leashed.

A thin ribbon coiled around Lewis. He knew something was wrong — and now it was confirmed. *The assimilation. I'm fucked.* The program that ensured he blended in, sounded native — without it, he was an alien abroad. His heart beat a tattoo in his chest.

Monk coughed. "It… appears it was deliberately corrupted."

"Deliberately corrupted? How corrupted?"

Monk was speaking fast now. "An English program. Regency period. About 1811. It's been downloaded. The two are running side by side — DZ168 circa 2025 and… the other one. Regency." Monk's voice faded to a mumble.

Lewis wasn't breathing. He remembered the last time he'd spoken to Scott. *"Assimilation's working,"* he'd said. *Scott, you did this. You bastard.*

"What? An old English program? Are you mad, Monk? How did this happen? What kind of damn security have you got there!"

Lewis could hear Rochester's rage, almost feel it.

I should be the one asking these questions.

"No security breach," Monk replied, more firm now. "We have the person responsible. We've got him under guard. It's Streathfield. Scott Streathfield."

"Eighteen years. I've waited eighteen years! Goddamn. I want to speak to Scott."

Lewis couldn't think. Panic like a heavy wet blanket was smothering him.

Monk's voice faded — then nothing but static.

He waited.

Faint whispery voices.

Then Rochester again: "Hello, Scott… And I thought you and Lewis were friends." He sounded almost sad.

"We are… we were… it was…" Lewis could hardly recognise Scott's voice.

"Was what, Scott?"

"Some kind of payback," Monk cut in. "A fight over a girl."

"And you downloaded what into the program, Scott?" Rochester's voice was like a kindergarten teacher now.

Lewis held his breath.

"It wasn't meant to—" Scott sounded desperate. "Two characters. From English history. Darcy, someone, and Byron. A poet."

"Darcy?" repeated Rochester.

"Guy in a book. I can't remember. I'm sorry. *LEWIS IF YOU CAN HEAR ME, I'M SORRY. I'M SORRY.*"

Silence.

Then: "You've got a man there, haven't you?" Rochester again. "He can fix this."

"No. He doesn't have the equipment," Monk replied.

"Really. That's short-sighted of the Bureau. I can send someone. One of my men."

More silence.

No way, thought Lewis. *Monk won't agree to that.*

"That's not possible. It's a government agency. Security won't allow it," Monk said.

"Is that so, Monk?" Rochester sounded bored.

Then: silence. Just the faint scramble of static, dancing in waves across his mind.

Lewis swallowed, again. Fighting down the nausea. He rolled his shoulders and stretched his arms, pulling the damp sweater tight across his back. *Can't fall to pieces.* He had to think. *Get through this. Make contact. Get extracted.*

He couldn't keep the panic out of his voice. They had to get him out. Monk couldn't leave him trapped here. Could he?

"Lewis to base," his voice echoed off the tin walls of the bicycle shed.

He had to think. He stared at the ground between his damp shoes. He had to... *Rochester! He wants the girl!*

That explained why Rochester was at the base. The mission was off the grid, and Rochester was the most powerful man in Perfection. He was going to send someone. He's waited eighteen years.

Lewis stood up. He prayed he was right. Until someone came to get him out of this mess, he was on his own—talking like who? He had to act fast.

England. Regency period.

He lifted his bag onto the bike rack, unzipped it, and pulled out his laptop. He typed into the search engine and read silently.

1811 to 1820, Regency Period, King George blah blah, ill, his son made Regent to rule in his place... blah, blah, period of elegance, etiquette, high fashion, romance, poetry...ugh... blah blah...

Lewis's fingers sped across the keyboard. He searched one word: **Darcy**.

He read: *Darcy, character in a novel. One of two central characters in 'Pride and Prejudice' by Jane Austen. Aloof romantic hero. Arrogant without knowing it. Tall and handsome. Lord of Pemberley. Loyal. Kind to friends. Television adaptation: Colin Firth...*

He stopped reading and searched YouTube. There were videos. He'd have to watch them later. Get some understanding of the character. Try to work out what he was being compelled to do. He glanced at a few photos. *For freak's sake.*

He typed in **Byron** and scanned the entries.

Lord Byron. English nobleman. Flamboyant. Notorious. Most fashionable poet of the day. Numerous affairs, notably Lady Caroline Lamb. She said of him: "mad, bad, and dangerous to know."

Lewis wiped his hand across his forehead. *You bastard, Scott.*

"Fuck, fuck," he muttered. "I'm acting like some... as though I'm—" He shouted above the rain pounding the tin roof. **"YOU BASTARD. YOU FUCKING BASTARD."**

That was it. He'd been talking like a twat.

He had to think. He was good at this. *Cool under pressure*, Monk had written in the mission recommendation. Think. He was going to have to learn fast. Model himself on the boys at school. He thought of Wide Shoulders: aggressive, ready for a fight. Somehow, he had to control the impulse...

Wait. Monk said they were running side by side.

What does that mean?

He shut down the laptop. "You're dead, Scott. I'm going to kill you for this," he said through gritted teeth.

A flash of lightning lit the sky. Lewis flinched, and an almighty crack of thunder broke the sky in two.

He didn't know how long she'd been standing there, next to her bike, in the shadows, watching him. He turned when he heard her gasp at the sudden noise.

The clap of thunder still reverberated overhead. She looked like a drowned cat—wet hair plastered to her face, lips... The words formed before he could stop them:

"A delicate shade of blue, like bluebells in—"

He muttered and clenched his jaw. Fuck. He hoped she hadn't heard him over the rain.

He knew he shouldn't speak. He needed time to work out how to manage the rogue assimilations. But they were part of him now, and they came naturally. He hadn't had time to recognise them, to rein them in.

Lewis inclined his head. He couldn't stop the small bow. He prayed that was okay. He needed her to keep helping him. *Don't speak.*

He swept his long, wet hair off his brow and moved closer, like a prowling panther, eyes glinting. The warning voice had grown faint and small. *Don't speak. Don't spe—*

"The rain suits you," he said, voice a husky whisper. "Diamonds in your hair." He reached out and touched the wet ends of her ponytail.

"What the—" She jumped back as though jolted by a cattle prod.

He gritted his teeth and thrust his hands into his pockets. He shivered. He was in trouble. The rogue assimilation was controlling him. He should be acting normal, like a typical DZ168 eighteen-year-old. But instead, he was behaving like some arrogant, pompous romantic idiot.

The word "sorry" hovered at the edge of his lips. Dare he say it?

"Sorry," he blurted, forcing himself to stay still. But he felt the urge to stand tall, bow, smile blindingly. He didn't move. He waited for a signal. He'd follow her lead. Copy her actions, her words.

She glared at him. "What's wrong with you? You're not in Drama, I checked. You're not even in Lit. Your subjects are all Maths and Science. Why do you keep acting like this?"

She threw her arm out. "Like that! Bowing and speaking like some character in a play."

He looked puzzled, as if she were speaking another language.

"CAN YOU HEAR ME?" she shouted above the rain.

He flicked his hand at her—a dismissal. Shut up. She bristled.

"You are so... arrogant."

He nodded. Why deny it? "Yes. Also, aloof. Although," he drawled, "I'm not supposed to be aware of it. But I'm kind to friends... and family."

She stared at him like he'd grown antlers. She had to get away. She bent, fiddled with her bike lock, and lifted her bike from the rack.

Lewis kept his hands under his armpits. He shivered. Cold and miserable. Why was she leaving school? It wasn't even midday. He flicked his hand at her bike. Raised his eyebrows.

She looked up at him from under her helmet. Her cold fingers fumbled with the clip. She dropped her hands.

"I'm going home. I'm not feeling well."

"Is that true? You look perfectly..." *Adorable tried to break free.* He struggled. No. Different word.

"Fine!" he spluttered. "Perfectly fine to me. In good health."

Her face turned a delicate pink.

"Stay. I need someone to... I need help... until fully recovered. Obliged to you," he said.

He needed someone to guide him around school. Speak for him until this nightmare was sorted. He flashed her his most romantic smile.

"Please."

He clasped his hands in a prayer. Looked at them. Couldn't believe he was doing that. How pathetic. *Darcy? Byron?*

He dropped his hands. Shoved them into his pockets. He felt cold to the marrow. He needed dry clothes.

Sports sweater!

He reached into his bag and pulled out a still-packaged green school jumper. He peeled off his soaked sweater, revealing a damp white T-shirt clinging to every muscle.

Violet said nothing. But she didn't look away.

He tugged off the T-shirt and quickly pulled on the dry sweater. She was chewing her bottom lip. Lost in thought.

She hadn't answered.

He felt warmer already.

Violet was thinking of school. Of Jenna. Of the video. Of what she'd done.

Her phone vibrated. A message:

Still waiting!!!

She stared at it. Then at Lewis. She held her finger on the screen until it went black.

Lewis watched her. No time to persuade her. He stepped forward, placed her bike firmly back in the rack, locked it.

"Good. That's settled, then. Come, fair Clorinda."

He hooked his elbow at her. "Shall we?"

No, you idiot. No more escorting. He smoothed back his hair.

Violet looked at the rain. It hadn't stopped. Then Lewis remembered. The little black thing in his bag. He pulled out a compact umbrella, popped it open with a flourish, and held it above her head.

"Let's go, then."

He didn't know why, but with this girl by his side, he felt like he could make it through the day.

"Where?" she asked, ducking beneath the umbrella, her cheek brushing his arm.

Drama, he thought. Somewhere wacky behaviour might go unnoticed.

"Drama?"

She shook her head. "No. Too much talking." She remembered Grade Nine. Mr. Benson. Cats. Licking. *Definitely not Drama.*

"Your next class is Physics. Room 20."

He raised an eyebrow.

"I saw your name on the class list. It's my class."

Lewis didn't notice her blushing. He was too focused on not reciting poetry.

"After you," he said, placing a hand gently on her back. The umbrella hovered above her. She didn't shake him off. The touch felt... safe.

They reached the school steps. He shook out the umbrella, collapsed it, and tucked it back into his bag.

And followed her inside.

CHAPTER SIX

They sat quietly in the back row. Lewis noticed the whole class was quiet. He did a quick calculation - sixty-five percent girls. The teacher—young, enthusiastic, female.

He kept his head down. Violet gave the laryngitis story again, then kicked him in the ankle to remind him not to stand and bow. Lewis winced.

After the teacher left, he whispered, "I hadn't forgotten. Thank you. Appreciated." He suppressed the dazzling smile—he'd seen what it did to Violet.

At lunch, he followed Violet to the canteen. Eyes locked forward, ignoring everyone. They found a corner table by a cold window. Violet finally asked the question that had been bothering her. She stared at him over her soup. Rehearsed the question in her head. Gave up.

"Do you have some form of Tourette's Syndrome?"

To what? Lewis blinked at her. Her greenish eyes sparkled—*like emeralds in sunlight. No. Candlelight.* He had to write that down. *No. Stop.*

"I shouldn't have asked," Violet said quickly. "Forget it." She looked away from his grey eyes, which were doing weird things to her insides.

Focus, he told himself. Two-something syndrome—maybe that could be his excuse. He touched his pocket. Phone. Info.

"Excuse me one moment..." he muttered. He wanted to say he needed the bathroom but bloody Darcy blocked him. He pointed at the toilet block and ran.

In the smelly cubicle, he googled it.

Tourette's Syndrome: a neurodevelopmental disorder characterized by involuntary movements and vocal tics.

It sounded awful.

Great. That's not it. He sighed. Why couldn't he be flamboyant and notorious like Byron? Women loved him.

He leaned against the wall. He didn't want to be Byron. Or Darcy. He wanted to be Lewis—focused, practical, calm. No eccentricity. No drama. He hated drama. Kind, yes—but not aloof. Not arrogant.

He wandered back to the canteen. Girls glanced up. He caught their eyes. The wicked smile came naturally. He was Byron. He swept his hair back. Hands in pockets.

Violet saw it. Her throat tightened. A small knot of anger hit her. She wanted to shout something savage, but just muttered under her breath, "Vain dickhead."

"So, Violet," he said, sitting sideways, legs crossed at the ankle. "To answer your question, which frankly I find rather—"

Violet held her hands over her ears, glaring.

He stopped. Dropped his head onto the table. Covered it with his hands. His heart thundered. It was like being controlled by an outside force. He raised his head. She wasn't glaring anymore. Just watching him. Worried. He clenched his jaw. He had to say it. In his own voice.

"Not Tourette's. Intermittent fault. Sorry. Not myself. Behaving like..." He couldn't finish. Dropped his head again.

"It's the lightning," Violet said. "You need a doctor." She reached over and patted his shoulder.

He didn't move. Her hand was warm. Calming. He didn't want her to stop.

He'd failed. The mission hadn't even started. Violet wanted him to go to the hospital. He couldn't fake this for a week. He needed to talk. Make contact. Find the girl. Guide her to the exit.

"We can get an Uber," she offered. "I'll come with you." Her voice softened. "Call your parents. Or I can speak for you. Or text."

Parents. Mother. The thought made him tense. His eyebrow lifted.

"Don't," Violet said. "You're about to say something..."

"Tw...at...ish," Lewis muttered.

She blinked. "Twatish?" She said it like *twotish.* "You sound posh. Like one of the King's kids."

"Which King?" he said dryly.

Violet rolled her eyes. He was impossible. Like someone raised in a bunker. Like time skipped him.

Lewis smiled. Brilliant and blinding.

Violet's stomach flipped. Like standing on stage. That stomach-drop-before-speeches feeling.

"Don't do that," she said. "That… thing." She gestured vaguely.

She didn't want to admit what it did to her. She'd known him less than three hours and already felt—*No*. She wasn't falling. Not again. He probably had a girlfriend. Or three.

Lewis sat up. His head pounded. Right eye pulsing. Something behind his ear vibrated. He couldn't last much longer. He had to get back to the apartment Cross rented for him. He hadn't given up. But it was over.

Monk would understand. Probably. The team would too. Maybe even Rochester. Scott… well, Scott was done. Career over. Violet said something. She looked flushed and awkward.

Lewis groaned. What now? Another trigger? His cheek vibrated violently. Lips wobbling. Then—screeching. Like bats screaming in a cave. He grabbed his bag and bolted.

"Wheeeeeeeeeee base to Lewis—wheeeeeeeeeee base to Lewis—wheeeeeeeeeee base to Lewis—"

Maybe—just maybe—they could still fix him. He ran. Down the corridor, out the doors, pounding the steps. Rain smashed into his face. No time for umbrellas. Just move. Just get to the shed.

His breath came in short gasps. His backpack thudded like a sack of wet bricks against his spine. By the time he skidded into the bicycle shed, he was soaked through and shaking.

He dropped to his haunches, hands on his knees, chest heaving. His head was splitting. Every heartbeat pulsed behind his eyes.

Then—just as fast as it started—it stopped.

The screeching. The buzzing. The jelly-face vibrating horror. Gone.

Relief hit him like a wave. He dropped onto his bag and closed his eyes. Let the rain pound above him. Let the world breathe.

He pulled out his phone. He tapped 'record'. "The rain beats like a—" He stopped. Stared at the screen. Deleted the recording. "Fuck off, Byron."

He sat in silence, listening. Rain on tin. A siren in the distance. A bird nearby. The school bell. Normal sounds. Earth sounds.

He jammed his fingers in his ears. Listened hard. Nothing. No white noise. No hum. He touched the transmitter under his ear. Still nothing. Panic crept in, tightening around his throat.

"Okay, okay… calm down," he whispered. "It's temporary. Monk shut it down. Probably fixing it. Just temporary."

He paced. Picked up his bag. Slung it over his shoulder. He could think now. That's what he told himself. He'd see Darcy or Byron coming a mile away. He popped the umbrella. Stepped into the rain. Back toward the school.

CHAPTER SEVEN

Miss French stood on the steps, staring at the grey sky. Free period. Next up: her Year Nines. Lion taming. Hormonal chaos. Testosterone and tears.

The boys were animals. The girls—lost. Trying too hard to be something. Anything.

She thought about Gavin. The brush of his lips that morning, barely there. No kiss. No "have a good day." Just gone. Something was off. She couldn't say what.

She wanted to call. Keep it breezy. Casual. Rehearsed it: *Hey babe. Roger sat with me at lunch. Showed me pics of his new boat. Bloody boring.*

Better: *Roger insisted. Wants to take me out.* More intriguing. More edge.

She scrolled to Gavin's number. Would he answer? Probably not. 'Working,' he'd say. 'Can't talk.'

She saw the umbrella first. Black. Moving toward her. Then the boy underneath.

"Lewis, isn't it? New boy." She smiled like a teacher was supposed to.

He shook out the umbrella. Nodded. "Yes. That's correct. I... yes, yes."

"Lewis, could I borrow your phone? Left mine in the staff room."

He blinked. "Of course. Delighted." He handed it over.

She held out her other hand. He stared at it, then reached toward her—was he about to kiss it?

"Umbrella," she snapped.

Right. He passed it to her.

She stepped out, punching in the numbers quickly. Breathless voice. Loud enough for Lewis to hear every word.

"Hi honey, it's me. Not my phone. Roger's. Had lunch together. He wants to take me out on his boat." Pause.

"You're running? In the rain? Who are you shushing? That's Roseanne's voice—don't lie. Don't you dare say I'm paranoid—say hi to Roseanne, you bastard!"

She stormed back, umbrella flailing. She tried to collapse it, failed, dropped it at Lewis's feet. The phone rang. She answered. "Fuck off." And dumped it in Lewis's palm.

Lewis watched her go. "Charming manners," he muttered. He checked the time. Thirty minutes. Violet—was she still in the canteen? He owed her some kind of explanation.

The canteen was nearly empty. Just a few kids left. Violet was still there, same seat. Talking to someone.

Lewis froze. Broad back. Tight black running gear. Curls.

Scott?

Violet said something. The guy turned. Pale. Worried.

Scott! What the fuck!

Lewis didn't think. He charged forward.

"Hi man," Scott said, holding out a hand.

Lewis ignored it. Grabbed Scott by the throat. "You contemptible ass. Damn you, Scott. Damn you to hell!"

Scott wrestled free, coughing. A small smile tugged at his lips when he heard Lewis speak.

"You're dead, Scott".

Silence fell in the canteen. Violet ran a hand across her throat—a signal. Shut up.

Lewis gave a weak smile and stepped back.

Scott sat again. "Violet was just telling me about the lightning. I told her you called me. Came to help. Medical attention, you know."

Lewis kicked his bag along the floor. Scott winced. Lewis stopped. Took a breath. Sat beside Violet. He'd let Scott do the talking.

Scott tried. "So… Violet says you two are in Lit together."

Lewis raised both eyebrows. His phone buzzed. He checked. *Under the Hood.* Only one person that could be. The teacher's boyfriend. He ignored it.

Scott turned to Violet. "Do you have another class later?"

"No. Well—yes, but I've got the material. Mr. Forrest doesn't teach 'til Wednesday. Double period." She hesitated. "I can photocopy the notes. If you want."

Lewis said, "Obliged." And glared at Scott.

Scott's mouth was a tight line.

The phone buzzed again. Lewis answered this time. A man's voice. Aggressive. "Listen, mate. Don't hang up. Stay away from Lisa. Or you're fucking dead."

Lewis didn't even think. Something wicked in him woke up. He smiled. "I intend to make her my mistress and lavish her with gifts." He hung up. Set the phone on the table.

Scott looked down. Violet stared at Lewis like she couldn't decide if she wanted to run—or stay.

"I think," said Scott, pushing back his chair and standing up, "I should be getting Lewis that help now."

Violet watched them go. Lewis stepped aside to let a group of girls pass, and she saw Scott grab his arm just as Lewis raked his fingers through his hair and gave a dramatic bow. Violet caught the words, "They walk in beauty…" before Scott hustled him away.

She was relieved Lewis had called Scott. She'd been close to talking to someone in admin. Underneath that ridiculous façade Lewis wore like armour, she couldn't help wondering who he really was. Tall, dark, hot—and he knew it. Probably a narcissist. She smoothed a hand across her forehead.

Violet pulled out her phone. Eight messages. Three missed calls. All from the same person. The last text made her stomach drop:

If u don't call back in 10 I'm coming to school!!!

That was fifteen minutes ago. She swore under her breath and quickly replied:

don't home soon

She didn't know if the threat would be carried out, but she wasn't taking chances. School was her sanctuary. She couldn't wait to leave home.

She slung her bag over her shoulder, ready to go, when Jenna appeared, storming toward her. *Here we go.*

Jenna planted her hands on her hips. "You've got some bloody nerve. You and your boyfriend."

Violet's heart thudded. At least Jenna was speaking to her. "He's not my boyfriend," Violet said calmly, staring at her clenched hands on the table. "He's new. That's all."

"Could've fooled me. He looked like your boyfriend. Holding your arm."

"It was a joke. It wasn't funny."

Jenna's tone softened slightly. "I saw the other guy, too. Not your boy-friend either?"

"Scott. Friend of Lewis. The one who—"

"—held your arm?"

"And deleted the video from your phone," Violet said, looking Jenna squarely in the eye.

Jenna waved a dismissive hand like swatting a fly. "They in class?" she asked, glancing around the emptying canteen.

"Gone home. Lewis wasn't feeling well. Scott went with him."

Violet wrapped her arms around her bag. Maybe this was the start of something. Maybe they could go back to how it was before.

"I've got to go home," Violet said. She didn't need to explain what that meant. Jenna used to know. Once, she might've even come with her. Not now. Violet hadn't done enough penance yet.

Jenna seemed to catch herself softening. Her mouth tightened.

"Your friend's a dickhead," she said.

CHAPTER EIGHT

They didn't talk in the Uber.

Lewis gave the address and stared out at the rain blurring the suburban streets. So, this was it. This world. Disappointing, really. Ordinary.

He sat in the front seat. He expected Scott to fight him for it, but Scott got in the back and left the door open like a peace offering.

The driver switched on the radio—bouncy Indian pop. Lewis shut his eyes. Silence would've been better.

The Airbnb was on the tenth floor of a faded beachfront tower. Lewis ignored the lift and took the stairs. One minute in an enclosed space with Scott and someone was going to die.

Scott kept pace until the fifth floor. Then came the wheezing. Lewis smiled slightly. Increased speed. By the tenth floor, both of them were pretending not to be dying. Lewis opened the door. The apartment was cramped and cheerful—blue, yellow, white. Nautical prints. A bowl of shells. Two bedrooms, tiny kitchen, and a laundry bathroom.

Lewis dropped his bag and opened the fridge. A half-empty carton of juice stared back at him. Scott hovered near the doorway, uncertain.

Lewis slammed the fridge and turned. Scott flinched. "You're dead," Lewis said. "And I don't care how twatty I sound when I thump you."

"Wait—Lewis—listen!" Scott backed up. "I get it. You hate me. You should. I messed up. But there's no time. We have to be ready."

Lewis forced his fists open. He flexed his fingers. Breathed. "You damned fool," he said. "Do you have any idea what your tomfoolery has done?" His voice was calm, cold and cutting.

Scott blinked. *Tomfoolery?* Really?

Lewis could see the grin tugging at the corner of his mouth. That made him even angrier. He wanted his old self back. The Lewis who could intimidate, who had command. Not this literary mash-up with a busted transmitter.

"You think this is funny?" he snapped.

Scott raised both hands. "Calm down. I'm here to help. I came to get you out." He moved past Lewis and stood at the window, watching the grey sea slam into the rocks.

Lewis stayed by the fridge, arms crossed, processing. How had Scott pulled this off? Monk wouldn't approve this. You didn't just walk out through a portal.

Scott slumped onto the sofa, hugging a bright yellow cushion like it might protect him. "What I did…" he said, "I didn't mean for it to go like this. Just a couple of activations. I was pissed, okay? After what you did. And then getting booted… I wasn't thinking." His voice faltered. Even he knew how weak it sounded.

Yeah, Lewis betrayed him. But Scott hadn't expected it to explode like this.

Lewis stared at his friend—his teammate. Two years of history between them. He thought he knew Scott. He walked over and stood in front of him.

"Why?" was all he said.

Scott raised his head and frowned, "Payback," he said quietly.

"Yes, yes, I'm fully aware of that," Lewis was flicking his hand at Scott, his eyes were steely, his nostrils flared. Scott had never seen Lewis quite like that before.

"But why the deuce, Darcy, Byron? Me talking like an arrogant twat," Lewis said, voice cold.

Scott didn't answer. He just looked at Lewis and raised both eyebrows.

"And what is that supposed to mean?" said Lewis. *What's he implying?!*

Scott threw the cushion across the room. It bounced off the flat screen and hit the floor.

"You're… arrogant. You think—" Scott stood up. Hands balled into fists. "Everything comes easy to you. You want it, you get it. And you don't care who you trample over. Win at any cost. That's your motto. You knew I liked—" he hesitated, "—you knew I liked her. But you had to show me."

Lewis opened his mouth. Nothing came out. That wasn't him. Was it? *And what about freaking Poppy?*

Scott's anger drained. His shoulders sagged. He brushed past Lewis and opened the fridge.

Lewis raised an eyebrow. "Wasn't expecting guests." He grabbed the cushion off the floor.

Scott returned with the juice, took a long swig, then handed it over. Lewis took it. Weighed it. He didn't trust himself to speak. Drained the carton.

***

Violet wheeled her bike to the front gate. One hinge. Always one. Ever since Derek kicked it. The garage door was open. His BMW was inside.

She felt sick. That old dread in her stomach. Home. She locked the back wheel, spinning the code, trying to think of anything but Lewis. *Don't. Don't go there.*

But the image came anyway—him tossing back his hair, that half-smile. The one that stopped her breath. She didn't want it. Didn't need it.

The TV was blaring. Always on. Always shouting.

Violet lifted the gate and slammed it shut. She looked at the house. Once red-bricked and pristine, now overgrown and hollow.

Her father had kept it neat. Since he died and Derek moved in, it felt like a different world. The garden was a mess. Curtains always closed. The place felt like it was asleep—and not in a peaceful way.

She stood still until the tears threatening her went away. Then she wiped her eyes, unlocked the door, and stepped inside.

CHAPTER NINE

Scott sat at the table, laptop open. "I'm ordering pizza. Paying online."

Lewis had changed into jeans and a sweatshirt. Barefoot. He said nothing, padded into the room, leaned over Scott's shoulder.

"Vegetarian spicy."

Two words. Short bursts. Safer that way. Anything longer, and the Regency crap might leak out.

They sat in silence, side-by-side at the table, buried in their laptops. When the food came, they ate without talking. Passed the lemonade bottle back and forth.

Scott burped loudly. Twice. He held the bottle up. "More CO_2 than home. And sugar."

Lewis tried to resist. Failed. Let out a long, loud belch. Scott grinned. It was hard to stay angry. But Lewis wasn't over it. Not while he was still talking like a literary freak.

He pushed the pizza box aside and stared at Scott. He had questions. "So," Lewis said, leaning back, "how did you get here?"

Scott looked up. Relief. A real question. Lewis sounded… mostly normal. "Same way you did."

"Not the portal. I mean—who gave you the exit pass?"

Scott didn't answer. Just stretched his fingers out on the table. Then he looked up. Grinned.

Lewis felt a chill. His stomach turned. "You didn't get an exit pass… did you?"

Scott didn't reply. Just stared at his own hands, as if they belonged to someone else.

"Small oversight. Couldn't wait for permission I wasn't gonna get," Scott said, casually leaning back. "No time to waste. Your transmitter went dead. I knew where you were and once I got here, I tracked your watch."

Lewis glanced at the red welt on his wrist where the watch had been. His shoulders sagged. A headache bloomed behind his eyes.

"And the rest?" he said flatly.

Scott shrugged. "I trained for this. Everything was in place. I just hacked the system, grabbed what I needed." He nodded toward the credit card and mobile on the table.

"You mean stole," Lewis muttered, tapping the tabletop. "You're an idiot."

Scott rubbed his forehead. "Had to, after what I'd done. Everyone was freaking out when your transmitter stopped. Monk lost it. Then Rochester showed up."

Lewis's head snapped up.

"Yeah. He was there." Scott gave a half-hearted shrug. "Didn't seem right, him being there. Too much security. He knew what I'd done. He was…"

"He was what?"

Scott frowned, searching the memory. "Angry, I think. But controlled. Like you get. Cold. Detached."

"Thanks for the comparison," Lewis said dryly, thoughts racing. Eighteen years. Rochester had said he'd waited eighteen years. This was his mission. The girl—they needed someone who could pass for eighteen to find her. She meant something to him.

Scott was watching Lewis carefully now. "What?"

"You're an ass," Lewis said, jabbing the table.

Scott smirked. "Could have been worse. "I'm sorry about the assimilation," Scott added. "The lightning—it corrupted the upload—"

"No. You corrupted it!" Lewis's voice was tight.

Scott nodded. "I'm sorry."

"You already said that…" Lewis narrowed his eyes. *He's lying. Rochester sent him.*

"Yeah, and?" Scott didn't like the way Lewis was looking at him, like he was a cockroach.

"The assimilation program," Lewis said.

"What about it?"

"You… Don't. Have. One." Lewis leaned in, each word clipped.

Scott let out a breath. "Phew. Thought you were gonna punch me."

"Don't change the subject."

"I don't need it," Scott said quickly. "The cultural download, the assimilator—I speak like they do. Barely any cultural difference. Haven't even noticed."

Lewis pressed a hand to his temple. "And you knew this before you left?"

Scott shook his head.

"You could have told me back there… back at the school."

"No, man, come on. I was rushing. Slipped my mind."

Lewis rubbed the node behind his ear. "I didn't need the download?" he said, almost to himself. "You saw the program?" he asked sharply.

"No. I just watched Tech Two build it. You know, the one with the… anyway, I watched her. That's how I knew how to—" He laced his fingers behind his head and stared at the ceiling.

Lewis's pulse was racing. *What's in my head?*

"It's gonna be okay, Lewis. We'll get out of this."

"What does Monk say? Does he want—" Lewis stopped. He saw Scott look down, hands clasped like he was about to say grace. A chill ran up Lewis's spine.

"You can't contact Monk, can you?"

Scott shrugged.

"You're shrugging?" Lewis's voice was ice. "We've got no way to get back. No comms. No base support."

Scott shifted, squirming in his chair. "It wasn't supposed to go like this…"

"Do you even have a plan?" *Of course not.*

Scott blinked. "Yeah, sure. We finish the mission. Go home. Get the bonus. I keep my place in the Agency."

Lewis stood and stretched. "Right. And before you left, did you check for any updates? Exit time? Location?"

Scott hesitated. "No changes."

Lewis stared him down. Scott turned to the kitchen.

He's lying, Lewis thought, heart sinking. *This isn't sanctioned. It's rogue. No one's coming for us.*

"So, your plan is we work together. Find the girl. Just one thing—how am I supposed to fit in at school? Today was a disaster."

Scott rubbed his mouth. "Ah, not sure if you've noticed… but it's not too bad anymore. Just a bit… posh. Mostly it kicks in when—"

"When?" Lewis slammed his fist down.

Scott flinched. "Girls. Mostly when they're around."

Lewis bowed his head, staring at a glob of pizza topping. His chest was on fire. Rage flared hot behind his eyes. He tried to breathe through it, clench it down.

He turned and stalked into the bathroom, shutting the door with a bang. Leaned on the sink. *Breathe. Think.*

Scott's "payback" was way out of proportion. Yeah, Poppy had kissed him. Yeah, he'd kissed her back—for a second. But he'd stopped. He'd shut it down.

He looked at himself in the mirror. Scott's words echoed: *You don't care who you trample over.* Was that really how people saw him? He shook his head remembering the confrontation with Scott back in Perfection. Scott's bunched fists and his own anger boiling over in the words he threw at him. He grimaced at his reflection. *Shouldn't have said all's fair in love and war. Idiot.*

Still. As angry as he was, he knew he had to be grateful Scott was here. The lightning had taken out his transmitter—that wasn't Scott's fault. But forgiveness? That was a long way off.

Back in the lounge, Scott was folding the pizza box.

Lewis stepped out. "I want to say one thing," he said. "I'm sorry for what I said. In Perfection. I didn't mean it. I shouldn't have said it. It was… provocative. I'm sorry."

"Yeah, I know," Scott said quietly. "I should've known you better. Forget it. You weren't the only one she…" he trailed off. "Dave Gilmour, too."

Lewis raised an eyebrow. "Sorry to hear that."

Scott shrugged. "It's done. Hey, I saw a corner store nearby. We should grab supplies. I'll go, if you want."

Lewis looked out the window. The rain had stopped. The ocean was still wild. "We'll both go."

Scott pulled a navy rain jacket from his pack. Lewis recognized it— Agency standard. Identical to his.

"Came here first," Scott said, noticing Lewis's glance. "Didn't want to look like a tourist at school."

Lewis said nothing. Scott had everything. Keys. Tools. Equipment. And he'd made him climb ten flights of stairs.

CHAPTER TEN

Violet went straight to her room and shoved a chair under the door handle. Mona had taken her key. No way to lock the door from inside.

She kicked off her shoes and changed into trackpants and a hoodie. Scanned the room. Had Mona been in here again? Probably.

Mona always wanted to know everything about her—and Violet gave her nothing. She took a breath, moved the chair aside, and went to find her.

Mona was exactly where Violet expected her—sprawled on the couch, some trashy afternoon show flickering on the screen, half-empty wine bottles on the table.

"It's just a glass with lunch, Violet," Mona had said once, eyes unfocused. "Doesn't mean I'm an alcoholic."

But Violet knew better. She'd tried speaking up once. Derek had shut her down.

"Don't disrespect your mother," he'd snapped.

"I'm not her bloody mother," Mona had said coldly.

Mona had banned Violet and Jamie from calling her "Mum" the second Derek moved in. "I'm too young to have a daughter your age. Besides, I'm not your mother."

Violet had stared at her across the kitchen bench. Said nothing. Jamie had pushed up his glasses and muttered, "We're too smart to be your kids."

It was the money. Violet knew that. The trust fund left when their dad died. She didn't know the exact amount, but she saw where it went—Derek's car, the Rolex, the long overseas holidays. "You and Jamie can't miss school," Mona would say.

As if they wanted to go anywhere with them.

Violet wanted to run away, escape Mona. But she didn't. Jamie, her little brother, meant everything to her. Just ten. She could survive. He couldn't.

And Mona didn't lift a finger to protect him from Derek's constant teasing. "He's got to toughen up, Violet. Derek's doing him a favour."

"There you are," said Derek.

He was in her dad's old chair, legs splayed, whiskey glass in hand. Smiling that sleazy smile. "You didn't answer my text. Mona's not feeling well. Thought you should get home and help."

Violet ignored him. Looked at Mona—half-conscious, hair in a messy top knot, face flushed. Mona stirred. "My head…" she groaned. "Splitting. You'll have to cook tonight, Violet. Migraine."

Like every night, Violet thought.

"I cooked yesterday. Casserole. We can eat that," Violet said, keeping her voice flat.

"You're a better cook than Mona," Derek said softly.

Derek pulled out his wallet and held up Mona's credit card. "Go down to the store. Get something for dinner. And fifty bucks cash. "Mona and I had the casserole for lunch," he added with a smile.

Violet's real mum had died when she was eight. Jamie was just a baby. Her dad had done his best—until Mona showed up at his office two years later.

At first, Mona was fun. Like a big sister. But after they got married, things changed. Babysitters. Partying. Mona wanted out. Always.

When her dad died suddenly, Mona stopped pretending.

"You're a burden. Both of you. I'm too young for this." She'd said it with a toss of her hair and vanished for the weekend with a new man.

"Dad's only been dead three months!" Jamie had shouted.

Violet remembered the will. The house in trust until she turned twenty-one. Half for her, half for Jamie. Mona only controlled the money while they were in her care.

And the clock was ticking.

CHAPTER ELEVEN

Scott led the way into the supermarket, grabbing a bright red basket from a stack near the door. He didn't wait for Lewis, just headed straight down the nearest aisle. The grey, thrashing waves outside had matched Lewis's mood; now the supermarket's fluorescent buzz only made it worse.

"Here," said Scott, tossing a loaf of white bread into the basket.

Lewis eyed the packet. "My preference is for wholemeal," he said, as if issuing a royal decree.

Scott rolled his eyes. A young woman nearby was scanning the shelves of packaged cakes. She glanced up at Lewis. He caught her eye, swept his hair back, and moved toward her with a deliberate smile.

Scott stepped in front of him and shoved the basket into his arms. "Carry this and follow me. Don't talk to anyone," he hissed.

Lewis narrowed his eyes. "I wasn't talking to anyone. I was talking to you."

"Yeah. I know," said Scott, dragging him by the arm down the canned vegetable aisle.

Lewis gritted his teeth. "You're a dead man," he muttered.

Jamie hated shopping. But with Derek always lurking at home, even the supermarket was an escape.

"Can you get some potatoes—the little ones—and whatever you want for school?" said Violet as she turned into the first aisle. She stopped. Up ahead: Lewis and Scott.

Lewis was jabbing Scott in the chest with one finger. "If you laugh, man, I'm thumping you!"

Violet hesitated. She could turn back—but she needed items from that aisle. No choice.

"Hi," she said, approaching with her basket. Keep walking. Don't stop.

Lewis turned. Light caught her hair, her blue sweatshirt, the red basket looped over her arm. Something stirred in his mind—an image, a phrase. Don't speak, Scott had said.

He failed. "By jove." Lewis murmured, "she walks in beauty like the night."

Scott elbowed him hard in the stomach. Lewis wheezed. "Hi Violet," said Scott quickly.

Violet ignored him. Her eyes stayed on Lewis. "Are you okay? Did you see a doctor?"

Lie. Keep it short. Let her know I'm alright.

Scott jumped in. "Yeah, he's fine. Just a headache. Tough as—"

"—I possess, madam, a constitution of iron, Lewis interrupted, – well able to weather tempest and the odd bolt from Olympus." He smiled—blindingly.

Scott turned away and coughed. "Anyway," he said, pointing to the basket in Lewis's arms, "better keep shopping."

They all moved along the aisle. Ahead, Violet's younger brother Jamie waved a bag of potatoes at her.

"This enough?" he shouted.

The bag split. Potatoes bounced and rolled in all directions.

"My brother," Violet muttered, bending to the floor to help him.

Lewis and Scott joined in, gathering the scattered spuds. Lewis placed his carefully into Violet's basket. Scott lobbed his in like he was on a basketball court. A potato bounced in, then straight out.

Violet frowned.

Lewis clenched his jaw. "Nincompoop! Addlepated turnip, what are you playing at?" he muttered. He straightened. He had to get away. Away from Violet. Away from this nonsense.

He bowed stiffly. "Take your leave," he muttered, dropping the basket at Scott's feet. Then he turned and walked briskly in the opposite direction.

"What did he call you?" Jamie's eyes tracked Lewis's retreating figure.

Scott kept his head down as he carefully placed the last potato in Violet's basket. It was worse than he'd thought, but he couldn't stop smiling. Watching Lewis was entertaining.

"Wait," said Violet as Scott moved to follow. "I told you, I saw what happened this morning—the lightning... I don't know how he survived. He's acting... I don't know... odd."

She couldn't figure him out. He wasn't like any boy she'd ever met. That smile he'd given her—warm, too warm. But she'd seen him aim it at other girls. *Don't be fooled, Violet. Don't make the same mistake again.*

Scott caught her concerned look. He furrowed his brow as though considering Lewis seriously. "Nah, he's always been like that. A bit... eccentric." That was safe. "He likes poetry."

"Likes what? Poetry?" Jamie scoffed. "That's weird."

Violet studied Scott. She wasn't convinced. Lewis didn't seem eccentric—just... different. And Scott wouldn't meet her eyes.

Scott bent to pick up the basket. It was almost full—not with junk food, but real food: bread, milk, cheese, vegetables.

"See you at school, then," he said quickly. He didn't want questions. He wasn't a good liar and knew it.

Violet caught up with them at the checkout. She stood behind Lewis, watching him unload the groceries.

"Who does the cooking?" she asked, nosy without apology.

Lewis hesitated. "His mother," he said, picking up a bag as Scott swiped his credit card.

"Do you live together?" she asked, tipping her basket onto the conveyor belt.

Scott raised an eyebrow. Lewis said, "Yes. Temporarily. While my parents are travelling abroad."

Scott blinked. That was a lie—and Lewis didn't lie.

Before Scott could shut him up, Lewis added, "I look forward to seeing you tomorrow, Violet of the greenish eyes and kissable lips."

His voice was velvet. His eyes sparkled. It looked like he wanted to kiss her—right there, under the supermarket lights.

Violet's eyes filled with tears. She bit her lip, her cheeks flaming.

Lewis's jaw clenched. *Hell. I only meant to say I'd see her tomorrow. What did I say?*

Scott wasn't smiling now. "Ignore him," he said. "He does that all the time."

Violet nodded. "I know. He's been doing it all day." But it wasn't that. He'd made her feel something—and that was the problem.

Outside, Jamie asked, "Is that your boyfriend? The one who wants to kiss you?"

"What?" said Violet.

"I said, is that your boyfriend?"

"No." Violet's voice was fierce. "He's just an idiot."

In the lift, Lewis hadn't spoken. He didn't trust himself. Finally, he said, low and bitter, "I made her cry. That's your fault, Scott. Damn you."

Scott stayed quiet. He'd seen the tears. He felt bad, but it wasn't the end of the world. While unpacking groceries, Scott said defensively, "I told you not to speak."

Lewis glared at him. He wanted to throttle him. Instead, he placed both hands on the kitchen bench and breathed through his rage.

He sat on the couch, opened a strawberry milk, and stared into it.

"She looks sad," he said to the TV. Then he drank.

"Forget it. It wasn't that bad," said Scott. "It was a compliment. Bet she liked it."

Lewis crushed the carton. "I doubt it. Some damned fool making a scene in front of her brother..." He stared at the floor. "No—I mean she looks sad. Just... sad."

Scott unpacked the rest in silence, worry gnawing at his chest.

"What's your plan, Scott?" Lewis asked finally. He flicked on the light, sat at the table, and waited.

Scott joined him, shifting uncomfortably. He didn't answer.

"There is no plan, is there?"

Scott grinned and held out his hands. That old gesture—you make the plan, I'll follow.

Lewis sighed. "Damn it, Scott. We're absolutely out of our depth. No contact with base. That's critical. Forget the mission? Have you even thought of that?"

Scott shrugged. "Got the credit card. We could go north. Explore."

Lewis stared him down. "Forget travelling. We complete the mission. That's our only shot at getting out of here."

Scott nodded, but the idea of travel still sat in the back of his mind.

Lewis pulled out a notebook. "Okay, brainstorm." He wrote: CROSS in the middle of the page.

"Cross," he said aloud. "The Bureau's man in DZ. Arranged everything. I met him at the exit point. Gave me the keys. Said he was leaving."

"Leaving?" Scott frowned. "He went back to Perfection?"

"Seemed like it. I didn't ask. Cold as hell, and he was in a rush."

Scott thought. "I don't think he left. Rochester mentioned a man in DZ— said something to Monk... get Cross to fix something..."

Lewis froze. "Cross. And you didn't think to tell me?"

Scott shrank. "I meant to."

Lewis rolled his shoulders, breathed slowly. "Okay. Forget Cross. We just need the exit point."

Scott blinked, his lips dry. He still hadn't told Lewis the worst of it.

"Exit point?" Said Lewis coldly. Picking up the pen from the table. He spun it between his fingers, flicking it across his knuckles with ease.

Scott blinked.

That was all Lewis needed. No need to ask again. *He doesn't know the goddam exit point.*

He waited.

Scott licked his lips, gave a feeble shrug. "I thought you'd figure it out," he mumbled, eyes darting away. "You're good at that...getting yourself out of a tight spot." His voice had an edge, the words twisted at the end. It sounded like an accusation.

The pen dropped, rolled off the pad, and rattled against the table. Lewis leaned forward and stopped it with the flat of his hand. The fridge kicked in. A low hum filled the silence.

Lewis shoved back from the table. He had to move – now – before he exploded.

He paced between the sofa and the kitchen bench. Three strides. Turn. Three strides. Turn. Air hissed through his teeth in short, sharp blasts, like he was building up to clean and press Scott over his head – and launch him through the nearest wall.

Scott wrapped his arms around himself. He didn't like the look of Lewis pacing. A small nut of doubt about Lewis's so-called genius hovered in the air. He batted it aside.

"Calm down man, Monk knows where we are," said Scott, studying the pen between his fingers like it was ancient relic.

Lewis stopped pacing. He turned to Scott, hands on hips, grey eyes blazing.

"And how exactly do they contact us?"

A beat.

"Thought about that, have you? No? Didn't think so."

The sarcasm in Lewis's voice was as thick as cold custard.

Scott looked up. Lewis was balanced on the balls of his feet like a man teetering on a cliff's edge and he was dragging Scott with him on the way down.

Scott ran a hand through his hair, fingers catching in the curls. He'd meant to get it cut. He smoothed it down, frowning, as if deep in thought. The way he saw it, it wasn't a big deal. These things got sorted. No one got lost in another world anymore. That was twenty years ago. Not now.

"Monk's working on it…fixing…your transmitter and the …" His voice trailed off. Bad idea to mention the assimilator.

Lewis's lips flattened into a hard line. *Dickhead* He touched the dot behind his ear, rubbing it with his finger. Lifeless. He hadn't let himself think about the consequences of a faulty transmitter. When he saw Scott – well, after he wanted to murder him – he'd felt a flicker of hope. Scott had come. That meant it was going to be okay. Scott was his parachute home.

Now? Lewis shut his eyes for a second. *Think, dammit. You can think your way out of this. Come on.*

CHAPTER TWELVE

Jamie was loading the dishes into the dishwasher. Violet watched Mona and Derek leave the house and smiled at Jamie.

"They've gone - at last."

"Yeh but they'll be back." He screwed up his nose.

Violet felt relieved whenever Derek left the house. Since the day he'd moved in she'd been on alert. He acted like he owned the place - like he had every right to sit in her father's favourite chair, sleep in his bedroom, use his things. The first time she saw him wearing her dad's jacket, something snapped.

"You can't wear that…it's my father's," her voice quivering like a plucked guitar string.

"This," he'd pulled at the lapels, "he's not here to wear it, is he? Is he? No, thought not."

His mocking tone made Violet's chest tighten a raging tiger trapped inside her chest.

Mona stormed out of the bedroom, her red high heels thudding on the polished floorboards. "What's going on?" she snapped.

She'd heard the exchange, Violet was sure. Mona was the kind of person who said, "*Sorry, what did you say?*" just for the pleasure of making you repeat yourself – while she stared you down.

Derek threw her a smug look. "The princess doesn't like me wearing this jacket."

"Don't call me that!" Violet's voice shook with fury. "Buy your own clothes…you parasite."

Derek stepped forward, his face darkening. His mouth pinched, one arm rising.

"If you hit her, I'll tell the police."

It was Jamie - standing in the hallway like a soldier, fists at his side, eyes blazing. He looked impossibly small and impossibly brave.

Derek spun around, but Violet moved fast, pulling Jamie into his room and slamming the door. She hugged him tightly. Her little brother. Fierce and fearless. She loved him more than anything in the world.

Now the house was quiet. Mona and Derek were gone. Violet and Jamie finished up in the kitchen. Violet wiped down the kitchen bench and rinsed the cloth, draping it neatly over the tap. She watched Jamie as he crouched, carefully placing the dishwashing tablet like it was a live grenade. He clicked the door shut and read the buttons aloud, "Rinse. Normal wash, Economy dry," He pressed the last one and the machine hummed to life.

Violet smiled. They never changed the washing cycle. A small ritual their dad had started—one of those little things that kept him close.

Jamie was like him. Same thick dark hair, same sharp blue eyes.

"Scottish ancestors, Jamie," their father had said once.

Violet remembered it clearly. Jamie had been six. He'd looked it up, then marched into the kitchen and declared he wasn't going to wear a skirt.

"It's called a kilt," their dad had told him, laughing. "Only worn for special occasions."

Jamie had rolled his eyes.

He was like their dad in other ways too—curious about how things worked, always asking questions. And smart. Everyone knew that. The school had accelerated him three years ahead, and now he was the youngest kid at the high school.

But brave? Jamie was braver. No, she didn't want to think that. Didn't want to compare. Her father had been a good man. That's what she needed to remember. Stay positive. He'd tried his best.

It was Mona who'd changed everything—like some twisted fairytale. The wicked stepmother. The woman who came in smiling and left them with nothing.

At seven o'clock, Violet left Jamie in his room, glued to his computer. She pulled the pink plastic retro radio off her shelf and unscrewed the back. It hadn't worked in months—not since she took out the batteries.

Inside was a rolled bundle of notes tucked into the battery slot. Mostly tens and twenties. Nine hundred and fifty dollars in total. She didn't steal every time Mona or Derek handed her the credit card—just here and there, whenever they asked her to get cash.

It's Dad's money, she told herself. *Ours. Jamie's and mine.*

Not enough to escape. Not yet. She needed at least three thousand: two thousand for flights, another to survive until she found work.

She added a ten-dollar note to the roll, slid the bundle back into place, and snapped the radio shut. It went back on the bedside table, next to her alarm clock.

She checked the time. Just enough for a run before Mona and Derek got home from the pub. Jamie would be fine. She'd left him alone before. The house had security locks.

***

Lewis stood at the window, staring into the darkening sky. Back home it was still summer. Blue skies, long evenings, the sun easing into the ocean like it had all the time in the world. Would he ever see that again?

He moved closer. Below, the sea shifted under a faint silver moon. The waves rose and folded back on themselves, hissing along the rocks. A flicker of movement near the window's edge caught his eye—a runner. A girl in a yellow windcheater and dark tights. Her stride was fluid, almost effortless. She moved like the pavement was soft beneath her feet, like the wind pushed her forward.

She lifted her head briefly, glancing toward his window. The light caught her face. Then she was gone.

Violet found her rhythm by the second block. Her feet skimmed the pavement, hips rolling, strides long and even. She kept her music off at night— no beats, no distractions. She wanted her ears clear. For traffic. For dogs. For Derek, just in case.

In the mornings she ran the beach track, weaving along the dunes with the other early risers. But at night she stuck to the footpath near the road, bathed in streetlight.

The wind hit her hard from the ocean side—rough going out, easier on the return. She focused on her breathing. In through the nose, out through the mouth. Just like the meditation app said. But clearing her mind was harder than it sounded.

Lewis.

The lightning flash. His silhouette. That impossible moment had seared itself into her brain. He was a contradiction. Vulnerable and arrogant. Mysterious and—definitely weird. He'd said he was a drama student. Total lie.

Still…

A man ran past with a dog, and Violet stepped wide. Dogs always waited till you were close before losing their minds.

Yeah, he's weird all right. She tried to land on the right word. Jenna would have helped. They used to rank boys in categories. Funny, smart, hot, undatable, etc. She ripped up the list in her mind. She didn't want to think about Jenna. Or lists. Or boys.

Violet picked up speed, legs burning, breath sharp in her chest. She passed the all-night supermarket, its fluorescent lights humming. She'd seen Lewis there earlier. That smile he'd given her—

Don't think about it.

She chanted in time with her stride. *Don't think. Don't think.* But Lewis was in her head again. Running beside her. His voice. His face. The way he called her *Clorinda*—what the hell was that?

Kissable lips. Her feet pounded out the rhythm on the pavement, one, two, kissable lips, greenish eyes.

Kissable lips,
Greenish eyes,
Kissable lips,
Greenish eyes.

She was nearing the large block of units she'd seen Lewis and Scott disappear into earlier. The white building stood stark against the indigo sky, its windows mostly black, a few glowing faintly with soft light. The ocean thundered against the rocks below.

Violet glanced up—and saw a dark figure in one of the windows. Even after just a few hours, she knew it was him.

She caught her breath and ran harder toward the statue of the nameless sailor, her turnaround point—beyond it the safety of houses gave way to thick brush that could hide anything. She turned before reaching it, her rhythm off, like she'd forgotten how to run. Her timing shifted. She slowed, lengthened her stride, let her arms hang loose. Her eyes locked on the distant surf club roof, shining silver under the streetlight.

As she rounded the curve past the club, she caught sight of the apartment block again. Her chest ached like she'd run a marathon. All day, ever since she first saw him, that feeling had been building inside her. A flutter. That awful, wonderful, flutter.

She knew that feeling. She remembered it. And she didn't want it.

If it hadn't been for that feeling, she and Jenna would still be friends. That feeling had flicked on a light after months of dark—but she'd followed it, and everything had gone to hell.

She bit her lip hard. *Don't think about him.* She hadn't thought about him for weeks. Not since he was expelled. Because of her. *It's not my fault.* What he did was—

She shut it down. She wouldn't have survived school if he'd stayed. But Jenna, his cousin, had stayed—and made sure Violet didn't forget.

And now, here it was again. That feeling. That flutter. *You're pathetic,* she told herself. *Someone says something nice and you melt. You are not doing this again, Violet Mackenzie, do you hear me?*

He's an idiot. And you're worse if you fall for it again. Kissable lips? Get real.

She gritted her teeth, set her jaw, and pushed harder. Arms pumping, lungs burning. She passed the apartment block without looking up—not even a glance. Just full-on sprinting. That idiot boy.

Up ahead, the man with the dog—now walking, the animal trotting at his heels. Violet veered off the pavement, into the road, not breaking her stride. She wasn't taking chances with dogs and their surprise ankle attacks.

Back up onto the footpath, she hit her stride again. The wind was at her back now, pushing her forward. She was imagining the dog biting her, the owner yelling—and then she saw him.

Someone jogging just ahead. Warming up. Tall, dark-haired. She knew who it was.

Lewis.

She checked her speed. She couldn't follow just behind him—not for five hundred metres. That would look ridiculous. She surged forward and sprinted past him like she was crossing a finish line.

She had maybe 500 metres left until she hit the turnoff. No way could she keep that pace. But maybe enough to put some distance between them. Then she heard him. Footsteps. He was behind her, gaining.

She couldn't go faster. This was it—she was at her max.

He drew level beside her, his hair bouncing in the wind. She didn't look. Didn't speak. Just nodded, barely.

They ran together. Side by side. Like this was normal. Lewis kept his pace slow, even though his body wanted to sprint, to clear his head.

He'd left Scott behind to come up with a plan. Said he needed space to think. At the Academy they always ran together—someone once joked they were joined at the hip. It didn't feel like that now. More like he needed a hip replacement.

Running next to Violet felt…right. She had a good stride. A natural. He wanted to say something—was fighting it down. He wasn't even sure what he meant to say, just that something was coming, and he couldn't stop it. He glanced sideways. Mistake. The words bubbled up.

He sprinted ahead to stop them from spilling out—but it was too late. He tossed them over his shoulder like a curse.

"Moonlight becomes you…" *Damn it, Lewis! More freaking poetry?*

He turned, jogging backward to see her face—and regretted it instantly. She looked like she'd just swallowed a dead fish left out in the sun.

Violet stopped. She gave him one withering look. He didn't see it. But he felt it. Violet crossed the road without a word. She wanted to run away, but her lungs were shot. Her chest burned. She was gasping like a baby taking its first breath.

Lewis chased after her. He didn't know why. He couldn't explain it—not to Scott, not even to himself. She made him feel…safe. That was the closest he could get to the truth. He angled across the road and stepped into her path.

"Sorry. Apologies. Don't mean to offend…" He made a slow circle in the air with his hand, and for a second Violet thought he was about to bow. But he didn't.

"Forget it. I don't care." She tried to brush past him.

He stepped sideways and folded his arms. "Wait. I…" The words lined up in his head—*I'm sorry if I'm being an absolute dick. My assimilator's fried because of Scott.* But he couldn't say that.

Or maybe: *You've been kind. I've been rude. I don't have a good reason but ignore it. I'm not great with words.* Yeah, that's what he wanted to say.

Violet stared at his chest. His white windcheater. And then, stupidly, an image from the bike shed that morning flooded her mind—Lewis, wet, dragging his shirt off, the muscles of his chest, the rain hammering the tin roof. Her hand against his heart.

She shoved her hands into her pockets. Looked up at him. He was backlit in the blue-black light. He didn't speak. And she wasn't going to rescue him.

Lewis held himself still. He felt the itch to bow, like it was breathing. Instinct. But something told him not to. Another part of him wanted to grab her, kiss her, shut up every part of him that kept blurting poetry.

He closed his eyes. "Walk... obliged if you... let... walk you home," he said, voice catching. He held out an elbow awkwardly.

Violet looked at it. His face caught the moonlight—serious, aloof. Raised eyebrows, practiced posture. But his eyes told the real story.

He doesn't know what he's doing. He's terrified.

She didn't speak. Instead, she pressed his arm down, firm and steady. Her fingers dug through his windcheater. Strong. Certain.

He nodded, relieved. He wanted to thank her—so he smiled. And the glow of that smile hit her heart like a tiny mouse leaping behind her ribs.

"You can walk me to the top of my road," Violet said. "No further." She didn't want him to see the house. It looked unloved, forgotten. "And stop smiling like that," she added. "It's insincere. No one smiles like that unless they're—"

Lewis was processing it all—her words, her body language, the things she didn't say. The arm thing. Right. Keep them folded. The smile? That was trickier. Wasn't it supposed to be friendly? Positive?

He shoved his hands into his pockets. Walked beside her. Tried not to look at her, not to feel her beside him. Tried not to let the rush of thoughts and feelings come pouring out of his mouth.

This is insane. I can't even have a normal conversation.

He clenched his jaw. She was kind. He didn't want to ruin it. He wasn't aloof. Wasn't arrogant. He was…reserved. Yes. That was it. Reserved. It had never occurred to him that might not be true. He batted the idea away like a mosquito.

They walked in silence, like a couple who'd had a fight and were still tethered by the weight of it.

Violet had stopped thinking the moment they'd turned away from the beach. Something about walking next to him just felt…easy. Her head came to his shoulder, and for some reason she felt like he needed her. Like he was reaching out. And part of her wanted to reach back.

"We're here," she said as they reached the crossroads at the bottom of her street. The supermarket glowed at the corner. She pointed ahead.

Lewis squinted across the busy road. Violet extended an arm across him. "Parallel road," she said, "just past that lamp."

He didn't want to leave her standing here alone. Every cell in his body was telling him *no way*. He didn't know if that was old-fashioned, chivalry, or just decent.

"I'll see you across. My pleasure… Clorinda."

Violet snapped her head toward him. Glared.

His brows pinched together. His forehead furrowed. She could see the corners of his mouth twitching. He was trying not to laugh. Lewis blew out his cheeks. The light turned green. He took her elbow and guided her forward. She shoved his hand off. He let it fall.

Her head was full of questions—but she didn't trust him to answer seriously. Maybe he couldn't.

"Where did you go to school?" she asked.

"Eton," he said, voice low, like it was sacred.

"Eton? The one in England? Where the King's grandsons went?" She stared at him. "Are you English? You sound it."

Lewis winced inside. Of course. His alter egos were English. They probably went to Eton too. He didn't answer.

"How long have you been in Australia?" she tried again, glancing at the time. Late. She had to get home before Mona and Derek did.

"A short while," Lewis said. He couldn't tell her the truth. Too many questions would follow.

She gave him a look. He was the most confusing boy she'd ever met. Evasive. Arrogant. Aloof. Infuriating.

She had a dozen words lining up in her head, about to burst out—But then he looked at her. Really looked. His gaze sharpened, focused. Like he was seeing her for the first time. She froze. Her heart slammed against her ribs. He was looking at her lips. One eyebrow lifted, like he was asking a question. Then he leaned in. Pulled her against his chest.

And kissed her.

Violet couldn't breathe. His lips were soft, warm, pressing gently into hers One of his hands at her back, the other at her neck. Her fingers slipped into his hair—until her brain kicked in and she pushed away.

"Stop," she whispered.

Lewis dropped his arms and stepped back. "Sorry… damn…" His voice was hoarse. "Beg your pardon. Forgive me, Violet." He turned his face to the sky. He couldn't look at her.

Then—A squeal of brakes. A car pulling up.

Violet spun around. Mona and Derek. Derek yanked open the door. The window rolled down. Mona leaned out. "Get in the car, Violet. *Now.*"

Derek's jacket flared open as he stormed around the bonnet. Violet shrank against Lewis. Her heart plummeted to her stomach.

Lewis hadn't quite registered the angry man heading his way—But he'd seen Violet flinch. Felt her recoil. He knew fear when he saw it. He put a hand on her shoulder. Gently. And squeezed.

"Go," he said. He could see the look on her face. *She's scared of what I'm going to say.*

Violet walked to the car. She pressed the back of her hand to her lips It had happened so fast. Had she really let him kiss her? *I should have stopped him. Who does he think he is?*

She wiped her hand across her mouth. *He knows. He knows about me.*

She slid into the back seat behind Mona and curled her hands into fists. It had to be Jenna. Jenna had told him.

The car reeked of alcohol. She rolled the window down. She could get drunk just breathing in the fumes. She needed to forget him. Forget the kiss.

Lewis walked toward Derek, one hand in his pocket, the other extended. Derek instinctively reached out to shake it.

"What's he doing?" Mona slurred.

Violet looked away. *Please don't bow,* she silently begged. *Don't say anything stupid. Just be normal. Please, Lewis. Be normal.*

"Lewis Green. You're Violet's father, right?" Lewis said, loud enough *for* them all to hear. "I'm sorry I kept Violet out late. Just asking about school— we're in the same classes. I only started today."

Every word landed clear. He sounded normal. Not English. Not pompous. Just…in charge. He looked relaxed, confident, hand in pocket, face serious. He looked older.

Derek shifted his weight, itching for a fight. "She's responsible for her brother. He shouldn't be left alone. It's-"

"—bloody irresponsible," Mona cut in, leaning out the window. Her voice thick.

Violet twisted her fingers in her lap. *Had they seen the kiss?*

Lewis stepped to the side and saw Mona. The calm mask on his face slipped. He could smell the booze. No need for a breathalyser to know she was over the limit.

He took a step closer, eyes locked on Mona. Violet sank down in her seat. Her face was burning. She couldn't look at him.

Mona was watching him now, twirling a strand of hair, her anger evaporating. She tilted her head as Lewis reached the window. She extended her hand. Lewis took it. And bowed.

It wasn't deep—but it was deliberate. He caught her fingers lightly, leaned forward. Mona smiled—syrupy and slow.

Lewis smiled back. *Why not?* he thought.

It lit up the car like fireworks.

"I hope to call upon you and Violet shortly," he said, stepping back.

Then he saw Violet, head down, lip between her teeth. He tapped on the window. No response. He tapped harder.

Mona hissed, "Violet."

She looked up. Her eyes sparkled—but not with joy. Anger. Embarrassment. Betrayal.

Lewis mouthed, "Sorry." She looked away.

Derek revved the engine and the car shot forward like he was drag racing.

Lewis didn't move. He watched the taillights until they blinked red and the car turned into Violet's driveway. Then he turned and headed back to the apartment block.

He had homework. Research to do. Two alter egos to understand and somehow control. He didn't want to think about kissing Violet. But every step he took, the memory chased him. The feel of her lips. He grinned like an idiot as he stepped into the lift and hit the button for his floor.

In the black mirrored walls, his reflection stared back. He didn't recognize himself. He looked…

No Get a grip, man. You just met her.

He grimaced.

Scott was asleep on the couch. A notepad lay on the floor. Lewis picked it up and flipped through the pages. Every plan—rubbish. The last note read:

Monk will rescue us.

Seriously? That's your grand idea?

Being rescued meant failing. And failing? Not an option. His dad used to say, "Not trying, Lewis—that's failure. Trying and failing isn't." Sure, he got that. But real life? Different. He liked winning. Always had. He remembered his mum cheering on the sidelines: "You were the youngest in the race, Lewis, but you beat everyone!"

It wasn't her fault, he told himself She didn't make him want to win. He wanted it.

He lay in bed with his laptop balanced on his chest, watching a YouTube video of *Pride and Prejudice*. He cringed as Darcy emerged from the river, his wet shirt clinging to his chest.

He remembered that morning—Violet staring at his wet T-shirt as he peeled it off.

Fuck.

He skipped through a few different versions of *Pride and Prejudice*, then searched for the novel itself. He speed-read the text, swiping through the pages.

The more he read, the more confused he became. Darcy? That arrogant fuckwit? Nothing like him.

Then he found a movie about Byron That made him groan. He'd have to stay away from girls entirely. If he started acting like Byron, he could get arrested.

Mad, bad, and dangerous to know. Brilliant.

He kept reading until the battery icon flashed. He shut the laptop, plugged it in, pulled the covers over his head, and dropped into sleep like he'd been drugged.

CHAPTER THIRTEEN

Scott was shaking him. "Get up, man—we're gonna be late."

Lewis opened his eyes. Blinding light. He groaned, rolled over, and buried his face in the pillow.

"Up, man!" Scott yelled in his ear.

Lewis propped himself up on his elbows. Scott was already dressed and ready for school. He grabbed his phone off the bedside table. A text had come in from *Under the Hood*:

SSTAY AWAY FROM LISA OR ELS

Lewis groaned and deleted the message.

Sunlight poured through the blinds, bouncing off the white walls. He shut his eyes again. He didn't want to face another day of being haunted by Byron and Darcy. But he rolled over, swung his legs onto the floor, and forced himself up.

In the shower, water beating down on his head, he rehearsed: *No bowing. No kissing hands. Definitely no kissing lips.* He groaned out loud, remembering the kiss. "Fuck you, Byron…you dickhead." It had to be Byron. Darcy would have asked first. *I say, I'd be terribly obliged if you'd let me throw my arms around you and plant a kiss on those inviting lips.*

Ponce.

He pictured Violet again. Her body pressed against his, his hands on her waist, the taste of her lips—blackcurrants. He imagined walking up to her: *Sorry I kissed you. Your blackcurrant jelly lips were too tempting.*

Crap. You're no Byron.

He scrubbed at his hair with the towel. He needed to focus. Everything about this mission pointed back to Rochester. He was the one funding it. He was the one who wanted the girl. And Lewis was starting to guess why.

***

On the train to school, the carriage buzzed with noise—students in uniforms yelling to each other over the din. Every seat was taken. Lewis and Scott squeezed into a cluster of students near the door.

Lewis kept his head down, earbuds in, listening to *How to Sound Like an Australian.* He needed to stop sounding like a Ponce. Drop letters at the ends of words. Say *Yeh* instead of *Yes.* He repeated the rules silently, doubting it would help. Overriding the program Scott had uploaded into the assimilator wouldn't be easy.

Scott had his back to him, talking to some girls. Lewis looked up—and locked eyes with the boy from the day before. Broad shoulders staring with menace flashing in his piggy eyes. Lewis looked away. Then he spotted Scott again, head down, laughing with a girl. He recognized her instantly. Jenna.

She showed Scott something on her phone. They both laughed. Lewis stared. At that moment, Jenna looked up—and saw him. Their eyes locked. Her face tightened, her eyes widened. She gave him a full-strength death stare.

Lewis didn't blink. He curled his lip and shook his head in contempt.

Scott turned and frowned at Lewis. *What the hell's going on between you two?* He said something to Jenna. She shrugged.

Lewis tried to ignore it, but his eyes kept drifting back to Scott. The way he was chatting easily with the girls, swapping numbers, snapping selfies. Classic Scott—charming, fearless, blind optimism in human form.

But optimism wasn't going to get them home. Not on its own. They had no plan. No portal. No way out. Just vague hope and the mission. Lewis felt the weight of it like a ticking bomb.

The train doors hissed open. The crush of bodies spilled out, and with it, the roar of noise. Scott waited for him on the platform.

"What was that death stare about?" he asked.

"Mistake. Thought she was showing you a video I deleted."

"That makes no sense."

Lewis didn't answer. He slung his backpack over his shoulder and kept his head down. *No poetry today. Please.*

But then the morning light caught a white gum tree near the school gates. The trunk gleamed. The leaves shimmered—blues and greens, sun flaring off them in flickers of gold and orange.

Lewis stopped, staring up at the canopy.

Scott followed his gaze. "What is it?"

Around them, students stopped too, craning their necks.

"It's a parrot!"

"No, boring, it's just a—"

"D'you see it?"

Scott watched Lewis's face, the goofy wonder in his eyes, like he was watching baby koalas do backflips. It made Scott twitch.

"Lewis, seriously," he hissed, tugging at his shirt. "There's nothing to see."

Lewis turned to him, eyes blazing with the kind of idea that made Scott nervous.

"Nothing to see?" Lewis swept out his arms. "Nature's mosaic written against the sky."

A nearby student frowned. "What'd he say? Something about a moose in the sky."

"Poetry," Scott muttered, dragging him away.

Lewis blinked, like he'd just woken from a dream. "Screw you, Scott," he muttered. He shook him off, shot a withering glare at a pair of gawking students, and stomped toward the school.

He wanted to turn around, walk back to the apartment, and lock himself in. He was sick of making a fool of himself.

The day started in homeroom—twenty minutes of rollcall and notices. Lewis groaned.

"What class are you in?" he asked as they crossed the yard.

"Yours," said Scott. "I need to be in every class you're in. Make sure—" He stopped himself just in time.

Lewis clenched his jaw. He could throttle Scott. And now, on top of everything else, he had to face Violet. Kissing her had been a mistake. Just like kissing Scott's girlfriend. That hadn't gone well either.

Still, kissing Violet? That hadn't been *him*. That was Byron. Bloody poetic narcissist. He couldn't even remember kissing Poppy, but Violet—her lips, her taste, the feel of her in his arms—that was burned into him.

And then she was there. Just ahead. Ponytail swinging.

Lewis slowed. He didn't want to overtake her. Scott glanced back and waved him forward. *C'mon, man.*

Violet disappeared into the classroom. Lewis hesitated, then followed. Scott raised his eyebrows. *What was that?* But Lewis didn't answer.

They grabbed seats at the back. The classroom was thick with heat. Violet sat two rows in front. He watched her pull a book from her bag, rest her chin on her hand.

Don't stare. Don't feel weird. Don't feel like you're about to skydive without a chute.

Scott drummed his fingers. He couldn't wait to charm the senior girls. This was his element.

The bell rang. Lewis bolted. He didn't wait for Scott. Just stormed off down the corridor.

Next class: English lit. Miss French.

And he already knew more about her than he ever wanted to. *Should never have let her borrow my phone.* Lewis sat in the back row and pulled out a notepad. Scott slid in beside him. "What's the rush? We're the first ones here."

"I want a seat at the back. Better for observation."

"Yeah, good idea." Scott scanned the room. Not many boys in this class.

The room filled quickly with noisy chatter. Miss French stood at the front, hands deep in the pockets of her long blue cardigan.

"Rude lot," Scott muttered. Lewis had thought the same thing yesterday. No one at his old school dared enter the classroom making that kind of racket. Every door had a sign: *Enter prepared for learning.*

"Good. Now we can start," said Miss French. "I've written a practice exam question on the board. I want you to tackle it in class today. You should all have read—" She stopped, eyes narrowing at Scott. "Another new face?"

The front row students turned. Scott stood like he was reporting for duty. "Scott Brown," he announced.

Miss French grabbed the roll. "You're not on the list. There are two English Lit classes. This one's full. You're meant to be with Mr Struthers. Room 13."

Scott scratched his head. He didn't want to leave Lewis. "Go," Lewis said under his breath. "I'll meet you at recess."

"Keep your mouth shut," Scott muttered, grabbing his bag.

"Obliged for the advice," Lewis said, teeth bared.

He turned to the board: *What is the relationship between Pip and Estella in Great Expectations?*

He picked up his pen and wrote hard and fast. Ten minutes in, he'd filled two pages. *That'll do.* He stood and held out the sheets. Miss French was staring out the window.

She couldn't take her eyes of Roger Thistlewaite, the phys-ed teacher, leading the pack—broad shoulders, easy stride, thighs like pistons.

Lewis cleared his throat. She turned, waved him forward. He didn't speak, just held out the pages.

Out of the corner of his eye, he saw Violet glance his way. Her face. Those lips. That flash of green eyes. *Damn it, don't smile—*

Too late. The killer smile was out. Violet flushed scarlet and turned away, gripping her pen like it might break.

Miss French noticed everything. She liked a classroom romance—short-lived, tragic, excellent practice for adulthood. "Yes?" she said, giving Lewis a knowing smile.

She took the papers, raised a pencilled brow. *Already?* She glanced at the pages—mostly scribble. She flipped them over. Some words were legible. Barely.

"You'll need to type this. Your handwriting's illegible. And no laptops in the exam."

Lewis forced down the bow. He managed the words instead. "Finished. Take your leave." He couldn't stop the smile or the flick of his hair off his forehead. Miss French noted it—an attractive flourish, and he knew it. She turned back to the window. Roger was doing push-ups now. She smiled to herself.

***

Lewis found Scott in the canteen, laptop open.

"What are you looking at?"

"Holidays. Look at this." Scott tilted the screen.

Lewis slammed it shut. "Are you out of your freakin' mind?"

Scott frowned. "Just gathering data. They've got camels in—" He stopped. Lewis's teeth were clenched, pulse ticking in his neck.

Scott pulled out his phone and scrolled through his photos. Not bad, considering they'd only been here 24 hours. He held it up. A selfie with Jenna and two other girls. Lewis recognized them instantly.

He hunched his shoulders. The photo hit him like a wave. He felt buried inside something bigger than him—a jacket two sizes too big. He had to claw his way out.

Lewis sat heavily at the table. His phone buzzed. He pulled it out:

you were warned.

Scott glanced over. "Who's got your number?"

"Under the Hood."

"Who?"

"Teacher's boyfriend. Don't ask." Lewis dropped his head into his hands.

"I've been thinking," Scott said. "Monk's gonna send someone. A courier. The mission's too important."

Lewis didn't answer. He was thinking about Violet—her eyes when she turned toward him. That look, right before the smile. The smile she told him not to give. *Why? Why had she said that?* Lewis couldn't remember why Violet had told him not to smile like that—but she had. And he'd done it anyway. Now that moment was stuck in his head, looping like a bad soundtrack. That look in her eyes before he flashed the killer grin.

"She looked lost," he whispered.

"What? Who's lost?"

Lewis looked up. Scott was staring at him.

"Who's lost?" he asked again.

Lewis waved a hand like he was brushing away smoke. He sat up straighter, slapped himself mentally. *Focus.* Scott's words finally registered. Would Monk really send someone? He might. But not unless he had to.

"Maybe," Lewis said. "But only if it's a last resort. He'll try everything else first."

He exhaled slowly. He had to stop spiralling and think his way out. "Okay. Show me what you've got."

Scott slid his phone across the table. Ten photos—ten different girls, all posing, all looking straight into the lens. Lewis was impressed. Scott had wasted no time. Lewis scrolled, remembering the only photo he'd taken – Violet, back in the bike shed.

"You've been busy."

He studied each face. The image of the girl they were searching for hovered in his mind. Monk had warned them not to trust it. "Assume she looks nothing like the projection," Monk had said. "But if you find someone who does... that's probably her."

"How many girls in the school again?" Lewis asked. "In the two senior years?"

Scott frowned. "Think the intel said nearly two hundred."

"Two-forty," said Lewis flatly. Scott had only skimmed the brief—he always did. "We focus on seniors," Lewis added. "If she stayed in school and didn't miss a year."

But Violet's eyes kept cutting through the fog in his brain. He shook his head hard, like a dog flinging off water.

"Start with Year Eleven?" Scott offered, brows raised. He was clearly proud of himself for having a plan.

"Yeah. Good idea," Lewis said, trying to look alert, like he hadn't just been frozen in Violet's arms. He *had* to focus. The mission was all they had now. If they finished it, maybe Monk would figure out a way home. Maybe he and Scott could get back to where they were before Poppy.

The school bell rang.

"You find out what classes Cross enrolled you in?" Lewis asked.

"Yeah, all the arty ones," said Scott, rolling his eyes. "Made sure we're not in the same classes. Just missed Dance. That would've been interesting. But I got Drama." He flung his arms wide, like he was about to perform Hamlet. "Meet you back here at lunch."

Scott studied Lewis as he slung on his bag. Lewis was still staring at the graffiti on the table like it meant something.

"You okay?"

No answer.

"Lewis?"

"Sorry. Yeah. Bit of a headache," Lewis mumbled, brushing his hair back. He stood and followed Scott.

"Take it easy," Scott said, then vanished toward the drama centre.

Lewis saw Jenna coming down the hallway, blonde hair gleaming in the sunlight. His jaw tightened. *Don't speak. Don't smile.*

She was smiling at him. He managed a polite nod.

"Finding your way around? What's your next class?" she asked quickly. Her eyes darted from his icy grey stare to his lips, then his jaw.

"Yes, fine thank you. Mathematics next," Lewis said, carefully scanning her reaction. Seemed okay. No glitch.

"We're having a party Saturday. My eighteenth. Marquee, band, everyone in my year. You can bring your girlfriend... if you've got one." She gave him a coy, wide-eyed look.

Lewis looked away before he said something stupid. "Delighted," he said, crisp and clipped.

Jenna laughed nervously. He sounded... weird. But hot. "Oh—and bring your friend Scott. More the... something..."

"Merrier. The more the merrier," Lewis said, straight-faced.

She laughed again. "Here—give me your phone. I'll put in the address."

He passed her the phone, shifted his bag and saw Violet. She stepped out of a classroom, spotted him, stopped...then turned and walked the other way. Lewis watched her walk away. Something twisted in his chest. He clenched his jaw. *Aversion therapy,* he told himself. *Don't avoid her—become immune to her.*

"Greenish eyes…" he muttered.

"What?" said Jenna, handing back his phone.

He ignored her. "Much obliged for the invitation." He turned and walked after Violet.

Jenna bit her lip. She was already having second thoughts.

Lewis followed Violet. *Speak to her. Crush the feeling. It's not you—it's the bloody assimilator. Master it. You can do this.* Then another voice burst through his thoughts. *Pull yourself together, Lewis. Stop acting like a fool.* Yeah. That voice. His mother. He knew it well.

Violet sensed him behind her. She sped up. Ahead, the girls' toilets. *Escape.* She slammed the door shut. She wasn't going to face him. He was insincere, a narcissist, a poser. Too good-looking for his own good. *It didn't mean anything. Don't fall for the BS. Guys only want one thing.*

Violet flushed the toilet, opened the door—Jenna was at the sink, brushing her hair. Lips glossy. Violet kept her head down and turned on the tap.

Jenna glanced at her in the mirror, stopped brushing. A thought flickered. She tapped her brush against the tap. Violet looked up. Jenna spoke to the reflection, voice casual—but it hit Violet like a slap.

"My birthday's Saturday. You can come if you want. Seven o'clock." She yanked the brush through her hair.

Violet let hot water pour over her hands. Her eyes burned.

Jenna walked to the door. "Up to you." She didn't wait for an answer.

"Thanks…" Violet whispered as the door clicked shut. She'd go. This was her shot to make things right with Jenna—to explain what *really* happened. She looked at herself in the mirror. Cheeks pink. But she didn't mind. It was going to be okay.

Violet felt lighter as she walked to class, like she'd left something heavy behind in the cloakroom. She wasn't even thinking about Lewis——until she saw him in the first seat by the door.

Don't look at him.

She passed without a glance and sat in the front row, next to Ben Church. The class nerd.

"Hi," Ben said, surprised. She never sat at the front.

Violet smiled. He had nice eyes—honey-coloured. She'd crushed on him in eighth grade… until she found out he only talked about *Phantom Pain*, some game he was obsessed with. He was nice. But totally, painfully boring. King of the nerds.

"How's Jamie going?" she asked, lining her books up with the desk and placing her pens precisely. Jamie was one of Ben's gaming crew—because of her. She'd asked Ben to let him in. She loved hearing that Jamie was keeping up with the older kids.

Ben gave a dramatic sigh. "Little swine's beating everyone. Gonna kick him out of the group." He smiled. "You know he's a genius, right?"

She did. Jamie had skipped three grades and was topping every subject.

"Mmm. I guess I do," Violet said, grinning wide.

Lewis was watching. The sad look was gone. Her eyes sparkled. She was *smiling* at that boy. Really smiling. Lewis wasn't noticing the green flash of her eyes or how the light caught her hair. He was too busy feeling like he'd been punched in the stomach.

He ground his teeth and looked away. *Concentrate. Immunity. Focus.*

He scanned the room. Any girl but Violet. They all blurred together. He forced himself to stare at the back of the head in front of him.

The rest of the class passed in a fog. Every time he looked up at the board, Violet's head was there. Once, she leaned closer to that boy—sharing a book. Lewis wanted to look away. He didn't. When the bell rang, he packed his books slowly.

Violet didn't look at him as she passed. But she'd felt him behind her the whole lesson, his eyes drilling into her back. When she turned and saw him still sitting there, her heart jumped. She hated him for that. She kept her eyes on Ben's back. Her cheeks flushed like she had a fever.

Lewis wanted to stick out his foot and trip the guy walking out with her.

He followed. His plan - talk to her. Clear the air. Crush the feelings.

Ben turned, noticed Lewis hovering. He didn't like the look he was getting.

"What's your problem?" Ben asked, frowning.

Violet kept walking. "Ignore him," she said, grabbing Ben's jumper and tugging him along. "There's something wrong with him," she whispered.

Lewis tapped her on the shoulder. "I need a word. It's important. Just talk—outside." He wasn't going to take no for an answer.

Violet swallowed. "You go ahead—save me a seat," she told Ben. She didn't want a scene. "It's okay. I know him."

Ben glanced between them. Lewis was smiling with his mouth, but his eyes were firing bullets—and Ben could feel everyone. Something was going on between those two.

Lewis stepped up beside Violet. He wondered what it would feel like to slip an arm around her shoulder, to feel her head on his bare chest...

"Focus," he muttered under his breath.

Violet glanced over. She saw a flicker of anger cross his face. She picked up her pace, cutting through the dawdling students, heading for the front doors. She didn't stop to check if he was following. She crossed the basketball court. The sun was high in the sky, casting long shadows from the bicycle shed across her path.

At her bike, she turned and faced him, chin lifted. Lewis brushed his hair back, rolled his shoulders, and stopped. She stared at him, feeling a knot rise in her throat. She wanted it to be anger. Anger was manageable. She could throw it at him and be done with it. She didn't want anything ruining the lift she'd felt when Jenna invited her to the party.

Lewis studied her. Her green eyes were dark like emeralds. Even in the shade of the bike shed, without any sunlight in her hair, she looked—He tore his gaze away. The basketball post still stood in the same place. No mark on it. Pain stabbed the side of his head. He touched the spot behind his ear.

"You, okay?" Violet said suddenly. She hadn't meant to. She didn't want to care. Didn't want to talk. She stared at his chest instead of his face.

Lewis frowned. Was he okay? She wasn't even looking at him. A low groan escaped through his clenched teeth.

"You didn't see a doctor, did you?" Violet's voice sharpened. "Why not? That makes no sense." She folded her arms. "Not that it matters to me," she added quickly.

Lewis leaned against a bike rack, hands in his pockets. "I'm fine."

He was trying to remember what words wouldn't make him sound like a fool. "I want to apologise. My behaviour last night…'

Violet licked her lips. Her face burned.

Lewis stopped. Kissable lips. Idiot. He screwed up his face and looked down at his shoes. "I'm sorry. Inexcusable. Won't happen again." He kept his gaze down. Ground. Feet. Pressure. Equal and opposite.

Violet looked at him. "Won't happen again," he'd said. Her teeth sank into her bottom lip. What did that mean?

"Okay," she said softly. "Forget it."

Forget it. If only I could. He looked up and gave her a small smile. It seemed real. She thought his eyes even looked… sorry.

He rubbed the spot in his chest. Still there. It had to go. He had to go. He forced himself to stare over her head. "Next class beckons. Don't want to be late."

"Wait. Tell me—why?"

Why I kissed you? Lewis raised his eyebrows, aloof without trying.

Violet didn't flinch. "Why didn't you get checked out? That was a serious hit—you could've—"

"—died. You've said that already. But I didn't." He waved his hand in front of his face. He didn't want to look at her anymore. She scrambled his thinking. It was the lightning. The malfunctioning assimilator. That bastard Byron. It wasn't him. Once he got home, he'd be back in control. He wouldn't be kissing girls on impulse. Not like Poppy.

"LEWIS!"

He turned. Scott was running toward him—and beside him, Helen.

Helen. Her dark hair flying. And—she was smiling at him. He didn't remember her ever smiling before.

She stopped in front of him and threw her arms around his neck. "Thank God," she said breathlessly. "You're both okay. I could kill Scott for leaving like that. Monk is furious—he—"

Lewis stepped away from Violet. His eyes flashed a warning at Helen.

Violet looked at Helen—flushed cheeks, bright eyes. Someone close. A girlfriend. Or close enough. Good. That makes it easier. She mumbled a hello and walked off without waiting.

Helen barely glanced at her. She had a job to do.

What are you doing here?" Lewis asked.

"Rescuing you two. And…" She planted her hands on her hips. "Making sure the mission gets done."

Scott exploded. "What?!"

Lewis turned to him. "You heard." He knew Monk would have chosen her—she was smart. Second only to him in the exams.

"Obliged," he said. "Can you fix this?" He tapped the side of his head.

Helen nodded. Monk had briefed her. "I've brought the tools." She slipped the strap off her shoulder and held up a black pouch.

Lewis felt like a balloon deflating. His legs gave way slightly and he reached for Violet's bike to steady himself. He hadn't realised how tightly he'd been holding it all together.

"Here, he said, gesturing behind the bicycle shed. "No one can see us."

It only took two minutes to replace the part.

"Don't move," Helen said, zipping up her bag. "Monk said you might feel dizzy when it switches on. Got your phone? He wants you to call right away."

Lewis pulled it out and powered it on. A flicker of heat pricked behind his ear. Then a low buzz.

"Lewis? Can you hear me?" It was Monk.

Lewis's mouth went dry. He licked his lips. He saw Helen and Scott watching him, like he'd just woken from a coma.

"Receiving, sir," he rasped.

"Good," said Monk, audible relief in his voice. "Is Scott with you?"

"Yes. He's here." Lewis glanced at Scott. "Good thing he came. Saved the day."

"Yes, yes," Monk interrupted. "We need to bring you home. Get you checked.

"I'm fine. Really. I'd like to complete the mission—with Scott and Helen. We've started already. Scott's got a bunch of images we can upload. We've come too far to stop now."

There was another reason. One he didn't want to examine too closely.

But he needed more time.

CHAPTER FOURTEEN

Violet walked up the school steps, mentally packing that kiss from Lewis in an envelope and posting it to "return to sender." It wasn't meant for her—wrong address.

She headed to physics, slipped into a seat at the back, pulled out her books, and exhaled. In three days, she'd be eighteen. She'd graduate, move out, and take Jamie with her. She wanted to go to university, but Mona had made it clear: "Get a job or move out."

Someone sat beside her. She didn't have to look—she knew it was Lewis. She opened her book, turned pages slowly, and stared ahead at the blank whiteboard. Mr. Robertson hadn't arrived yet.

"Violet," said Lewis, resting his arms on the desk, watching her profile. He took a long, slow breath. He felt okay. Calm. Cool.

He didn't know what to say. He wanted to make things right. It was the decent thing to do. He wasn't the kind of guy who forced himself on a girl. He barely knew her—but he wanted her to... what?

Violet didn't turn. "What?" she said.

"How's your brother?"

"Jamie? He's okay." Her brow furrowed.

Lewis nodded. "And you? Was everything alright… after the other night?"

Her heart squeezed. He sounded different. Normal. Concerned.

It had haunted Lewis all night—the drunk couple, the awkward goodbye. He remembered seeing Violet in the back seat, twisting her hands, not meeting his eyes.

They're not our parents—Jamie's and mine," she said, voice firm. "Our parents are dead."

"Oh. I'm sorry."

Mona's my stepmother. Derek's her boyfriend." Violet twisted her pen in her fingers, bracing for something awful.

"That must be tough… losing your parents." Lewis felt himself relax. No wonder she looked sad.

Violet turned toward him. He smiled. "So, no trouble from the drunks?" He raised an eyebrow.

"Not much," she said with a faint smile. She wasn't about to tell him how Mona had grilled her about Lewis. "You should invite him around," she'd slurred. "That was no hug."

No way.

"So," Lewis said, "we're in a lot of the same classes. I take it you're into science, not the arts?"

"Yeah, but I like the arts too. Not one-dimensional," Violet replied.

He shouldn't ask, but he couldn't resist. "Speaking of dimensions… any thoughts on parallel universes?"

Violet frowned. "That's sci-fi stuff, isn't it?"

Lewis shrugged. "Open mind. Quantum mechanics. Who knows?" He had to stop. Monk would lose it if he knew Lewis was blabbing. His transmitter was off. Too much buzz in his ear.

Mr. Robertson walked in. Lewis opened his books. He didn't pay attention. The material was prehistoric. He wondered how long before this world figured out another universe was pressing against it. Hopefully never. He didn't want them wrecking his home the way they'd trashed this one.

When the bell rang, he waited for Violet to finish packing. "You going to the canteen?" His eyes sparkled.

"You go ahead. I'll meet you there."

She wouldn't. She planned to avoid him. She'd been an idiot over a boy once—never again. She forced herself to remember how that felt: curled in bed, sick with shame. If that was love, she didn't want it.

When Lewis left, Violet slipped out, crossed the oval, and hid behind a tree to eat her lunch.

***

Lewis made his way to the canteen. Scott and Helen had found a table by the window, laughing with Jenna and some students—including Wide Shoulders and a blonde boy. Phones out and loud voices.

Lewis grabbed a sandwich and juice, dragged a chair over, and sat at the far end, facing the window.

Helen was asking Jenna about the party, tapping notes into her phone. "Last count? A hundred and twenty," Jenna said proudly. "Most of my year. Cousins. Others." She waved around the table. "Girlfriends too," she added, eyes flicking to Lewis.

Lewis tapped his fingers on the table.

Scott leaned across and looped a finger through Helen's. "Boyfriends too?" Helen yanked her hand away.

Jenna ignored it. "Oh, you're invited. I asked Lewis to bring you."

Lewis didn't register the change in Scott's face—grin fading into grimace. He was too busy wondering where Violet was. Okay, so she was ignoring him. That was good. Easier. He finished his sandwich—gritty lettuce and all. Jenna was twirling her hair. Danger.

He'd need to invent a girlfriend. Someone from England, maybe.

Helen took over. She could see Jenna wanted to ask questions. She was good at this, building a story on the fly. "Our dads work for the same global company. Known them forever. So, your dad has hired a what band?"

"A reggaetón band," Jenna looked thrilled to explain. "My parents are from Chile."

Helen blinked. Blonde hair, blue eyes. "Chile?"

Jenna smiled. "Yeah, adopted when I was a baby."

Scott kicked Lewis under the table. Lewis glanced at him. Scott raised an eyebrow. Girl. Right age. Adopted. Bingo?

Lewis was staring out the window when he suddenly stood, grabbed his bag, and strode out of the canteen. Scott opened his mouth to ask where he was going, but Lewis was already gone.

He took the side doors that led across the car park, cutting toward the oval. He'd seen her—Violet—slipping out from behind a tree. Hiding. Why?

She didn't see him until he was right in front of her, blocking her path. He was out of breath, face flushed. She could see his clenched jaw. That dimple in his cheek gave him away—he was angry.

He dropped his bag at her feet and held out his arms. "Okay, I get it. You're still mad. I get that." He drew a shaky breath. "But what happened... that wasn't me. The other day, I mean."

He dropped his arms to his sides. "You were right. The lightning—something happened. I can't explain it. It's just... too weird."

Violet didn't move. She was focusing on not letting the fizzy feeling in her chest explode. His blazing grey eyes. His mouth. His nose—yes, focus on the nose. Straight nose. Totally not kissable. Just a... nose.

Lewis ran out of words. She wasn't saying anything. She was staring at his nose. He wiped it with the back of his hand.

He tipped his head back and groaned. Immunity wasn't working. Who was he kidding?

He dropped his gaze. Her eyes sparkled. A line from a book floated into his mind—*one word from you will silence me forever.* He almost said it.

But he caught himself. *Pull yourself together, Lewis. Don't go full Darcy.*

"Tell me what you want, Violet."

She lowered her chin to her chest. Didn't look up.

"Leave me alone," she whispered.

He stepped back. "Don't... I'm sorry, okay?" Her tears hit him hard. "Don't, Violet. Please."

He reached out and brushed a tear from her cheek with his thumb. The contact undid him. He felt like he was melting. His mother's voice rang in his ears—*Stop acting like a fool. Get the mission done. Get home.*

"Okay. I hear you." He picked up his bag and turned. Walked straight to the school gates. As he left, he pulled out his phone and fired off a text:

Going back to apartment. Headache.

Violet watched him go. She saw him leaving the school grounds. Guilt settled in her chest like a stone. She should've said it was okay. That she forgave him. That she understood. But instead, she'd acted like he'd shattered her heart.

Better this way. She curled her fists so tightly they left red half-moons on her palms.

***

The afternoon sun was high and pale yellow. Lewis walked halfway down the road toward the beach. He hadn't taken the train. He needed the air. Needed space.

He pulled off his school windcheater and shoved it into his backpack. His white T-shirt clung to him. His jeans felt hot. The band of grey-blue ocean shimmered on the horizon, and for a second, he thought about diving straight into it.

Violet's eyes. That look. It wouldn't leave his head.

What are you doing? She forgave you. She said so. She didn't sit with you. She hid. What more proof do you need?

His phone buzzed. Scott.

Monk said turn on your transmitter!!!

Shit.

He reached behind his ear. Touched the transmitter. That familiar low buzz started in his head. He pressed his phone to his ear.

Monk's voice hit like thunder. "Where the hell have you been? You were barely connected for ten minutes before going dark. What's going on?"

Lewis paused at a crosswalk. Red light. A woman stepped into traffic, ignoring it completely. Lewis recognized her before she saw him.

Mona.

She called out. He turned away.

"Sorry, sir," he said into the phone. "Citizen approaching. One moment."

"Playing hooky?" Mona purred, tapping his chest with a long red fingernail. She gave him a smile meant to be flirtatious. "Hope you're not a bad influence on Violet. She's easily led astray."

Lewis arched a brow. No smile. A poem came to him—something about violets destroyed by cruel words. *You're a destroyer, Mona.* His brow stayed lifted. His stare turned cold.

The smile slid off Mona's face. She straightened her mouth, pulled her eyebrows down.

"She dobbed—well, her last boyfriend got into trouble. Expelled. Police involved. Then he dumped her. Left town. That's all I'm saying."

Lewis blinked. His frown dropped. Mona was a snake. She'd betray Violet in a heartbeat. What else might she do?

"How terrible," he said gently. Tilted his head. His mother once told him he looked endearing like that.

Mona looked smug. "You should come over. Violet's a great cook. Come to dinner." She raised her eyebrows like she'd just proposed a scandalous idea they were both in on.

Lewis gave her a slow nod. Thought about winking. Didn't. He waved, stepped into the street, and pulled out his phone again. Still on. *Dammit.*

"Lewis here."

Monk was already mid-rant. "You've only been in the country two days and already some mother's worried you're corrupting her daughter. That's not what you're there for, man."

Lewis stayed silent. Monk didn't pause to breathe.

"Explain yourself!"

Lewis took a beat. "Nothing to explain, sir. Mistaken identity. She thought I was someone else. She'd been drinking. I let her talk, didn't want a scene. Lots of weird people here."

He swallowed. Monk didn't need to know what Violet meant to him—or how badly he was failing to control it. He'd work on that. Starting with a freezing dive into the ocean.

The cold water made Lewis gasp. He drew a breath, then dived beneath the waves and started swimming toward the floating raft anchored two hundred metres offshore. He was a strong swimmer—back home, he and Scott swam two or three times a week. They'd trained together for the last two years, and their sculpted bodies showed it.

Lewis reached the raft, pulled himself up, and lay on his back, arms spread wide. The wood was warm beneath him. He closed his eyes. Thought about Violet. Wondered what had happened to her.

He sat up suddenly. He'd managed not to think about her for almost thirty minutes—the time it had taken to change and swim out. "That's why," he murmured as the waves slapped against the raft. "Some bastard did something to her."

He lay back down, feeling the sun on his skin. No need to beat himself up. She was recovering—from a disaster boyfriend.

He swam back to shore, then sprinted along the edge of the waves, driving his legs hard, pumping his arms. Pushing Violet out of his head.

By the time he got back to the unit, it was close to five. He figured Helen and Scott would be home. They were in the kitchen, cooking. One look at their body language and Lewis sighed. Helen was falling for Scott—if she hadn't already crash-landed.

***

Lewis pushed his plate away. He couldn't eat. His stomach felt tight. He *should* be hungry—he hadn't eaten since breakfast.

"What's up, man? It's not bad. Tastes fine. Full of every vegetable we found in the fridge," Scott said, glancing over.

Lewis couldn't afford to be sick. They had work to do. Time was ticking.

"You okay?" Helen asked, as Scott got up to clear the plates.

"Yeah, fine. Just not hungry. Thanks for the meal." He stretched. "Okay, let's see what we've got." He nodded toward the kitchen. "Leave the dishes. I'll do them."

"That's the plan," Scott said, smirking. "We cooked, you wash."

But Scott watched him. Something was off. Lewis had looked spaced out at lunch. Staring out the window. Then walking off.

Lewis returned with his laptop. He had to look focused. This had been *his* mission—time to show some initiative instead of vanishing all afternoon.

Helen fetched hers too. "What happened at lunch?" she asked. "You just disappeared. We were worried."

Scott called from the bedroom, "Yeah, don't do that again. We spent the whole afternoon searching for you." The irritation in his voice was real.

Lewis looked up. "I sent a text. Said I had a headache."

Scott walked in, pulling out his phone. "Didn't get anything."

Lewis checked his phone. The message was still unsent. "Sorry." He held it up. "Didn't go through. Okay, what've we got?"

He didn't want questions. He needed a distraction.

Scott met his eyes. Something was wrong. Lewis didn't fold over a headache. This wasn't about that stupid kiss with Poppy—it was deeper. Maybe they should abort. Lewis wasn't really here. Take Lewis home. Get his brain scanned.

"We've got shots of forty girls," Scott said. "Not discriminating. Just scanning them all through facial recognition. Jenna's a strong candidate."

"Jenna?" Lewis asked.

"Lunch," Helen said.

"Right." He vaguely remembered something about a Latin American band. Mostly he remembered Violet, slipping out from behind that tree. Hiding. From *him*.

"We struck lucky," Scott said. "If you hadn't shown up, Helen, we'd still be chasing shadows."

Helen waved off the compliment. "Don't know about that."

"Wrong eye colour," Lewis said, remembering Jenna's stare. "Blue. As I recall."

"Greeny-blue. Aquamarine," Helen said, already sensing her win slipping away.

"I'm with Helen," Scott added. "Blue green."

Lewis gave them a flat look. "Brief said *green*. Not bluey-green. Not seafoam, not ultramarine. Just... green." He held his hands out. "Like emeralds."

"Yeah, well, Monk said we weren't to discriminate," Scott reminded him.

Helen tapped her keys. "The description said 'hazel, possibly greenish'. We include every shade, or we risk missing her."

"Fine. We include every girl," Lewis said..

Helen shrugged. "I'll upload what we've got. While you were... recovering," she said, side-eying him, "Scott and I photographed thirty more girls." She turned her screen to show them.

An hour later, they got Monk's answer.

"Negative."

Lewis should have felt disappointed. He didn't. He was relieved. He wasn't ready to leave.

"If she's here, we'll find her," he said, standing to do the dishes.

Scott flicked on the TV. A movie about an alien invasion started. He and Helen curled up on the couch. Lewis could see Scott making his moves. Helen wasn't stopping him.

"I'll move in with you tonight," Lewis called over the noise. "Helen can take my room."

Helen glanced at Scott.

"Nah," Scott said. "Her stuff's in my room. Two beds. And you were shouting last night."

"Shouting?" Lewis frowned.

"Yeah. Loud. Kept me awake."

Lewis couldn't tell if he was joking. "Up to you, Helen," he said.

"Thanks," she said without looking away from the screen. "But I'm a light sleeper."

CHAPTER FIFTEEN

It was hard to sleep that night with rain battering the windows and thunder rolling like distant cannon fire. A crack of lightning split the sky sometime around midnight—just when Lewis had finally drifted off. He jolted awake, heart pounding, his fingers instinctively reaching for the metal dot behind his ear.

In the morning, he stood at the window, looking down at the street and the wide pools of water still glinting from the night storm. The sky hung low and grey, threatening more rain.

He had to face Violet again. Aversion therapy was backfiring. He thought about her every minute of the day. And then there was the dream.

He'd been running across the school oval, calling her name, shouting. She hadn't answered. He found her behind a tree, legs tucked up, reading a book. He couldn't see the title. He was furious.

"I was calling you. Why didn't you answer?"

She didn't lift her head. Didn't move. Didn't see him.

He crouched in front of her, breathless. Put his hand over the page.

"Violet."

She finally lifted her face. Eyes still closed. Lashes golden. Cheeks flushed. Skin pale and perfect.

"Look at me, Violet. Please—look at me."

Then the alarm went off.

Lewis rubbed his face and shook his head. He had to stop thinking about her. He rolled his shoulders and headed for the shower.

Scott's door was still shut when Lewis emerged from the bathroom. He slammed it on purpose. Still no movement when he came out dressed. They were going to be late.

He banged on Scott's door as he passed on the way to the kitchen.

Scott staggered out, scratching his head. "Not going in. Helen's jet lagged. Gonna hang back, explore. We got loads of data yesterday."

"Jet lagged?" Lewis raised a brow.

Scott grinned. "You went AWOL. You've got catching up to do."

"Fair enough," Lewis said.

The sky was still overcast, a pale watery grey. Lewis checked the forecast: "light showers throughout the day." This weather made no sense—sunshine, storm, then this.

He threw on his windcheater, slung his bag over his back, and jogged down the apartment stairs. An icy wind whipped in off the water, stirring up white caps that pounded the beach. He yanked his hood up and hunched his shoulders against the chill.

As he climbed the hill away from the ocean, the buzz of his transmitter kicked in.

"Sir?" he said, tapping his phone.

"The exit date has changed," Monk's voice crackled. "You don't have three weeks. At most—three or four days."

"*Four days?*" Lewis stopped dead. "But—how? Why?" He wasn't ready. He couldn't leave. Not yet.

"Climate shift. Weather's unpredictable. We've lost some of the known contact points. No one predicted a storm like that. And it's acting like winter, not summer."

"But that was factored in—"

"We can't take the risk, Lewis. Just do your best. All of you. Out."

Lewis stared at his phone like it might offer a better answer. *Damn. Four days. Forget Violet. Stay focused.*

He shoved the phone in his pocket and ran the last stretch to the train station. The train was already at the platform. He fumbled for his swipe card, found it just in time, and sprinted to the doors as they began to close. He slipped into the crowded carriage.

And there she was.

Pressed against him. Bag clutched to her chest.

Violet had seen him running, fumbling with the scanner. She'd tried to vanish into the crowd, but they were packed too tightly. She got an elbow to the ribs for trying.

Now she stood with her head down, chin resting on her bag, pretending she wasn't there. Pretending he wasn't either.

She wished she had brought earbuds, music, a podcast. Anything to explain why she couldn't look at him. But she could feel him. His heat. His breath. The face she'd tried not to think about. The smile she'd tried to forget.

She'd thought about it last night, cooking spaghetti. Stirring the sauce while replaying that smile in her head—the one that made her stomach fizz and her chest go tight.

Then the train lurched. Lava sauce. Boiling thoughts.

It had to be the lightning, she'd told herself. It changed him, scrambled him. He was normal now. Right?

Someone called out, "Hi, Lewis." He answered over her head.

The train stopped. More students piled in. Lewis was pushed closer.

"Sorry," he whispered to the top of her head.

She didn't answer.

"I said sorry, Violet." He caught the scent of oranges in her hair. It made him want to lean in and breathe her in.

"Violet," he said again, louder this time.

She raised her head. Looked down at the cord on his jacket.

"Look at me," he said softly. "You'll see I mean it."

She raised her eyes—and she saw him. Her mouth trembled. Her gaze darted.

He didn't know how hard it was for her to look at him. To feel that falling feeling again. The electric happiness. The way love once felt. And how it had ended—in pain.

Lewis drew his eyebrows together. He wanted to wrap her in his arms. He wanted to say, *I'd never hurt you.*

But he didn't. He smiled instead.

"Friends, okay? No hard feelings?" he said. "I'm leaving in a few days. Not coming back. You won't have to see me again."

She blinked, did he say he was leaving?

The train entered a tunnel. Screeching wheels. Shadows. She thought she'd misheard him.

He could tell she hadn't heard a word. The train slowed. Students shuffled off. The crowd shifted. She stepped away. The carriage lurched, she stumbled. He reached out. She grabbed his arm.

"Whoa," he said over the noise. A boy nearby looked up, then glanced back at his phone.

She let go. "Thanks." She leaned against the rail.

The train emerged into light. Lewis watched the red in her hair glow under the sun. She turned away. Wet her lips. He noticed.

He shrugged, looked out the window. Green lawns flashed by. Pale sky.

"I said before... you probably didn't hear me. I'm leaving. In a few days. Not coming back."

Violet blinked. It felt like someone had thrown her a life raft—only it had a hole in it.

"You've only just got here!" The words flew out before she could stop them. That wasn't what she meant to say.

She blushed. "I mean… oh, really? Where are you going?"

Lewis was ready. "Dad's got a job. Other side of the... world."

Universe, he thought. He couldn't tell her the truth. Not ever.

"It was on the cards—just happened sooner than I thought," Lewis said. He lifted one shoulder and gave a half-smile, as if to say, *So there we go. No need to hide behind a tree.* He smiled out of the corner of his mouth.

It stung Violet's heart.

She was wondering what would have happened if he'd stayed. It was good he was leaving. Trying to squeeze your feelings into a small ball and hurl them away didn't work—because a ball that small never flew far. The wind just blew it back. And if it was too big, you couldn't throw it at all. You had to carry it around, picking at it, trying to make it the right size.

"I wasn't hiding," she said. She didn't care about lying. *He* had been the idiot. *He* kissed *her.* She didn't think about how her hand had touched the back of his neck before she pushed him away.

The train stopped. Lewis stepped off with her. The wind had dropped. A vague golden glow tried to break through the grey.

"Where's your bike?" he asked, shifting his bag to the other shoulder so he could lean in closer.

"Stolen last night. I thought I'd locked it to the veranda post, but it was gone this morning."

"That's rotten luck." *But I get to walk with you.*

She glanced at him. He almost sounded pleased.

"I loved that bike," she said flatly.

"Did you report it?"

"What's the point? It's gone."

"Was it insured?"

"Mona said the house isn't covered for contents. Just the building."

Violet had been trying to figure out how to buy a new bike with the money she'd saved—without Mona finding out. An idea sparked.

"Do you have a bike, Lewis?"

"Nope. Sorry. If I did, you could borrow it."

He wished he had one. It could have been his parting gift. Something she'd remember him by.

"I wonder if I could ask a favour," Violet said, slowing her pace. The sun broke briefly through the grey, casting lacework shadows across the path. She looked up at the gum tree ahead of them. Sunlight shone through the canopy.

Lewis followed her gaze. He smiled and whispered in her ear, "Nature's mosaic written against the sky."

Violet's eyes lit up. "I love that. That... do you write poetry?"

"Nah. It's the Byron in me. Comes out when I least expect it."

"Byron?"

"Yeah—nineteenth-century romantic poet. Wildly eccentric. Flamboyant. Passionate," Lewis's voice dropped an octave. "Wild affairs."

Violet shivered. "Lord Byron?"

"That's the guy."

She stopped in front of the tree and reached out to touch the white bark.

Lewis stood behind her, holding back the urge to quote more poetry. He wanted to impress her. Make her fall madly—*No. You don't want that. You're leaving.*

Violet was thinking about the first time she'd seen him. The way he dazzled everyone. The poetry. The charm. The eccentricity.

She stuck out her chin. "Is that your hero? The man you model yourself on?" Her tone was biting. "That smile you do. And the other thing..."

She trailed off. She wasn't going to say *kissing me*. That would make her go beetroot-red.

"No! No way. But..." Lewis looked puzzled. "What's wrong with smiling?"

Her eyes flashed.

"What's the *other* thing?" Then he saw her flush. She didn't have to say it.

He remembered too late. He wondered what Byron would say. He didn't care what Darcy would say—Darcy was a dick. Byron made women fall in love.

They hadn't moved from under the tree. He needed to change the subject.

"So, what's the favour? Ask me anything." He flung his arms wide in a theatrical gesture.

He was never going to forget this girl. Violet standing under this tree. The distant train rumbling. The rustle of leaves. Light in her hair. Her eyes. She looked so...Lost. Alone. He would carry this moment with him forever.

Violet bit her lip. She couldn't stay angry and ask a favour.

"I've saved some money. Enough to buy a bike, but... Mona doesn't know. I was thinking—"

Lewis cut in. "You buy the bike and we say I gave it to you. Or sold it to you for—"

"—Peanuts!" Violet's face lit up. "Will you?" She held her hands together, mock pleading. It was ridiculously endearing.

Lewis was helpless. *Good job I'm leaving. If I stayed, I'd be putty in her hands.*

"Of course. But it can't be *my* bike. You may have noticed—I'm taller than you. Long legs." He stuck one out for her inspection.

"Do you have a sister?" Violet crossed her fingers.

He grinned. "Ha! I do now. Little sister. About your size. Never rode the thing. Practically new. Going cheap because of Dad's posting. You'd be doing my family a favour."

Her smile was dazzling.

Lewis soaked it up. It was infectious. He grinned back.

"Thank you, Lewis. I'll never be able to repay you."

He couldn't stop the warmth rising in his chest. And other places. "It's nothing," he said, looking down into her shining eyes.

His ear buzzed. Monk was calling. Lewis ignored it. Not now. Not while she looked at him like that—as if he'd just pulled her from a burning building.

His heart pounded. Could she hear it?

Running footsteps broke the spell. Students were rushing past toward the train station.

Ben waved. "Storm last night—school's flooded! Day off! Oh, and Violet—Jamie's coming to mine. Gaming. All day!"

Violet's heart sank. School was her refuge from Mona and Derek. She didn't want to be trapped at home. Or sit in the library all day with retirees reading themselves into oblivion.

She moved behind the tree. Lewis looked over his shoulder and saw Jenna and a group of girls heading their way.

"Let's go get that bike," he said. The sun was trying again. It looked promising.

"We can walk... if you like." He didn't wait for an answer.

Violet had to jog to keep up. His strides were double hers. He slowed when they turned the corner.

"I'm nineteen," he said suddenly.

"Oh." Violet blinked. "Were you kept back?"

Lewis winced. Mistake. Now he'd have to lie. "Something like that. How old are you?"

"Eighteen in three days. Same day as Jenna. We used to pretend we were twins."

"When you were friends?"

"Yeah."

Lewis remembered the birthday invite. "You going to her party? I hear it's going to be big."

"Yeah. You?" She hoped he would. She needed someone there. Someone who didn't know *everything*.

Lewis hesitated. He wasn't sure he'd still be here.

"Do you want me to come?" He immediately felt pathetic.

"Why do you ask?" she said coolly.

"Forget it. I'm going. If I'm still here."

"That soon?"

He thought he heard something in her voice—like she might miss him already.

He *should* go home. Tell Helen and Scott the timeline had shifted. That the party might be their last shot at identifying the target. But he didn't care. He wanted to help her get a bike.

"That soon?" she asked again.

"Could be. Where are we going?"

"Home first. I need my money."

"Then Mona will know you're not at school," Lewis said. "I'll buy it. With my card. You can pay me back later."

"Okay. Thanks."

He was leaving in three days. Maybe four. She'd never see him again.

Lewis's ear buzzed again. He'd been ignoring it too long. If he didn't answer, Monk would message Helen—and then he'd have to explain everything.

This wasn't like him. Breaking protocol. Making up stories. He hadn't been able to think straight since the lightning. Since Violet. Since the kiss.

Which, right now, was *exactly* what he wanted to do. But they were at the bike shop. Violet handed him her backpack. "Hold this, please." Then she was off, walking the rows of second-hand bikes, scanning and rejecting them in seconds.

Lewis dropped both bags and leaned on the counter. He watched her move. Every time he looked at her, his chest ached. *Think of her like a sister,* he told himself. *An annoying little sister.* Right?

She bent to check a gear, turned, and flashed him a grin. Lewis grinned back. He was done pretending. She wasn't his sister. And he couldn't lie to himself anymore. But just when he thought he might surrender—fall completely—he stopped.

What would this do to her? He couldn't be that selfish. That much of a narcissist. Could he?

"What kind of bike are you looking for?" The shop owner stepped up beside Lewis. He was an older guy, fit, wearing tight black pants and a red jersey that read *I'm a cycopath* across his chest. He folded his arms and squinted at Violet.

Lewis nodded toward her. "She knows what she wants."

"Your girlfriend?" said Cycopath.

"Sister," said Lewis. He was trying it on for size. It felt safe. Safer than what he actually felt.

Cycopath raised an eyebrow, flicking his gaze between Lewis's dark hair and Violet's red ponytail. He'd seen the way Lewis had been watching her.

"This one or this one," Violet said, pointing to two bikes. "What do you think?"

Lewis liked that—she barely knew him, but she still wanted his opinion. Probably knew more about bikes than he did.

He walked over. "Give me the specs."

Violet rattled off the features: "Eighteen gears versus twenty-two. The second one's fifty bucks more but lighter."

"Go with the lighter one," Lewis said. "Can you swing $300? Looks like it's in better shape."

From behind the counter, Cycopath chimed in, "That one cost over a thousand when it was new."

"Yeah. Ten years ago," Lewis muttered.

Violet looked worried, like she was draining her entire savings. Lewis could tell how much she needed this. Her bike was freedom.

He handed over his credit card.

"It's only ten o'clock," Lewis said as they finished up. "We can leave the bike here and pick it up later."

"Later?" Violet said, hesitant. She didn't know how much more time with Lewis her heart could take. He was too perfect. *Shut up. He's not perfect. Don't be stupid.*

"Sorry. Wasn't thinking," Lewis said. "Do you want to go home?"

The last thing Violet wanted was home—Mona, Derek, the suffocating quiet of her room.

She shook her head. "Not particularly."

"Okay then!" Lewis glanced outside. "Sun's out. Let's catch a bus somewhere—get lunch, sit by the water, do nothing."

Outside, he got another idea. "We'll swing by the apartment and drop our bags."

"Are your parents home?" Violet asked.

"No." Not technically a lie. "They like to get out. Outdoorsy types."

His ear buzzed like an angry bee. He flinched. Violet gave him a worried look.

"You okay?"

"Yeah. Not my head—my back. Old injury." He sounded like his dad.

He turned away and answered the call. "Sir?"

"What the hell is going on, Lewis? I've called three times in the last hour. You're supposed to be working."

Lewis clenched his jaw. "Sir, the school's closed."

"I know. I've already spoken to Helen."

"I was getting to that," Lewis said tightly. "Ran into a student—got invited to a party. Last shot at intel."

Monk went quiet. Lewis wondered if the call had dropped.

"I'll deal with you when you get back," Monk snapped. The line went dead.

Lewis stared at the phone. *Threats. Great.*

"Everything okay?" Violet asked. He looked flustered.

"Sure," he lied. "That was my old man—stuff he needs me to do later. Still got a couple hours free."

He thought he saw disappointment flicker across her face. Wishful thinking?

CHAPTER SIXTEEN

They walked along the beach road. Waves crashed against the sand like a warning bell. Lewis stared at the horizon. Somewhere beyond it, was his world, nudging this one.

Violet followed his gaze. He'd gone quiet. Maybe he was changing his mind.

"We don't have to hang out," she offered.

"Yes, we do," he said, almost to himself.

"It's fine, really."

No, it's not fine, Lewis thought. But instead of saying that, he grabbed her wrist and pulled her across the street toward the apartment.

"Come on. No time to waste."

He hoped Scott and Helen weren't home—but he didn't care if they were. He felt reckless. Reckless felt good.

They rode the lift up. Violet stared at the floor numbers. Lewis stared at her profile. He imagined her red hair spilling across a pillow. Her cheek pressed against—

The lift jolted to a stop. Lewis blinked. It was too hot in here. The doors slid open—and there stood Scott and Helen.

Scott barely glanced at Violet. Helen stared.

"Hey man," said Scott, stepping back to make space. "Why aren't you at school?"

Lewis ignored Helen, who was giving him a look—alarm mixed with amusement. Her smile twisted. Lewis gave her a look back: Drop it.

"Hi… Vi-o-let," Helen said, dragging out the name like a warning.

Lewis bristled. Helen was doing it again. Being smug. Being dangerous.

"So, what's up?" said Scott.

"School's flooded," Lewis said. He kept his eyes on Violet, who'd turned crimson.

Helen smirked. Lewis glared. Helen shrugged. She knew she'd hit a nerve.

As the lift doors closed behind them, Helen called out, "Have fun, you two!"

Scott turned to her. "Why'd you say that?" He'd seen Violet go bright red.

Helen pressed her lips together. She felt a twinge of guilt. "That was mean. She didn't deserve that."

Scott looked relieved. He didn't want anything ruining the way he felt about her.

At the door of the apartment, Violet hesitated. The place looked empty. Too clean. Like a model home. She could see the lounge room—blue sofa under the window, a black jacket flung over the arm. Light spilled across honey-coloured boards. I'll wait here," she said. Just standing in the doorway made her uneasy, like crossing some invisible line she couldn't uncross.

Lewis heard it in her voice. "Okay. I won't be long." He held out his hand. "Want me to take your bag?"

Violet unzipped the front pocket and pulled out her purse—five dollars inside. Her phone was in her back jeans pocket. She grabbed her cap and the tube of sunblock she never left home without.

She watched Lewis walk down the hall, silhouetted in bright light. His broad shoulders made her throat tighten. She looked away. Then she heard running water—and suddenly had to pee. Legitimate reason to step inside.

"Can I use the toilet?" she called, taking a step into the hallway. Lewis didn't answer, and she took another step. Then he was there, blocking her path. "Toilet?" she repeated. "I really need to go."

"Sure." He stepped aside, nodding toward the open bathroom door. Helen's things were scattered across the bench.

Violet hadn't meant to snoop, but she noticed things. A bra hung over the shower taps, underwear draped across a towel rail. Helen was living here. No parents. Just the three of them. Freedom. Violet wanted that—her and Jamie, no Mona, no Derek.

Lewis stood at the window when the door clicked shut. He turned and nodded toward the view—blue-grey water stretching to the horizon.

"There's a ferry nearby. We could go to the island," he said. "I'd like to see it before I leave."

"Rottnest?" Violet said. She hadn't been there since her eighth birthday with her dad. No cars, just bikes and an old island bus.

She walked over and followed his gaze. You couldn't see it from here, but on clear days, it rose like a faint shadow on the horizon. The sea looked rough. Her stomach clenched.

Lewis glanced sideways and saw her biting her lip. Her bottom lip. Cherry red. "No?"

She hesitated. "It's not that, I just…" She flicked her hand toward the ocean. "I get motion sick. Sometimes."

Lewis turned back to the water. "Too rough?" He shrugged. "Let's check the ferry. We'll decide then."

He didn't wait for her answer. His bedroom door was open—he caught a glimpse of the bed. Not helpful for his mental state.

The lift ride was awkward. Their reflections stared back. Violet brushed his arm and then quickly clasped her hands in front of her. He leaned his head back, sighed—more like a groan.

She glanced at him in the mirrored wall. Their eyes met. Her ears buzzed. His eyes were asking her something, and whatever her answer was, she was already giving it, without knowing the question.

Lewis didn't move when the lift stopped. His chest felt tight, like his heart needed more room.

Violet stepped out. "You okay?"

He had no idea how to answer that. He just knew he was totally infatuated with the girl standing in front of him.

He smiled. It hit her like a sucker punch—brighter than any Lord Byron charm.

She scowled. "Byron," she muttered.

Lewis looked confused, then laughed. "Nope. Just me." He swept his dark hair off his forehead and lightly touched her elbow. "Promise." He led her down the steps and into the wind rolling off the water.

***

They sat up top on the ferry, facing the open sea, wind slapping their faces. Lewis's hair whipped across his forehead. Violet shouted over the engine noise, "There it is! The island!"

It was just a grey smudge on the horizon—like a stranded whale.

"I see it!" Lewis yelled. His arms were folded against the cold. His windcheater wasn't enough. He looked over. Violet's nose was red, but she didn't look seasick. She looked…

"You okay?" he leaned close, shouting in her ear.

His lips were warm against her frozen ear. She hugged herself tighter. Below deck was warmer, but ten minutes in there and she'd be throwing up.

"I'll get us hot drinks—chocolate?" he asked.

She nodded.

"Don't fall overboard while I'm gone."

He returned five minutes later, walking carefully with two paper cups. "Here."

She wrapped both hands around hers, holding it under her nose.

"You're supposed to drink it," Lewis said. Then he took a sip. "Ugh. Tastes like cardboard."

She sipped anyway. He'd bought it for her. He'd paid for the ferry. He wouldn't even let her chip in. "Don't worry," he said, grinning. "The old man's paying. He's loaded."

"Feels delicious," she said, holding the cup to her cheeks.

He saw her shivering. She had on a thin windcheater like his. "We should've worn our windbreakers," he muttered. He'd left his back at the unit. Not thinking straight.

As the boat slowed, the wind eased. Sun broke through the clouds, sparkling off the water. This was going to be a good day—he could feel it.

They walked down the wooden jetty onto the island. A few low buildings made up the town centre. No one really *lived* on Rottnest—just shop owners and staff.

"What now?" Lewis asked, stretching. "We could rent bikes… or take the bus," Violet said, unsure. Bike hire cost money.

He heard it in her voice. Pulled out his wallet. "Old man to the rescue!"

If anyone asked questions, he'd reimburse the Bureau. But he didn't care. Not today. He was building a memory. She looked guilty, but she smiled back at him. He was leaving. It would be okay. She'd have fun today. He was just a friend, nothing more. Remember that, Violet.

If only he would stop smiling at her like that. The Byron smile. What had he said about Byron? Passionate, eccentric, flamboyant.

Eccentric had suited Lewis the first two days, but now he seemed more... reserved.

They headed toward the bike rental shop, a family ahead of them with two little kids. Lewis bumped her shoulder with his. "More bikes, Violet. Exciting, huh?"

She nudged him back. "I love bikes," she said seriously.

He raised an eyebrow. She grinned. "I dream about them, too."

"You're kidding—dream about bikes?" *Dream about me instead.*

She was kidding. She just loved that she could be herself around him. She laughed and ran ahead. "Can't wait," she called over her shoulder.

Lewis found her among a sea of bikes, old and new, bright colours everywhere. They had to wait for the family to finish.

She waved him over to a tandem. He raised an eyebrow. "You thinking this?"

"No, not really. I've never ridden one. Ha! I'd make you do all the work up the hills!"

"Looking at your skinny legs… I will be doing all the work. And not just on the hills."

Violet glanced at her jeans. "My legs aren't skinny. How would you know?"

"Saw them in those thigh-revealing running pants you were wearing the other evening." He arched an eyebrow at her.

She refused to go pink. "Lucky you," she said coolly.

They skipped the tandem. Violet didn't want to stare at Lewis's blue windcheater—or the back of his neck—all day. She liked to see where she was going.

They cycled out of the little village and onto the coastal road. Less than two kilometres in, they reached a bay. Pale green water lapped against white sand. Violet stopped at a sandy path winding through the dunes.

"Do you want to stop here?" she asked.

Lewis scanned the beach—forty people or more. Kids shouting, families everywhere.

"No, it's beautiful, but let's go further." He pointed toward the red-and-white striped lighthouse in the distance. "Let's cycle there."

They rode in silence. The sun was stronger now. Violet felt sweat on her face. Her helmet kept slipping down her forehead.

A steep hill loomed ahead. Her gears clunked as she shifted. She had to stand on the pedals, swaying to climb the final stretch.

Lewis pulled up beside her, breathing hard. "Wow, what a view." He unclipped his helmet and hooked it on his handlebars. The lighthouse loomed close now, perched on the island's headland.

He reached back and pulled his windcheater over his head. His white T-shirt lifted. Violet looked away quickly.

He leaned his bike against a fence above the path leading down to the beach.

"Let's explore," he said.

Violet was fumbling with her helmet. Her face was flushed. She needed sunblock. Shade.

"What's the problem?" he asked.

"Just… this." She tugged at the strap digging into her neck.

"Here, let me." He turned her shoulders toward him. Bent close. His fingers brushed her chin. She stared at his eyebrows—dark and thick—and those lashes, unfairly long.

He glanced up. Her mouth was close. Too close.

No, you can't.

"Got it," he said. "Did I hurt you?"

A red mark sat under her neck. She wiped her damp forehead with her forearm. She turned away and stripped off her windcheater, tucking her T-shirt into her jeans.

"Wait," she said, I need my sunblock from your backpack."

He watched her smooth the cream over her pale skin. She glanced up and widened her eyes at him. She wanted him to stop looking at her like that. *He's leaving. Remember that Violet.*

Lewis walked ahead, picking his way down the zigzagging cliff path. At the bottom, he turned to see Violet leap the final rock.

He held out a hand. She hesitated. "It's okay," she said, landing beside him.

Lewis slipped his hand into his pocket, covering the instinct. The bay was perfect—almost like a cove, with rocks on either side and the cliff behind. Just the two of them.

They found a shady patch near a boulder smoothed by years of waves. Lewis stretched his legs. His jeans felt warm. They should've worn shorts. Or swimmers.

Violet sat beside him. What was she doing here, on a deserted beach, with Lewis? It felt unreal. One moment she was putting her bike away in the rain. Then lightning. Then Lewis reaching out.

He was watching her runners. Her soles reached his calves. Her head barely met his chin. He would have to bend down to kiss her. He should thank Byron. Without Byron, that kiss might never have happened.

He turned. Violet was sifting sand through her fingers, looking thoughtful.

"What are you thinking?" he asked.

She smiled faintly. "Nothing important." A lie.

She leaned back, closed her eyes.

I wish you weren't leaving. I wish I'd never met Lincoln. I wish...

"What are you thinking?" she asked, eyes still shut.

A bird screeched above, its cry tearing a hole in the sky.

Lewis hesitated. Then: "You'll think this is weird, but I was thinking I wish I were more like Byron. Impulsive. Passionate. I know I shouldn't have kissed you, Violet... but I haven't thought about anything else since. And I want to do it again."

Violet opened her eyes. He wasn't looking at her—he was staring out to sea.

"Out there," he said, "is another world. That's where I'll be tomorrow." He turned. "And I'll never see you again."

Violet pressed her lips tight. He sounded dramatic. Like Byron. Over the top. He could see her again if he really wanted to.

"There's FaceTime," she said, not bothering to hide the edge in her voice. "If you wanted to... we could still be friends."

She ignored the part about wanting to kiss her again. She knew where that could lead.

"Can I tell you something?" Lewis asked.

His phone buzzed.

"Sorry, someone's trying to reach me. I have to take this." He fished out his phone. Three missed calls from Scott. It had to be urgent.

"Sorry, Violet. Just a second." He stood and walked to the water's edge.

"Scott?"

"For fuck's sake, Lewis—I've been calling you—"

"Yes, and what's the urgency?"

"The transfer is tomorrow. I just got the details from Monk. You better get back now. That's it." Scott ended the call.

Tomorrow. Lewis stared at the phone. This is what happened when you let feelings surface. You did irrational things. You lost your place in the world. He'd been in the grip of madness.

Violet could tell the phone call had rattled him. He wasn't smiling anymore. He looked like he was ready for a fight. She watched him roll his shoulders, then pocket the phone and walk back across the sand—a tall black silhouette against the glare.

He bent to pick up his backpack. "Sorry, Violet. That was the old man. I've got to get home... pack. He's booked me a flight for tomorrow."

The best-day-ever balloon she'd been floating on popped quietly. She pressed her hands to her knees, determined not to let him see her disappointment. She hardly knew him. He was weird. He was leaving. *Get it together, Violet.*

She forced her voice steady. "Okay. I've got to get back by four... pretend I went to school."

She jumped up, brushing sand from her jeans. "It's been fun. I haven't been here in ages. I used to come with my dad. Want to see the lighthouse before we go?"

"Sure." He took off up the rocks fast, not checking to see if she followed. Violet's heart beat hard as she scrambled after him. She saw him pause at the lighthouse entrance. For a second, she thought he was waiting—but he didn't look back. He disappeared inside.

Violet felt it in her gut. He was just like Lincoln. Get angry, kill your feelings, repeat. She followed.

The lighthouse was a heritage site. Usually someone was there, answering questions about light wattage and colour schemes. She heard Lewis's voice, low, and then another man's. The guide.

She froze at the top step. That voice. No. It couldn't be. But it was. It was Lincoln. She backed away. Her heart slammed against her ribs. She saw him—obscured but unmistakable. He turned his head. Her stomach dropped.

She ran. Helmet forgotten, she pedalled hard down the hill. She left the bike inside the rental shop and bolted to the ferry. One was docked, but the sign said it wouldn't leave for 30 minutes. No ticket. No cash. Lewis had the tickets.

She sank onto the end of the jetty, hugging her knees, trembling. It was nearly noon. The breeze chilled her. She pulled her windcheater over her head—her ponytail caught, and when she yanked it free, Lewis was suddenly there.

He looked confused. "Hey... you didn't wait." She covered her mouth with a shaking hand. "You okay?"

She nodded. "Had to find a toilet." Her voice wobbled. She turned away, hugged her knees. "Cold."

He sat beside her, elbows on knees. "I'm sorry. I wish I wasn't leaving. I wanted more time. To know you."

Violet lifted her head, "It's fine. I hardly know you." She tried to sound strong and not some trembling mess. *It's not about you! Get over yourself!*

She pushed to her feet and made her way to the far end of the jetty. The lighthouse stood behind her like a witness – and so did Lincoln, face twisted, voice bitter. "You went to the police. I've been expelled. It was just a photo…"

Lincoln had waited for her outside the school gates. She'd raised her chin and stared him down. "You're not supposed to talk to me."

She drew in a shaky breath. Seeing Lincoln and hearing his voice had catapulted her back to that day. She bit her lip hard. She had to stop herself playing the scene in her head. *Think of something else.*

Lewis watched her. Something was wrong—really wrong. Her hands were over her face, and her shoulders shook like she might fall apart.

He stood, frozen. What was he supposed to do? He wanted to run the other way, leave her crying at the edge of the jetty. Instead, he stepped forward and threw an arm around her shoulders. She was trembling hard. Panic lit up in his chest.

"Violet? What is it? What's wrong?"

She pressed her hand tighter to her mouth. She had to stop. Keep it together. Why did he have to be here? Why hadn't he gone, like Jenna said?

She tried to say, *I'm fine.*

Nothing came out. She brushed at her face. No—she wasn't going to cry over him. He wasn't worth it. She tipped her head up to the sun and took a long, shuddering breath.

Lewis reached out and gently wiped a tear from her chin with his finger. Violet stepped out of the circle of his arm.

"I'm okay," she said, giving him a small, shaky smile.

He looked at her like he didn't buy it—guilt all over his face.

"It's not you," she added with a hiccupped breath, pressing a hand to her chest. "Promise."

She pushed her hair back, tugged the elastic free, and let it fall loose before gathering it again into a ponytail.

"See?" she said, forcing a smile. "Totally fine."

Lewis raised an eyebrow. He wasn't convinced. As far as he knew, nothing had happened between the call and her walking away at the lighthouse. But something *had* happened—he could feel it.

Lewis checked the time. 25 minutes until the next ferry. He glanced at Violet. Awkward silence or... a walk?

"No, you're not." He pulled her close. "Let's skip the ferry." He jerked his head toward the water. "Let's walk the beach." He crooked his elbow and smiled.

She imagined him saying, *"Shall we promenade along the shore, madam?"* but he hadn't gone full-Darcy all day. That side of him seemed to have vanished. She thought he'd drop his arm when she got close—but he didn't. So, she curtsied.

"Thank you, kind sir," she said, forcing a smile.

"What was that?" Lewis laughed.

"Supposed to be a curtsy. Bit hard in jeans, in case you hadn't noticed."

He had noticed. He noticed everything about her.

Violet kicked off her runners and walked toward the water. Lewis followed, peeling off his shoes and rolling his jeans like she did.

"Should've worn shorts," he muttered, stepping into the shallows beside her. His voice stayed light, but he was waiting—for her to talk.

They hadn't gone far when Violet crouched to pick up a shell. She rinsed it in the surf and held it out. "Look at this."

Lewis turned it over in his hand. "Snail shell?"

"Isn't it beautiful?"

Her green eyes sparkled. For a moment, she was just a girl on a beach. Trying to forget.

But then Lewis bent down to grab his own shell, and Violet froze. She saw him—*Lincoln*—just a few metres away, walking the jetty.

She dropped to her knees in front of Lewis, trying to disappear. He turned sharply. "Violet—what is it?" Then he followed her gaze. The guy on the jetty.

"You know him?"

"I don't want him to see me." Her voice shook. "Please—don't let him see me."

Lewis didn't hesitate. He stood, pulling her to him. Her face was against his chest.

"Who is he, Violet?"

She didn't answer. Her body was trembling.

"It's okay," Lewis whispered. "He can't see you." He risked a glance over his shoulder. "He's getting on the ferry. He's gone."

Violet clutched his shirt in her fists. She was shaking harder now.

"Hey," Lewis said softly. "We'll wait for the next one. We've got time. Let's head up the beach." He gently pulled her hands from his shirt and wrapped one arm around her, steering her away from the jetty. They kept walking until the ferry was out of sight behind the curve of the beach.

"Up there," Lewis said, nodding at a wooden staircase leading to the village road. "Let's find something to eat. I'm starving."

Violet didn't answer. The thought of seeing Lincoln again had turned her inside out. She felt sick. He blamed her for everything.

Lewis didn't let go of her until they hit the road above the dunes. He glanced at her—she looked pale, her lips pressed into a thin line.

She's scared. He scared her.

"This looks good," he said quickly, pointing at a small bar facing the ocean. "Fish and chips? What do you want to drink?" He led her toward a table on the patio near the railing. "Sit. Don't move."

"Water. Just… water," she said, her voice thin. "I don't eat—I'm vegetarian." Her mouth felt like sandpaper. Her hands were shaking under the table.

He came back carrying a glass of water and a beer. He wanted to try one before he left. He handed the glass to Violet's outstretched hand and sat opposite her. Their table faced the ocean—the ferry and the jetty now out of sight.

"I ordered a vegetarian burger and chips. That okay?"

She wasn't hungry, but he was being kind. She nodded. "Thanks."

He took a sip of beer. "Want to talk about what happened?"

Violet hesitated. Then: "He went to my school. Seemed nice... but he wasn't. He posted photos. I didn't know he'd taken them."

Lewis clenched his jaw. "That's illegal here, right?"

"He got expelled. Community service. He's Jenna's cousin."

Lewis shook his head. *Figures.*

"Was school hell?"

She nodded, tears welling. The waitress arrived with food. Violet turned away, pretending to look at the ocean, wiping her fingers across her eyes. Her hand trembled as she reached for her glass.

"Burger and chips for two," the waitress said brightly, setting the tray between them. Violet moved her glass, her hand shook. She gripped the edge of the table like it was a cliff face.

Lewis tried to lighten things. "Massive servings." He said trying to shift the energy. "Hope you're hungry."

He'd changed the subject – moved on – and Violet felt both grateful and disappointed. Talking about it hurt, but now that she had, she wished he knew more. She didn't want to be remembered as the girl who'd been used, exposed and humiliated. She hadn't told him the details. She couldn't.

Lewis sipped his beer, held the glass up to the light. He didn't drink often. But he was thinking. He hadn't changed the subject to avoid her pain – he was just giving her space.

"You okay Violet?" he asked, setting the glass down and tilting is head. She looked so small across the table. Vulnerable. He'd been right.

Violet nodded. *Not really.* Lincoln had torn her apart and left her in pieces. But she was getting over it. Slowly.

"Just a few more months util the end of the year. Then what?" Lewis asked. His mother's voice echoed in his head. *Don't wallow. Life's short. Move on.* That advice had buried his own pain when his father had left.

"That's better," Violet murmured. "Think about the future." She picked up a chip. She wasn't really okay. School was ending and then what.

"Have you got a plan?"

She picked at her food. "I don't really have a plan. Just to get away. With Jamie. I'm saving up so I can leave – find a job."

Lewis looked at her. "Not much of a plan. More a leaky boat."

She smiled weakly. "You're right."

"Let's make a plan then."

She smiled for real. "Okay."

"All plans start with an idea." He was good at making plans.

"Okay," she said all wide eyes.

He felt himself falling into those green pools of light. "Beautiful eyes Violet. I'm…ignore me. Okay the plan. Give me the details."

"Details?"

"Yes I need to know all about you." He wanted to know everything, the white scar on her temple, everything.

He pointed at her temple. "That scar?"

She touched it. "Derek. Threw a plate. Said he meant to hit the wall."

"What?…Has he hit you?"

She hesitated, then nodded. "But I can't leave Jamie."

She told him about her father's will the trust fund he set up. Mona and Derek's holidays the BMW.

He wanted to help but all he could do was make suggestions. "You have free legal advice here?"

"Legal Aid. They came to the school."

"They could help. You need a lawyer to help you with the Trust. Trustees aren't allowed to use the money like that."

She nodded. "Is your dad a lawyer?"

He didn't answer. The ferry horn echoed.

"We should catch this one," he said.

She didn't answer. She was glad he was leaving.

He didn't want to go. Being here with Violet was the best part of the whole damn mission. He didn't want to say goodbye. They sat on a bench at the end of the jetty. The sun was out, but the breeze off the water was cold. The ferry bobbed gently below them. Violet kept her eyes on the ocean, trying not to look at the boat.

Lewis checked his phone. They'd be back by three-thirty. She could still get home like she'd been at school all day.

"Violet," he said quietly, "do you mind if I take a photo? I'd like one. Just… a memory."

He sounded unsure. She shivered.

"You've already got one," she said softly. "The one you took. Before the lightning."

He frowned. The photo in the bicycle shed. She'd remembered.

"Yeah. Trying out the camera. Sorry about that." It wasn't a lie. Not exactly. "But it's not a good photo."

He pulled out his phone, angled it away from her, flicking past the girls he'd photographed—until he found it.

Violet looked at the photo. The light was bad, but it was clearly her. She looked fierce. She'd never seen herself that way before.

"Mmm," Lewis murmured thoughtfully. "Just wondering… maybe that lightning bolt? That was you, huh?"

She nudged his ribs with her elbow. "I wish."

He grinned. "Okay then. One more?"

He tilted his head and smiled—unguarded, hopeful.

She nodded.

He held the phone at arm's length and draped his arm around her shoulders, pulling her in close. His cheek brushed hers as he snapped the photo.

He didn't move. Neither did she.

He loved the feel of her face against his. His heart was hammering.

"A goodbye kiss, Violet?" he whispered.

She didn't answer. But when he turned his face toward hers, she didn't stop him.

Their lips were almost touching. She stared into his eyes. *This is a bad idea.*

He waited, not moving—giving her the choice. She reached up and wrapped one arm around his neck. His heart stopped. He stood, pulling her with him, sliding his phone into his pocket. His arms wrapped around her, holding her like she might vanish.

He was going to kiss her—more than once.

Violet laced her fingers and rested her head against his chest. He wondered if she could hear his heartbeat over the slap of the waves and the shrieking seagulls.

He cupped her face, traced a thumb across her lips. *Kissable.*

He rested his chin on her head. He knew—even before he kissed her again—that he didn't want to leave. He wouldn't call it love. Not yet. His mum's voice echoed: *It's your hormones, Lewis.*

Maybe. But that was part of it.

Then he kissed her.

His mouth met hers, soft at first. Then everything blurred—his arms, his lips, the burn in his chest. Violet's fingers slipped up the back of his neck. He groaned into her mouth. She was killing him—slowly, beautifully. His tongue brushed hers. Her nails scratched lightly at his skin. He crushed her closer, lost in her.

Then she pulled back. Pressed her hands to his chest.

"Stop. Please," she whispered. "Please stop."

He froze, then gently let her go. He held her face in his hands, breathless.

"It's okay," he said softly. "Just a goodbye kiss."

A tear slid down her cheek.

"Damn, Violet," he murmured, brushing it away with his thumb. "Was it that bad?"

She didn't answer. Part of her was glad he was leaving. The second boy to show interest in her, and she'd kissed him like that. Not such a princess, Mona had said when the photos came to light. Mona hadn't even wanted her to report it.

Violet bit her lip. This is why kissing was dangerous. It messed with your head. Made you forget everything you'd promised yourself.

She turned away as a group passed them on the jetty.

Lewis grabbed the backpack, slung it over his shoulder. He shoved his hands in his pockets and watched her walk toward the ferry.

He didn't follow—not yet. She needed a second to pull herself together. He owed her that. He shouldn't have kissed her like that. It was supposed to be a goodbye, not a make-me-stay kind of kiss.

She reached the end of the jetty and turned around. Her face was serious, like someone had just delivered bad news.

She pointed toward the ferry. "We should go. Find a seat up top."

Lewis nodded. "I just want to say this, Violet—I'm sorry I'm leaving. I'll never get the chance to prove I'd never hurt you."

He didn't wait for a response. He threw an arm around her shoulders, held her tight. When they reached the gangplank, he let her go.

They couldn't find seats on top.

"Here," Lewis said, spotting a space at the back, facing the retreating island. He braced his legs and leaned against a metal chest full of life jackets.

The boat rocked against the waves. Violet lost her balance and grabbed his arm. He pulled her in, settling her between his legs, her back to his chest. He didn't ask. He just held her—one arm wrapped tight around her waist.

His arm felt like steel across her body. She didn't know how long he could hold her like that. She couldn't relax. His warmth was everywhere. She dropped her chin and closed her eyes.

He was kissing her again. On the jetty. His lips, his arms, his voice. *Don't. Don't think about him.*

The ferry bounced against a wave. Lewis's grip tightened. His breath was warm against her ear. "Look at the horizon, Violet. It helps."

She did. She watched the island shrink until it was gone. Only the sky and sea remained.

She didn't know when it happened—when she stopped tensing and started leaning into him. Her head found his chest, her breathing slowed. The ferry rocked and Lewis stayed still, holding her as if he could shield her from everything.

He felt her relax. He closed his eyes. This girl, with her fiery hair and fierce eyes, was nothing like the mission brief.

The engine shifted gears. The boat slowed. He'd have to let her go. He stretched his back and gently unwrapped his arm. His shoulder ached. He flexed his fingers.

His eyes searched hers. "You okay?"

She nodded. She wasn't. Not really. But this weird, gentle boy had kissed her and held her like she mattered. And, somehow, she trusted him. Even though she'd probably never see him again.

The passengers stirred. People stood, gathered bags. Lewis picked up the backpack and took her hand. He didn't let go until they stepped off the boat and onto the stone jetty.

He brushed his hair back. His fingers grazed the transmitter. *The transmitter.* He pulled out his phone. It was off. He wasn't going to make that mistake again.

CHAPTER SEVENTEEN

The apartment was empty when they got back. Afternoon sun flooded the small lounge room. Lewis dropped his bag on the floor, headed into the kitchen, and opened the fridge.

"We've got juice, chocolate milk… or water?"

"Water, thanks," Violet said, walking over to the kitchen bench. She pulled the elastic from her hair and ran her fingers across her scalp.

Lewis glanced at her, "Beautiful hair… no, correction—glorious hair."

"Thanks," Violet said softly.

Lewis found two glasses, filled them at the tap. He handed a glass to Violet and walked over to the table and sat down. Violet didn't move, she watched Lewis stretch out his legs. He tilted his head toward the chair opposite.

"Sit for a minute. Tell me what you're going to do." It was the least he could do—help her find a way out from Mona and that creep, Derek.

"The plan to get away from Moaning and Dickwad?" He raised his brows and gave her a grin.

Violet spluttered into her glass, she grinned at him, "I like it!"

Lewis grinned. "Exactly."

A knot twisted in Lewis's chest. She looked beautiful—pale skin, freckles, the sun catching the copper in her hair. Those sea-glass eyes. Lips he couldn't stop thinking about. He looked away, afraid she could read everything on his face.

Violet's smile faded. "After school Monday, I'm going to talk to someone at Legal Aid. About the trust." She sighed like the weight of it all had just landed on her again.

"You think you can handle that on your own?" Lewis asked, quiet.

She heard something in his voice. Pity? She stiffened. "I'm not helpless," she said, a little too fast. "Of course."

She stood and walked her glass to the kitchen. Lewis heard the tap running. He glanced over and saw her staring at the water like it held answers.

She turned and caught him watching. Her face flushed. She cupped her hands under the stream and splashed her face.

Don't think about him like that. He's leaving.

"I have to go," she said suddenly. But she didn't want to. She wanted to stay with him until the moment he stepped on a plane and vanished into the sky.

"Right," Lewis said, trying to sound upbeat. He walked over as she rinsed his glass. Her movements were casual, domestic—like they lived here. Like they were a thing. A couple. The ache in his chest spread.

He watched her at the sink. She didn't turn around. The tears would spill if she blinked.

He didn't think—he just asked. "Violet… can I have a lock of your hair? To remember you by."

She turned, startled. "You've got a photo. That's weird."

"Yeah, I know. It's me. Please."

He found scissors in the drawer. Violet stood still as he pushed her hair back and snipped a small lock. "You won't notice where I cut it," he said.

"Is this something Byron did?" she asked, watching him fold the hair into a notebook.

Lewis smiled. "I think girls wanted Byron's hair."

She said nothing. She didn't want keepsakes. She wanted to forget.

He rinsed the scissors under the tap. It was the only sound in the apartment.

"My bike," Violet said suddenly. "I have to get it."

"Wait." Lewis reached across the bench and touched her wrist.

She didn't pull away. Instead, she turned her hand and traced his palm with her fingers. He closed his hand around hers, held her gaze.

He swallowed hard. She was breaking the heart he didn't know he had.

"I'm glad I met you," Violet whispered. "You might be the nicest thing that ever happens to me."

"Me too," he said, his voice low and rough. "Let's go get your bike."

"You don't have to come," she said, but her voice was hopeful.

Lewis picked up her backpack and slung it over his shoulder. He didn't answer. Just headed for the door. Outside, the sun blazed.

Lewis tugged the brim of her cap. "You need a bigger sunhat, Violet."

"I'm careful. I wear sunblock every day," she said, stepping into the patch of shade his body cast across the pavement.

He bit his lip. She'd be safer back home. Healthier. She'd never get sick. Not like here.

Without thinking, he reached for her hand. "Do you mind?"

She didn't. Not one bit. His fingers laced through hers, warm and steady.

They passed the beach where the floating raft bobbed in the waves. Lewis pictured her lying there beside him, both of them dripping wet, skin to skin. He squeezed her hand.

"Lewis!" Scott emerged from the dune path, towel around his waist.

Violet pulled her hand away, but Lewis held on tight. He didn't care what Scott thought. To hell with him.

Scott met Lewis's eyes and read the message there. He backed off. He knew better.

Helen popped up beside him. "Hi guys," she said to Lewis. "We wondered where you were."

A reminder. Time was running out.

"Just walking Violet home," Lewis said, jerking his chin toward the horizon. "Went to the island."

Violet tugged at his hand again.

"I'll see you back at the apartment," Lewis said, turning away.

Violet looked up at him and smiled. It sliced right through him. He had one more idea. One last chance.

"About Jenna's party tomorrow… I think I can make it. Before I leave. I could pick you up?"

Violet bit her lip. She wasn't sure it was a good idea. Holding his hand, brushing her arm against his—it felt nice. Safe.

She glanced at him. He was watching her from under the brim of his cap, waiting.

"Would it be a good idea?" she asked.

A cyclist rang a bell behind them and zipped past. Violet stepped closer to Lewis.

"A good idea?" he said, throwing his arm around her shoulders. "No. terrible. But let's do it."

Then, quieter: "Might help you, maybe—"

"Help me what?" She narrowed her eyes. "You mean, move forward?"

He shrugged. He thought of Lincoln, what seeing him might do. What *not* seeing him might mean too.

"Jenna's cousin will probably be there," she said. Her voice was flat.

Lewis didn't answer right away. He imagined being her. Living her story. "You were the victim, Violet. He should be the one ashamed. I'll be there. You won't have to face him alone." He pulled out his phone. "I'll give you my number."

Outside the shop, Violet collected her bike. Lewis pointed out she didn't have her helmet, so she couldn't ditch him.

He pushed the bike uphill beside her. She was quiet, thinking. At the red light, Violet blurted, "Will you keep in touch?"

Lewis swore silently. How could he explain the impossible?

"Forget it," she said quickly. "It was just a thought."

"Violet, I want to. I really do. But where I'm going…" He hesitated. "There's no communication."

"I said forget it." Her voice was sharp. Of course. He had a girlfriend.

They reached her road. He still hadn't let go of the bike.

"Thanks," she said, stopping at her gate. She reached for the handlebars.

Lewis blocked her. "Hands off. I'm telling Mona I sold it to you. My dead sister's bike."

"Oh—I forgot. I have the money at home, I can—"

"I don't want the money. It's not mine anyway. Consider it your birthday present."

"It's too big," she said quietly. "I hardly know you."

He had hurt her. He saw it. "I will write. I'll try to find a way."

Liar, liar, liar, she thought. But she gave him a small smile. "Okay."

They reached her house. Mona and Derek were ready to leave. "Just in time," Mona said, brushing past Lewis without a glance. "Back late." She stopped outside the garage door and gave it a kick.

Derek eyed the bike. "Whose bike?"

Lewis jumped in. "Violet's now. It was my sister's. We don't want it anymore."

Violet blinked at how smooth he sounded.

Derek sneered. "Better lock that one up tighter."

"I didn't forget to padlock it, did I?" Violet said, staring him down.

Derek scowled. Lewis glared, fingers tightening on the handlebars. He looked across at Mona kicking the garage door.

"What y'doing?" Derek shoved her out of the way and grabbed the handle. The garage door jammed halfway. Mona screeched. Derek cursed and yanked it open with a bellow. Doors slammed, and the car roared out of the driveway.

Violet's face was pale. Lewis could feel the heat of her anger. He nodded toward the porch. "He did it, didn't he?" He chained the bike up.

She nodded. "Thanks."

Lewis lingered, hoping she'd invite him in. He glanced at his shoes. Anything to stay. Violet stood in the doorway, unmoving.

His phone buzzed. Monk.

"Wait," Lewis said. "It's the old man." He answered without walking away. "Sir."

Violet closed the door.

"Change of plan, Lewis. You found the target. It's your photo."

Lewis froze.

"I'm sending the image. It's a perfect match—with the mother."

"My photo?" Lewis asked, stunned.

"Yes. Sending it now."

His phone buzzed. He looked. His stomach flipped.

Violet. In the bicycle shed.

Another buzz. Text from Scott:

Just heard the news. How did you know????

Lewis didn't reply. His mind was spinning. Perfect match with the mother?

Violet's mother was dead. No. No, it couldn't be. He stared at the house.

She's in there.

She's the target.

And she would never leave without Jamie. He stepped toward the door.

Inside, Violet stood frozen. Her heart pounded with every knock.

"Violet, open the door!" Lewis's voice cracked. "Please!"

Violet covered her ears.

"Please, Violet. Please."

She opened the door. He looked awful. Face white. Hair wild.

She'd seen him like this before—one hand on the basketball post, the other reaching for her. Now his hands were buried in his pockets. Shoulders hunched.

She met his frantic eyes and her stomach dropped.

He didn't pause – just pushed the door wider, urgency crackling off him. She stepped back blinking.

"Sorry." *Calm down idiot. Breathe.* He forced a smile "I needed to talk to you." He pushed the door shut. "Is Jamie home?" He said softly.

Violet narrowed her eyes. She folded her arms. "Yes, he is," she said pointedly.

Lewis exhaled, long and shaky. "Okay. Is there somewhere we can—"

Violet stared him down.

Lewis tried to read her face. *Hurt? Angry?*

"I need to talk to you," he almost whispered. He glanced down the hallway. A door ajar. Her room. Her bag on the floor. He took a step. She blocked him. Planted herself in his path. Just the thought of him near her bed made her stomach turn.

He caught it then—her glare, the set of her mouth. It landed hard.

"I said talk," Lewis snapped. His voice went cold. He grabbed her arm and pushed her gently but firmly into the bedroom.

The room was small—just a narrow bed, a bookcase, a plastic pink radio on the side table. He sat on the bed. She didn't. She tied her hair back fast, her fingers jerky.

Shame. He'd liked it loose, wild. Like a flame framing her face. He brushed his own hair back, trying to think, trying to line up his lies in a row.

She stood, arms crossed, shoulders tight. "You look like you've seen a ghost," she said flatly.

"Good news," he said finally, flashing her a quick, crooked smile. "I've got a few more days. The old man changed the departure date."

He waited for her to smile. She didn't.

Her face went blank. Pain blank. He watched her twist her fingers together. "It's not good news," she said. "It's just more time to drag this out." Her voice cracked. "I don't think it's a good idea. Spending more time together. You're leaving. I'm staying. And it's harder for the one who stays."

Lewis nodded slowly. "Yeah. I get that."

He thought of his own dad leaving. The silence afterward. His mother's bitterness. The way loneliness curled in your gut and stayed.

"But I'm thinking," he said, leaning forward, "we use the time. I go with you to Legal Aid. I've got the old man's card—he gives me a stupid allowance. I can pay—"

"No." Her voice was sharp. She stepped back.

"Just hear me out," he said quickly. "We can set something up before…" he hesitated.

"—Leave," she finished. "And never contact me again."

They didn't hear the front door open.

Derek charged in, swinging the bedroom door wide like he owned the place. He looked smug. Triumphant.

Lewis stood fast, positioning himself beside Violet. "Ever heard of knocking?" he said. His voice had a dangerous edge.

Derek sneered. "What, and miss catching you at it?" He pointed at Violet, jabbing a finger close to her face. Lewis stepped forward, shielding her. She grabbed his shirt.

"She wasn't doing anything," Lewis said. "Neither was I. We were talking."

Derek's eyes darted around the room, as if expecting to find someone hiding under the bed. Violet stepped forward too. She didn't want to cower behind Lewis.

Derek's sneer curled deeper. "Lucky I came back for my sunnies. Who knows what I would've walked in on." He turned to go, but not without one last jab. "Better check his phone for photos, Vi. After."

Then he was gone, the door left hanging open.

Violet's stomach twisted. She couldn't look at Lewis. Could barely breathe. A car horn sounded. Short and sharp.

"Shut up!" Derek shouted, stomping down the hall.

The front door slammed.

Silence.

Just the sound of their breath.

Lewis unclenched his fists. "Sorry about that. Are you okay?" His voice was soft again.

Violet didn't answer right away. She couldn't. The heat still hadn't left her face. "Yes," she said eventually. "He's a bastard. What did you want to talk about?" she asked, moving away. "You said you wanted to talk."

She sat on the bed. Lewis joined her, quiet for a beat. He caught sight of the pink radio.

"I keep my savings in there," she said, following his eyes. "I can pay you back."

He shook his head. "Told you. It's a birthday gift. "He gripped his knees, his hands tense. The room felt smaller than it had before. Her life, her neat world—he didn't belong in it. He stared at her bookcase. Just a handful of old books.

"The books," she said. "Most of them were Mum's."

He blinked. Monk's voice echoed in his mind: *Perfect match with the mother.* He stood. Knelt at the bookcase. Old paperbacks, unfamiliar titles. He scanned the spines until one caught his eye. *The Idea of Perfection.* He pulled it out. Flipped it open. Inside, in careful handwriting:

Ailsa Mackenzie. And underneath: *Perfection is a prison.*

"It's a novel," Violet said, "about a bridge."

But Lewis wasn't listening. His blood was rushing too loud in his ears.

"Do you have a photo of your mother?" he asked, voice tight.

Violet frowned. "Why?"

He closed the book slowly. "Just curious. Wondered if you looked like her."

She hesitated. Then reached for a dictionary on the shelf. A photo slid out, worn and folded. "This is all I have," she said. "The album was… lost."

She didn't like saying it. She didn't like remembering. Mona had thrown it out. She was sure of it.

Lewis took the photo. Her mother. Blonde. Slight. Jamie a baby on her lap. Violet leaning into her mother's side. Her mother's arm wrapped around her shoulders.

Same smile. Same eyes. Same mouth.

Perfect match.

"Where was your mother born? Not here?" said Lewis, his voice neutral.

"Scotland," said Violet, "She migrated to Australia when she was twenty-two."

"Your father, he's from there? You were born here?"

It felt like an interrogation. She nodded, "Yes I was born here, not long after they got here."

"They both look young," said Lewis. He studied her father's face. Dark, curly hair like Jamie's.

"She died not long after the photo was taken." Violet managed to say it now without breaking. But the sadness still clung to her like damp clothes.

Lewis looked at her, questioning. She answered before he could speak.

"They didn't know why. She just didn't wake up one day." She took the photo from him.

Lewis nodded slowly. It didn't add up. If both her parents were from Scotland—then why did Perfection want her? Why did Rochester?

Violet fell quiet. She thought of her dad often. The loneliness after her mum died. How he tried so hard. The way things shifted when Mona arrived at the mine. "You like Mona, don't you?" he'd asked. Back then, Violet had. As a babysitter. But not as a stepmother.

He changed. Always trying to please Mona. Time with him grew rare. And then—he died. And they were left with her.

Lewis had more questions. But he needed to pace himself. She looked brittle.

"I don't know when they're coming back," Violet said. She turned from the room.

He caught her arm. "Violet, come to the party with me."

She didn't answer. Her eyes clouded. He saw it coming.

"Don't say no."

She wanted him gone. He hadn't moved, hands in his pockets, like he'd asked her to a prom and expected dental surgery. Her stomach twisted.

"Okay."

He blinked. "You will? Great. I'll call for you at six—that okay?"

He touched her shoulder as he turned. At the door, he looked back. She was still by her room.

"I'm going to find a way, Violet. I promise you."

She didn't answer. She didn't believe promises anymore.

The door clicked shut.

She squeezed her eyes tight. She didn't want to see Lincoln. But there he was—in her memory, his hands on her skin, his mouth close, whispering promises.

"I love you, Violet. I'd never tell anyone. Promise."

Just words.

"Just words," she whispered to the closed door.

***

Lewis didn't go straight back. He sat on a bench overlooking the ocean. Waves pounded the rocks below. He could get Violet to the Exit. But he'd have to lie.

He watched the horizon. Thought of the island. The beach. Her. He saw it like a daydream—Violet, Jamie, a dog named Fetch. A beach near Perfection. Her eyes sea-glass green. Him watching her, heart full.

He folded his arms. Leaned back. Gave himself a mental slap. Then another.

Focus.

A bicycle passed. Running feet. The memory of her kiss ignited again. Groaning, he dropped his chin to his chest. Suppressing thoughts of Violet made everything worse. *Girls, Lewis. This is what you get.* His mother's voice. He hoped she'd like Violet. His dad would. He'd love her.

But what was waiting for Violet in Perfection?

When he returned, Helen was on the couch, laptop open. Scott emerged from the bedroom, still pulling on a shirt.

Helen looked up. "Wow, Lewis. What a piece of luck. You and Violet— she likes you. It's going to be easy."

Scott grinned wide. The bonus.

"Yeah, man. You knew. How did you know?"

"I didn't," Lewis said. "Coincidence." He tugged at his shirt. "Need a shower." Scott raised an eyebrow. "Been running," Lewis added. He'd answer their questions later. Or not.

138

CHAPTER EIGHTEEN

Violet didn't sleep much that night. Too much had happened—the island with Lewis, the kiss, seeing Lincoln, and then Lewis asking her questions about her mother. She'd seen his face when he picked up the book and turned the page. He looked as though he'd seen a ghost—and then he'd smiled at her. She turned over. Light behind the curtain. Saturday. She pulled the covers over her head. The house was quiet. Derek and Mona always slept in.

She hadn't heard them come home last night. She'd gone to bed early after making dinner for Jamie. It had been hard to drag him out of his room and away from his games, but at least they kept him safe from Derek—and Mona, who had joined the bullying lately. *When will it end?*

She rolled onto her back, stared at the ceiling. Jenna's party. You're the victim. He should be the one hiding. *Is that what I'm doing?* She flung back the covers. She was going to that freaking party. She'd text Lewis the message in her head. **I'm coming.**

The curtain snapped open. Early morning sun. She changed quickly, running gear, earbuds. She knew the music. She grabbed her phone from the bedside table. Music queued. Cap on. Earbuds in. She twisted the door handle. Pulled. It didn't move. She pulled again harder. Yanked out her earbuds. Listened. The door rattled. Locked. They'd locked her in.

A hot wave of anger surged. Because Lewis had been in her room? Because they needed something to control? She looked around the room, desperate for a way out. Nothing. The window was unlocked. Opened. But the thick metal grill bolted into the frame sealed her in.

She sat on the bed, runners kicked off. No way out until they let her. Not the first time. Mona had done this before. Her fists clenched. She rolled onto her side, tears blurring the pale pink sky outside. Her thigh pressed against something. The phone. She pulled it out. Earbuds back in. Music. That's what she needed. Then she saw the message from Lewis, she hadn't heard the ping.

you up? want to run?

Even if she could… did she want to? She remembered that night, running side by side, their steps in perfect rhythm, the kiss the look in his eyes, like he was possessed. She held her forearm over her face. The memory wasn't painful anymore. It warmed her. She typed out a reply. Plugged the earbuds in. Hit play and let the tears fall.

Lewis had already run the beach path toward Violet's. Now he was jogging on the spot, scanning the street, willing her to appear. He'd sent the text five minutes ago. Not a whim. He'd planned it, thought of it as he drifted to sleep. *Go running with Violet.* Then sleep had wrapped around him like a blanket.

He rubbed his hands up and down his arms. The ocean wind was biting. His ears stung. The music throbbed in his ears, urgent, pulsing. He wanted to run up the hill, cross the road, find her, pound on the door and shout… and then he heard the ping and read the message:

I can't they've locked me in

What the fuck!" he shouted—and he was already running. No plan. Just legs pumping. Until he was outside her bedroom window. He killed the music. Breathing hard now, not from the run -from rage.

He tapped the window. Inside, Violet froze. The tapping came again. Not a polite knock. A furious tattoo. She pulled back the curtain. Lewis. Grey eyes blazing. Jaw clenched. He looked like he'd fight anyone who came near.

She didn't know whether to laugh or cry. She shrugged. Palms up. Resigned. Lewis stepped back. His gesture clear: What the hell is this? He pulled at the iron grill bolted to her window. It didn't move. What if there were a fire. Violet bit her lip. She knew he couldn't break her out. She watched him turn to leave. This would be the last time she saw him. The grill blurred her view. He disappeared.

She pressed her face to the glass. Then—wha-wha-wha—the car alarm screamed.

Urgent.

Wild.

Lewis flashed past the window, crouched against the wall.

Then the thud of Derek's feet pounding down the hall. The rattle of the front door. A blur—Lewis again, ducking low. The click of her bedroom door. Then Lewis inside. Back to the door. Finger to his lips. His eyes were sparkling. He waited for the silence. The click of the front door. Derek's footsteps fading. Then he grinned and held out the key.

"Let's go, Violet."

They stopped running when they reached the ocean path.

"Okay if we walk on the beach?" said Lewis.

He didn't wait for her answer. He was already heading for the steps through the dunes.

The beach looked deserted, but a blue striped towel dropped in the sand said otherwise. Lewis scanned the water—grey waves, grey sky.

"Sharks," Violet muttered, and shivered.

Lewis didn't want to think about sharks. He had other things on his mind—like how to get Violet and Jamie to come with him. Would he have to lie?

Yes. He couldn't tell her the truth.

They walked along the water's edge, his apartment block behind them. Ahead was a sheltered cove ringed with boulders polished smooth by the sea.

"Have they locked you in before?" he asked.

"Yeh. A couple of times." She kicked at the sand. "But now I've got the key, I'll be locking myself in. And them out."

"Derek's a swine," Lewis said softly. "You and Jamie need a better life."

Violet didn't answer. She couldn't look at him. This was the life she had. Only she could make it better.

"How many days before you leave?"

She followed his gaze to the small bay. A popular spot for families. Empty now.

"Here," he said, "let's sit. Out of the wind."

They sat with their backs to the rockface. Lewis dug his shoe into the sand.

Violet waited. Still no answer.

"I'm not sure," he said. "Depends on… I think I've got a few days."

"Aren't you flying? Don't you have tickets?"

Her voice was too sharp. She heard it. He's lying.

That familiar shadow of disappointment swept over her. She stood up.

"Violet—"

He reached for her hand. She pulled it back. "It's okay. Let's go. Run to the statue." She tried to move. He didn't let go.

"Just wait." He rose and faced her. "Violet, just give me until six o'clock. I'll tell you everything. I promise."

She didn't trust promises. Especially from boys. Especially not now.

He took off his cap, raked a hand through his hair. "You're still coming tonight, yeah? The party? I'll call for you. Uber, okay?"

She didn't answer. Her mind was folding in on itself. She didn't know what she thought anymore.

He saw it in her face—like the lights had gone out. He dropped her hand, held her shoulders.

"Listen to me. Everything is going to be okay. Trust me. Please." Then— "Come on. Let's run."

They ran in silence to the statue.

Violet didn't stop. She turned and kept running. As they neared her street, she thought he'd peel off—but he stayed with her. At the corner, she stopped. He didn't. He ran on up the hill. She watched him go. She knew he'd come back to the house. Of course he would.

"Thanks for the jailbreak," she said at the gate.

"I'll wait until you're inside," said Lewis. His jaw clenched. He didn't know what he expected—only that he wanted to stop anyone from hurting her. *This is what feelings do to you, Lewis. They're irrational.* His mother's voice. And she was right. But he didn't care. It felt good. Like being alive for the first time.

Violet opened the front door. Quiet. Everyone still in bed. She turned and waved. "It's okay."

"Six," he whispered. He looked solemn. As though he'd just come from a funeral.

Scott and Helen were in the lounge when he got back. He went straight to the kitchen, grabbed a glass from the bench and drank four in quick succession. They were watching his every move. It made his skin itch.

"Can you stop looking? I went for a run," said Lewis, putting the glass down harder than he meant to.

"Yeh, we saw you," said Helen. "From the window."

Damn. They saw Violet too Lewis tugged at his t-shirt. It was damp. He'd practically sprinted back.

"Impressive," said Scott. "And surprising.

"What d'you mean by that…surprising?" Lewis hadn't meant to say it aloud.

"Well, just that—man, you're…" Scott didn't like the belligerent look Lewis was giving him. "Nothing. Just fast work, that's all."

Lewis caught the nudge Helen gave Scott.

"So," Helen said, "we need to talk about how we're going to do this. What have you found out about her?"

"Later," said Lewis. There's no 'we', he thought. I'm doing this on my own. "I'm taking a shower."

He took his time There was something about the extraction that kept bothering him—and it had everything to do with Rochester. Something he couldn't quite see. The hot water ran down his back. He let it.

"Hey, when are you coming out?" Scott banged on the door.

Lewis twisted the taps off. He wasn't looking forward to the grilling. He wasn't good at being evasive. Violet was different. He didn't want to share what he knew about her—not with anyone. Thirty minutes later he walked into the lounge room. Scott was on the sofa, giving him a look.

"Where's Helen?" Lewis asked, sitting at the table.

"In the bedroom. Talking to Monk."

Lewis glanced toward the closed door. He didn't like the way it made him feel.

"Don't ask me. Monk called her," Scott said, just as Helen came back in.

"Yeh," Helen said, slipping her phone into her pocket. She looked directly at Lewis. "Just a check-in to see how you're going. They want extraction tomorrow morning. Think you can do it?" It wasn't a question.

"What?" Lewis exploded. Too soon. He needed a day. At least. There was Jamie. He wasn't leaving him behind.

He looked between them. Helen was inspecting her nails. Scott stood, hands on hips, watching Lewis.

The silence crouched in the room. Lewis could feel it pressing against him. *They know.* About Violet. About him. But how? He had to hold it together. Keep his face straight.

"It's too soon," he said flatly, and turned into the kitchen. He opened the fridge. Empty. He looked across at Scott, still watching.

"I just need a day. I'll talk to Monk." He shut the fridge door. "There's no food. I'm starving. You eaten?"

"Yeh, sorry," said Helen. "We finished the cardboard. Wheaties or whatever. But we could go out. Mac something. Try it before we go home." She was talking too fast. It was worse than the silence.

Lewis walked to the door. "Coming?" he asked Scott.

CHAPTER NINETEEN

McDonald's was packed. Noise bounced off every surface. They took their trays to a window table. Lewis sat facing out to the street. He needed time to work out what he was going to say about Violet. He watched cars snake through the drive-through. Kids scrambled over plastic tubes in the play area.

Helen unwrapped her burger like it might explode. She bit it. Chewed. Swallowed. "Tastes… processed," she said. "But not bad."

"So," said Scott, dabbing at his mouth, "you've made a lot of progress with…" He let it hang.

Lewis flared his nostrils. "Progress?"

"Yeh," said Scott. "Monk told Helen."

"Told you what?" He looked at Helen.

Scott slurped his drink. "That you're making progress. Thought you wouldn't have trouble getting her to the exit point. Said he was impressed."

Lewis's mind was racing. How did Monk know? He hadn't said a thing about Violet.

"You must've mentioned something. When you saw me with her?"

Helen shook her head. "Nope. Didn't see the relevance."

Lewis went still. That only left one possibility. They were being monitored. He checked his phone. Off. He touched the transmitter behind his ear. Warm. Just as it should be. An icy trail slid down his spine.

They've bugged me. Bugged us.

Lewis folded his napkin. Tight. Like a blade. He'd have to be careful—until he found out what Monk really knew.

"So," Scott said. "You don't need tips from me? The master's hand?"

Lewis raised a brow. "Master's hand?"

He balled the napkin and threw it at Scott's head.

They walked the ocean path. Lewis tried to head off talk of Violet. He couldn't avoid it. The sea was blue. Sky cloudless. He looked to the horizon—thought of Violet on the beach, knees in the sand. Afraid.

"She's almost eighteen," he said. "Parents dead. Her father four years ago. Mother, maybe ten. She has a brother, Jamie. Genius. Three years ahead in school. There's a stepmother."

"Step-mother?" said Helen.

"Mona. Came when Violet was twelve. There's a boyfriend."

"She has a boyfriend?" Scott again.

His name's Derek. He's thirty-five."

"What!" Scott almost shouted.

"Mona, not Violet." Lewis felt weary. "She runs. Cycles to school. You've seen her."

"And your plan?" said Helen.

"Party. Tonight. I'll figure it out then."

"A lot riding on it," Scott said.

"You mean the money."

"I'll get her to the exit," Helen offered. "She'll trust me."

Lewis clenched his jaw. "No. I've got this."

"Okay," said Scott. "Just making sure. Monk said we might need—"

"—persuasion," Helen cut in.

Force. That's what they meant. Lewis changed the subject. "Free day. What're your plans?"

"Train south. Mandurah," Helen said. "You coming?"

"No. Checking the exit with Monk."

Scott pulled him back. Whispered, "Already checked."

"What? When?"

No answer. Scott caught up with Helen.

New team, huh?

***

Back at the apartment, Lewis rounded on Scott. "What's going on?"

Scott poured water, calm. "Chill. No big deal."

Helen slipped to the bedroom. Scott opened his laptop. "Monk sent this. Didn't send it to you. Thinks you've got a brain injury."

"I'm fine."

"He's worried."

Lewis studied the coordinates. *A valley. Wrong.* He jotted numbers. Did the math.

"You've been there?" he asked.

"Just mapped it," Scott said. He didn't like the way Lewis was staring at him. He folded his arms. The green light on his Sixty-Six watch pulsed. Lewis's heart jumped. *The watch.* Lewis scribbled on the pad.

It's recording us — take it off.

Scott frowned. Paranoid. But removed it.

Lewis led him to the bathroom. Tossed his own watch onto his bed.

"What now?" said Scott.

"You said Monk told you I was making progress. Did you speak to him?"

"No. Just a message."

"How did he know?"

"We saw you two."

"You told him?"

"No. Thought it didn't matter. Figured maybe, for once, you were happy."

Lewis flared his nostrils. Violet was serious. She wasn't Scott's idea of a fun time.

"What about Helen? Did she say anything to Monk?"

"Could be. I don't think so. Ask her," said Scott.

"Wait. Not yet. I need to figure out what we're going to do. You know the co-ordinates are wrong, don't you?"

"What?"

"Think, Scott. Think. Where are they?"

"In... Arlon Valley," said Scott, drawing his brows together.

"Yes, that's right. And?"

"No need to talk to me like an idiot."

"I'm not. I'm waiting for the neurons to fire, for fuck's sake."

Scott's eyebrows shot up. His eyes registered alarm. "A valley."

"Yes. Exactly."

"Can't have an exit point in a valley." He was remembering something. Not the details, but close. "Not a valley," he repeated. "Hey, why don't you call Monk and check it out?"

Lewis shook his head. He didn't know if they could trust Monk. He couldn't risk alerting anyone.

"They—whoever they are—we don't know. They're not planning an exit. Or if they are, we're not part of it. I don't know why they want Violet, but I know it's not the story they've spun us."

He paused. "This is Rochester. He wants her. She's important to him. Said he'd waited—"

"Yeh," said Scott. "He said that back... when... at... could—" Scott looked at Lewis. His eyes widened, as though he'd been hit over the head. "Could she be related... to Rochester?"

Lewis felt the room tip. *Related!* It hit like the lightning bolt that had struck him in the schoolyard.

"Eighteen years," he said. "He said he'd waited... Rochester. That's it. That's it..." He held his head in his hands. "I read it, Scott. I read..." He clawed at his hair, dragging the memory up.

"Damn." He leaned on the washbasin, stared at his reflection. Closed his eyes. Willed the image to come.

"Rochester's wife and unborn child died in a fire nearly eighteen years ago... what if..."

"Didn't die. Someone... kidnapped her," said Scott.

"Or she ran away. From Rochester. Didn't want to be found. Came here."

"Why?" said Scott. "Why would anyone leave Perfection?"

Lewis gripped Scott's shoulders. "Don't know. But we're going to find out. We're not taking her back until we know."

He should have made the connection before. Idiot. It had never felt right. He was talking to himself now. Piecing it together aloud. He turned on the tap. Splashed water on his face.

Scott bit his lip. He could see the bonus slipping down the drain.

"Cross," said Lewis, slapping the basin. "You said you didn't think he went back to Perfection. He's still here. He's working with Rochester. Not Monk sending the messages. It's Cross. He's Rochester's man. And he works for the Bureau."

"Fucking bastard," whispered Scott.

"Hey, you two, I need to use the bathroom." Helen banged on the door.

Scott opened it. Helen raised an eyebrow. "Men's business, I suppose.

"Sorry. Personal," said Lewis.

Helen pursed her lips.

Lewis shoved Scott out and returned to the living room. He picked up Scott's watch still winking on the table, carried it into his room, and set it beside his own. Closed the door.

"Okay. What now?" said Scott.

"One thing first," said Lewis. He looked toward the bathroom.

Scott didn't know what it meant. But it had to do with Helen.

They sat in silence, listening to the flush, then Helen joined them in the lounge.

"You two sorted?"

"Yeh," said Lewis. He went to the kitchen, filled the kettle. "I was wondering if you saw Rochester before you left?"

Helen looked at Scott on the sofa. She didn't want to feel disappointed—they weren't going to Mandurah now. Lewis had stopped that.

"Who?" she said, choosing a chair at the table, away from Scott.

"Rochester," said Scott. "Advanced Laboratories."

She frowned. "Victor Rochester? Why would I see him?"

"No reason," said Lewis. He lifted the lid off a tin of drinking chocolate, shook some into a mug. Held it up.

"No thanks," said Scott. "We're heading off."

Helen didn't answer. Lewis walked over to the table without the mug. One sip was enough. He wasn't used to drinking liquid sugar.

"You spoken to Monk since you got here?" he asked Helen.

"Just to let him know how you were. Nothing else."

Her glare was sharp.

"Here." Lewis turned the laptop toward her. "Exit location. Tomorrow morning. Scott said he got them from Monk today in a coded message. I just looked."

"I was going to show you—after Lewis," said Scott.

Helen leaned in. It was an aerial shot. Fields. Trees. Coloured specks. She zoomed in.

"What's that?" she said.

"Hot air balloon," said Lewis. "Popular spot evidently."

Helen studied the balloons. The baskets. "Did you check the co-ordinates?"

"Yeh. Same result," said Scott.

She rubbed her lips. "Did you come through this valley?"

"Did you?" said Lewis quickly.

She lifted her head. "What's going on? Is this a test? I'm here because I came second in the exams. You both needed rescuing!"

She glared at Scott.

Lewis winced. "Sorry."

She stepped forward. "I came in at the same location. Grantham Hill. Ninety-three metres above sea level. Just made it. Monk told me—co-ordinates came from him. Personally. Not a coded message." She jabbed a finger at the laptop. "That's a contact point. Not the exit!"

Lewis stepped back. *A contact point?* He hadn't known that. "And you know it's a contact point how—not an exit point?"

"This is a bloody test, you've got a nerve…who the hell do you think you are! You're an arrogant bastard everyone.."

"Shut up, Helen," Scott cut in. "Just answer the freaking question."

Helen glared at him. Scott stood up and ran his hands through his curls. "Sorry, Hell. We're wasting time—you and me, the train trip to… wherever." He smiled, hoping to break the tension.

Helen turned to Lewis. His eyebrow was raised, lip curled. That look could cut glass. She'd seen it used on others. Never on her.

Lewis didn't care what everyone said. He needed to be sure about Helen before letting her in.

Helen drew a breath. "I know it's a contact point because I did my research before I left." She paused, couldn't keep the sarcasm out. "I thought it might be important info in an emergency… but I didn't know the exact co-ordinates."

She frowned. "And that's not the exit. It has to be at least ninety metres above sea level with a clearance of two hundred. If it's there," she nodded at the laptop, "then something's not right."

Lewis let out a breath. Smiled. A real smile that softened his eyes.

"Sorry. It was a test." He flicked his hair back. "Sit down. I'll tell you what Scott and I worked out. Then you and I can figure out how we're getting out of this world… and then you can catch that train."

They sat around the table for two hours. They had a plan. Of sorts. Then Scott and Helen left. And Lewis called an Uber.

CHAPTER TWENTY

Violet moved around the kitchen as quietly as possible, careful not to rattle the cutlery. She ate toast and drank juice at the bench, laptop open "The Law of Trusts" stared back at her.

"What are you looking at?" Mona's voice snapped through the silence.

Violet jumped, changed the screen. "School stuff. English. Dickens."

"The Law of Trusts," Mona said, rounding the bench. "Why would you be looking at that?"

Violet closed the laptop. She was leaving the room. She wasn't doing this today—not on her birthday. But Mona was faster.

"Derek! Derek!" she shouted.

Violet backed up against the wall.

Derek came pounding down the hall, in nothing but his underwear, hair wild. "What's up?" He blinked, disoriented.

"Her. That's what's up."

Derek hadn't even noticed Violet. "What she do?" he asked, squinting toward the window.

"She was reading about trusts." Mona spat the word.

"Yes," Violet said quietly. "Researching what you should have done with the money Dad left for Jamie and me. How you were meant to hold it—in trust—until I turned twenty-one."

She stepped forward. "I'd like my laptop, please."

Derek sneered. "Good luck with that. Mona's entitled to expenses for raising you."

"There's none left," Mona said her lips twitching.

"What?" Derek spun to her. "None left?"

"Not much," Mona corrected. Too late.

All gone. Five hundred thousand. Violet felt like collapsing.

"Anyway," Mona added, "he wasn't your father."

Violet blinked. She must've misheard.

"Don't look at me like that. It's true. He knows." Mona jerked her head at Derek.

"She should know," Mona hissed. "He met your mum in Scotland. Jamie's your half-brother."

"I'm going back to bed," Derek muttered. At the door, he turned. "The Beemer—that's mine. You said it was a present."

"It's leased," Mona replied. The door slammed.

Violet blinked away tears. Could it be true? She didn't care. He was her dad. Jamie, her brother. Nothing could change that.

She was eighteen. She could leave. But there was no money. She locked herself in her room. Made a new plan. Or tried to. She picked up her phone, typed a message. Deleted it. She wanted to talk to Lewis. But she couldn't rely on him. She had to do this herself. The doorknob rattled.

"Let me in, Violet.

Jamie. She opened the door. His hair stuck up, sleep in his eyes.

"What was that about?" he said, flopping face-down on her bed.

"Were you up late?" she asked, ruffling his hair.

"Homework."

"Good. We've gotta do well."

"I know. Part of our escape plan." He left, returned with an envelope. "Happy birthday. I didn't forget." A card. Roses on the front. "I know you like roses." Inside: "To the best sister in the universe. Going to buy you a present when I get a job."

"Thanks, Jamie. I'm going to think of something expensive." She hid the card. She didn't want Mona seeing it. She didn't want to remind her she was officially an adult.

"What was that about? Jamie said again. He sat beside her, waiting.

She didn't have answers. She wasn't even sure what the question was. Her dad, Jamie's dad wasn't her biological father. What difference did it make? She wasn't going to think about it.

"Don't treat me like a baby," said Jamie. "Tell me Violet." He sounded angry.

"I don't treat you like a baby Jamie, that's not fair. I just sometimes think we both don't have to be worrying about all this…shit."

"Yes, I do, if you're worrying about it then…we're in this together." He pushed his glasses up.

"Okay. You know that daddy left money for us in trust, that means – "

"-I know what that means,"

"You do?" said Violet.

"Yes, I googled it. I read dad's will."

"You did?"

"Yes, I heard Mona telling Derek about it, ages ago. So, I found the will…it's in dad's desk…in the study."

"Why didn't you talk to me Jamie?"

He waved his hand across his face, "Just didn't," said Jamie, he looked at the floor.

Violet could read that look, there was something he didn't want to tell her.

"Did you find anything else about the will or anything…?"

"Nah nothing." He wasn't good at lying, Violet knew that about him. He hated telling a lie, he didn't care if the truth got him in trouble.

"You did, didn't you? Something about me…wasn't it?" Violet put her arm around his shoulder. "You can tell me…Mona said something just now." She tried to smile but it was hard when you were trying not to cry.

Jamie jumped up, his fists were clenched, "What did that…what did she say? No don't tell me." He swiped his hand across his eyes.

"We're a couple of orphans, "said Violet, "but we've got each other. You are the best thing ever," she stood up and hugged him. "Love you Jamie,"

"Love you too… big sister."

He'd never called her that before. It was true then and Jamie knew. She wasn't going to think about that…ever again.

"Okay, now tell me about our money," Jamie said.

"Mona said there's no trust money. I was researching trusts in the kitchen…I know…but it was early, I didn't expect them to be up. Lewis told me I should see a lawyer." Violet shrugged her shoulders. "She saw me. I heard her tell Derek there's no money left."

"Bastards…both of them, effing bastards."

"Shh Jamie, it's too late now, have to think of something else. Still going to see a lawyer. We'll figure something out. What are you doing today, anything fun?"

"Yeh, I'm going over to Ben's this morning, trying out a new game; she knows," he said jerking his head towards the door. "I didn't ask for permission I just told her I was staying overnight. I knew she wouldn't object; anything to get rid of me," he grinned.

"Good, I'm going to a party at Jenna's. It's her birthday party but I'm going to be celebrating mine."

"Okay, I'm going back to bed."

Violet lay back on the bed, she looked at her phone, it was still early, she had hours before she saw Lewis and the party. She threw her arm across her face, she had to get out of the house. She could hear Mona shouting at Derek, "You can't take the car, I've hidden the keys." And then the sound of feet running down the hall and the bathroom door shutting.

CHAPTER TWENTY-ONE

Lewis took an Uber out to Arlan Valley. The driver was telling Lewis all about the area. "Really popular with couples; hot air balloons," he pointed to the roof of his four-wheel drive, "get engaged up there. They think they're being original, don't like to tell them they're not." He slowed down carefully as the lights changed red. He was driving as though Lewis was a little old lady.

He looked at Lewis in the rear-view mirror. He had a sudden thought, "Sorry mate, is that what you're going to do?"

Lewis wasn't listening, he'd been thinking about the plan, it had flaws, big ones. He had to lie to Violet when he'd promised her he wouldn't do that. He stared back at the dark eyes looking at him,

"Sorry, did you say something?"

The driver looked back to the road, the lights were green. He stretched his neck, "Nothing mate, just making conversation." He put his foot down and the car shot ahead as the seat belt snapped hard across Lewis's chest.

The rest of the drive was in silence, the driver's mood seemed to have changed like the weather, but Lewis was looking ahead, he could see hot air balloons rising into the sky.

"Here," said Lewis when they got closer and he could see the field in the distance and the sign on the corner of the road that read,

BREATHTAKING SUNRISE

IN HOT AIR BALLOON

$300 PER COUPLE

"Drop me here thanks." He wanted to walk the rest of the way, he didn't want to miss anything. He slung his backpack over his shoulder and took his phone out of his pocket and started taking photos.

***

Violet stayed at the public library until it closed at four o'clock, then cycled home, stopping at an op shop to search for something—anything—for the party. She found an emerald, green blouse for five dollars.

As soon as she stepped inside the front door, she froze. Books lay scattered in the hallway, pages torn and fluttering. She ran into her bedroom. The bookcase had been overturned, her clothes strewn across the carpet, and the pink radio smashed in pieces. Mona had found the money.

Violet dropped to her knees, clutching her stomach as her legs gave way.

"Looking for this?" Mona's voice was slurred. Violet didn't turn. She didn't want to see that face.

"You little thief." Mona staggered into the bedroom, shoved her foot into Violet's back. Violet hit the floor, her cheek striking the edge of the bedside table. She pressed a hand to her face, steadied herself, and stood. Her cheek throbbed.

Mona's face was red, mascara smeared like bruises under her eyes. "Your fault he's left." Mona waved the roll of money. "This is what he wanted." She stumbled, sliding down the wall until she sat crumpled on the floor. "You can leave too. You're old enough. Take him." She gestured vaguely at the open door, like Jamie might be standing there.

A strange calm swept over Violet. "I will leave, Mona. Monday. I'll take Jamie. But I need time. And I need money." Her voice came out steady, calm—surprising even herself.

"Not getting this," Mona slurred, clutching the money tight. "This is mine. My money for giving up the best years of my life."

Violet didn't answer. What was the point? The money was gone. She had no plan. No backup.

Mona staggered to her feet and left the room. "Monday," she mumbled as she disappeared down the hall.

Violet set the bookcase upright, gathered her books and the torn pages from the hallway. Only two had survived. Her mother's name was still written inside both.

She didn't want to go to the party. But she wanted to see Lewis one more time. She'd tell him everything. He said he'd write. He won't.

She checked her phone. Two hours. She couldn't stay in this house. She grabbed her party clothes and locked herself in the bathroom. She washed her hair. She didn't cry.

Violet pulled on her jeans and the emerald, green blouse. In the mirror, she folded the sleeves and tucked the shirt in. Her shoes were worn runners—the only pair she owned.

Her hair still damp, she pulled an elastic over her wrist. She'd tie it back later. She touched the red mark on her cheek. No makeup. Just sunscreen. She slung her bag over her shoulder, unlocked her bike, and pedalled toward the beach—and Lewis.

He saw her the moment the Uber turned the corner. Red hair blazing. Green shirt flashing. Lewis tapped the driver's shoulder. "Can you stop? Let me out ahead of that girl on the bike."

The car pulled over. Violet slowed, confused, as Lewis stepped out and waved. She stopped pedalling.

"Hey, you coming my way?" he said, walking beside her. "Let me wheel your bike." He took the handlebars from her gently.

"This is…" he started, wanting to say, this is perfect, I get to see you again—but he reined it in.

"Nice blouse," he said as she took off her helmet. He held out his hand for it and hooked it over the handlebars.

Violet shoved her hands in her pockets. Seeing him cracked something in her chest. "Thanks," she said, unable to meet his eyes.

"What did you do today?" she asked quickly, needing to keep him from asking her anything.

"A bit of sightseeing. A last look around. You?"

She winced. She could have gone with him. Could have avoided Mona. Saved herself. She nodded vaguely. "Where?"

"Oh, out in the country."

They reached the apartment. She stopped at the entrance. He glanced over his shoulder. "Just need to change shirts. Scott and Helen aren't going to the party." He jerked his head. "Come on."

He leaned her bike against the hallway wall. "Be safe there," he said. "No Derek around to cut the lock."

He grabbed a drink from the fridge. "Orange juice?" he asked.

Violet shook her head. She spotted the open bedroom door and clothes on the bed. Her chest tightened. *No, Violet. You're on your own.*

She walked to the window, trying to block the memory of the island. He appeared beside her.

"What's that?" he asked, pointing to the red welt on her cheek.

Violet touched it, startled. "Fell," she said. "Bedside cabinet."

Lewis gripped her shoulders. "Did that bastard hit you?"

She shook her head. "Get changed. I'll tell you everything."

"Okay. Sit tight. Five minutes."

He was back fast, wet hair brushed back, dressed in jeans and a white long-sleeve windcheater.

"Bit short on party gear," he joked, flicking his hair. He sat beside her. "Okay. Talk to me."

She did. About the money, the trust, the books. "I've got to leave, Lewis. Me and Jamie. We can't stay there."

"Fuck. That's awful." He meant it. And it made what he was planning easier.

"Mona's throwing me out. I turned eighteen."

He blinked. "Your birthday. Today?"

She nodded.

"Happy birthday," he said softly. One she'd never forget. He looked at his phone. Time ticking. He had exactly sixty minutes.

"Violet… would you mind if we skipped the party?" She opened her mouth but he pushed ahead. "I've got a surprise. A kind of birthday present. It includes Jamie. We've got to pick him up."

She narrowed her eyes. "What kind of surprise?"

"Wouldn't be a surprise if I told you. But it'll be exciting."

She frowned. "I thought… I had something to face."

"Forget it. We've got better things to do."

He looked around. He wasn't taking anything except his backpack and laptop. He checked the time. "Jamie at home?"

"No, with Ben. I'll call him." She frowned. "He might not want to come."

"He doesn't have a choice," Lewis muttered to himself.

Jamie didn't want to leave. "I'm winning!"

"Let me talk to him," Lewis said, taking the phone. He walked into the bathroom. "It's a surprise," he called to Violet.

A minute later, he emerged. "Done. He's coming. Let's go."

Lewis stopped beside a white rental car.

Violet blinked. "You hired a car?"

He nodded, tossed his bag in the boot.

"Where are we going?"

He raised an eyebrow.

"Right. Surprise," she said. "Of course."

He opened her door. She climbed in, heart hammering. He drove fast. Just under the limit. They picked up Jamie, who was bouncing with energy.

"Don't forget. It's a surprise," Lewis said.

"Yeh, yeh," said Jamie.

Lewis switched on the radio. Jamie looked curious but didn't ask more. Violet watched the scenery shift. She knew this road. Her mouth went dry. *No. Please not that.*

Lewis turned off the road. Through a gate. Into a nearly empty carpark. A sign flashed past. Hot air balloon. Her stomach dropped. In the sky: a rainbow-striped balloon.

Lewis checked his phone. Twenty minutes and four seconds.

"Come on. We've got to run."

Lewis couldn't see Scott and Helen, but he'd spotted the hire car in the car park. They had to be there, waiting in the balloon's basket.

Violet wasn't getting out.

Jamie had already bolted towards the launch site, chatting with a man in a leather jacket who was helping him climb into the wicker basket.

Lewis grabbed his backpack and opened the passenger door. "Come on, Violet." He held out his hand. She didn't take it. Her eyes stayed locked on the balloon, on the flames flaring orange-blue beneath the rising fabric. On the sky.

"It's not that—" she whispered, swallowing. "The balloon… is it?"

Lewis wasn't listening. He was watching Jamie, watching the basket, waving toward someone.

Then he leaned in. "No time," he said, voice tight. "We have to leave now."

She didn't move. She was clutching the seat. His eyes met hers—green, wide, frightened. "Don't think about it, Violet. You have to do this. Trust me. Please."

Something in his voice—urgency, something close to fear—battered her resolve.

"The weather," he said, trying to smile, "small window before it's too late."

Violet still didn't move.

Lewis ran a hand through his hair. "It's going to be amazing. One of those memories. You'll never forget it."

Her body sank back, further into the car. Lewis reached in and took her hand—it was ice-cold. He tightened his grip.

"I've… already paid. It cost a fortune. No refund."

That did it. She flinched, then let go of the seat. He tugged gently, and she followed—stumbling from the car, hand in his, running across the field. She would remember this. Just not the way he thought.

The balloon loomed closer. Jamie was already inside, beaming. The flames hissed into the burner. Another man in a matching leather jacket was untying ropes at the base.

Lewis's hand pressed against her back. "Here," he murmured. He guided her up the steps and lifted her into the basket. Scott caught her by the waist and set her down

"Surprise," said Helen from the far side.

Violet didn't answer. Her stomach had already dropped. Lewis climbed in after her.

The pilot turned. "Sorry mate—no luggage. Over the side."

Lewis dangled his backpack over the edge… and watched Bill finish untying the final rope.

"Chocks away," the pilot called.

He turned. Shouted again. "Chocks away!"

Lewis and Scott moved in unison. Hands on the pilot's shoulders. A heave. The man toppled. A yell. A thud.

Scott hauled the ropes up, out of reach. The balloon rose. Lewis pulled the lever. The flame burst higher. Violet clung to the basket. She'd seen it. They'd thrown the pilot out.

Her stomach turned. She looked at Jamie. Calm. Grinning. Like this was part of a game.

"Backpack," Lewis said. Scott handed him the laptop. They huddled.

"We're on track," Scott said.

Helen nodded from her corner. She shouted to Violet, "It's going to be okay."

Violet couldn't speak.

"Everyone sit!" Lewis shouted.

The balloon was climbing too fast. Helen dropped. Hands braced. Jamie obeyed instantly. Legs crossed, palms on knees. Teeth chattering. Grinning like Aladdin on a flying carpet. Violet couldn't let go of the basket. Her hands had locked.

The light exploded—too bright. She shut her eyes. Slid sideways. Her head hit the floor. Jamie fell into her. She wrapped her arms around him. A body shielded hers.

The wind howled. Someone was shouting—Lewis? Scott? They were falling.

If she survived she was never going to forgive him. The body lifted off her. The basket steadied.

They floated. Cracking wicker. Moaning wind. She opened her eyes. Jamie stood. Leaned over the edge.

"Jamie!" She couldn't move.

Lewis gripped the side. They were over a coastline. Hills in the distance.

"Altitude, wind direction?" he yelled.

"Ten thousand feet! Wind 270, north!"

Lewis muttered, "Thank the Gods." They were drifting inland.

"It's amazing," Jamie said. "Where are we?"

Violet couldn't answer.

"Don't move, Jamie," Lewis warned.

Violet folded in on herself.

Scott grinned at Helen. Violet blinked. *They're all mad.*

"Where are we, Scott?" Lewis said.

He opened the laptop. "Eighty k's south of the Foxtail delta. We'll land before the hills. Rosalinda Bay on the other side—harbour, train, small town."

"I've been there," said Helen. "Holiday place." "Yeh, I see the train track," said Scott.

Lewis was squinting toward the distant hills. "Where does the train go? Can you find a route into the Capital?" He tried to keep the urgency out of his voice. Everything depended on them getting there before Rochester.

"Yeh, we're looking," said Scott.

Violet struggled to her feet. She'd never heard of a place called Foxtail Delta. Gripping the side of the basket, she didn't look down. Instead, she scanned the landscape—low trees, a glint of water, distant hills. Nothing familiar. No houses. No roads. No skyline. Just a strange, open quiet.

"How could we have flown so far?" she muttered. But it wasn't the geography that bothered her. Not now.

"Why are you doing this, Lewis?" she shouted.

This wasn't a birthday present. It was something else. Something she wasn't in on.

She tried again. "Why?"

Lewis didn't answer. He couldn't. Not yet. Not while they were still airborne. Not while someone might spot the balloon and alert Rochester.

"We can do it," Scott shouted. "We'll need to change trains, but we can get to the Capital."

Lewis kept his focus on the horizon. The balloon's shadow skimmed the treetops. They needed to get down. Now. Too fast. *Water!* He swore and pulled the lever. The flames surged. The balloon lifted just enough to skim the river. The shadow shot forward across a patch of green.

A forest loomed. They brushed the crown of one tree, then another. A clearing. A sudden drop. Sticks cracked. The basket tipped, then crashed. Everyone spilled out as the balloon lifted again, wobbling in the air before collapsing in a rainbow heap.

Helen was on her feet first, brushing off her jeans.

Lewis stood up, everyone was ok. He pulled Jamie up, "You okay?"

"Lost my glasses," Jamie squinted. "Everything's a blur."

Lewis jogged back, waving the glasses. "Crack in one lens."

"We'll fix it," Scott said—then stopped. Lewis was giving him a look.

"Later," said Lewis. "We've got to move."

Violet pushed herself up. Her knees stung. She scanned the grass.

"What game is this?" Jamie grinned. "That was epic." He though Violet had a really cool boyfriend, but he didn't like the way Violet was looking at Lewis. As though they weren't a team.

"The laptop?" Lewis asked.

Scott unzipped his jacket. "Looked after it like a baby."

"Good. Find the route to the nearest town." Lewis stepped away, pulling out his phone.

Violet watched him. He was just… calling someone? After what had just happened? After tossing a pilot out of a balloon?

He slipped the phone back in his pocket and breathed deeply. "You okay?" he asked gently, stepping toward her.

Violet turned away. She crossed to Jamie.

"What's next, Scott?" Jamie asked, eyes shining.

Violet wished she thought it was a brilliant game and she didn't feel so scared and betrayed.

CHAPTER TWENTY-TWO

Lewis walked beside Violet for hours. She didn't speak. Her silence burned hotter than the sun. Ahead, Jamie skipped between Scott and Helen, full of questions. His world was full of powers, quests, missions. This was the best game ever.

They reached the top of the hill. Rosalinda Bay spread below them—boats in the river, white buildings clustered along the shore.

Jamie tugged at Lewis's arm. "What now? A boat?"

"No," said Lewis. "A train."

Jamie ran ahead. Violet stayed back. When they were alone, she spoke. "Are you going to tell me?"

Lewis sighed. Brushed his hair back. She stared him down. "You lied to me."

Lewis frowned. Had he lied? He hadn't told the truth was that the same thing? "I haven't lied. I just haven't told you everything." He started to walk down the hill. Violet followed him.

"We could have been killed," she couldn't keep the anger out of her voice. "And what you did to that man…he could be…"

"…he's alright. It wasn't a big drop. We had no choice. I saw him stand up and run…" He took a breath. He was going to tell her. *She'll think I'm crazy.*

"This," he threw a hand out in a sweeping gesture, "is part of Perfection. It's a Parallel universe to yours." He spoke quickly, "This is where I come from, Scott and Helen too. My world sent me…us to find someone." His grey eyes turned to her. "It turned out it was you."

Violet glared. He looked so serious. Her eyes glittered.

"Violet, I know it sounds mad. Just hear me out." Violet listened in silence as he filled in the details. The Bureau, the transmitter, the lightening, her mother's books.

"Perfection. Your mum wrote in it. Remember that?" He sounded desperate

She did every one of those books. Torn. Ruined. "Perfection is a prison," Violet whispered.

The words scraped out of her throat. Ahead, the town shimmered in the distance. She was thirsty, bone-tired, and half-convinced she was losing her mind.

"Did you ever wonder why she wrote that? Or even what it meant?" Lewis's voice dipped, cautious. "Violet…I don't think your mother was from Scotland. I think she was from here. From Perfection. And-"He cut himself off. He couldn't tell her the rest. Not yet.

Violet was silent. The mark on her cheek like a red flag against her pale skin.

"You okay Violet?" He stepped closer. He wanted to hold her but he resisted. "I know it sounds crazy. It's a lot. "He turned away toward the town "Not far now. We'll get something to drink there. Maybe food"

She was hungry. Thirsty. But she wanted answers. She felt like she'd fallen down some rabbit hole and couldn't find the ground.

"Answer me this, then,". Her voice was edged, disbelieving, almost sarcastic. "Who sent you to find me - and why?"

Lewis froze. The hardest question. *How much should I tell her.* What if he was wrong? What if the truth wrecked her completely?

"I thought it was the Bureau. The one I told you about." He swallowed. "But now I think it was Victor Rochester. He's powerful. More powerful than anyone. He runs the most advanced medical laboratories in Perfection. And he wanted you found."

"Why?" she folded her arms.

He didn't answer. He kept walking. The silence hung between them like a hot air balloon.

The town drew closer. The roads and buildings taking shape. Jamie ran ahead. He stopped outside a white painted café with a wooden bench outside and blue pots with bright yellow flowers Violet didn't recognise.

Jamie pumped his fist in the air. "Let's eat here. I'm starving." He glanced at Violet. He didn't want her to say no.

Violet pressed her fingers to her forehead. She needed to sit.

Lewis was watching her, eyebrows pulled tight. Worried? Thoughtful? He couldn't tell. He didn't know her well enough.

She'd been a fool to trust him, she thought.

His hand touched her shoulder, light but certain, guiding her toward the open door of the café.

Inside was crowded, voices echoing against glass and chrome, but they slid into a table by the windows. Beyond the glass the bay stretched wide, water flickering, boats rocking with the tide.

"Rosalind Bay Café", Jamie read aloud, lifting the menu. He studied it like it was hiding clues, as if the answers were tucked between cappuccinos and fish burgers.

"You okay Jamie?' Violet could see he was. She wished she felt like Jamie.

"No steak sandwich," Jamie couldn't hide the disappointment.

"Here," said Scott he scanned the menu. "There, Vita B delight. That's what I'm having."

"Is it vegetarian here?" Jamie couldn't imagine not eating meat again.

"Violet?" Lewis waited. He thought she might be in shock. He walked to the counter pulling out his credit card.

Helen read the look on Violet's face. "It will be okay Violet. You can trust Lewis…you can trust Scott." She glanced at Scott who was explaining the menu to Jamie. "and me; you can trust us, Violet, promise."

Violet didn't think she could even trust herself. Her world had gone mad. She looked out of the window. A family walking across the lawn toward the Harbour.

The food came. But Violet didn't move. She stared at the plate as though it was some ancient artifact.

"Are you eating that?" Jamie said.

Violet pushed her plate across the table. "You can have it." She'd drunk the juice—some kind of fruit she couldn't even recognise.

They sat in silence. All around them people were talking. Scott started to say something but Lewis silenced him with a flash of his grey eyes.

Scott stood. "I'm going to look at the boats. You coming, Jamie? Bring the burger." He looked at Helen. "You coming, Hell?"

Violet reached for her glass. Her hand was shaking. She blinked back the tears now threatening to show how afraid she was. Lewis saw her hand tremble. He was too far down the table to reach her. He stood and moved beside her. He didn't care if it was the wrong move—she was shaking.

He slipped his arm around her shoulders. "Violet, let's go outside."

He didn't wait for an answer. He helped her up and steered her toward the door and into the bright sunlight and the street thick with holidaymakers. He didn't take his arm away until they reached a bench down by the harbour.

Scott and Jamie were on the jetty. Helen was somewhere close.

"Here, Violet. Sit."

She looked at the bench as though she couldn't place what it was. She shivered. Couldn't stop shaking. "Cold," she said. "So cold."

"Violet, you're in shock." He pulled her against him, wrapped his arms around her. He could feel the tremors running through her body.

Fuck. Didn't plan for this.

"I'm sorry," he whispered against her cheek. "I didn't tell you... you wouldn't have believed me. The way I acted when we first met—you'd have said I had a brain injury." He squeezed her tighter, hoping to still the shaking.

She pushed him away. Held her hands under her armpits. Didn't want him confusing her more. She looked out at the jetty. Jamie was pointing down the river. "He thinks it's a game."

"I know. I'll tell him later."

"Later? How much later?" Her voice caught. "We haven't brought anything—no clothes, no toothbrush. We have to go back and get—"

"—can't go back, Violet." He said the last part louder. She needed to get it. She pressed her lips together. A couple walked past with a white fluffy dog.

"They have dogs here then?" she said.

Lewis narrowed his eyes. Didn't answer. They couldn't stay. He took out his phone and checked the time. They had to keep moving. They were being tracked by Rochester, Monk or both of them.

"Scott!" he shouted, waving an arm. The others came running. "How far to the station?"

Helen answered, "Checked already. Ten minutes. Train's due in twenty."

"You lead," said Lewis. He stepped forward.

Violet didn't follow. He turned. "You're coming. Okay?" His voice was quiet—but it sounded like a warning.

She saw the others running. She started running too. She wasn't letting Jamie out of her sight.

They reached the white-painted train station. It looked like something from a picture book. Not real.

"Cute," said Helen. "Must be the original."

Lewis walked to the ticket booth and bought their tickets. Violet paced the platform, hands deep in her pockets. Lewis left her and sat beside Helen. Scott and Jamie were further down, talking.

Lewis glanced their way, then at Helen. "He's telling him it's not a game?"

Helen nodded. "He thought he should."

Lewis nodded once.

They heard Jamie shout. "What? It's not a game?"

"Keep your voice down, Jamie," Scott said quickly. "Remember—secret."

"I know that!"

But Jamie was already racing down the platform. He shouted at Violet. "Did you know?"

Lewis winced. One Mackenzie down, one still hating him.

Jamie was shouting, "We never have to see them again, Violet. Never!"

He swiped a hand across his eyes. "Best news ever. I hated them. I hated how they treated you..." His shoulders shook.

Violet wrapped her arms around him. "Jamie, you should have told me. We're in this together, remember?"

Lewis turned away. He couldn't hear her words. But he saw Jamie crying. And his heart sank.

"You did the right thing," Helen said softly. She'd been watching it all. And she'd seen that troubled look flicker across Lewis's face.

It was the right thing he knew that. It was just his feelings he had to handle.

"Great Kid," said Scott, "asked a few questions. Said it was like some game he played. Thanked me and.." Scott smiled.

"And?" said Lewis.

Scott grinned, "Said he was glad you were Violet's boyfriend."

"Not her boyfriend," Lewis said his voice clipped. He looked down the track, "Trains coming."

***

167

Violet sat by the window, watching the holiday town slip away as the train pulled out of Rosalinda Bay. The train was speeding through waving fields of sun ripe corn. She leant her head against the window. The rhythmic click-clack of the train lulled her to sleep.

Lewis sat behind her with Helen. He couldn't trust himself to sit close without the urge to take hold of her. He felt tired but he couldn't fall asleep. He needed to be alert. He didn't know what was waiting for them.

CHAPTER TWENTY-THREE

Nearly eighteen years ago in Perfection.

Dave Callum stirred his coffee noisily. His knee bounced against the leg of the dining table that dominated their ranch-style kitchen. He stared toward the wall of windows at the far end. He wasn't really looking at the three horses in the paddock or the green hills of their horse farm—he was thinking.

Jenny, his wife, watched him from the kitchen. She could tell something was wrong. She lifted a poached egg from the simmering water and held it aloft until the dripping stopped. She'd meant to buy one of those new poachers—perfect rounds, neat yolks—but lately, she had bigger worries. Like how to convince Dave to leave Advanced Laboratories.

When he'd landed the job straight out of university, it had felt like winning a gold medal. And he had, in fact—an actual gold medal at the world science competition. Offers poured in from the top labs, but Advanced was the crown jewel. The position felt like a miracle.

At first, it had been everything. The money erased every worry. They bought a beautiful house, luxurious cars, extravagant holidays. Everything was amazing. Even their twins—just four years old—were talking, running, astonishing. Dave used to say "amazing" about everything.

But he barely said anything now.

He rarely came home. He practically lived at the lab. Jenny hardly saw him. And when she asked what was going on, he'd say, "Don't ask me, Jen. I can't talk about it. Top secret."

She wanted to scream. Top secret? What was more important than the twins? "You'll wake up one day and they'll have left home," she had told him.

He didn't look like her Dave anymore. He looked older than his boss, Victor Rochester—who must be pushing sixty, though you'd never guess, not with the treatments he received from the lab.

Jenny placed the plate in front of him. "Here, sweetie. You have to eat."

Dave stared at the egg and pushed it away. It reminded him of work—of the embryos. All the animal trials he'd run over the last three years, and now... a human embryo.

He walked to the window. Outside, the twins were on the swings. They waved at him. He didn't wave back. His mind was elsewhere.

That bastard Rochester. Anna thought the injection had been routine—help with the baby. But it wasn't. And now Dave was part of it. Part of the lie.

It wasn't just unethical. It was criminal.

Jenny scraped the cold egg into the sink disposal, rinsed her hands, and dried them on her apron. She looked at Dave's back. His shoulders were slumped. He looked defeated.

Then he squatted down at the window, pressing his nose to the glass. The twins ran over and did the same, laughing. He stayed there for a moment. Stood up. Straightened his back. Squared his shoulders.

"I'm going to tell her, "He said aloud. "What he did. What I tried to stop him doing. And then I'm going to resign."

Jenny froze. Her hands clasped in front of her. "Tell who?" she asked, her voice small.

He turned to her. He hadn't realized she'd heard. But he saw the fear in her eyes.

"Rochester's wife," he said grimly. "And you. I'm going to tell you too. To hell with the consequences."

CHAPTER TWENTY-FOUR

The train pulled into the Capital four hours later. Violet was still asleep, dreaming she could fly. She swooped over treetops like a bird until a hand landed on her shoulder.

"Wake up, Violet."

Lewis stood by her seat, phone in hand. Tense. He turned to Scott. "He's here. Two streets back, Plymouth Street. Underground carpark. Level three."

Scott nodded. "Know it. Across the tracks. Over the footbridge."

"You go with Violet and Jamie. Blue car. Mercury Six. I'll take Helen. We'll go out the front. Helen—cap on. We buy time. You know the plan."

Violet sat up, confused. The tension hit like a punch to the chest. Even Jamie looked like he was suiting up for battle. And she—she still didn't believe it. Not really.

"What's happening now?" she asked.

"Getting off this train. Getting somewhere safe." Lewis raised his phone. "One photo. All of us. Move in." They crowded in and Lewis took the photo.

Violet watched Helen hide her hair beneath the cap. "Is this dangerous?" she asked. She already knew the answer.

Helen gave a half-smile. "Hope not."

The train doors opened.

"We go first," Lewis said. "They won't be on the platform. Too public."

He turned to leave. Violet caught his hand. "Will we see you again?"

He paused. That flutter in his chest again. "That's the plan," he said flatly, but she saw the flicker in his eyes. Then he was gone.

Scott grabbed Jamie's hand. "Run." They ran. Across the station. Down streets Violet didn't see. Past cars, strangers, traffic. No time to look. No time to think. Scott veered down a ramp.

"Underground," Violet muttered. "Level three."

"Got it." Scott didn't break stride.

"Mercury Six. Blue." Jamie was out of breath but focused.

"There." Scott pointed.

A tall man stepped from the car. Familiar face. Grey eyes. "You're Scott? Where's Lewis?"

"He's okay, sir. This is Violet and Jamie."

"John Carlyle. Call me John." He looked past them. "Wasn't there another girl?"

"Helen. She's with Lewis. They're creating a diversion."

John nodded, jaw tight. "Alright. In the car. Let's move."

Jamie said. "What kind of car is this?"

"Solar-powered Mercury." John smiled. "Hop in front. I'll tell you all about it."

He opened the passenger door. "Your glasses, okay?"

"Used to it," Jamie said.

Violet slid in behind him. Said nothing. Her head throbbed. She wanted a shower. Sleep. A reset button. She leaned against the seat. John's voice faded into the background, talking to Jamie. Solar panels. Batteries.

Her mind drifted to Lewis. To what he'd told her. To the knife Mona had plunged in. She wasn't an idiot, she could connect the dots. Rochester could be related to her… might be her father. She squeezed her eyes shut. Pulled the knife out again.

The car moved silently. Up. Out. Into sunlight.

***

Lewis and Helen paused at the station's entrance. The street ahead buzzed—people waiting for transport, spilling out of shops, dodging traffic. Carpark to the right. Tall towers beyond. A mall. An apartment store up ahead. And right in front? A lineup of cars, engines humming, waiting to scoop up train arrivals.

"Cross the road, head for the apartment store," Lewis said. "You watch right, I'll take left."

They stepped to the crosswalk. Four lanes of roaring traffic. Helen kept her head down. They were halfway across when Lewis caught it—dark-windowed car, peeling away from the curb, swinging toward them. Two men ahead, watching.

"They've clocked us. Turn back," Lewis muttered. "We cut through the car park. Lose them on foot."

They spun, dodging pedestrians. Sprinting. Weaving through bumpers and bonnets. Lewis glanced back—yep, they were being tailed. Two men, closing fast. He ducked behind a van, Helen right beside him.

"Mall," he panted. "Shops. Cover."

They burst from the lot and into the mall crowd, blending instantly. Music. Fluorescent lights. Chaos.

"That shop," Helen pointed—surf gear, beachy kids, noise.

Ten minutes later, they emerged in disguise. Helen now in cobalt blue, red cap tugged low. Lewis in green, white cap. She slid her arm around his waist, playing the part. He looped an arm over her shoulders, tried to match her easy confidence. Tried and failed.

She grinned, bumped his shoulder, kissed his cheek. They looked ridiculous. But believable. They laughed and talked and acted like tourists in love. Until they passed two of the watchers. Until the shout came.

"Damn. They're on us."

They ran again. Back through the car park. Deeper into the city. Lewis's heart hammering. He needed that buzz from Scott—needed to know Violet and Jamie were safe. Helen looked wrecked. So did he.

They ducked down a narrow alley. A car blocked the exit. Lewis's phone buzzed. One word lit the screen: **gone**

He opened the photo of them all he'd taken on the train. Pressed send on the prepped message.

"All good," he told Helen just as the hands clamped down on their arms.

"We're not resisting," Lewis said, calm and loud. "I'm Carlyle. This is Jones."

The walk back was silent. A phone buzzed beside him. "They got Streathfield. Girl's not with him." One of the men said.

Scott was waiting at the station wall, flanked by agents. He stood when he saw them. "You, okay?"

"Yeh," Helen said, wiping her face. "You?"

Scott nodded. A black car pulled up. They all recognized the man stepping out.

"What now?" Scott asked.

"I'll tell you what," Monk said. "You're coming with us."

Lewis smiled, slow and razor-sharp. "Good time to call…"

A ringtone cut him off. Monk's pocket. Lewis arched a brow.

"Probably him now."

Monk answered. "Monk." He listened. His expression didn't shift, but everyone knew who it was.

He pocketed the phone. Jaw tight. "Where is she?"

"Safe," Lewis said. "And we're leaving. News crew will be here in… now." He checked his phone. "Hot scoop of the decade. Tell Rochester we'll be in touch."

"Yeh," Scott added. "And we expect the bonus."

Lewis shot him a glare. Bonus? Not on his list.

Monk rocked on his heels. "Carlyle. Think hard about what you're doing."

Lewis stepped forward, voice low and lethal. "I have. This mission? Rotten from the start. We were never making it back. Rochester made sure of that. And you knew.

Monk's jaw clenched. He didn't deny it.

"You knew," Lewis repeated, fury rising. The betrayal stung.

Scott's hand clamped Lewis's arm. "Lewis. They're here."

A car rolled up. Red letters across the door: "PWNN".

"Perfection World News Network," Helen said cheerfully, like she was announcing the beginning of a movie.

Lewis pursed his lips. "We'll be going now." He nodded at Scott and Helen. Monk didn't stop them. Just watched as Lewis turned one last time.

"Tell Rochester," Lewis said. "We'll be in touch."

CHAPTER TWENTY-FIVE

Violet turned her head away from the window. Endless green fields. Waving grass. Passing trees. In the distance—purple hills, soft as pressed lavender. "Where are we?" she asked

"Nearly there," John said, catching her eyes in the rear-view mirror. "This is Caxton. Big crop-growing area."

"I haven't seen one cow," Jamie said, frowning.

Neither have I, thought Violet. Not even a sheep.

"Well spotted," said John. "You won't find many livestock around here. No cows, sheep, or... pigs. Not too many carnivores in Perfection."

"What!" Jamie looked personally offended. "There's more vegetarians?"

"Yep. We worked out a long time ago it's better for the environment and better for the animals." He glanced in the mirror again. "I'll explain when we get home."

Home. Violet flinched at the word. *Do I even have one?*

They turned off the main road, heading toward the low, violet-tinted hills.

"Up ahead," John said, "is one of the biggest radio telescopes in the world. One of over a thousand tracking the universe."

"What's it tracking?" Jamie asked, already leaning forward in his seat, hungry for answers.

Violet twisted her fingers. Smoothed them against her jeans. She tried to stay calm. Tried not to feel like she was still in that nightmare-dream.

"I'll show you both when we get there," John said. "I work at the station." He seemed to remember she was still sitting in silence. "How are you doing, Violet?"

"What happened to Lewis? The others?"

He hesitated, eyes flicking to the mirror again. "They're okay." He hoped that was true. He reached into his pocket. "Lewis messaged about an hour ago. " He handed her the phone. Violet read the screen aloud.

Done.

John's shoulders dropped and he let out a breath. "That's good," he said. Despite his faith in Lewis, he'd been tense.

Her stomach fluttered.

"Now check the news," John said.

Jamie twisted around to look. It wasn't much but he knew it meant something. Violet straightened. And there it was. The photo from the train. Lewis. Helen. Scott. And her. No Jamie.

She read the headline in her head. "Missing Daughter of Rochester Rescued After Eighteen Years."

That's me. She couldn't breathe. She handed the phone to Jamie.

He read aloud, voice full of awe. "Missing daughter of Victor Rochester, billionaire owner of Advanced Laboratories, rescued after eighteen years…"

He stared at the image. "That's you!" he whispered. Then grinned. "A billionaire. We're going to be rich!"

John cursed under his breath. He should have warned her.

"I'm sorry, Violet," he said softly. "I thought you knew."

Jamie was still reading. "…rescue team from the Bureau of PWIB… daring escape from a designated disaster zone… exclusive interview airing October 4, 7pm…

Violet turned back to the window. Everything blurred. Her reflection stared back at her—pale, blank. Why was Lewis doing an interview? She closed her eyes. Pressed a hand to her forehead.

Violet," John said, gently. "This was Lewis's idea. To keep you safe. He hasn't betrayed you."

But he didn't tell me the truth. Isn't that a betrayal?

Jamie had more questions. But he stayed quiet....

***

Rick Jarvis drove the so-called heroes to a hotel booked by the network. He was twenty-two. Fresh out of journalism school. Six months at the desk. This story? This was going to make his career.

"'The Star,' as requested," he said proudly as they pulled up.

Lewis sat in the front, silent. Scott and Helen rode in the back.

"Thanks," said Lewis. "We'll need a few hours. To clean up. Prep."

"No clothes," Helen muttered. "We travelled light."

"I'll organise something," Rick promised. "Just strange there wasn't a welcoming party. Would have thought Rochester…" he trailed off.

Lewis dragged a hand through his hair. "The weather stuffed the exit point," he said flatly. "Lost contact. Didn't know who was watching. Couldn't risk the wrong people showing up for the cargo." *Cargo.* Violet would hate that.

Rick nodded, thoughtful. He'd heard stories—people who made it out of disaster zones, only to disappear after quarantine.

"Still. Rochester's daughter. He would have moved fast. VIP treatment."

"Couldn't risk it," Lewis repeated. "Needed to give the boss time. To make it right with the authorities." *And figure out how to get Jamie in.*

Helen nudged Scott. She liked how calm Lewis sounded. Almost bored.

A beat later, they rolled into the hotel driveway. Lewis was first out of the car, dodging more questions.

Reception was smooth. Too smooth. Scott caught the receptionist's look of recognition. She smiled. Scott grinned back. This was going to be fun. Right after he got a haircut.

CHAPTER TWENTY-SIX

Lewis had just stepped out of the shower when his phone rang. He let it buzz a few times. Then answered.

"That you, Carlyle?"

Lewis took a breath. *Rochester.*

"Yes."

"What game do you think you're playing?" Rochester's voice was sharp.

Lewis stared at himself in the mirror. Frowning. Worry lines. He wrapped the towel tighter and walked into the bedroom.

"I said—what—"

"I heard you," Lewis cut in. "It's not a game. It's survival."

"What nonsense—"

"Cut the crap," Lewis snapped. "We're not idiots. This mission was under the radar for a reason. And your 'rescue' didn't include the rescuers."

"I don't know what you're talking about—"

"Cross. The wrong co-ordinates. The wrong time. Your man. Don't deny it." Lewis dropped his voice. "Why did you want her?"

There was a pause.

"She's my daughter," Rochester said coldly. "I've been looking for her for eighteen years."

"No," said Lewis. "You've hidden the truth. Your wife and unborn child didn't die in that fire. You lied."

"I had my reasons."

"Then you can share them tomorrow. PWNN. Ten a.m. Better call Monk and get your story straight. I've told them the storm scrambled the exit point. I gave them a sample of Violet's hair. World Security's confirming it now."

"I have spoken to Monk," Rochester lied.

"Good. Then I'll see you there. Or I'll take it to the next level."

Lewis hung up. He called Scott. Told him everything. Then sent a message to his father. **Ask Violet to call me. All as planned.**

John Carlyle tried to stay calm. He relaxed his grip on the steering wheel when he heard the phone buzz.

"Can you get that, Jamie?" he said.

Jamie read out the message, then handed the phone to Violet.

"Here. He wants you to call."

He made it sound like she didn't have a choice. Violet took the phone. She didn't want to speak to Lewis.

All as planned. She felt like nothing in her life was hers anymore. Every choice had been taken from her. People were making decisions for her, and she was just expected to go along.

She pressed the phone to her lips.

Jamie shouted, "There's the radio telescope!"

Violet looked up. A great glass dome glittered in the middle of a green paddock, surrounded by a cluster of small buildings.

Jamie twisted in his seat and shot her a glare. "You have to call him, Violet." His voice was firm. "Scott's on our side. Lewis too. You have to keep in touch with the platoon leader."

Violet rolled her eyes. *Platoon leader. Seriously?* "Are we nearly there?" she said.

"Yes, just a few minutes. Why don't you call Lewis when we get out of the car?" John said. "I expect you've got a lot to say to him." Probably more than he knew.

They drove the rest of the way in silence.

Jamie was glued to the giant antennae reaching into the sky, firing questions at John about galaxies and signals and light years.

John was impressed. Jamie may have come from a world fifty years behind, but he kept up.

"Violet, did you hear that?" Jamie said. "Different galaxies!"

She didn't answer. She was thinking about her mother, and what could have made her leave this world behind.

At the top of a hill, the car stopped at locked gates beside a small guardhouse. John rolled down the window.

"Hi Mac. Two visitors I arranged passes for—Sarah and Robert Miller. My niece and nephew."

Jamie caught on fast and smiled at the guard.

Violet bit her lip and turned her face toward the field of telescopes. They looked like giant crystal raindrops.

The gates opened. John drove slowly down a gravel path, into a grassed courtyard bordered by four whitewashed houses. He pulled up outside one of them.

"This is home," he said. "For now. Hop out. Violet, you might want to sit on the bench there, and call Lewis. Jamie and I are going inside."

The bench was tucked under a tree in the middle of the lawn. She didn't want to sit. She wanted to run. But she walked over, leaned against the trunk, and called.

"Violet. What took you so long?" Lewis sounded annoyed.

She bit her lip. He had no right to be angry.

"Hello?" he said again. "You there?"

"Yes. I'm here."

He could barely hear her. Before he could speak, she said, "When did you make the plan?"

Lewis crossed the hotel room and sat on the edge of the bed. He tried to sound steady.

"I made it the day before your birthday. When I found out who you were. And before you start—I couldn't tell you. I'm sorry, Violet. But it's done. Going public was the only way to keep you both safe. Look... this world isn't exactly welcoming to migrants. We keep them out."

"Migrants?" Her voice had gone flat. "Is that what we are? Jamie and me?"

Lewis walked to the window. Outside, the sun was falling into the ocean. Vermillion sky. Families on the beach. It could have been perfect.

"Violet, our world's known about yours for over a hundred years. We've avoided the problems destroying your planet. There are laws. We don't let people in. And if they do..." He hesitated. "It's serious."

"What happens to them?" she demanded.

"They're... kept out. Quarantined sometimes. Citizenship takes years."

"So why are they going to let me and Jamie in?"

"Because you're Rochester's daughter. You're a citizen by birth. They just need DNA confirmation."

"Who's they?"

"World Security. They've contacted the news station. Monk. Rochester. They'll be at the interview."

Her breath caught. "Rochester? He's going to be there?" She sounded small. Scared.

Lewis pressed a hand to his chest. "I won't let anything happen to you."

Violet didn't speak. Tears stung her eyes. He'd let so much happen already. He'd pulled her into this world—this lie—and she hadn't even known she was falling.

"Violet, please... just trust me, okay? I don't have all the answers, but I know this much—if what Rochester said is true, then this whole mission wouldn't have been covert. They wouldn't have left me, Scott, and Helen behind. That was the plan: no witnesses. But we know Rochester. The world sees him as a hero. I'll tell you everything tomorrow. Just trust me."

"My name's Sarah now... evidently," she said quietly.

Lewis turned from the window. "Tomorrow, Violet. Just listen to my dad, okay? You can trust him."

"Your dad?"

"He didn't tell you?"

"He said his name was John Carlyle."

"Yeah. That's my name—Lewis Carlyle. I guess he figured you knew."

Violet didn't answer. Inside the house, she could hear Jamie's excited voice echoing through the open door. No fly screen.

"Violet?"

"Yes."

"Just do what Dad says."

"He's letting in the mosquitos," she murmured.

"What?"

"Mosquitos. There's no screen on the door. Jamie's allergic."

Lewis frowned. "We don't have mosquitos here that can harm humans. I'll explain everything tomorrow. Okay?"

"Jamie!" Violet's voice broke as the question hit her. "Wait—what about Jamie? Will he..."

Lewis closed his eyes. The one question he hadn't wanted to answer.

"Be given citizenship?" She already knew. Jamie didn't fit into any category.

"It'll be okay. I'll talk to you tomorrow." And with that, Lewis ended the call.

He was betting everything on Violet being the key. If they shared the same mother, then maybe, just maybe, Jamie's DNA would be enough.

Violet stepped back inside. She found Jamie and John in the kitchen.

John was feeding oranges into a sleek silver juicer, the soft hum of the machine filling the space. He looked up and smiled.

She should've known he was Lewis's dad—same eyes, same way of smiling like they saw through you.

"Everything okay, Violet?" he asked. "Did you get some answers?"

She shrugged. "Some. He told me you don't have mosquitoes that harm humans."

"Mosquitoes?" John frowned.

"Jamie's allergic. If he gets bitten…"

"Oh. I see. That was your worry?" John smiled. "No, we don't have those kinds of mosquitoes. He poured a glass of juice and held it out to her.

"Drink this. I'll show you around. We can talk through tomorrow's plan. I'm guessing it's all been…a lot."

He had a kind smile. Too kind. Violet blinked hard. She wasn't used to kindness. Not without a price. He turned away, rummaging in the fridge.

"Oh—and I'll find you and Jamie some t-shirts for tonight. Leave your clothes outside the door. I'll wash and dry them for morning."

She turned her face. Too much like Lewis.

"We'll need to pick up proper clothes too." He smiled, light and easy. "Lewis said you're vegetarian. Makes dinner easy."

"He told you that?" Violet asked.

"Yeah, we spoke." He held up a freezer bag. "These are good—delicious bites, all healthy stuff. I've got veggies too."

He looked over the fridge door at her. "Want to help me chop?"

CHAPTER TWENTY-SEVEN

The pulse in Rochester's temple was beating hard. That punk Carlyle—threatening him? Take it to the next level? Who the hell did he think he was? A cadet. A kid. Rochester swiped the sweat from his forehead.

He hurled his phone onto the couch, snatched the remote and flicked through channels until he hit PWNN. There it was: a red ticker screamed across the bottom of the screen.

BREAKING NEWS: The PW Investigation Bureau claim to have found the daughter of Victor Rochester in DZ.

He stared at the headline, the fury rising fast. With a snarl, he flung the remote at the TV. It bounced harmlessly off the unbreakable screen and hit the floor.

Pacing to the side table, he grabbed the wedding photo—silver frame, wide smiles—and stared at it.

His lip curled. Then he dropped it. The frame landed with a soft thud on the carpet. He didn't stop. Just ground his heel into the glass until it shattered.

Then he picked up the phone and called World Security.

***

Lewis felt hot under the studio lights. He pulled at the collar of his shirt. It was new, stiff, and it itched. Across from him, Scott leaned forward, murmuring something to Helen.

Stuart Richardson, the PWNN anchor, spoke into his earpiece. Monk and Rochester hadn't arrived. Lewis swallowed. No Plan B.

Stuart's fingers tapped a rhythm on his knees. "Did you send a car? Okay… okay. Who's trying to contact them?" He turned toward Lewis. "Five minutes, then we're running something else."

The network was twitchy. They couldn't afford to alienate someone like Rochester. The PWIB students' credentials were legit—but was the story?

Stuart had spent hours with them last night. Lewis had been convincing. The others had backed him. Research had pulled Rochester's file. It had to be true. Confirmation would come with the DNA results from World Security.

Stuart tapped his mic again. "Good. Get them into makeup. Delay with a promo for tomorrow's show." His shoulders dropped. A lost daughter. A billionaire. A world exclusive. The ratings would explode.

***

The drive gave Rochester time to rehearse. Not all lies, he told himself, staring at his reflection in the tinted window. Ahead, the Bureau car with Monk. He hadn't wanted to ride with him. That man was digging too deep. Carlyle was smart. Too smart. The real threat. Rochester clenched his fist. He'd deal with him. And Cross. And where the hell was Cross?

His reflection stared back, sharp-suited and composed. Curious, perhaps, about the child—but only mildly. He flexed his long fingers. Had she inherited those? Or her mother's stubby ones?

He'd seen the photos. The girl looked gormless. Eyes wide and vague. She looked like someone who didn't know what time of day it was.

But the hair... that was unmistakable. Rochester hair. His own had been genetically altered years ago—dark auburn now. School had been hell with that orange mop. Anna had been a redhead too, before he made her blonde.

He'd never taken women seriously. Annoying creatures, always trying to please.

He'd chosen Anna because she was compliant. Or so he'd thought. She should have been grateful. A nobody, adopted by a low-level employee. But no—she'd fled.

He still didn't understand it. Yes, there was a risk to the baby. But sacrifices were necessary. For greatness. He'd lost a wife. That meant nothing. The baby though—fame, prestige, data. All gone.

He pressed the button to seal off the driver. Made the call. "Found his father's location?" Pause. "A niece and nephew... how old?" He almost smiled. Raised his eyes. Red hair. Teen girl. Younger boy. "And the boy's still at the house?" He pinched the bridge of his nose. "Yes," he said, a smile curving his mouth. "Get him. Take him to my estate." Cross had done his homework.

Rochester checked his watch. He'd be late. Let them wait. The girl couldn't enter Perfection without his claim. And the results—they'd want drama. On air. Let them have their show.

The car slowed. Two men stood beside Monk. World Security, in their black uniforms. Rochester stepped out. Smoothed his jacket. Ignored the assistant's outstretched hand.

"Rick Jarvis," the boy chirped.

Rochester didn't blink. Nodded coldly at the officer from yesterday—the one who'd taken his DNA.

"You lead the way," he said.

Monk trailed behind, uneasy. He hated the spotlight. But he had to keep appearances. Civility, for now.

***

Violet hadn't slept. John had told her everything. And now she was going to meet her father. On national TV.

They'd left early. Just the two of them. Jamie was hidden. They couldn't take chances.

"Everything points to you being Rochester's daughter," John had said. "Once that's confirmed—"

"Jamie? Quarantine?" Violet had whispered.

John didn't deny it. "We'll find a way. He'll be okay. The station is secure."

"He was safe at home," Violet said. "We were safe."

"He'll be safe today," John promised. "He's smart. He'll be busy."

She twisted her fingers. Nothing could happen to him.

They arrived as the shops opened. John gave her his card. "Buy what you need—clothes, shoes."

She stared at the card. *The old man's loaded, he said that.* But he wasn't she could see that now. He worked at the tracking station. *Another lie.*

She took the escalator to the young women's fashion floor. The store was empty. She picked the first thing she saw. A dark green dress. She changed into the dress in the changeroom. She looked down at her runners. She wasn't going to buy shoes. She didn't care what she looked like. She didn't want to look good for Rochester or Lewis.

John saw her coming. The green dress made her hair burn like fire. Still in the runners. He smiled. He was starting to see why Lewis had risked it all.

"No shoes?" John said taking the card from her.

"Didn't see anything I liked." She tossed her old clothes in the back.

"Okay. Were just twenty minutes from the studio. You feeling okay?" Her eyes seemed wider, greener, as though she couldn't take in this world.

She didn't answer.

"What happens to me after?" she asked.

John didn't reply. He was parking the car. He didn't want to tell her. She would never be anonymous again.

"Let's go," he said softly. He opened her door, took her hand. Her fingers were ice. "It's going to be alright." He released her hand.

The glass front of the studio glittered. Reporters surged forward. Cameras flashing. It didn't register—they were here for her. Security stepped in. Cleared a path.

Violet smoothed the dress. Looked up at the gold lettering: PERFECTION NEWS NETWORK.

She licked her lips. She needed water. Sleep. To wake up from this. She didn't know how she felt about Lewis. About any of it.

The security guards led them inside. At reception, Rick Jarvis waited with two men. John's face changed when he saw them. He knew who they were - World Security.

"Miss, you'll need to come with us," one said.

Rick looked apologetic. "I didn't know—"

John took Violet's hand. "It's just precaution," he said. "They're doing their job."

"Can I go with her?" John asked.

"Sorry," He shook his head. His face grim as an executioner.

Violet's grip tightened. Her stomach turned.

"Tell me where you're taking her," John said, "She's Rochester's daughter. A citizen."

The man raised an eyebrow. "Wouldn't know. Orders are orders."

"Probably just questions," the other added.

Violet wasn't moving. Not without John.

"Let me go with her," John said. "Then you can ask your people if I can stay."

He looked at Violet his eyes full of concern. She nodded. What choice did she have?

John wasn't allowed past the front gates. He watched the car roll across the courtyard with Violet inside, two World Security men beside her. The vehicle stopped. Violet got out, and the dark-suited men escorted her through the glass doors.

She kept her head high but her hands were trembling. Her shoulders too. The doors slid shut behind her and she was standing in a dim ante-room, cameras blinking red above her head. A screen lit up with her own image—her face pale between the two unsmiling men. Blue lights flashed.

Another set of doors opened. Guards waited. One of the men behind her tapped her shoulder with a single finger. She flinched, twisting away. People were already appearing in the glass corridors, slowing to stare.

She was the girl from DZ.

They led her into a room with glass walls, a sofa, and two chairs angled toward a large flat screen. The men stayed outside. She felt like a goldfish in a bowl.

More faces drifted past. She gripped the chair, trying not to show her hands shaking. She hated Lewis. She hated all of it.

A woman walked in—short blonde hair, red lipstick. She set a jug and glass of water on the table, poured, and nudged the glass toward Violet. "You can watch...," she said, indicating the screen. But she didn't finish the sentence. Everyone knew what was coming. Violet nodded. Her lips were too dry for words.

The screen came to life. The woman left as Violet reached for the glass, the water sloshing against the rim. She needed it to stop—the shaking, the whole thing. She wasn't ready to meet a father she didn't know, not while grieving the one she'd always believed was hers.

And then her hand jerked. Water spilled down her dress. The screen showed a studio. Lewis. And a man staring into the camera with cold green eyes was her father.

Stuart Richardson adjusted his earpiece and glanced at the man seated beside him. Victor Rochester. He looked calm. No—indifferent. Stuart had heard stories. Psychopath. Narcissist. No empathy. No conscience.

"On air," said the floor director.

Stuart straightened. His voice dropped an octave, weighted like the news of a world ending.

"We have in the studio, on my right—Lewis Carlyle, Scott Streatham, and Helen Jones, the three heroes from the PWIB who achieved the remarkable rescue of the girl from DZ believed to be the daughter of Victor Rochester. And..." he turned, "...we have Victor Rochester."

Rochester stared ahead, unmoving. His face like stone. Lewis crossed his legs and leaned back in his chair.

Stuart gestured to Monk. "And Sampson Monk, Director of the PWIB."

He turned back to the students. "This was a dangerous mission. You haven't even begun full training. Why did you agree?"

Lewis opened his mouth to speak but Scott got in first, laughing as he said. "Well, the bonus we're all getting was a pretty good incentive."

Lewis snapped his head sideways. *You idiot. I didn't do it for the damn money.*

"A bonus?" Stuart said, interested.

Scott's grin vanished. Rochester stared at his hands like he was imagining Scott's throat between them.

"Hardly a bonus," Monk said quickly. "A stipend. A salary of sorts."

"Yes," Helen added smoothly. "Just the standard." She glanced at Scott, wondering whether he was going to be worth the effort.

Violet watched Lewis glare at Scott. It was true a bonus, a reward, not a salary and it was coming from Rochester. Worse than Lincoln, she thought. Lewis was worse than Lincoln.

She barely heard Stuart ask Monk, "Who initiated the mission? And why under the radar?"

Monk flinched—like someone had just pulled a trigger. "All our missions are...as you put it…under the radar." He gave what Lewis thought was a patronising smile to Richardson. "We certainly don't broadcast world threats to our borders and how we're going to deal with them."

"This was hardly a world threat. This was a rescue operation," said Richardson. He didn't wait for an answer. "It was believed that Mr Rochester's wife and unborn child died in a fire in Advanced Laboratories eighteen years ago. Mr Rochester, can you explain that?"

Rochester's pupils seemed to dilate. "Yes, I can explain that," he said, voice edged. He didn't have to explain himself to anyone. "At the time my wife went missing and my laboratory—and important research—was lost by fire, espionage was considered the most obvious explanation. The police were involved and then, of course, the Bureau. The research at my institute has world importance." Rochester clenched his jaw. The world owed him. "I haven't stopped looking for my wife and my child. But I never imagined she would have been taken to DZ."

"You suspect your wife was kidnapped and taken to DZ?" said Richardson.

"All I know," said Rochester, voice sharp with irritation, "is that my child, my daughter, was located there. I understand my wife died some years ago." He sounded resigned.

Richardson turned to Monk. "Can you tell us how she was located?"

Monk looked grim. He didn't want more questions. "We received information that led us to believe she was in DZ, and acting on that information we quickly deployed three of our students to locate her and bring her back."

Monk was waiting for the one question he couldn't answer—was she really Rochester's daughter?

Then Rochester spoke. "Of course, before she was rescued I—" he paused and corrected himself, "—the Bureau confirmed a very high probability that she was my daughter." He gave a small nod to the cameras. "I'm confident the confirmation testing will prove us right."

Lewis felt the back of his neck prickle. Something about Rochester made his skin crawl. *He wants her for a reason, and it's not because she's his daughter.*

Richardson shifted. "We're about to find out the results. We have personnel from World Security with the test results. Earlier samples of DNA were provided by Mr Rochester, and a hair sample was made available from Miss Mackenzie.

Violet sat and watched. The camera panned to Lewis. He looked guilty.

Hair sample? Her fingers dug into the arms of the chair. The lock he'd asked for—it had been for this. *Liar. Liar. Liar.*

The camera followed an official walking forward, envelope in hand. He held it out toward Richardson.

Lewis felt a bead of sweat on his top lip. He should have thought this through. Violet would never forgive him. And she had to. She just had to. He turned to the camera. *Please be watching.* He placed his hand over his heart. *Trust me, Violet. Please trust me.*

"I think Mr Rochester should read the results in private," Lewis said.

Rochester flinched. He should have said that, not Carlyle. He hated agreeing with him.

"Yes. Carlyle's right. This is an extremely important moment for both Violet and me." He gave a strained smile. "As much as everyone would like to know the answer, I ask for just a small window of privacy. And" he turned to Richardson, "I don't believe the envelope is addressed to you."

The official glanced at the label. It was addressed to the Director of the Bureau. He handed the envelope to Monk, who passed it on without looking to Rochester.

Rochester meant to walk off camera, but instead he tore the envelope open and read the single sheet inside. He glared at Richardson.

"That settles the matter. I'm going to see my daughter. And the cameras aren't coming." He stormed out of the lights.

Violet twisted her fingers. *I'm his daughter.* The blood roared in her ears. She crushed the fabric of her dress between her fists. There was no going back. She was here now. Forever.

She looked back at the screen. The camera was on Helen—she looked like she'd been asked a question she couldn't answer. Then Scott, running a hand through his curls. And then Lewis. He was already standing, pulling the mic from his shirt, avoiding the camera.

Chasing after Rochester. Chasing the bonus. That's how it looked to Violet. He'd placed his hand over his heart. *Liar. Liar.* He was just like Lincoln.

Stuart Richardson watched Rochester storm off set. His producer was screaming in his earpiece: "Don't let him go! Get his thoughts, his feelings on camera!"

Richardson flared his nostrils like a horse. He wasn't an idiot. He turned to the camera, raised an eyebrow, and gave a knowing look. "I think that was pretty conclusive. Understandably, Mr Rochester wants to see his daughter. That's all for the special from PWNN. And now for our regular news with Linda Fox." He yanked the earpiece from his ear.

He should've seen that coming. Rochester had no interest in sharing feelings. Lewis was already moving through the shadows of the set. Scott and Helen started to follow.

He turned. "Don't follow me. I have to see Violet. I have to stop her going with him."

He ducked past cameras and production crew. Rick Jarvis was off to the side, phone to his ear. Lewis pushed past someone and approached him fast.

"Where's Violet?"

Rick flinched. "What?"

Lewis stepped closer. "Where's Rochester's daughter?" His voice cracked. He didn't care.

Rick covered his phone. "Rochester's daughter?"

"Yes! Where is she? She's in the studio, right? Somewhere in the building?"

Rick shrugged. What was his problem? She was the richest man's daughter now.

"Gotta take this," he said, turning away.

Lewis's phone buzzed in his pocket. A message from his father.

I'm out the front.

Lewis sent Scott a text and bolted from the building.

John was standing beside his car, hands in his pockets. He smiled when he saw Lewis. It had been over a year. Lewis smiled back.

"You alright?" John asked, reading his son's face. "Let's go. Rochester's ahead of us."

They pulled away from the curb. "Sorry, Dad. It's good to see you. Everything okay?"

John nodded. "Fine with me. Not so fine with you, huh?"

Lewis exhaled. "I don't know how this ends. But Violet—she's important to Rochester, and not because she's his daughter. I don't buy the kidnap story. It's been eighteen years."

John nodded again. "And the fact you and Scott and Helen were going to be left behind."

"Exactly. He wanted this buried."

They drove in silence. "Busy this morning," John said as he edged through traffic. "Have you thought about how we're going to get Jamie through World Security?"

"Jamie! Damn. Is he okay?"

"I left him a message an hour ago. He was glued to my computer—totally engrossed."

"Did he text back?"

John handed him his phone. "Last message I sent him. Go on—check in."

Lewis opened the phone. His heart stopped. The message from Jamie:

Two men coming.

"Fuck. Dad, they've got him."

"Call him," said John, calmly but firmly.

Lewis dialled it went to Voicemail "They've taken him," Lewis said, panic flooding his voice. "They've taken him. No one knew we brought him. Not Cross. How the hell—He stopped.

"You, Dad. That's how. They found you."

Up ahead, the Bureau compound came into view. "She'll never forgive me, Dad," Lewis said, voice cracking. "Jamie's her brother. All she's got."

John reached across and placed a hand on his back. "Let's find out what's happened first," he said. "And I hate to say it—but if anyone can pull strings, it's Rochester."

CHAPTER TWENTY-EIGHT

Rochester walked down the corridor of the World Security building. He had got the clearance and his plan was to take Violet home. He put his hand in his pocket and took out a crumpled piece of paper. He scanned the DNA report again and found the conclusion:

100% DNA match between:

i). hair sample (Lab.Code328), identified as Violet Mackenzie, provenance, Lewis Carlyle, and

ii) buccal swab taken from Victor Rochester by Lab technician, Code 337.

That was good enough for Rochester. She was his daughter and if that useless genius Callum was right, she was the ticket to… and there she is.

Rochester paused at the glass door and stuffed the paper back in his pocket. He saw her look up and her eyes widen as she stumbled to her feet. He had to proceed carefully, she was like a skittish colt, ready to bolt at any moment. He noticed the wet patch on her dress, clumsy like her mother no doubt.

He stepped inside and stood with his back to the door. "Hello Violet," he said as softly as he could. He watched her wring her hands. "Violet, I've come to take you home. We can talk when we get there." Rochester studied the pale face, the trembling lips. He should feel something, but he didn't. Only impatience. He had to get her out before Carlyle came rushing in on his white horse. Rochester almost curled his lip at the thought.

Now for the Ace. "Jamie's at my… our house waiting for us."

He felt almost triumphant when he saw her head lift and the expression on her face turn to relief.

"Jamie, he's alright? He can stay?"

"Of course," he gave her a small smile, "he's family too. Shall we go?"

He held the door open for her, and they walked silently to his waiting car.

"Sit in the back, Violet. I'll sit next to the driver."

She felt relief. He couldn't be that bad. He'd saved Jamie, and he was considerate, not making her feel uncomfortable by sitting next to her. He wasn't peppering her with questions she didn't want to answer. She closed her eyes as the car drove out of the World Security gates and past the blue Mercury six on the other side of the road.

"There, Dad. It could be Rochester's car. You've got to stop it, Dad. Pull in front."

A sleek black car with darkened windows paused at the guard house and then sped through the gates as soon as they parted.

"It's Rochester," said Lewis. "Look at the number plate. He's got her. Dad, he's got her."

He sounded defeated. There was no plan B. No way he could explain to Violet about the lock of hair or the bonus.

John read the number plate, 'AL 1'. "Advanced Laboratories. It's him, alright. Do you want me to follow him?"

The car was speeding away. Lewis twisted in his seat. He thought he could see a Violet-shape in the back seat. He shook his head. It was pointless trying to follow Rochester. He had to get help.

"Dad, can you drop me back at the Academy? I've got to speak to Monk. He owes me. He owes us all… and Violet. Does he know why Rochester wants her?" He dragged his hand through his hair. "I've got to see her. Talk to her. And Jamie. We've got to find him. Dad, can you call the tracking station and find out what happened?"

Violet opened her eyes when she heard the crunch of gravel as the car swung into the drive of Rochester's home. She sat up and watched the tree-lined drive slide away until the car reached the steps of the house.

Jamie was there waiting for her on the steps, looking anxiously towards the car. She tried to undo the car door, but it was locked. Then Rochester was opening the door and Jamie was hurtling down the steps and into her arms.

"It's okay, Jamie," Violet whispered. "It's going to be okay."

She'd been wrong about Lewis. And Lewis had to be wrong about Rochester. He had to be. She couldn't see an alternative.

Rochester watched the two hugging. He was impatient to start the testing, but he knew he had to wait, gain her confidence. Carlyle couldn't have told her anything. He didn't know why she could be the rarest thing on the planet.

Rochester nodded at Jamie. "You must be Jamie, Violet's brother." He lifted the corner of his lips a fraction—it could have been a smile.

Jamie thought he looked unfriendly, as though he was sneering. But he ignored it, because he was going to be living in this mansion if everything turned out alright.

Jamie grinned. "Yes, her only brother."

"Let's go inside, shall we," said Rochester, leading the way into the house.

They were met at the door by a woman with dark hair tied at the nape of her neck. She glanced at Violet and then nodded at Rochester.

"This is Rose, my housekeeper. She'll look after everything. Find them bedrooms, Rose. In the far wing." *As far away as possible.*

They all walked down the wide polished floorboards. Rose led the way to the room at the end of the house.

Rochester stood at the entrance to a room. "The most important room in the house," he announced without a hint of a smile, "this is where you'll find my chef most of the time."

He led them into a huge kitchen. A short dark-haired man stood before a long marble bench in front of a gleaming bank of steel ovens. He was preparing vegetables. He didn't look up when Rochester spoke, his every attention on the knife in his hand.

"This is Dom, my chef. He'll make you anything you ask for."

Dom stopped chopping and looked over at Rochester and the children. His knife was poised. He'd never seen young people at the house before.

"He'll make us anything?" Jamie said, his mind filling with his favourite foods. "Is there anything you can't make?"

Dom waved his knife in Jamie's direction. "There is nothing I can't make."

He straightened his shoulders. What request could a boy make that he couldn't deliver with his eyes closed?

"I'll leave you with Rose. She can show you around the rest of the house and…" he looked at Violet's dress, his eyes travelling to her worn runners, "mmm… some clothes, I think. Rose, arrange to have some clothes brought in for Violet."

He hadn't sorted the issue with the boy yet. He didn't want to arouse suspicion by having clothes brought into the house for him. He would send Rose out to buy something. Something for her grandson. Yes, her grandson who was staying with her.

He nodded to himself. The boy was a means to an end. The girl was the end. He didn't intend to let Violet leave the house unless he was by her side.

"I'll leave you two in the capable hands of Rose." He wasn't smiling, and he didn't wait for a reply. He just turned away. But as he reached the door Jamie said, "Sir, can I call Scott?" Rochester didn't break his stride and he didn't answer Jamie's question.

Violet pressed her lips together. She didn't feel a thing when she looked into those icy green eyes. She wondered how old he was; she thought he had the kind of face you couldn't tell if he was old or young.

Rose folded her arms and drew her brows together. She knew who Violet was—everyone did—but the boy, who was he? She didn't ask. You never asked a question unless you absolutely needed to know the answer, and you never spoke about Rochester or the household if you wanted to keep your job—or get another one.

"Why don't you two explore the place, and I'll meet you in the far wing. I'll show you where it is, and you can pick out a room."

"How many rooms are there?" said Jamie. He felt as though he'd entered another game, where his avatar was the son of a billionaire. He intended to explore them all. He'd already explored the ground floor.

"Come and look at this room, Violet. It's full of sofas and chairs and there's a giant flat screen on the wall."

Violet followed Jamie. She walked over to a wall of French doors that opened out onto the garden. It looked like a park. She walked slowly around the room, just looking, not touching anything.

She stopped in front of a side table with photos. She recognised Rochester. She moved closer and heard glass crackle beneath her runner. The moment she saw it, she knew what it was. A wedding photo.

She carefully picked it up, the glass was shattered, the pieces fell onto the carpet. She couldn't recognise her mother but it had to be her. He hadn't changed, he looked exactly the same, standing stiffly at her mother's side. Violet swallowed, she felt a flutter in her chest. He must have done this— why?

"Come on," said Jamie, "let's pick a bedroom, I want one with a view."

Violet carefully placed the photo on the side table. She smiled—at least someone was enjoying themselves. She didn't think Jamie had a thousand wings beating in his chest.

"I think all the rooms will have views—the house is in the middle of a park," Violet said, following Jamie up the wide marble staircase.

They chose bedrooms next to each other on the top floor. They had a connecting door and shared a large balcony that overlooked an enormous pond. In the middle of the pond, water gushed from a large stone fish that seemed to have been caught mid-air as it leapt.

Violet stood on the balcony and looked out towards the distant skyline—the city she had just come from. Somewhere out there was Lewis. And John. John had said to trust Lewis, but John couldn't have known about the money. She turned away and went back into the bedroom.

***

A young woman employed by the store had been sent to help Violet put together a wardrobe of clothes suitable for the daughter of Rochester. She had stayed for three hours, making Violet try on clothes Violet thought she would never wear—dresses in all shades of green.

"Lovely with your hair. You just have to have this one—a special occasion dress."

Violet lost count of how many times she heard that. After she'd gone, Violet lay on the bed in her new jeans and a pale green T-shirt. She looked over at the open door of the walk-in dressing room that held more clothes than she'd had in her entire life—and it was still almost empty.

She thought she should be more excited, but she couldn't rid herself of the 'what if' fear at the back of her mind—that Lewis could be right. All she knew for certain was that Lewis had lied. It was all about the money. Everything was about the money.

She didn't want to think about him. She got off the bed and went to find Jamie. Jamie was in the kitchen talking to Dom, explaining the mysteries of a BLT.

"It's got bacon in it—lettuce and tomato. I like cheese in it too."

Dom didn't look up from stirring the pot on the stove. He wasn't used to having young people in his kitchen and he'd never been asked to make something he'd never heard of before.

"It's alright. It doesn't have to be real bacon. But do you have something that tastes like that? Please?"

"Jamie, let's go into the garden," said Violet.

197

Dom looked at Violet standing in the doorway. "Go," he said to Jamie. "I'll find something… like bacon but not bacon. Go."

They walked across the lawn to the fountain. Jamie sat down next to Violet and trailed his hands in the water. He wondered what fish they had here. He looked up at Violet.

"What's up?" He knew that worried look she was trying to hide.

"Nothing. I just wanted to get out of the house."

He didn't believe her. "Are you going to see Lewis?" He didn't wait for an answer. "I want to see Scott. And I want to explore this city."

"I don't know how to get in contact with them. I don't have a phone." She didn't want to tell Jamie about the bonus Scott would be getting.

Jamie looked puzzled. "There's a phone in the house. Lots of phones. and you know who they work for. The PWIB." He hadn't forgotten.

Something caught Violet's eye and she looked up. Rochester was standing at the window. Violet's heart jumped. She didn't know why. She stood up. She could see him moving toward the glass doors that led out into the garden.

"He's coming," she whispered to Jamie.

She felt as though they were on parade and had to look their best. She was wearing new clothes. Jamie wasn't. He was still a secret. He needed to be safe.

"Hello, you two," said Rochester. "Come inside, Dom's made something for you, Jamie."

Jamie ran up the steps and headed for the kitchen.

Violet smoothed her hands down her new jeans. "Thank you for the clothes," she said.

"Yes, good. That's better," he said, looking her up and down. He frowned. "I hope we have clothes other than jeans and…" he looked down at her feet. "You do have shoes, yes?"

Violet nodded. "Yes. A woman came and she… chose everything…"

"Really?" said Rochester. *Everything.* It was disappointing to think that his daughter was as witless as she looked.

He led the way back into the house and into the lounge room with all the pale-coloured sofas. As they walked past the side table with the photos, Violet saw the wedding photo of her mother and Rochester was back with the other photos. The glass unbroken.

Rochester sat in a chair with his back to the window. He indicated a chair opposite his, and Violet sank into it.

"So," said Rochester, steepling his fingers. "How has your first day been? Not too challenging?" He tried out a smile.

Violet shook her head. Her mouth felt dry. She'd never felt this afraid or unsure of herself living with Mona. It had been miserable, but she knew what to expect with Mona. But the man sitting opposite her was a stranger. She didn't know anything about him. Only that Lewis had said she couldn't trust him—that he wanted her for something, not because she was his daughter.

Who can I trust?

"Tell me about yourself, Violet. All the years I've missed." He pressed his lips together as though he were holding back some emotion. He leaned forward.

"You know, Violet, I've a lot to catch up on… but not all at once. We've plenty of time."

He crossed his legs and leaned back. He noticed she was sitting on the edge of the chair, her fingers twisting in her lap. She looked pale. He had a flash of memory of another young woman twisting her fingers, her eyes full of fear.

Violet ran her tongue over her dry lips. She couldn't form the words. Rochester tapped his fingers on the armrest and nodded to Violet. He was waiting. He suppressed a sigh of exasperation. He hated indecision. *Let's start with something easy.*

He waved his hand in Violet's direction. "Have you finished school? What were you planning to do? What are your interests… that sort of thing?" He tried not to sound impatient. He wanted to get to the real questions but was prepared to wait.

"I almost finished school. I had a few weeks to go… when this happened."

"By this, you mean when you were found and brought home—here?" He hated imprecision.

"Yes," said Violet. She was struggling to think. Her mind was in a fog.

"And?" he said.

"And?" said Violet, her voice full of puzzlement. She thought she could hear Jamie somewhere. She willed him to come into the room.

"And your plans? Your interests, Violet?"

My plans? Her plan had been to escape Mona and Derek. Live somewhere in her world with Jamie. Just the two of them. Not here. Not this.

"I don't have any plans," she said.

Of course, she doesn't have any plans. He was going too fast. Not giving her time. "Yes, of course, Violet. Forgive me." He gave a small smile and pushed down the irritation that was barely beneath the surface.

He drummed his fingers on the armrest of his chair. *What does she know?*

"Too soon for plans. Violet, this must be a big shock for you. When did you find out about…?" He left his question suspended mid-air.

When did I find out you were my father?

When did I find out Lewis lied?

Violet took a breath. This had to be real. This world. This man sitting opposite. He had to be her father… why would he hurt her?

Violet closed her eyes. Her heart beat faster. She knew what she was going to do.

She stood up and walked over to the side table and the photographs. The wedding photo was back in place, the glass unbroken. She took the photo and walked back to Rochester and thrust the photo in front of him.

"This is a photo of you and my mother, isn't it? I saw it earlier—it was broken." Her voice was full of accusation.

Rochester looked at the photo in Violet's hand. He reached forward and took it from her. He knew how to lie.

"Yes," he whispered as though it was a secret to share. He smoothed a finger over the photo, "that's your mother, Anna. I believe she called herself Ailsa in your world." He didn't look up he wasn't sure his acting skills were that good. "I loved her Violet, we were so happy, we were going to have our first child…you…and then she disappeared and for all these years…" His voice took on a bitter tone. "For years, I thought someone had taken her. But when I heard you'd been found in DZ…" His eyes darkened. "I realised she left me…for another man."

He looked at Violet. "I was angry. But as you can see—" he nodded at the glass, "I was sorry I broke it. I had it replaced right away. She was your mother. I'm sure you loved her. She hurt me. But let's not talk about that."

The lie was wearing thin. He stared at the photo again, at the woman whose eyes shimmered with fear. Then he flipped it over and set it on the armrest.

"Sit down, Violet." He checked his watch. "Almost lunchtime. But first—tell me about yourself. Do you ride?"

Violet didn't answer. Her mind spun. Her mother had left him for someone else. Not the man Violet had thought was her father. Another man. Someone she didn't know.

"I said," Rochester repeated, his voice sharp, "do you ride?"

Violet felt a bead of sweat trickle down her face. Her heart was thudding. "Ride?" She echoed, confused. "A horse?"

No, an elephant! Rochester nodded tightly. "Yes. A horse. I have stables here. You'll ride."

She shook her head.

"Pity. But you must learn." He leaned back, pretending to soften. "Your mother was an excellent horsewoman." Another lie. But it hit the mark. He saw it in Violet's eyes.

"She was?" Violet blinked. "I don't think I knew that."

"She rode every day." He closed his eyes, painting the picture—but all he saw was her terror, her first time on horseback, her sobbing in the grass after he made her fall. He'd laughed. She never rode again.

"Interests?" he barked out the words and then caught himself. Softer this time: "What do you like, Violet? Hobbies?" He took a long silent breath. He had to be more patient. He had to get her trust. Who knew what that punk Carlyle had told her.

"Reading, I like reading…books." She bit her lip.

"Books?" He smiled faintly. "Novels that sort of thing?"

"Old ones. Dickens. Austen."

"The DZ classics." He nodded. "We have them here. Your mother loved reading, too." *All she ever did.*

Violet had a sudden thought. "Do I have grandparents?"

Rochester shook his head, *no thank heavens* "No." His voice lowered, trying for sympathy. "We can talk ancestry later."

He stood. "I've calls to make. No more questions today. We'll talk again—after dinner. I'll take you and Jamie around the estate."

"Best BLT that wasn't a BLT ever," Jamie said, appearing in the doorway.

Rochester winced. The boy had a penetrating voice.

Violet looked at Jamie standing in the doorway, a smudge of something red, like ketchup, on his chin.

"Why don't you both explore," he said. "Swim. The pool. Or the beach— it's private."

"A private beach?" Jamie's eyes lit up.

Rochester clenched his jaw.

"Can we go into the city?" Jamie asked. "And school—what school will I go to?"

Rochester stopped at the door. "I'm afraid you can't leave. Not yet." He looked at Violet. "Did you explain it to him?"

"Explain what?" Jamie demanded.

"I'm afraid you're an illegal immigrant, Jamie. No one knows you're here. Until I sort that out, you can't be seen outside."

"It's going to be okay," Violet said quickly. "You're my brother."

"Half-brother," Rochester corrected.

Violet flinched. "Still family. Still blood."

Rochester let the weight of that settle. Then, "Of course. I'll take care of it. And," he smiled and looked at Jamie, "school—I have one in mind. But for now, low profile." He had a school in mind, far away, a boarding school.

Violet looked at Rochester, the smile had gone. He was already miles away, thinking of something else.

Violet stepped forward. "Can I make a call?"

"To whom?" He raised his brows like it was all a little joke.

"John Carlyle. Lewis's father."

"You have the number?"

She didn't.

"I'll get you a phone. But here—" he held out his own. It was already recording.

She glanced at Jamie. "Do you know it?"

Jamie grinned. "All primes. First is—nineteen."

Violet took the phone. Rochester handed it over with a tight grip.

Jamie listed the rest. Violet pressed call.

"John? It's Violet."

"Violet!" Relief poured through the line. "Are you okay? Is Jamie?"

"We're both fine." She glanced at Rochester.

"Lewis is worried. He wants to explain."

She remembered the hair. The bonus. She said nothing.

"Can I give him a message? Please, Violet."

"I'm fine. Tell him that." *Tell him to leave me alone. Tell him he's a liar.*

She saw Rochester's shoulders stiffen.

"Tell him," She said, louder, "Jamie's safe. My father's already fixing things."

Rochester smiled to himself. *I'm quite the hero…tell that to the punk.*

John's voice dropped. "Violet, you have to hear him out. Please."

"I don't have a phone."

"I'll give you his number. Jamie?"

"Got it," Jamie said. "Multiples of five and my birth year. Tour of the tracking station soon?" he asked.

"Soon as we can," said John. "Take care, both of you."

Violet handed the phone back. Her lips were trembling. Her eyes shimmered.

"I'll see you both at dinner," said Rochester. "Six sharp. Until then, explore. Violet, the library's on the second floor." He dropped his voice. "Your mother's favourite room."

Violet froze.

"Oh no," he said with mock horror. "I'm never going to see you again, am I?"

"Going to find the library," she muttered. "You coming, Jamie?"

"Nah. I want to talk to Dom about dinner."

CHAPTER TWENTY-NINE

The library was bigger than her old school library. Books in glass cabinets, just like a museum. Violet walked slowly through the room, pulling out books one by one. She noticed the order of them—rows too precise for chance. Rochester must have a librarian.

She was disappointed. They were all non-fiction. Not a single novel. She glanced up at the gallery lining one of the walls. Books there too. She climbed the spiral staircase tucked into the corner.

Muted light fell across a blood-red velvet sofa nestled between two towering bookcases. Violet stepped toward the glass. Her reflection should have looked back—but for a moment, it wasn't her. A young woman with honey-coloured hair and dark eyes stared out instead.

She blinked.

Gone. Just her. Pale face. Red hair. Green eyes.

She turned away, heart fluttering. Then she saw the books. She stopped. A hand to her throat.

She knew these titles. "Pride and Prejudice." "Great Expectations." "The Complete Works of Shakespeare."

Her mother's books. Her mother's world.

Her eyes scanned the shelf—every single one of them. These were the books her mother had read. She looked down at the velvet sofa. *This was where she read.*

Violet opened the cabinet. Her hand trembled as she pulled out a leather-bound copy of "Persuasion". The book fell open at a page. She started to read.

Rochester found her there when the sun had gone down and the room was lit from the garden lights outside. The book lay open on her lap, her eyes closed, red hair spilled across the velvet cushion. He stood watching. Familiar. Too familiar. He clenched his jaw. *Like mother, like daughter.*

Violet woke with a start. Mona had been in her dream, tearing pages from books, hurling them across the floor. Rochester was there too, a shadow behind her. She gasped and the book slid from her lap.

"I see you're awake," he said, lifting the book, smoothing his hand across the embossed lettering. His lip curled when he read the title.

She couldn't think. The dream clung to her—Mona, the books, the room. She pushed herself upright. Her head throbbed.

Where am I? Her head felt heavy. The light had gone and he was there, Rochester, her father, string down at her.

She followed his movement as he placed the book back in the cabinet. Slow. Careful. Letting her see it was something valuable. The glass door clicked shut. He wondered briefly when he would have the library locked.

Not yet, he thought. Not just yet.

Violet tried to stand, then sank back. Her limbs were heavy, her eyes too full of sleep. He offered his hand.

"You must still be tired. Early night for you—but first, dinner. Dom's made something different. At your brother's request. Spaghetti bolognaise."

He led her toward the stairs. "I think Jamie's proving a bit of a challenge to poor Dom," he added with a faint laugh. "Hope he doesn't leave me under all this pressure."

He saw her smile. Good. He was getting better at the casual stuff. It was exhausting, but it was working. He needed her trust.

In the dining room, Jamie's voice rang out. "Tastes perfect! As good as Violet's. No—better. Don't tell her I said that."

Rochester hadn't paid Jamie much attention. The boy was a complication. A loose thread.

He glanced at Violet. Her eyes were shining. "I heard that," she said as she entered the kitchen.

Jamie stood at the bench, spoon in hand. "Sorry, Violet. But it is. He's a chef. He should be better. Makes sense."

Dom waved him out. "Go. It's ready."

Rochester lingered in the doorway. Revising. Rethinking. Perhaps it was time to shift focus. His mouth tightened. *He has to go.*

He waited until the meal was over. Forced himself to chew the claggy mess clinging to pale spaghetti. "Different," he murmured covering his grimace with something like a smile. He pushed the sauce around his plate.

"I was thinking," he said lightly. "Tomorrow—why don't we take a trot around the place?"

Jamie blinked. "A trot?"

"Horse riding. You should both learn."

Violet's brows lifted. She'd ridden ponies when her dad was alive. It had bored her senseless.

Rochester dabbed at his mouth with a napkin. "Does that appeal?"

"Great!" Jamie said.

Rochester winced. He turned to Violet. "Not something you'd like?"

"No—I mean yes. I'd like to try."

"Good." He stood. "I have a meeting tomorrow, so let's ride early. Be ready by eight. Stables are at the far end."

Violet nodded. Early was easy. For the past two years, it had been her refuge—running along the beach at dawn.

Jamie pumped a fist. "Fantastic! I've always wanted to ride a horse."

"I had riding clothes delivered. They came yesterday." He smiled at Violet. *Getting quite good at that too.* "Let's see if you take after your mother."

Violet met his eyes. Chin lifted. "I'm in," she said. And smiled.

CHAPTER THIRTY

Lewis paced the corridor outside Monk's office. Four days since Rochester drove off with Violet.

"Hey man, stop pacing. You're making me dizzy," Scott said, leaning against the wall. Helen stood beside him, hands in her pockets. She glanced at Lewis—dark circles under his eyes. He hadn't slept since they got back.

"Lewis," she said, touching his shoulder, "from what you've told me, Violet's cautious. She doesn't trust easily. She barely knows Rochester. She'll be wondering why her mother ran. We've got time. Whatever Rochester's planning, he'll be trying to win her over."

Lewis squeezed his shoulder blades together. He was exhausted. His rational mind hijacked by feelings he couldn't shake.

"Yeah, you're right. Just need answers from Monk." He stretched his arms overhead. Monk had been gone for days. Now he was back—and Lewis wasn't leaving without a conversation.

Monk's secretary opened the door. "The Director will see you now."

The three stepped inside. Lewis braced himself. Monk couldn't discharge them from the Academy. He could bluster—but he had no grounds.

Only Monk wasn't blustering. He looked drained. Four days with World Security had taken their toll. He spoke first.

"Despite the drama, a good result," he said, leaning back. "Why don't you sit?"

No one moved.

"Won't take long, sir," Lewis said. He'd rehearsed this. "We're back. We expect to resume at the Academy. We know there'll be an investigation into the mission. We'll cooperate fully. But…"

Monk leaned forward. "But what?"

"Depends," Helen said. Lewis raised an eyebrow, letting her finish.

"On what you're willing to share with us."

Monk stood, hands in his pockets. They thought they had him cornered. He almost laughed. "Sit down. I'll tell you what I know." *Just enough to shut you up.*

"I want to know where they are," Lewis said.

Monk gave him a withering look. "They're at Rochester's home. As far as I know, they're settling in. What I can share is this: When Rochester's wife Anna disappeared, she was six or seven months pregnant. That same day, Advanced Laboratories' main research wing burned down—twenty years of work, gone."

He waved off Lewis's next question. "Genetic modification. That's all I can tell you."

"Surely some research was saved?" Lewis asked.

"Yes. But it vanished too. Rochester suspected espionage, maybe kidnapping. No ransom demands ever came. The chief scientist was suspected—but nothing stuck. He left soon after. Moved to a university on the coast."

Monk continued, "All employees were monitored. Phones tapped. We stopped after two years, but Rochester insisted we keep surveillance on Callum—the chief scientist. We scaled it down to just phone taps."

"Three months ago, we heard something. Callum's wife got worried—he missed his flight home from a conference. She said something that triggered alarms. She was afraid he'd gone to DZ… to visit Rochester's wife."

Monk spread his hands. "No one expected that. DZ isn't a place people escape to. But it started to make sense. Callum's brother works at World Security. We're pretty sure he helped her—but he covered his tracks. No proof."

"Why?" Lewis asked quietly. "Why would she do it?"

Monk shrugged. "Marriage problems? She was younger. Maybe another man?" Even he didn't believe it.

Lewis waved the suggestion away. "Callum must know something. What does he say now that Violet's been found?"

Monk's face hardened. "Not our department. World Security's handling it."

He shifted in his seat. The Bureau was under investigation. Rochester's involvement had been sanctioned—but someone had infiltrated the system and had planned to leave Lewis and the others behind. Violet was brought to Perfection under the radar.

"Why would Callum help her?" Lewis asked again, mostly to himself. Monk heard. He'd asked Rochester the same thing. No answers.

"You can find Callum. We need to talk to him," Lewis said.

Monk's eyes narrowed. "We need to do nothing. The girl is safe. She's with her father. She has no family in DZ. She'll have a wonderful life here."

Lewis didn't flinch. "Like the wonderful life her mother had. The one she ran from. She burned down his lab, destroyed everything, and vanished. She didn't want to be found. She chose DZ."

Monk sighed. "Enough, Lewis." He leaned across the desk. "Rochester spent eighteen years searching for her. He wants his daughter. She's going to be fine."

Lewis stared back. He didn't trust Monk. Not his ties to Rochester.

"I want to see her," Lewis said.

Monk frowned, glanced at Scott and Helen. They didn't seem as invested now. Monk stood, staring at his desk. He didn't want to make an enemy of Rochester—but it was inevitable. Rochester didn't know World Security had Callum and his brother in custody.

Monk checked his watch. He had a meeting with the Minister. He wasn't looking forward to it.

"You three need to focus on the Academy," he said sharply. "The adventure's over. Mission completed." He squared his shoulders. "Meeting over."

Lewis was already out the door when he heard Scott say, "And we want the bonus. You can tell him that."

Lewis groaned. *Not the bloody bonuses again.*

He headed toward the library. He didn't know what he was looking for—anything that might help.

His phone rang. It was his father.

"Dad."

"Lewis, Violet called me two minutes ago. She said to tell you she's fine. You don't have to worry."

John knew how it would land—not with relief, but disappointment. Lewis listened, hand at the back of his neck. It wasn't good news. "That's all she said. That she's fine? Did you tell her I need to talk to her? Explain everything?"

"Yes, Lewis. I did. Give her time. It's been a shock. She's trying to make sense of it. And she has Jamie."

"Yeah. Monk told me."

"Thank heavens," John said.

"I figured he got to him. But Dad—Violet thinks I betrayed her. Lied to her. I have to find a way to talk to her. Someone helped her mother escape. Monk thinks it was a scientist who worked for Rochester. I need to find him. He knows something."

"Lewis, listen. The world's watching. Violet and Rochester—it's the story of the century. He's going to parade her around. This is the daughter he's telling the world that he's been trying to find for eighteen years. Nothing's going to happen to her."

John tried to sound reassuring. But he remembered—there was no plan to bring Lewis or the others back from DZ.

"And if it wasn't world news, Dad? What then?"

John sighed. "I don't know. But you need to act like you've accepted it. Get back to your studies. Keep a low profile. Oh—and I gave Violet your number. You never know. She might call."

CHAPTER THIRTY-ONE

Violet woke in the middle of the night. The third dream about Lewis in as many nights. This time they were running along a beach road. Not her world, not even close—an alien one, with acid green skies and a blood-red ocean. Lewis was shouting, "Don't stop! Keep running. Don't let him catch you."

She bolted upright. Blankets tangled around her legs. Heart pounding.

She lay back, eyes on the ceiling, waiting for the dream to fade. It didn't. She hadn't given him a chance to explain—she knew that. She rolled onto her side and hugged her knees. *I'll call him. Hear what he has to say.*

But the phone Rochester had promised still hadn't appeared. He'd claimed he had forgotten, but she couldn't tell if that was the truth or just another tactic. She didn't know him well enough to know when he was lying.

She'd asked at dinner. Jamie had already left the table. Rochester had sighed. "Sorry, Violet. I've been distracted by Jamie's situation. It's proving more difficult than I thought."

"But it will be alright, won't it?" Her voice broke. "You said it would." She couldn't keep the accusation out of her voice.

He stared at her his face blank. She couldn't tell if he was angry. Then— he reached out and tapped the back of her hand. "Don't worry. His application's with World Security. They'll clear him." He added quickly, "Just keep a low profile, okay? People get paranoid about aliens and what they might bring into our pristine universe."

He paused, voice darker. "They send them to islands or lock them up. Just like your world. And they stay there... a long time. But I'll make sure Jamie gets citizenship. That's a promise. "Just a few more days, Violet. Then we can go out together. A trip. A proper holiday."

She'd believed him or tried to. Now, at midnight, the clock glowing dim on the bedside cabinet, she couldn't sleep. She wondered where Lewis was now. She pictured him lying in bed, staring at the ceiling like her.

Stop it. He's probably dreaming about the damn bonus.

She yanked the blankets over her head. She didn't need him. Didn't need to hear a thing. Today, they were getting out of the house. Finally.

Rochester was taking them horse riding.

Jamie had joked he was going "stir crazy."

"You've only been confined for two days," Violet had said, laughing. "Back in our world they lock illegal immigrants up for years. But it won't happen to you. My father promised."

The days had been long. Lazy. Too quiet. The estate offered tennis courts, a lagoon pool, a secluded beach—but none of it felt real. None of it felt hers.

***

Violet stood in front of the mirror. The jodhpurs fitted perfectly.

She tucked the short-sleeved white silk shirt into the waistband. The riding jacket was still wrapped in silver tissue paper on the bed. She peeled it open. Black velvet. She let her fingers skim the fabric, shimmer catching in the light. She slipped her arms into the silk-lined sleeves and pulled it tight across her chest. A hiccup of laughter escaped her lips. She stared at her reflection.

"Who do you think you are, Violet Mackenzie?" she said to the image reflected back to her. She didn't recognise the girl in the mirror. She wiggled her toes in her polished riding boots.

Rochester was waiting for them in the dining room. Her boots squeaked as she walked in.

"I see you found the clothes," he said. "You look very smart, Violet. Everything fit alright?" He didn't wait for her answer. His frown snapped toward Jamie.

"Didn't your jacket fit?"

Jamie looked at the floor. "I don't like jackets."

Violet knew why. The last time he'd worn one was at their dad's funeral.

Ungrateful boy, Rochester almost muttered.

He handed out the riding helmets. "And what about these? Don't tell me you won't wear one."

"Of course I will," said Jamie. "I'm not stupid."

Rochester drove them past a golf course, winding through fields where horses grazed. The road curved to a stop in front of a large white building. It looked like something out of a movie.

"Is this a house?" Violet asked.

"It was. The original one. Now it's the stables. Built three hundred years ago."

He opened the car door. "I'd knock it down, but it's heritage protected."

"It's beautiful," Violet whispered. She meant it.

He led them to a row of low, whitewashed stables. "Phew!" Jamie muttered. "What a stink."

Violet caught Rochester's look of irritation. The smell hit her —horse droppings, damp hay, wet earth. Violet's nose stung. She didn't blame Jamie for wrinkling his face. From inside the stable, horses shuffled and a man's voice echoed.

"I've asked my stable master to saddle a couple of horses for you both," Rochester said, stepping aside. "Here he is. Stewart, meet my daughter Violet and our guest, Jamie."

Stewart emerged from behind a horse, tall and wiry, white hair clipped close. His eyes narrowed. He could spot rookies from a mile off—and these two screamed beginners. He tried to keep the troubled look off his face. Rochester had told him what horses to get ready and who was riding them. He knew better than to question Rochester.

"I've got them ready, sir. Whistler for the young lady, and this one—Vector," he nodded at the massive black horse behind him, "for the lad."

"He can't ride that," Violet said, sharp.

"Yes, I can," Jamie shot back, chin high.

"I could saddle another, sir," Stewart offered.

Rochester ignored him he glanced sideways at Jamie. "What do you think? Up for it?" There was challenge in his voice and something else.

Jamie stepped toward Vector, hand out. The horse jerked back, stomping hard on the cobblestones.

Violet's eyes snapped to Rochester. He was testing Jamie. She didn't like it.

She moved to Vector, voice soft. "You're a beauty. Black Beauty." Her hand hovered under his nose, then brushed his forehead. She leaned her head against his flank. "I want to ride him. Look—he likes me." Her heart thudded. Jamie would try to prove something. She couldn't let him.

"That's not fair," Jamie said. "He was chosen for me, wasn't he?"

Stewart looked to Rochester, silent question in his eyes. Rochester clenched his jaw. Damn the girl. She couldn't handle Vector. Nothing could happen to her.

Violet still had her back to him, murmuring to the horse.

Jamie hadn't moved. "I'm meant to ride him," Jamie said again, but his voice cracked.

Violet didn't turn. "I'm riding him. You take the other."

"You've ridden before?" Stewart asked, cupping his hands to boost her up.

"A couple of times. Years ago," she said, gripping the reins.

"I'll put him on a leading rein," Stewart said, eyeing Rochester, who was already leading his own pale horse.

"I'll take that," Rochester said, grabbing Vector's rein. "You lead the boy."

Don't call him that. His name is Jamie. Violet glanced at Rochester, then pressed her heels down, knees tight. She looked back—Jamie's horse looked tiny.

She leaned forward, patting Vector. "You're beautiful. How old is he?"

"Four," Rochester snapped.

Violet frowned. Why was he angry? This was his idea. But she was starting to enjoy it—the height, the sway, the power beneath her.

Behind her, Stewart murmured instructions to Jamie. Violet held the reins loose. Was that right? She was glad Rochester had the lead. She could feel Vector's energy, coiled and ready.

"You want to gallop, don't you?" she whispered.

"Take Whistler to the other paddock!" Rochester barked.

Vector sidestepped hard. Violet slipped, reins sliding through her fingers. She lunged for the pommel as the horse bolted, leading rein yanked from Rochester's grip.

"Violet!" Rochester swore, swinging onto his horse. He kicked hard. He had to catch her. Nothing could happen to the girl.

Violet bounced in the saddle, every jolt slamming her chest. Vector's ears pinned back, hooves thundered, wind whipped her face.

"Hang on! Grip your thighs! Pull the reins—hard! Don't panic. Animals sense fear." Rochester's voice faded beneath the roar of hooves.

She touched the reins. *Don't panic, Violet. Don't panic.* Rochester's voice was a blur, drowned out by the thunder of hooves.

She had to stop bouncing. Every jolt in the saddle slammed through her chest. She pressed her heels down, leaned forward, fingertips brushing the reins.

Rochester watched her bounce like a rag doll. Any second now, she'd fall—just like her mother. He urged his horse faster, but Vector was untouchable. He cursed himself. "Idiot, idiot," he muttered, watching Violet lean over Vector's neck. For a moment, he thought she was going down.

She hooked the reins with one finger, worked them under her grip, then yanked hard to one side. Vector's head twisted, his hind legs skidding sideways. She'd stopped him. But staying upright was a whole new battle. She twisted with the horse, refusing to let go.

Vector's eyes flashed white—he was wild. The ground churned beneath him. Hooves pounded nearby. Rochester was shouting, but she couldn't hear him over the chaos and the blood roaring in her ears.

Rochester pulled up beside her, his horse snorting.

"What do I do now?" Violet asked, trying to sound calm.

Rochester jumped down, grabbed Vector's bridle. "Good girl!" he said, breathless. "A one-handed stop? How'd you know to do that?"

Violet wiped sweat from her lip. "Instinct," she said, voice shaky.

"Instinct. That's good. You okay?"

"I think so." She wasn't sure. Why had Rochester picked this horse for Jamie? Vector was no beginner's ride.

As if reading her mind, Rochester shook his head. "What was I thinking, Violet? I should have picked one of the older horses for you."

"You picked this one for Jamie," she reminded him. His jaw clenched. He tugged Vector's bridle, knuckles white.

He led the horse around the paddock in silence. Across the field, Jamie looked like he was having the time of his life.

"Good," Rochester said once they were back at the stables and Stewart took the horses. "For a first lesson, I'd say that went pretty well, wouldn't you?"

Violet nodded. She hadn't expected to enjoy it—but she had. Even when Vector bolted. "Yeah. I think I might like horse riding," she said.

***

Violet hesitated outside the dining room. She'd swapped her riding gear for jeans and a white tee. Still no phone from Rochester, and she needed to call Lewis.

She'd had time to think about her talk with John. He was right—she hadn't let Lewis explain. But it wasn't anger she felt. It was hurt.

Hurt that Lewis had played her. Made her believe she mattered. That it wasn't just a mission. The lock of hair. The bike. The island. *No. Don't go there.* The jetty. His arms around her— *Stop. Don't think about it. Shut up, Violet. Shut up.*

She shook her head, trying to clear the images *I'll call him. Hear him out. Then that's it.*

Rochester sat at the table, one hand propping up his head, eyes on his laptop. Jamie was already seated, looking like he was about to devour the table.

"Ah, Violet, finally," Rochester said. "Jamie and I are ready to eat a horse."

Violet smiled. A joke—sort of. "Sorry, did I keep you waiting?"

Rochester shook his head, nodded at Jamie, who gripped his knife and fork like he was in a food duel. She sat opposite Jamie. Rochester was in his usual spot at the head. Dom came in with a dish.

"Another of Jamie's challenges?" Rochester asked, eyeing him.

Violet glanced at him. He seemed... different. Relaxed. Friendly. She'd been worried, thought he didn't like Jamie. And Vector? That horse was dangerous. Jamie could've been thrown.

Rochester waited until Dom left. "So," he said, "after this morning's success, I'm thinking Violet, I should buy you a horse. Jamie, you'll get Whistler—the pony you rode. Violet, you need something bigger. Spirited, but not like Vector. That was a mistake. I should've listened to Stewart."

Jamie swallowed his bread. A pony—not a horse. He knew he should be grateful, but still.

Violet felt heat rise in her cheeks. Her eyes stung. She hadn't expected this. "Thank you," she stammered.

Rochester drummed his fingers on the table. Good—she liked the idea. *Now for the coup de grâce.*

"Oh, one other thing," Rochester said casually. "I've invited your friends over this afternoon."

Violet blinked. "My friends?"

"The three you came to Perfection with…" He dropped his voice, dramatic. The heroes." He stood, wiped his mouth with a napkin, and tossed it onto the table.

Violet's heart stopped.

Jamie whooped. "Finally!" He shoved his glasses up, eyes wide.

Rochester looked straight at Violet. "I'll be back at three when the heroes arrive. I have to present the bonuses they were promised for finding you. I keep my word. I think they'll be very pleased… especially the team leader. Lewis, isn't it? He gets double." *How do you like your hero now, Violet?*

Violet stared at Rochester's retreating back. Her appetite vanished. She shoved her chair back and stood.

Rochester walked down the corridor, then turned and nearly collided with Violet as she rushed out. "Steady," he said, hands light on her shoulders. "Not hungry?" He didn't wait for an answer.

"I forgot to mention—your phones are arriving this afternoon."

"Do I get a phone?" Jamie called from the dining room.

Rochester kept his hand on Violet's shoulder, guiding her to the doorway. He wanted her to hear this.

"Yes, Jamie. Yours will be loaded with games. Once your citizenship's sorted, you'll be online in no time."

Jamie pumped his fists. "Yes!" His cracked lens distorted the shine in his eyes.

"Must get those eyes fixed too," Rochester said.

Violet clutched his arm through the thin fabric of his shirt. "Thank you…" she hesitated. She didn't know what to call him. To her, he was just Rochester.

He squeezed her shoulder. He could wait. Everything was falling into place.

"Oh, and Violet," he added, "I'll leave the refreshments to you. You probably know what they'd like."

***

Scott didn't have to search for Lewis. He was exactly where he'd been since they got back from DZ—buried in the library.

Scott knew what he was hunting for: some clue about why Rochester wanted Violet. They'd talked two days ago, when Scott tried dragging Lewis out for a drink.

"Get over Violet," Scott had said. Big mistake.

Lewis had snapped, eyes blazing. "Get over—I don't know what you're talking about. I feel responsible for her. And Jamie. We brought them back. You forget we weren't supposed to come back. We were meant to stay in DZ forever. Slipped your mind, did it?"

Scott hadn't answered. He knew Lewis wasn't giving up. And he definitely wasn't being honest about his feelings for Violet.

Lewis didn't hear Scott approach. He was glued to the screen, scrolling fast.

"What you looking at?" Scott leaned in. "Scientific advancements in genetic modification," he read aloud.

Lewis leaned back, stretched. Hours of digging through archived journals—nothing. He'd chased every mention of Advanced Laboratories, followed every reference. Still no answers. He stood, needing air. "What's up, Scott? What brings you to your least favourite place on campus?"

Scott grinned, leaned close. "Just saw Monk. He said Rochester invited us—me, you, Helen—to his place this afternoon. Bonus time."

Lewis jerked his head. *Damn the bonus.* His eyes flared. Scott clenched his jaw. He wasn't letting Lewis ruin this. He wanted the money. Lewis was only acting noble because of Violet.

Lewis swallowed his reaction. "You said Rochester's house?"

"Yep. Two-thirty. Helen's driving."

Scott saw the flicker in Lewis's eyes. *Yeah, you're hoping to see Violet.*

Lewis checked his watch. Thirty minutes. "I'll meet you at the gates," he said, shutting down the computer.

As they left, Lilian glanced across the library. The blonde girl in the corner had been watching Lewis—and now she watched him leave, tracking every move.

Lilian sighed. She wasn't the first girl trying to catch his attention since DZ. But Lewis stayed cold, distant.

Still, he nodded at her as he passed her desk. A quiet acknowledgment. Nothing more.

Poppy stood and shut the file she'd been pretending to read. At first, it was a game—she wasn't used to being ignored by boys. But Lewis? That night still burned. *I don't like myself and I don't like you.* Who did he think he was? She smiled bitterly. She knew exactly who he was—an arrogant nobody. Not a game anymore. She tucked her hair behind her ears, lips pursed. He didn't know who she was. No one did. She had kept that secret locked tight.

***

Violet wanted to hide in the library all afternoon, avoid Lewis entirely. But she had promised John she would hear him out.

She stood at the entrance to her dressing room, overwhelmed by choices. Her eyes landed on the green blouse—the one she wore when she first arrived in Perfection. She hadn't let Rose throw away her old clothes. They were the last tangible objects connecting her to a life where she had parents who loved her.

She pulled out a black silk shirt and black jeans. Tied a black scarf in her hair. Sneakers. She stared at her reflection. All black. *A funeral.* She looked paler than usual.

Jamie's voice rang out from downstairs. "Violet! I see the car—they're here!"

Rochester was waiting at the foot of the stairs, watching Jamie race toward the front doors. Violet paused at the top step. She saw Rochester tense, fists half-formed. Then he looked up and saw her.

"All in black, Violet?" he said, eyebrows raised. He smiled to himself. "I think your heroes are here."

My heroes. Her mouth was dry. Her chest fluttered. She couldn't speak.

Rochester waited until she reached him. He glanced at his watch. "Early," he murmured, leaning close. "Can't blame them, can we? They're eager for their reward." He nudged her toward the open door. "Let's meet them on the steps."

Through the doorway, Violet saw the car pull up. Jamie waved both hands like a kid at a parade.

Her legs felt like lead. Rochester glanced at her, grabbed her elbow, and jerked her beside him. She moved away, shoved her hands into her pockets.

Rochester drew closer, resting his hand on her shoulder—just long enough for Lewis to see.

Lewis spotted her the moment he stepped out. He saw Rochester's hand, knew exactly what it meant. But he didn't care. He only saw Violet.

She stared at his chest, then lifted her eyes. For a second, he thought she was glad to see him. But the look vanished. She stared at him like he was a stranger.

Scott bounded up the stairs. "Hey Jamie, man! How you been?"

Rochester watched as Scott and Jamie exchanged some weird handshake.

Helen stepped out, glanced at Lewis—still frozen, still staring at Violet. She walked past him and hugged Violet. "Good to see you, Violet. You okay?" Helen thought she looked pale. Tired. Blue shadows under her eyes.

Violet nodded. "Yeah. And you?"

Lewis clenched his jaw. Helen was in the way. Talking too much. He had no time. Rochester's hand was still on Violet's shoulder, and now he was steering her inside.

"Lead on, Violet. To the lounge," Rochester said. "We'll do the presentations there. Did you organize the refreshments?"

Violet mumbled something. Her lips were dry. She just wanted this over.

Rochester led them into the lounge. He didn't speak, just gestured for them to sit.

Lewis held back, watching Violet. He needed to sit near her. Needed to talk. Not across the room. She sat by the window. Too far away to talk. Lewis cursed under his breath.

Rochester waited until everyone was seated. "Violet, would you…"

Would I what? Her mind blanked. Everyone was staring.

Rochester frowned. "The refreshments, Violet." His voice was light, but the irritation simmered beneath.

"Sorry." Violet crossed the room, passing so close to Lewis he could have grabbed her hand. No one saw him lift a finger from his knee and brush her hand as she passed.

Jamie was telling Scott about the phone Rochester promised him.

"You'll be able to play games with me—if you know how," Jamie teased.

"What! If I know how?" Scott laughed. "That's a challenge you'll regret. I'm the Fortitude champ. Right, Lewis? Beat you every time."

Lewis wasn't listening. He was watching the open doorway, waiting for Violet to come back. She hadn't looked happy to see him—if anything, she looked anxious. And now he couldn't stop worrying. This was going to be harder than he thought.

Violet stood frozen in the kitchen, holding her hand. Had he touched her? She wasn't sure. She squeezed her eyes shut. Nothing had ever felt like this before—her heart pounding in her throat, her brain fogged up like glass in winter.

Rose was already stacking cakes onto the trolley. "I'll bring them in," she said, smiling gently.

Violet didn't move. She could still feel Lewis's eyes on her, like he was willing her to turn around. She rubbed at the centre of her chest.

When she stepped back into the lounge, Rochester was standing with three envelopes in his hand. He waited for her to sit down before he spoke.

"I owe you three an enormous debt of gratitude." He held up the envelopes. "This is a small reward for everything you've done. I can never thank you enough for finding Violet—" He glanced her way and smiled. "—and bringing her safely home. Of course, not forgetting..." He nodded toward Jamie, who was helping himself from the trolley.

Lewis shifted in his seat. *You don't fool me.* He didn't know how much more of this he could take. Then Violet looked at him—and the accusation in her eyes cut straight through. He shook his head. He wanted to yell it. *I never did it for the money. That's not why.* But all he could do was shake his head.

Rochester crossed the room, handing envelopes to Scott and Helen. No protest from them—Scott was practically beaming.

Then Rochester moved to Lewis and held out the last white envelope.

Lewis didn't move. His eyes locked on Violet. *Read my face,* he begged silently. *You have to see it's not true.*

Rochester raised his voice. "And for you, Lewis—just like we agreed—your bonus is double."

The blood roared in Lewis's ears.

"What?" said Scott, pulling out his cheque.

Helen hadn't even opened hers—she was still staring across the room at Lewis.

"There was no agreement," Lewis said, his voice like ice.

"Wasn't there?" Rochester replied smoothly.

"No." Lewis turned to Violet. *Please. Believe me.*

"Oh, I don't usually make that kind of mistake." Rochester waved the envelope in front of him. "Go on. Take it. You earned it." He smiled. "I'm sure Violet agrees."

Violet surged to her feet. *Liar. Liar.* "Yes," she snapped. "He earned every cent." Her eyes were blazing. "Excuse me," she added, voice trembling. "I have to get something from my room."

She brushed past Rochester, fists clenched. She didn't run, but she wanted to. She had to get out of that room. She couldn't breathe with Lewis in it.

"You got double?" Scott said, stunned.

Rochester dropped the envelope into Lewis's lap. Lewis stood. The envelope hit the floor. He didn't care. He only cared about one thing now—Violet. And no one was going to stop him.

Rochester smiled to himself. *Go on. Explain that. Punk.*

At the doorway, Lewis stopped. He turned, eyes blazing. "There. Was. No. Agreement." Each word a hammer on stone.

Violet was halfway up the stairs. She heard him. She didn't stop. "Violet, wait! Just—hear me out!" he called.

She kept going, swiping at her eyes. The tears were hot now. He couldn't see them. She wouldn't let him. She reached her bedroom door. Lewis was right behind her. He followed her in and shut it behind him. She spun around, furious. "Get out."

Lewis lifted his hands, palms out. "Listen—please. This is what he *wants*. He's trying to make you hate me. Don't you get it?"

"You were wrong about him," she said coldly. "I don't believe a word you say." She backed away until her legs hit the bed.

"I'm not wrong about *him*. But you're wrong about *me*." His voice cracked. He took a step forward—then stopped. She was still furious. He shoved his hands into his pockets and closed his eyes, trying to slow his racing heart.

"You *are* wrong about him," she repeated.

Lewis looked at her—really looked—and gave a slow nod. "Okay," he said quietly. "I hear that. Okay." *Let her believe it for now. If that's what she needs.* He nodded again. "Good. That's good, Violet." He gave her a crooked smile and raked a hand through his hair. "That's good," he repeated, voice low.

Violet folded her arms. She didn't believe him—and he could tell.

He leaned against the door. A wave of déjà vu crashed over him. Another bedroom. Violet. Same arms folded. Same fire in her eyes.

She blinked and sank onto the bed.

"This feels familiar," he said, raising an eyebrow.

She remembered. Her fingers curled into the silk brocade bedspread. She couldn't meet his eyes—not without crying.

"Violet, listen." His voice was soft now.

"I know how this sounds. But hear me out. Rochester *did* say there'd be a bonus—if we were successful. We weren't getting paid by the Bureau. It was a mission." He stepped closer, not too close. "But there was *no* agreement like he said. That part's a lie." He looked her straight in the eyes. "Believe me, Violet. I didn't do it for the money. I don't *want* his money. I never did." He exhaled. "I just want you to believe me. Please, Violet."

Violet fell back onto the bed, her arm flung over her eyes. She couldn't look at him. Couldn't trust herself. *What about the lock of hair? Something to remember me by.*

She sat up abruptly. She wasn't ready to talk about that. Not what it meant. Not what it stirred up. "Okay. I believe you. Is that all?" she said flatly.

Lewis heard it in her voice—the distance. The switch flipped. She didn't even look at him as she pushed off the bed and walked to the door.

He didn't move. *Is that all?* What else could there be? If it wasn't about the money... then what *was* it?

Violet ran her fingers through her hair. The elastic on her ponytail was giving her a headache. She tugged it loose. Her red hair spilled over her shoulders like fire. Lewis saw it catch the light—amber and copper and gold. He remembered the first time he saw her. That hair. That pale skin. She hadn't even looked at him—and he'd been wrecked.

Violet gathered her hair up again and twisted the elastic back in place. She stood waiting for Lewis to move from the door. "I have to go back downstairs. My father's expecting me. And your friends... I need to go."

She waited. But he didn't budge. He was staring at her, and she could *see* the hurt in his eyes. He had no right to look hurt. *She* was the one who'd been lied to. *She* was the one who got played. The kisses—she raised a hand and brushed the back of it across her lips. A mistake. Lewis finally stepped aside. She was so close. He could have reached for her. Could have pulled her in. Instead, he caught her hand.

"Wait, Violet. I need to show you something."

She twisted the doorknob.

"It's important," Lewis said, his voice hardening. "At least, I *think* it is. I know you think I lied, but I never lied about… you and me."

Her heart lurched. *You and me.* She shook her head. There is no *you and me.*

"Just let me show you. On my phone. A photo. Please."

She frowned but didn't leave. Lewis scrolled quickly, then held out his phone.

Violet squinted at the screen. A tiny, fuzzy shape curled up on a table. She frowned harder. "What am I looking at?" Lewis glanced at the photo, then back at her.

"It's… you. I mean, it's yours."

He zoomed in. Not a small animal—A curled, reddish lock of hair.

"I had to give it up," he said. "It was the only thing I had to prove who you were. To keep you safe." He tucked the phone back in his pocket. "I didn't want to. It meant something to me, Violet. I wasn't lying." He gave a crooked smile, shifting on his feet.

"And you took a *photo* of it?" Violet wrinkled her nose.

"Yeah. I know. Super weird." He shrugged. "I used to be perfectly sane until I met you."

She raised an eyebrow. "Byron? Darcy?"

Lewis relaxed a little. She wasn't looking at him like he was radioactive anymore.

"Oh, well, there *was* that lightning strike…" He folded his arms and leaned in slightly, his voice soft. "But I was looking at you when it happened."

"No, you weren't. And stop being Byron." She pushed past him. "I've got to go, Lewis."

"Can we talk? Somewhere else? Not here?" He glanced toward the lounge. "Will *he* even let you leave?"

Violet paused at the top of the stairs. "Of course he will. I'm not a prisoner, Lewis." Her voice sharpened again. "He's been very kind. To both of us."

Lewis bit back what he wanted to say. He had to be smart. If she thought this was about taking sides, he'd lose her.

"Good," he said carefully. "Then… when can I take you to see my dad?" He followed her down the stairs. At the bottom, she paused. She wasn't sure she could be alone with him that long. She wasn't ready to let him all the way back in. Not yet. But for the first time since arriving in Perfection… she didn't feel completely lost.

"Soon, I'll call you as soon as I get a phone." she said. She hid the smile tugging at her lips as she stepped back into the lounge.

"There you are, Violet. "Rochester leaned back in his armchair, eyebrows raised like he expected an explanation. He glanced at Lewis standing beside her. His eyes narrowed—then slid away.

***

"Did you get a chance to talk to her?" Helen asked as she turned the car out of Rochester's driveway. She flicked a glance at Lewis in the rearview mirror.

He still looked grim. The dimple in his cheek barely masked the tension in his jaw.

"You didn't?" she said, surprised. They'd been gone long enough for him to stammer out *something*. She'd spent the whole time with Rochester, keeping the conversation going, covering for Lewis while he chased after Violet. She hoped it hadn't been for nothing.

"What did Rochester give you?" Scott asked. His tone had an edge. Helen caught it—resentment. This wasn't going well.

Lewis didn't answer. The envelope Rochester handed him had slipped to the floor, untouched. He was thinking. Hoping Violet would keep her word. *"I'll call you as soon as I get a phone,"* she'd said. He wanted that to mean something. That she'd call *him*. That he'd see her again. Part of him wished he'd never met her. He was falling apart. He should feel better. But now he was hooked.

"You gonna tell us?" Scott asked, glancing over his shoulder.

Lewis frowned. "Yeah. I spoke to her."

"No, not that. The money."

"He doesn't know," Helen said, pulling up at a stop sign. "I've got his envelope. He dropped it. It's in my bag."

"Should've left it there," Lewis muttered. "I'm not interested in a reward."

"Rochester asked me to give it to you. Said to make sure you got it."

Scott tore open the envelope. "Are you kidding me? It's double what we got." He handed it to Lewis. Lewis glanced at the figure, shoved it in his pocket.

"Changed your mind?" Scott's voice dripped sarcasm.

Lewis looked at him from under his brows. He wasn't going to argue. He got it—Scott was angry.

"I'll fix it, Scott. Later, okay? But you both know me. I had no deal with Rochester. He lied." His voice cracked with anger.

Helen stayed quiet, waiting for Scott to respond. Lewis sucked in air through his teeth. "What, you want a lie detector test? I'll take one. Whatever it takes."

Scott's face was pale, eyes blazing. "Sorry, Lew. I believe you. What did Violet say? You think she's safe? She seemed… okay. Jamie said Rochester's buying her a horse."

"A horse?" Lewis repeated. He was glad for the shift. The tension in the car eased.

"Yeah, Jamie wouldn't shut up about it. Rochester's sending him to some fancy school once World Security clears him."

"Did he say when?" Lewis asked.

Helen slowed at a red light. "No, but it matters. Violet's close to Jamie. If Rochester wants her on side, he'll make sure Jamie stays."

Lewis nodded. She was right. But something about Jamie didn't sit right. He didn't think the boy was part of Rochester's plan.

Scott twisted in his seat. "I don't get it. Maybe we were wrong about him."

"That's what I was thinking," Helen said, eyes on the lights.

Lewis felt the anger flare. He unclipped his seatbelt and opened the door. "I need air. I'm walking."

He slammed the door as the light turned red. He wasn't wrong. He just had to prove it. He checked his phone. Walking back would take an hour. He couldn't waste that time. He crossed the street and waited for the bus to the Academy.

***

For two days, Lewis waited for Violet's call. He couldn't focus. "You take the notes, Scott. I'll be in the library."

"What? You always take the notes. I suck at it."

"Get Helen's. She's organized."

Lewis rubbed his eyes. He'd been staring at the screen for hours, digging through articles on genetic modification. The library was about to close. His back ached. He stretched and scrolled again.

"Hi."

The voice broke his concentration. He knew it—Poppy. She'd been sitting in the far corner. He'd made sure not to look her way.

He looked up. She stepped closer. He closed the screen. She glanced at the Academy logo now showing. *Like that, huh?*

She leaned on one hip, clutching her laptop and books. Lewis rested an arm over his notepad. "Hi." His voice was clipped. He wanted her gone. Seeing her didn't feel good. He didn't blame her. He blamed himself. Poppy was dangerous. And now she was standing there like nothing had happened.

"So… what was it like?" Her eyes widened. "Everyone envies you."

He drummed his fingers on the desk, shook his head. "Sorry. It's classified."

"Oh." She pouted. "That's not fair. Everyone knows you went there."

"Yeah, but until we get clearance, no specifics. Sorry." He glanced at the screen. "Okay, when we get clearance."

She didn't leave. He waited. He could feel it—she was going to say something personal.

She hugged her laptop tighter, looked down at her shoes. "I'm sorry. About that night. It was my fault. I was mad at Scott. He was flirting and I wanted to… anyway, it was wrong. I'm sorry."

"Forget it. Equal blame. It's in the past," Lewis said.

"Okay then." She turned to leave. "Hope we can have a drink sometime." She smiled. "When you get that clearance."

"Sure thing." *Not happening.*

He waited until she walked away, then reopened the screen. And there it was. A small article in an obscure journal.

Poppy was still smiling when she passed Lilian on her way out. She wasn't waiting for clearance. Now she just had to find Scott and fix things there. That would be easier—he had a girlfriend now.

An hour later, Lewis left the library, hands deep in his pockets, head down.

He had to know more about the science that vanished the day Violet's mother ran and Advanced Laboratories burned. He'd found a clue. One article. No other references. Three years before Rochester's wife disappeared, Advanced Labs had received approval to take their genetic research to the next level.

He'd read everything he could. Genetic modification was tightly controlled. Government panels. Strict limits. Only for eradicating disorders. Lewis pushed open the cadet club room doors. He knew Scott and Helen would be there in some quiet corner. They were and so was Poppy. He turned to leave—too late. Poppy looked up, raised her glass.

Damn.

He took a step toward them. His phone buzzed. His heart stopped. It was Violet. He turned and walked out, down the tree-lined path toward the dorms.

"Hi," he whispered.

"Hi. Is this a good time to call?"

"Sure. How are you?"

"I'm fine. We're both okay."

Violet was in her bedroom. Rochester had given her the phone two days ago—but she hadn't called until now.

Lewis heard the hesitation in her voice. *How long had she waited to call?*

Behind him, the club doors opened, noise drifting into the evening breeze.

He stepped farther away. "Good to hear," he said. "So, when would be a good time to visit Dad?" Take charge. That's what he needed to do. "How's tomorrow?"

"Tomorrow?"

Violet crossed to the window. The sun was nearly gone, long shadows stretching across the lawn.

"I can pick you up at ten. It'll take a couple hours to get there."

She watched Rochester walking across the lawn, phone to his ear. He paused. Looked up at her window. Turned away. Suddenly, it felt like he might be on *this* call too.

"Okay," she said quickly.

She walked to the bed and sat down. "I'll see you tomorrow then… ten."

Lewis didn't want to hang up. "Wait, I… okay. I've missed you, Violet." He winced. *Idiot.*

Violet closed her eyes and flopped back on the bed. She *had* missed him. But she wasn't ready to forgive him. Not for everything. Not for kidnapping her and Jamie. For taking away her choice.

The silence pounded in his ear.

"Right," he said stiffly. "I'll see you tomorrow, then." It came out like an order. He ended the call and stared at his phone. *She hasn't forgiven me.*

Violet rolled onto her side, knees to her chest. *I missed you.* The words looped in her head. "Stop that," she muttered. She sat up and stormed downstairs to the dining room.

"You're going *where?*" said Rochester, though he'd heard her the first time.

"I'm going with Lewis. To see Mr. Carlyle. At the tracking station."

She lifted her chin. She knew Rochester didn't like Lewis.

"Mmm. I thought we were going to buy you a horse tomorrow."

Violet bit her lip. *How did I forget that?*

"I'm so sorry. I forgot. I can call Lewis back and cancel."

"No, that's alright," he cut in smoothly. "It's important that you have friends here." His tone was mild, but his eyes flicked toward the open door. Jamie stood at the kitchen bench, talking to Dom.

Rochester turned back to Violet and raised his voice. "So, you're going to the *tracking station* with Carlyle?" It came out mocking. Sarcastic. Like Derek.

Violet didn't answer. But her eyes flared green. Rochester saw it. *Yes,* he thought. *I knew I was right about that punk—and the girl.*

"I'm coming!" Jamie yelled from the kitchen.

Perfect, thought Rochester. *Jamie can be the chaperone.* He smiled, glancing between Violet and Jamie, now in the doorway.

"I'm sorry, Jamie," Violet said, wrapping an arm around his shoulder. He was nearly her height. "You know you can't leave the house." She brushed his hair back. "Soon," she said softly. "It'll be soon, won't it?" She looked to Rochester.

"As a matter of fact," he said smoothly, "I just heard this morning." He turned to Jamie and tried to smile. "It was meant to be a surprise."

"Really? I'm a citizen?"

"Of course. You didn't doubt me, did you, Violet?" His puzzled look was too perfect. It made him look annoyed.

Jamie jumped in. "No, we've never doubted you. Have we, Violet?"

"No, of course not." *But she had.*

"Then I can go," Jamie said quickly. "I'm a citizen now."

Rochester raised an eyebrow at Violet. "I'm not sure Violet wants company. Do you, Violet?"

Violet's face went hot. "Of course you can come, Jamie. Mr Carlyle would love to see you."

"Yes, he *would*," said Jamie. "He said he wanted to show *me* the tracking station. Not you."

"That's settled, then," Rochester said. "What time is Carlyle picking you up?"

"Ten o'clock," Violet said.

"Good, good." Rochester nodded. He had two hours to get Jamie's application processed.

Once they were gone, he pulled out his phone and called World Security.

***

Lewis checked the clock. Ten minutes early. He eased the car to a stop at the end of the long driveway. At two minutes to ten, the gates opened.

Jamie was already on the steps. Then Violet appeared beside him. They ran down together. She wasn't smiling. Lewis could feel it—the tension. She knew Rochester was watching.

"Hey, Jamie," Lewis said. "How's it going?"

"I'm coming," Jamie grinned. "I'm a citizen!"

Lewis looked at Violet. "Yes," she said quietly. "Yesterday. My father told us."

"Wow. Great news. Dad will be pleased to see you, Jamie."

Violet hesitated, then stepped toward the car. "Jamie, hop in the back," Lewis said quickly, opening the passenger door for Violet. "I want to talk to Violet."

Violet slid in. She didn't look at him. Her hands were clenched on her knees.

"Seatbelt," Lewis said, stepping on the accelerator. The car lurched forward. "Sorry—not my car. It's Helen's."

"You don't have a car?"

"Motorbike. Figured that wasn't a good idea." *And I wanted to talk to you.*

"No, I don't think my father would have liked that."

Lewis nodded. *I bet he doesn't like you being with me either.*

Almost like she read his mind, Violet said, "I was supposed to go out with him this morning. I forgot. But he said it was okay. He… thinks I should have friends."

Lewis nodded again. "Mmm. Good."

"He does," Violet said firmly.

Lewis didn't answer. He didn't trust Rochester. But if he argued now, he'd only push her away. He had to get her trust back. Without forcing it.

"So where were you going with Roch—your father?" he asked, trying to sound casual.

"He was going to buy me a horse."

"A horse?"

"Yes. He's got stables. We went riding the other day… I liked it."

"Great," said Lewis, though it didn't feel great at all. It felt like she was slipping further away.

The car fell into silence. Sunlight flickered through the trees. Lewis cleared his throat. "How's Perfection treating you, Jamie?"

"Haven't seen much. I've been confined to barracks. Until today." He grinned. "Veedad's finding me a school. A real posh one too."

"Veedad?" Lewis looked at Violet.

She shrugged. "That's what Jamie calls him. Not to his face."

"I bet he wouldn't mind," Jamie said from the back.

"What about you, Violet? School?"

She shook her head. "No. Home schooling. Private tutors, just to get me through the final year."

"And after that? What's the plan?" He was asking too many questions. Violet stared out the window at the sprawling houses. Huge, rambling things set back from the road, each surrounded by perfect lawns.

Lewis followed her gaze. "Millionaires' Row," he said.

"Yeah, that's us too," Jamie chimed in. "We're probably multi-billionaires. Trillionaires. Billion-trillionaires. Or tril.."

"Shut up, Jamie," Violet snapped.

"Why? I bet Lewis is a millionaire now that he's got the reward. What did you get?"

"Jamie, that's rude. You know better," Violet said, biting her lip. She didn't want to think about the reward.

Lewis gripped the steering wheel tighter. He knew the amount. He'd wanted to send the cheque back to Rochester—but he'd banked it. His plan was to share it, and he would."

"You should have bought a car," Violet said flatly.

Lewis didn't answer. He wanted to change the subject, but nothing came. A weight pressed against his chest.

"Look!" Jamie leaned forward, thrusting his wrist past Lewis. "It's a Sixty-Six. Veedad gave it to me. I can play games on it. And look—" He swiped the screen.

"Lewis is driving," Violet said sharply. "Show him later."

But Lewis wasn't listening. A chill ran down his spine. He knew what that watch could do. *The bastard's tracking us.*

"Great watch," Lewis said lightly. "I had one, but it broke. Lightning strike." It hadn't. But once he knew Rochester could track him through it, he never wore it again.

"What? It's supposed to be indestructible," said Jamie.

"Took a fierce hit," Lewis said. "Didn't totally destroy it."

Violet glanced at him. Her cheek dimpled as a memory surfaced. That weird boy, standing in front of the glass cabinet at school. Lewis raised an eyebrow.

"Byron," he murmured. They both laughed.

Warmth bloomed in Lewis's chest. Maybe everything would be alright— But then he remembered - Rochester was probably listening to every word.

Violet broke the silence. "There's a library at the house. The same books my mother had back at... the other place." Her voice grew soft.

"Do you miss it? Them? Mona and Derek?"

"No. Not them. But I… it's…" she shrugged. "It's complicated. He's been good to Jamie and me," she added quickly.

"You feel like a fish out of water?"

Violet sighed. He got it. She didn't need to explain. "Yeah. A small fish, and a whole lot of water."

"Speaking of water…" Lewis crested the hill, and the view exploded into the blue stretch of ocean.

"Are we going to stop?" Violet asked.

"Yes. There." Lewis pointed at a grey stone building perched near the edge of the sea. "Bydard Castle. Oldest building in Perfection. Dates back to the Bydard invaders."

"Never heard of them," Jamie said.

Lewis laughed. "Different history books in your world." He turned to Violet. "Want to take a look? We've got time. Dad's not expecting us till lunch."

Then over his shoulder, "Jamie? You'll have to walk. No cars allowed on the approach. It's steep."

Jamie leaned forward. "That's a Motte and Bailey castle! The round stone tower, the teeth-shaped battlements—those are called crenels. That big square bit is the living quarters."

Lewis glanced at Violet, impressed. "He knows a lot," she murmured.

"It's interesting," Jamie said defensively.

"Ditto, Jamie. I love castles. How many have you seen?" said Lewis smiling.

"None. This is my first!"

"Alright," Lewis said. "There's a car park down the road. I'll drop you here, Jamie. Save us a spot in the queue—it's popular."

As Jamie stepped out, Lewis added, "You can use your Sixty-Six to measure the incline. I think that's a feature."

"It can do everything," Jamie said proudly.

Once Jamie was gone, Lewis turned to Violet. "Do you have a Sixty-Six too?"

She shook her head. "No. But my father gave me this phone." She pulled it from her purse. It looked normal. But Lewis knew better. It could track her. Monitor everything.

"Here." She held it out.

Lewis didn't want to touch it. Instead, he watched the rearview mirror as he backed into a space.

Suddenly, a shrill bell tone rang. Violet nearly dropped the phone. Lewis clenched his jaw. *Rochester. I bet.*

Violet answered. "Hello? Oh. Jamie's just ahead. We're visiting a castle… Bydard Castle, yes." She glanced at Lewis. "My father wants to talk to you," she said, holding out the phone.

Lewis stared at it like it was a ticking bomb. He didn't move.

"He wants to talk to you," Violet hissed.

Reluctantly, Lewis took it. "Hello?" Nothing but buzzing static. "Hello?" he repeated. Still static. Lewis shrugged and handed it back. "No answer."

"He probably hung up," Violet muttered, dropping it into her purse.

Lewis reached up, touching the metal dot behind his ear. Warm. He brushed his hair back, eyes narrowing. "You look ravishing," he said, a crooked smile on his lips.

Violet was halfway out of the car. She froze. "What did you say?"

Lewis got out of the car and walked towards Violet, his eyes were glinting with some unspoken purpose.

"What did you say?" Violet demanded. She held her hand up to keep him away.

What did I say? He shoved his hands into his pockets, clenched his jaw. He couldn't trust himself to look at Violet. The light on her hair, her emerald green eyes. *Don't say it.* He spoke slowly as though he'd forgotten how to.

"Said you look ravenous. Repast….something to eat." Lewis shook his head he couldn't stop looking at her lips. He knew he was going to say something he'd regret.

***

Rochester smiled into the phone, he almost laughed. He turned it off and slipped into his pocket. *That's finished the punk.*

Lewis ran to catch up with Violet. What had he said? He groaned. *Idiot, idiot.* "Violet wait."

She didn't stop. She blinked back the tears. She waited for him at the entrance to the Castle. "So sorry Violet," he forced himself to look at her feet. He couldn't trust himself to speak. Violet narrowed her eyes. He was bowing, "Beg your…"

"Shut up," Violet slashed the air with her hand. "Don't speak. I don't like you acting like Byron."

Byron! No fucking way. Rochester. The phone. He grabbed Violet by the arm. "Can't talk," he whispered hoarsely. It took an effort to get the words out.

He pointed to the entrance to the Castle. He couldn't talk. Violet looked sideways at him. His face was white. His jaw tense. His lips a hard line. His head felt weird. He recognised that weirdness. He felt sick, his head was buzzing, a low steady white noise.

Violet tried to pull her arm away. Lewis gripped his fingers harder, He couldn't let her go. Lewis searched for his wallet with his free hand. Found it and thrust it at Jamie. "Pay," he said through gritted teeth.

"You're hurting," said Violet. Lewis let go of her arm and put his hand on her shoulder. She could feel him trembling. She glanced sideways. He looked like death. He swayed. She slipped her arm around his waist.

A couple turned and stared. The man raised his eyes at Violet in a question. He didn't like the way Lewis gripped her arm. Violet shook her head at him.

"Clorinda," he gasped. The light suddenly went out.

"Stand back Give him some air." Someone cried.

"Does he need CPR" said Jamie, "I did that at school."

Lewis opened his eyes and pushed himself up onto one elbow. Violet was kneeling by his side. He looked at Violet his eyes pleading for help.

"He's okay," she said. "Low blood sugar. He does this often. Here can you stand?"

Someone helped him up. Lewis grunted, "Obliged." Violet thanked the man.

"Jamie, you buy the tickets. We'll wait on that bench." She helped Lewis move to a bench against the stone wall.

Lewis held his head in his hands. The ocean pounded the rocks below. He touched the spot behind his ear. It was hot.

"Why?" Violet said, "I thought it was fixed."

Why? Helen had disabled it. He was supposed to have had it removed. No time. He was a fool. Something had triggered it. He groaned his brain wasn't working.

"Was fixed, something amiss, something…" the effort too much.

Jamie came back with the tickets. Lewis waved him away.

"Go…Jamie. Violet castle. I'll sojourn here…until…"

"You what?" Jamie's brows met in the middle.

"He'll wait here until he feels better and then he'll find us." Violet said.

Lewis reached out and squeezed her hand, "Go." He didn't move until they were at the Castle entrance. Violet glanced back and lifted her hand.

She stood at the castle gates, a last farewell….shut up! He shook his head. Words were forcing their way into his thoughts. He took out his phone and called Scott.

"What's up?"

"Problem, need assistance." His voice sounded thin and distant..

"Yeh what kind of problem?"

"Problem," Lewis said more firmly.

"Yeh, I heard you. What is it? Talk. I'm in the supermarket."

Lewis tried to form the words; they rushed at him. "Damnation!" he shouted.

Scott stared at the phone, *Damnation?* "Okay, what's up?"

Lewis screwed his eyes up. "Listen, you nincompoop. I'm….Byron." He shouted into the phone.

"Byron? What?"

"BYRON," Lewis shouted hoarsely.

"How…how. You had it removed the translator…."

"Forgot. Too busy."

"What enabled it?"

Lewis struggled for the words. "Earpiece. Violet's. Rochester. No words, just infernal noise."

Scott scrambled to make sense of it. "Earpiece? Violet's?"

"Yes. On. It. Now." He emphasised each word.

"The phone!" said Scott triumphantly. "Phone activated it. Rochester did it. Okay got it. Stay put, I'll get help." He made a call.

Helen jumped out of her car and ran to Scott. She was holding a small silver case. Scott recognised it. He raised his eyes at her.

"Never gave it back." Scott stared. "No one asked for it. Souvenir. Here. Call him."

The phone rang twice. Lewis answered, "Yes." His voice clipped.

"It's Helen. This might work." Helen brought the transmitter close to Scott's phone. It was sending a signal.

Lewis closed his eyes. White noise roared down the phone. An explosion in his head. He reached for the wall and fell. The silence engulfed him. "Fuck." He said. He wiped the sweat from his face.

"Say something else. Where are you and where is Jamie and Violet?" said Helen.

"At the Castle" his voice cracked.

"Good. You sound Okay. I'll hand you back to Scott."

"The bastard," said Scott. "You sure it was him?"

"Yeh. No doubt." He wiped the sweat from his brow.

"Why?" The words were coming.

"Make me sound like a fucking idiot in front of Violet. Can't think of any other reason. He must have known. I hadn't had it removed. I'll just keep away from Violet's phone and Jamie's Sixty-six – Rochester gave him one."

"And did you?" said Scott."

"Did I what?"

"Sound like a dick."

"Yeh… no… probably." He grimaced at the thought. "She doesn't realise it was Rochester. I can't tell her and burst that bubble…not yet."

"What you going to do now?"

"Rochester's monitoring her. Listening in….so keep making an idiot of myself until I get to the Academy and get it removed.'

"Who's helping Rochester…Monk? "

"Don't know. Could be. Figure it out. Stop talking now." He could see Jamie and Violet leaving the castle entrance."

"Just like the castles at home." Said Jamie,

"Not impressed." Said Lewis raising one brow.

Violet narrowed her eyes, "You okay?"

"Excellent," he crooked his arm, "shall we depart." Violet shot a wide-eyed warning look. Lewis mumbled something and put his hands in his pockets.

They walked back to the car in silence. As they reached it, Violet caught his arm, leaning close. Her whisper barely carried. "We should go back. You should get it sorted." Then, louder for Jamie's sake: "We can come another day to see your father."

"Oh no," Jamie piped up. "Lewis is fine now, aren't you? Don't let's go home. I want to see the tracking station."

"Excellent health," Lewis said, flashing Violet a blinding smile as he opened the door. Her stomach flipped. It's not him, she thought. He can't help it. Jamie filled the back seat with chatter, rattling off castle history in obsessive detail.

Lewis kept his eyes on the road. If he was going to fool Rochester, he needed to sound like Byron. All he could dredge up was that line from DZ—some woman calling him mad, bad, and dangerous to know. Not exactly useful. Poetry. He needed poetry.

The car crested a hill. Below, rows of lavender spilled across the fields, the distant hills drowned in violet haze. Lewis cleared his throat. "Yonder mist-covered hills, their beauty clothed behind a silken veil of purplish mist—"

"A silken veil of misty purple," Violet corrected softly.

Lewis grinned. "A veil of misty silken purple."

"Lavender?" Violet teased.

"It's blue," said Jamie, leaning forward. "Light properties. Scattering molecules. That's why the sky's blue."

Lewis laughed. "Not a poetic bone in his body. As I was saying—before my muse was interrupted—"

"Do one line, I'll do the next," Violet said. Lewis reached for her hand and squeezed it, silent thanks.

The security gates of the Tracking Station lifted without a hitch. Jamie leapt from the car before it stopped. "Wait for it to stop, you brat," Lewis muttered, stomping the brake.

"Violet, how are you?" John's voice carried across the drive. "You both look well. I can see your father's looking after you."

"Yeah," Jamie said, bouncing. "We've got a cook. No—a chef. He makes anything I ask for. Mostly no meat." He grimaced. "Still tastes good though."

John laughed, ruffling Jamie's hair. "Easy to please, then." His eyes flicked to Lewis, a warning in them. Fear. Something that needed saying alone. You two head inside," John told Violet and Jamie. "Lunch is ready." Then to Jamie: "No comparisons, alright?" Lewis jerked his head toward the car and followed John back down the garden path, away from the house.

"How are you, Lewis?" John asked once they'd reached the car. Lewis glanced back, making sure Violet and Jamie weren't within earshot. Then he spoke quickly, spilling what had happened.

"Bastard," John spat, the word sharp and sudden.

"Got to keep up the pretence," Lewis said. "Make him think I'm still affected." His brow furrowed. "But the bigger problem—someone at the Academy must be helping him. He knew I hadn't had it removed."

"And he knew how to switch it on. But all that, just to make you look a fool?"

Lewis shrugged. "Why else?"

John's hand closed over his shoulder. "After lunch, lie down. Say you're unwell. I'll show Violet and Jamie around. Buy you a little reprieve from playing Byron."

Three hours later, they were finally heading home. Jamie fell asleep approximately three seconds after the car left the tracking station—classic.

Lewis, meanwhile, hadn't exactly been lounging around while Jamie geeked out with his dad. He'd been glued to his phone, whispering updates to Scott and Helen.

Scott had already spoken to Monk. "His reaction seemed legit. Called you a damned idiot, said he warned you to get it removed. Basically, you brought this on yourself."

"Wow, thanks for the pep talk, Scott. Any word on the lab?"

"Yeah, Monk sorted it. You're heading straight there."

"You didn't mention Rochester, did you?"

"Of course not. We haven't crossed Monk off the suspect list yet."

Violet glanced over. "You okay?"

He nodded. "Why?"

"You're quiet. Is your head acting up again?"

Before he could answer, Violet's phone rang. Lewis flinched. Rochester. Had to be.

"It's my father," she said, already answering. Lewis subtly leaned away, like her phone might bite.

"We're heading home now. Yes, it was interesting. No, everything's fine. Did you want to speak to Lewis?"

Lewis's heart did a full-body slam. He waved frantically, shaking his head like a man possessed.

"Sorry," Violet said, dropping the phone into her bag. "I forgot."

"No apologies necessary, Clorinda," Lewis muttered, his head pounding in sync with his pulse.

Rochester was listening. He could feel it. And if the man wanted theatrics, Lewis would give him a show. Violet thought he couldn't help himself—so he leaned in.

"I can't sleep for thinking about you," he said, voice low and dramatic. "You invade my dreams. Do I haunt yours?" He smiled, barely. It felt fake, but also real. He wanted to know.

"Be quiet, Lewis. You'll wake Jamie—and he doesn't need to hear your romantic nonsense."

"But I mean it," Lewis said, pressing the accelerator. He needed to get them home. Fast. Before he cracked.

"I know why you're saying all this," Violet hissed. "Don't forget that."

Lewis clenched his jaw. "Of course I do," he drawled. "You've bewitched me. Your beauty, your charms—"

"Shut up! Don't speak. Doesn't this car have a radio? Use it."

Lewis flicked it on, letting the static fill the silence. His shoulders dropped for the first time all day.

When they reached the Rochester mansion gates, Violet asked, "Are you going to be alright?"

Lewis didn't answer. He wasn't driving up to the house. Not with Rochester possibly lurking. He got out, circled the car, and opened her door.

"Of course I'll be alright," he said, taking her hand with theatrical flair. Then, before she could protest, he kissed her—quick, soft, gone in a blink.

It was a performance. Byron would've done it. And Lewis had wanted to.

Violet gasped, stepping back.

"I hope to see you again soon, Violet. For another... jaunt."

"I'll call you," she said, lips still tingling.

CHAPTER THIRTY-TWO

Lewis didn't waste time. He headed straight to the tech lab the moment he got back to the Academy. Scott was already there, pacing the floor.

"All set," Scott said. "Monk pulled strings."

Lewis nodded, barely. Inside, he sat stiffly as the technician prepped the headgear. The robot arm loomed overhead, humming like it had opinions.

Minutes later, Lewis emerged looking like he'd seen a ghost—or maybe been one.

Scott threw an arm around him. "How you doing, buddy?"

Lewis exhaled hard. "Never again." He touched the spot above his ear, half-expecting a crater.

"They seal it as they remove it," Scott said, trying for reassuring. "That's what they told me."

Lewis didn't look convinced.

"Okay. What's next?" Said Scott.

"Two things: figure out who's helping Rochester—and find Callum. I think I've got a lead. Dug up something in the library archives."

"What kind of something?"

"I'll tell you later," Lewis said quickly. The fewer people who knew, the better. He trusted Scott, but Scott trusted Helen—and Lewis wasn't ready to go there.

Scott dropped his arm, shoved his hands into his pockets. "Fine by me."

"Help me find Callum," Lewis said, catching the edge in Scott's voice.

"Where do we start?"

"Monk. He said they'd been monitoring Callum's phone. He must know something."

"Leave it with me," Scott said, checking his watch. "Meeting Helen. I'll get her on it too."

Lewis nodded and started toward the library. His phone buzzed. Violet. He smiled. "Hey."

"Hi. You okay?"

"Yeah, headache's gone. When can we meet? Helen and Scott want to hang out again. There's a band playing in the city tomorrow night—actual music, not whatever Rochester calls culture. I could pick you up at five, grab dinner, hit the gig. What d'you think?"

"I'd like that," Violet said..

"Done. See you then."

Lewis hung up, knowing full well Rochester would hear every word.

Violet stared at her phone, wishing the call had lasted longer. She could feel it—Lewis was slipping back into her heart, and she wasn't stopping it.

She tossed the phone onto the bed and peeled off her riding clothes. She'd been out with the horse Rochester bought her.

It was big like Vector, but mellow. No sudden lunges, no wild eyes. Rochester didn't do risk—not with Violet.

He'd watched her from the paddock fence, arms folded, eyes calculating. Stewart jogged beside her, trying to keep up. Rochester noted her posture, her grip, the way she held herself.

Not bad. With effort, I might grow quite fond of her.

His watch blinked red. Violet had used her phone. He raised his own to his ear, listening.

His lip curled. So that didn't work.

He pulled out his phone and made a call. Time for Plan B. Lewis had to go—and this one should do the trick.

"So, where are you off to, Violet?" Rochester's tone was casual, but his eyes were anything but.

She stood at his office door, swinging her bag at her feet like she was trying not to bolt. Her hair was loose. Blue jeans. Cream cable-knit sweater. Of course. Always jeans. He disapproved—except today. Today, jeans meant Lewis. And Rochester didn't trust Lewis.

"I'm going to see a band. Lewis invited me this morning. He's going with some friends."

Rochester tilted his head, eyes narrowing. "Hope his girlfriend Poppy doesn't mind."

Violet's stomach dropped. Her heart leapt into her throat.

She stared at him. "Girlfriend?"

"Didn't you know?" His voice was syrupy with fake sympathy. "She used to be Scott's girl. Until Lewis stole her."

Violet's fingers clenched around her bag strap. Her chest burned.

"He's just a friend," she said, turning fast before he could see her eyes shimmer.

Girlfriend. Didn't you know? The words echoed, sharp and cruel.

She walked slowly to the front door, down the steps. Lewis was waiting by the car, smiling like nothing had happened.

"Right on time," he said, then instantly regretted it.

"Yes," Violet replied, stiff as steel. She reached for the door. Lewis jumped to open it, trying to read her face.

He could tell something was wrong. He started the car, silence stretching between them like fog.

"Did you follow any bands back in DZ?" he asked, trying to sound casual.

Violet flinched. She hated that nickname. "In Australia?"

"Yeah. Sorry. Back there. Any bands you liked?"

"A few. Mostly indie. Doubt you've heard of them."

"Try me."

"Post Notes?"

"Nope."

"Collected Thoughts?"

"Still nope."

"Crushed Hearts?"

Lewis raised an eyebrow. "Sounds tragic. Were they all heartbreak and doom?"

"One of my favourites, actually. Not depressing. The lead singer named it after his girlfriend…" She bit her lip. "She slept with his best friend."

Lewis blinked. "She what?"

"Doesn't matter." Violet turned to the window.

But it did matter. Whatever it was had shut her down. The air in the car dropped from cool to ice.

"That's the Law Courts," Lewis said, pointing to a granite building glowing pink in the sunset.

"Beautiful," Violet murmured.

"Granite from the north. They limit mining to protect the landscape." He pointed again. "That dome ahead? State Theatre."

"Looks like a church," Violet said.

Lewis kept talking, naming buildings, filling the silence. The sky darkened. City lights flickered on.

He'd lied. No Scott. No Helen. He'd tell her soon. Hopefully she'd forgive him.

"That building with the blue lights? That's us."

He turned off the main street and drove down into the underground lot. Past empty bays. Down, down, down—six levels underground.

"Why here?" Violet asked, uneasy.

Lewis didn't answer. He checked his phone. No reception. Good.

"Yours working?" he asked.

"Didn't bring it," Violet said.

Lewis laughed, hollow. "Damn."

"Sorry," she said. "Will yours work outside?"

"Yeah." He turned to face her. He had to fix this.

"Violet, I don't know what to say to make you trust me. But I need you to."

She didn't answer.

"Yesterday felt right. Didn't it?" He didn't wait. "If it was the Byron thing—I need to explain."

Violet leaned away, pressing into the door. "You don't owe me anything," she said, voice cold.

"That. That wall you're putting up. Just tell me what I did."

Violet blinked. Tears threatened. She opened the door, ducked her head back in. "Your girlfriend!"

"My what?" Lewis jumped out, caught her arm.

"Let go," she snapped, eyes blazing.

"Sorry. But you're the only one I want. I don't have a girlfriend."

"Then who's Poppy?" Violet asked quietly.

"Poppy? No. Never. Not even close." He shoved his hands in his pockets. "I'm not good at this, Violet. Wish I was more like that twat Byron."

Violet wiped her eyes. Lewis pulled her into his arms.

"I want it to be you, Violet. Always have."

"Liar," she whispered into his chest.

"Okay, maybe not the first second. But close."

"I don't know who told you about Poppy, but I want to explain. Okay?"

Violet lifted her head. She didn't smile. But she nodded. "Okay."

"Let's sit. Band's not till ten. And… no Scott and Helen."

Violet shook her head, but she was glad they hadn't come.

They sat in the car while Lewis told her everything.

"And that's all I've got on Poppy," he said, looking into the greenest eyes he'd ever seen. "I think she's trouble. I don't trust her. Told Scott that this afternoon. I looked for her today but couldn't find her. She's off campus. But when she's back—I'll sort it."

"Okay," Violet said.

Lewis frowned. "Who told you about Poppy?"

"It was my father. You said he knew about the argument with Scott. I think he was protecting me." She added quickly. She knew what Lewis thought about her father.

Lewis ground his teeth. If Rochester was protecting Violet, it wasn't for the right reasons.

Lewis smoothed his hands around the steering wheel, debating whether to say it. Whether to tell her what he suspected — that Rochester was recording her every move, every word.

"I know you don't like him," Violet said quietly. "But he's done nothing wrong. He's been—"

"—Yeah, I know. Kind." Lewis cut in, voice tight. "Violet, I just want you to keep an open mind about what I'm going to say. You don't have to believe it. Just… allow for the possibility. Okay?"

She studied him. He looked like he'd just heard something awful.

"Okay," she said, cautious.

Lewis took a breath. "I think it was your father who activated the assimilator in my head. Made me act like Byron. And I think he did it through your phone."

Violet blinked. "My phone?"

"It happened right after you said Rochester wanted to talk to me. You remember?"

She nodded slowly. "Yes. But you didn't speak to him."

"No. There was just static. That's when it happened. It must be."

"Couldn't that be a coincidence?" Her voice was small. A dread like black fog pressed down on her. She didn't want it to be her father. She wanted things to work — for her, for Jamie. For Lewis to be part of it.

"No." Lewis leaned forward. "I called Scott while you and Jamie were exploring the castle. Pure luck — Helen had kept the transmitter switch. Said it was a souvenir. She held it to Scott's phone and it worked."

Violet pressed her fingers to her temples. "It sounds…" She closed her eyes. "It sounds mad."

Lewis reached for her hand. She let him take it. Her fingers were ice.

"I know it sounds impossible. But Violet, I know it happened."

"It is crazy." She pulled her hand away. "Why? You don't know the answer to that, do you?"

Lewis heard the fear in her voice. He didn't blame her. She was scared. And he got that.

He was close to understanding — if he could just talk to Callum. But he couldn't tell her yet. Not now.

"Let's get out of the car," he said, opening the door. "We need air."

They stood in silence as the lift carried them to ground level. Violet watched her reflection in the mirrored walls, her face just visible behind Lewis's shoulder.

He turned, eyes full of concern. "You okay?"

She couldn't speak. She shook her head, pressing her forearm to her face as tears welled. Her legs buckled.

Lewis caught her, arms around her shoulders, pulling her close. She trembled against him.

"Violet, don't cry," he whispered into her hair. "Don't cry. It's going to be okay. Promise."

She was still crying when the lift doors opened. Heaving sobs, like her heart was breaking.

An older couple waiting outside stared. Lewis ignored them, eyes straight ahead. He wrapped his arm around Violet and guided her past, out into the street.

The night air was cool. The street buzzed with young people. Violet muffled her crying behind her hand.

"Let's cross," Lewis said gently. "We'll walk down to the foreshore. It's not far."

He took her hand, threading through traffic. He cursed himself. He shouldn't have said anything about Rochester. He was a fool. Should have waited. Gotten proof.

Lights from the boats flickered across the dark, oily river. They sat in silence as the wind curled around them. A boat passed on the far side. People moved on deck, silhouettes in the glow. Music drifted across the water.

"That sounds like a fun party," Violet said, trying to break the silence. Trying to show him she was okay.

She'd looked after herself for years. And just when she thought she could stop worrying — that someone might take care of her and Jamie — Lewis was unravelling it.

Lewis looked up. A party. He was glad he wasn't there.

"I hate parties," he said. "Wouldn't find that fun."

Violet glanced at him. He wasn't joking. His profile was sharp, serious.

"What's to hate?" she asked.

Lewis turned to her. "Everything. Drunk people. Boring conversations. People pretending to care."

She clasped her hands in her lap. That wasn't what she wanted to talk about.

"Tell me why you think my father had the Bureau send you to bring me here. To this world." She gestured wide.

Lewis hesitated. He owed her an answer. But he wasn't ready. Not yet.

"I need to talk to Callum first," he said. "Then I'll know."

Violet frowned. "Callum?"

Lewis looked at her. "He worked for Rochester. Are you ever sick?" The words came fast.

She blinked. "What?"

"Are you ever sick?" he repeated.

"No. But I've got a good immune system," she said.

Lewis didn't respond. But something in his expression shifted — like he'd just confirmed a theory he wasn't ready to share.

"Have you ever been sick?" Lewis asked.

Violet blinked. "I've thrown up. Food poisoning."

"That's different," he said. "That's your body reacting to something toxic. But I bet you've never had a fever. A cough. A cold. The flu still kills people in your world."

"So?" She shrugged. "Just lucky, I guess. Good genes or something." Her brow furrowed. "Is that it?"

She stood. A chill crept over her skin. Lewis watched her, silent. He wasn't explaining himself, and she could feel the tension building.

She turned to face him. "I thought no one in Perfection got sick."

Lewis ran a hand through his hair. He didn't know how far to take this. He stood and walked toward her. Her arms were bare. He thought he saw her shiver.

"You're cold," he said. "Let's get out of the wind." He took her hand, slipping it into his pocket.

"I still get cold. I guess I could freeze to death."

"Judging by this block of ice in my pocket? Definitely a possibility."

Violet wiggled her fingers. They were warming.

Rochester stood in Violet's room, staring at the phone lying in the middle of her bed.

He swore loudly, pulled out his own phone, and made a call.

Jamie heard it from the next room. The door between them was ajar. He'd just taken off his headphones after two hours of research, trying to catch up before school started.

Veedad was the best not-your-real-dad you could ask for. He didn't care if Jamie stayed glued to his computer all day. Violet disagreed.

Jamie knew she was looking out for him. He also knew Rochester didn't have to be so cruel — not like this morning, when he'd snapped at Violet.

"You're not his mother," Rochester had said coldly. "Or his guardian. I am, Violet. Not you."

It was nearly 1 a.m. when Lewis pulled the car to a stop at the edge of Rochester's street. He turned off the engine. Silence settled between them.

"Thanks," Violet said at last. "It was a great evening."

She'd already told him how much she loved the band. They'd talked music the whole way home.

She'd mentioned songs she used to listen to — ones Lewis had never heard.

"I might be able to access the DZ archives," he'd said. "They update them all the time. Just give me a list."

"Is that possible?"

He wasn't sure. But her excitement made him want to make it possible.

"Sure," he said, leaving no room for doubt.

"When can I see you again?" he asked. He wanted to see her every day.

Violet smiled into the dark. Lewis leaned in. She met him halfway. Their lips touched, soft and searching. He cupped her face in his hands. His lips traced hers. Violet pressed her palms to his chest. She could feel his heart pounding beneath her fingers. A voice in her head whispered: *Stop. You know what happens next.*

But it was Lewis who pulled away.

"Killing me, Violet," he said, hand over his heart. "This is beating out of my chest."

Violet gave a shaky laugh. "Mine too."

"Good," he said. "I don't want to be the only one who's…"

He didn't finish. A car pulled up behind them. Light flooded the interior. Lewis checked the rear-view mirror.

"Rochester," he said through gritted teeth.

"Oh," Violet breathed. She twisted in her seat, fumbling for the door. "I'd better get out."

Lewis said nothing. He opened his door and stepped out.

Rochester was walking toward them. His face was hidden in shadow, backlit by his headlights.

"A little late, isn't it, Violet?" he said. "It's past one. You didn't answer your phone. I was worried."

Lewis didn't hear concern. He heard accusation. "My fault, sir," Lewis said. "I should have told Violet the band didn't start until ten."

Rochester ignored him. "Get in my car, Violet. I assume you've had plenty of time to say goodnight." He turned and walked away.

Violet's face flushed. She was glad it was dark. But the old anger flared — he sounded just like Mona.

She straightened her shoulders and glanced at Lewis. The headlights caught his eyes. He gave her a look: *Be careful.*

He looked fierce. Like some avenging angel. Lewis placed a hand over his heart and bowed.

Violet couldn't help it — she laughed.

Rochester spun around, face tight with fury. "You find this funny, Violet?"

"Sorry, sir. My fault."

"Really," he said, voice thick with sarcasm. "Seems everything is your fault tonight."

Lewis didn't respond. He knew better.

"I'll pick you up tomorrow. Same time?" he said and walked back to his car.

Violet didn't want to get in with her father. He had no right to be that angry. She was eighteen. She could stay out all night if she wanted.

Rochester didn't speak until they reached the house.

"I was worried about you, Violet," he said softly. "I tried to call. When you didn't answer, I thought the worst."

He took a shuddering breath. Brushed at his eyes. "You'll think that's foolish of me, I know."

Violet touched his arm. "No, I don't." Her eyes filled. *He really cares about me.*

Rochester smiled. "Just keep your phone with you. For my peace of mind. Now off you go. I'll see you in the morning. I've got news for you and Jamie."

Violet ran upstairs. Stripped off her clothes. Brushed her teeth. Crawled into bed.

She lay on her back, staring into the dark. She tried to see it from her father's side. Of course he'd be worried. That made sense. Didn't it? But then the phone. Lewis said it was tracking her. Recording everything. She remembered handing it to him at Bydard Castle. Was it a coincidence? It had to be. It was too weird. She turned her face into the pillow.

She wanted to trust Lewis more than anything.

CHAPTER THIRTY-THREE

Lewis looked at Scott's lecture notes, closed his laptop, and sighed. He'd have to do the reading himself. Scott's notes were next to useless—vague, scattered, full of holes. He checked his phone. Missed text from Scott.

Meet me on the oval.

He was about to leave when Scott jogged up.

"Sorry. Frosby ran over. Bored us all to death."

"Why did you need to see me?"

"I found Callum."

Lewis straightened. "Where?"

"World Security. His brother too."

"Monk told you?"

Scott grinned. "Nope. I did some digging. Used my charm."

"Charming to who?"

"The women, Lewis. Monk's secretary, Sylvia. She likes me. I might ask her out."

"What? Aren't you with Helen?"

"I am," Scott said, grinning wickedly.

Lewis rolled his eyes. "How long are they being held?"

"No clue. Both families were found two days ago on an island in the South Sea. Claimed they were on holiday. Total coincidence they left the day Violet made headlines."

"What about Rochester? Any leads?"

Scott shook his head. "Drew a blank."

"Thanks for the info. I need to talk to Callum before Rochester does whatever he's planning with Violet."

Scott looked down, scraping the grass with his toe. "You think you might—"

"Be wrong? Not a chance," Lewis snapped. "I'd bet my life on it."

"Okay. It's just... he's not stopping you from seeing her."

"He can't afford to. He needs Violet to trust him. And I need her to trust me more. Rochester's playing the long game."

They walked back toward the main campus.

"Have you seen Poppy?" Scott asked.

Lewis stopped. "Poppy? Why would I?"

"She said she saw you the other night."

"Oh, that. In the library. She came over, apologized... that was it."

"Not what she told me," Scott said. "Asked if I'd mind if you two went out."

"What?! That's crap. I barely said two words to her. Maybe I said we could grab a drink, just to be polite. That's all. She's trouble."

"Better steer clear then."

"Yeah. No. I'll deal with it. Make sure she knows where I stand. No time now though. Picking up Violet in thirty."

"Your plan must be working."

"No plan," Lewis said, and jogged off.

CHAPTER THIRTY-FOUR

Rochester was already seated in the dining room when Violet and Jamie arrived. He hadn't joined them for breakfast since the second day. Mornings, he claimed, required silence—and Jamie, apparently, didn't come with a mute button.

So many questions. Rochester had nearly choked on his tea when Jamie asked if there was another Jamie and Violet in Perfection. He'd covered it with a laugh. "I hope not. I couldn't cope with two Jamies and all those questions."

Violet was exhausted. She hadn't slept well, but she was determined not to give her father a reason to bring up last night.

"So—good news, Jamie," Rochester said, slicing into his toast. "You're starting school next Monday. Merton College. All boys. Excellent science program. Sports. Every facility. I'm sure you'll enjoy it. Uniform arrives this afternoon."

Jamie whooped. "Great!"

"And Violet, your studies will begin soon." Rochester leaned back in his chair. "Jamie, you'll need immunisation before you attend."

Jamie frowned. "What kind? I've had all my shots back home."

Rochester sipped his coffee, eyes steady. "You'll be tested first. And we'll fix your eyes—get rid of those glasses. Test first, glasses second."

"What about me?" Violet asked. She was confused. He'd let her out of the house, to a band, into crowds. Why was Jamie being treated differently?

Rochester blinked at her, as if the question hadn't registered.

"If I've got to have the needle, then so do you," Jamie said, miming a syringe before disappearing into the kitchen for seconds.

"Your DNA," Rochester said, recovering. "You're not at risk like Jamie. But you'll be tested for…?" He faltered. "Autoimmune. Genetic markers."

Violet stiffened. She didn't like the sound of being tested. She'd had all her vaccinations, same as every other kid back home.

Rochester stood. "I'll see you both at dinner."

"I'm going out," Violet said quickly. "With Lewis. We're seeing a movie."

He paused, pushing his chair under the table. His gaze locked on hers. She couldn't read him. But then—just for a second—his lip curled, and something flared in his eyes. Anger. Gone as fast as it came.

"Two nights in a row?" he said lightly. "Is he bringing his girlfriend this time?"

Violet smiled sweetly. *Two can play this game.* "I hope not," she said, arching her brows.

"And Violet," Rochester added, voice flat now. "Don't forget your phone again. I expect you to have it with you at all times."

It wasn't a request. It was an order. Violet felt it like a collar tightening around her neck. But she couldn't see a way out.

Jamie wandered back in, holding a toasted sandwich. "You'll get fat if you keep that up," Violet teased.

"Nah. It's got no actual food in it. And I've been swimming every day."

"What do you know about the school?" Violet asked.

"Nothing. I'll look it up after I finish this." He spoke around a mouthful of sandwich. Violet was glad Rochester had left—Jamie's eating habits drove him mad. Honestly, everything about Jamie seemed to annoy him.

Violet stood behind Jamie as he searched for Merton College. It looked impressive. Two hundred years old. Jamie read the curriculum aloud; it was heavy on science.

"But where is it?" Violet asked. "It looks like it's in the middle of nowhere. Fields. Hills."

Jamie scrolled, then clicked on a map. "It says it's in Merton. Wherever that is." He searched the distance from Perfection.

"What?" Violet leaned in. "It says 3,000 miles. That's nearly 5,000 kilometres. You'd have to board. You're not going there." *He's not sending Jamie away from me.*

Jamie's excitement drained from his face. He looked small suddenly. "I don't want to leave," he said quietly. "I want to go to school. Make friends. But I've never been away from you for more than a week."

"Exactly. We've only just arrived. You can go to a local school. Who cares about some snobby rich school full of posers?"

"He's already ordered the uniform," Jamie said. He sounded defeated.

"So what? He should've talked to us first. He can't just make decisions like that." *I won't let him.*

***

Lewis woke a second before his alarm buzzed at 6:45. He threw on his running gear, clipped music to his ear, and headed for the park beside the Academy. The dormitory stretched long and narrow, split by a courtyard shaded with trees and scattered benches. He used to share a room with Scott—until the end-of-term test thinned the student numbers. Scott had moved to the quieter wing, the one mostly housing girls.

Poppy leaned against a tree, legs tucked out of sight. She checked her phone. One more minute. Then she'd step into his path. He never missed a run. So predictable. So punctual. She smiled. She could already hear the rhythmic thud of footsteps. It had to be him.

She stood, one hand braced against the trunk. Her tongue flicked across her lips. Any second now.

Lewis ran with effortless grace, the early light casting long shadows across the path. His music played low in one ear—his favourite band, the one he'd taken Violet to hear. He was trying to clear his head, but the thoughts kept circling. The Callums had answers. He was sure of it.

He glanced at his watch. Thirty minutes in. Fifteen more and he'd be back by 7:30. The sun filtered through the trees, dappling the path—just as Poppy stepped out.

A flash of colour. A body. Lewis swerved, too late. He clipped her shoulder, sending her sprawling sideways. She hit the ground with a cry, brushing against the tree before collapsing onto a pile of leaves.

Poppy lay flat, eyes closed. She'd nearly cracked her head—but twisted just in time, landing on the soft cushion she'd prepared.

Fuck. Not her. Lewis yanked out his earbud and dropped to one knee, winded from the elbow jab he'd taken mid-fall. "You okay?"

Do I look okay, you idiot? Poppy groaned, tried to sit up, then slumped back. Lewis narrowed his eyes. The leaves beneath her were suspiciously arranged. He hadn't seen her fall—he'd been doubled over, catching himself.

"Poppy?" He reached for her earbud. It was silent. She stopped his hand, opened her eyes.

"It's you," she whispered.

Lewis didn't like the sound of that. He should probably apologize—but she was the one who'd thrown herself into his path.

"Here, let me help." He slid a hand under her shoulder, lifting her gently. She leaned back, forcing him to steady her with an arm around her shoulders.

"I… just give me a minute. I feel dizzy." She turned her face into his chest, clinging to him as he helped her to her feet. She didn't let go.

Lewis clenched his jaw. "You okay?" He tried to peel her hand off his shoulder, but she looped her other arm around his waist.

"Can you help me back to my room?" she said. "Ouch—my ankle." She rotated her foot, then abandoned the act. "Oh, my head. I think I hit it. I should get checked out."

No, you didn't. You landed on leaves.

He'd meant to talk to her—about what she'd told Scott. But he'd been distracted. Now she was gripping him like a lifeline, and he couldn't push her off without looking cruel. He didn't trust her. Not for a second.

He guided her toward the path, arm still around her. She tilted her head up. "Lewis," she said, like she was about to ask something important.

He looked down. Her face was upturned, smiling—radiant. *What the hell?* The hairs on his neck stood up. He turned away—and saw a boy jogging toward them, eyes glued to his phone.

Poppy suddenly straightened, dropped her hand from Lewis's waist. "Thanks," she said coolly. "I'm fine. Just needed to stand up." She turned and jogged after the boy.

Lewis watched her retreat. The boy was ahead, glancing back at her before veering off the path into the trees. Poppy kept running.

Poppy swore under her breath. *You idiot. I said meet up later. I bet Lewis is watching.*

"Fuck," Lewis muttered. He replayed the moment—Poppy's smile, the boy's glance, the phone. Someone who knew her? Someone she'd planned to meet?

Poppy stopped jogging. Her phone pinged. She was out of sight now. She checked the screen.

A photo. Lewis's arm around her. Her face tilted up, smiling. She laughed. Almost perfect—except for the blank look on Lewis's face. She scrolled, found the number, and forwarded the image.

Lewis could barely contain his anger. He sprinted back to his room, tore off his running clothes, and stepped into the shower. Arms crossed, hands tucked under his armpits, he stood motionless as water poured over him.

She was waiting for me She timed it. Engineered the fall—on a pile of leaves. She wasn't hurt. She pretended. Why?

He closed his eyes, replaying the scene. It was going to come back and bite him. He could feel it.

He shut off the taps and stepped out. No more delays. He had to find the Callums. He had to talk to Monk -wherever he was.

Fifteen minutes later, he walked into the canteen. It was packed. Students never missed meals. He spotted Scott and Helen at their usual table.

"You're late," Scott said. "We've already eaten."

"You coming to class today?" Helen asked. She sounded worried. Lewis had once been the Academy's most diligent student. Now he barely showed up.

Lewis shook his head. "No time. Monk's back—I'm going to see him."

"Where were you last night?" Scott asked. "We came looking."

"Out," Lewis said.

"Yeah, like out where? And who with?" Scott's grin tugged at the corner of his mouth.

"Tell you later. Gotta go." Lewis turned to leave—and saw Poppy at a nearby table. Her blue eyes locked on him, icy and unreadable. She was smiling, but not at him. She'd just read a message. Instructions. And she couldn't wait.

Lewis didn't slow. He left the canteen with his head down and his stride sharp.

He ignored Monk's secretary and the protocol. It was exactly nine o'clock—Monk's official availability window. Lewis pushed through the office door.

"Is Monk in? I need to see him."

"Mr Monk to you," Sylvia Saxon said, rising from her desk. "And please go outside, knock, and wait to be invited in."

She was slight, almost fragile looking, but her stare could flatten anyone. Lewis paused, took a breath. Idiot.

He gave her a rueful smile, brushed his hair back.

"My apologies," he said, channelling Byron. "Terrible manners. I'll knock and wait."

"You're here now," Sylvia said, lips pursed. She knew who he was—everyone did. Even before his trip to the other world. Top student. Perfect scores. Monk had shaved a few marks off, for his own good. Sylvia hadn't asked why. She knew. Lewis was arrogant enough already.

She rolled her pen between her fingers. "He's not in. Came early. Left for the day." She glanced at her laptop. "I can book you for ten tomorrow."

Lewis wanted to kick her desk. He exhaled slowly, forcing calm. "Any chance you know where he is?"

She did. But she wasn't about to betray Monk's trust. She'd seen the look on his face ever since Mr Rochester's daughter arrived from that crumbling world. She'd overheard Violet's name once—before Monk shut his office door. He was talking to World Security.

That's where Monk was now. She didn't know why. But she knew it was about Violet. She stared at Lewis. His grey eyes seemed to read her thoughts. She blinked, looked away. For a moment, he thought she might tell him. Then she said, briskly, "No. I don't know. Do you want the appointment?"

She's lying. Lewis nodded, turned, and left. Nothing more he could do. Time was running out. Violet had something Rochester wanted. And when he got it…

Lewis clenched his jaw. As long as he kept seeing Violet, Rochester wouldn't move. Rochester wanted him gone. Then no one would be watching Violet. No one would be protecting her.

He checked the time. He'd missed half of first class. He sighed. He was barely keeping up. And then he remembered Poppy. That look she'd given him across the cafeteria. She was up to something.

He wanted to avoid her. Not because she annoyed him. Because she scared him more than dangling from that damn hot air balloon. He went looking.

The lecture room buzzed louder than usual. Lewis stood with his back to the door, scanning. The professor leaned over his desk. Students clustered in groups, whispering loud enough to sound like a hurricane.

The whiteboard was covered in geometric analysis. He spotted Scott next to Helen—Scott chewing his pen, Helen scribbling furiously.

But no Poppy.

Lewis slipped out before the professor noticed. He checked the library. The cafeteria. Finally, her dorm room.

He knocked hard. Took a step back. He'd rehearsed what he was going to say. He mouthed the words silently as the door opened.

"Lewis," she said, surprised. Her blue eyes widened. She started to smile—then stopped.

He wasn't smiling. He looked carved from stone. Jaw tight. Eyes narrowed.

"I don't know what that was this morning," he said. "Your… injury." He let the word hang, glancing at her perfectly fine ankle. "But this campus is small. I don't want any mis—"

Poppy slammed the door.

Lewis stared at the wood. Swore under his breath.

***

What can you do about it?" Jamie held up the blazer like it might bite him. Striped maroon and blue. "Look at this—it looks like a clown's jacket." He dropped it back on the bed like it burned his hands and grabbed the round box sitting next to it.

"What's this?" His voice was pure disgust.

Violet leaned in. Inside, nestled in tissue paper, was a pale straw hat.

"It's a straw boater," she said, grinning. She plucked it out and jammed it on his head. "My, don't you look posh."

"Straw *bloater*? It's stupid." Jamie spun it on his finger.

"*Boater*," Violet corrected. "I think you wear it when you go boating."

"No, you don't." He grabbed the glossy pamphlet and stabbed a finger at a picture. "See? It's the uniform. They wear it all the time."

Violet squinted at the neat row of boys in maroon and blue, straw boaters perched perfectly.

"They're not in boats," Jamie said flatly. "That settles it. No way. You've got to talk to him, Violet."

She glanced at the clothes laid neatly on the bed, her stomach twisting. She didn't care how much it had cost—Jamie wasn't going.

"Don't worry," she said. "I'm calling him now."

"Violet," Rochester said, sounding genuinely surprised. He covered the mouthpiece and waved his secretary out of the office.

"I wanted to talk to you this morning," she said, "but you had already left."

"Yes. And what was it you wanted to talk about?" His tone shifted, curious now. She'd never called him before.

Violet took a breath, fingers tight around the phone. "It's about Jamie. I don't want him going to a school so far away I'll only see him at the end of term. He's never been away from home and… And we've only just got here. Everything's… new."

Silence stretched. Rochester pressed his thumb against the pulse in his temple, letting the pause hang before he spoke.

"I understand, Violet. I should have discussed it with you both. Forgive me. We'll find another school. One closer. A beat. *"Damn it, if I have to put up with that irritating child and his endless questions,* I'm coming home early this afternoon. We'll discuss it then."

Violet blinked fast, tears stinging. He hadn't argued. He'd listened. He was going to change the plan. Lewis was wrong about him. He had to be. "Thank you," she said softly.

She looked over at Jamie and grinned. He dropped back onto the bed, arms flung wide.

"You saved me from having to wear a bloater!"

"*Boater*, you idiot. A bloater's a fish. A dried one."

"I'd rather wear that on my head than this thing!"

The image of Jamie parading around with a dried fish as a hat sent them both into fits of laughter so loud Rose called up the stairs to check they were alright.

***

Rochester stared at his phone as though it had betrayed him. Then, without warning, he hurled it across the room. It hit the far wall with a heavy thud and crashed to the floor.

He waited, jaw tight, daring it to move, to give one last gasp before dying. But the phone lay still.

He crossed the room, scooped it up, and swiped the screen. Still working. Of course it was. Indestructible, like him.

He found the number he wanted and pressed it to his ear. No introduction, no preamble.

"I need you tomorrow. Take a liver sample. Laboratory, 2:30 p.m. I can't wait any longer."

He had to know.

Rochester paced the covered terrace that ran the length of the house. Irritated. He'd come home early, expecting to confront Violet and Jamie—only to find them swimming at his private beach.

He squinted against the sun sliding low in the sky. Beyond the manicured lawn, a strip of dark water shimmered past the trees. It was getting late, and his visitor had arrived. The plan couldn't fail. It couldn't. He had to get Lewis out of the way.

Jaw clenched, he turned just as he spotted them—white towels flashing between the shadows of the trees. He waited until they crossed the lawn, then turned and went back inside.

Rochester sank into the armchair, glass of amber liquid in hand. He took a slow sip, set it down on the marble coffee table, and leaned his head back.

His visitor sat opposite, silent, waiting.

The French doors shut softly. The sound of footsteps padded across the marble hallway.

"Is that you, Violet?" Rochester called out.

Violet stopped just short of the doorway, squeezing Jamie's arm. She whispered, "You go get changed. I'll talk to him first." She smoothed back her wet hair and thrust the damp towel at him.

"Yes," she said carefully, stepping inside. "I've just been—"

She stopped. Rochester was smiling. And there was someone else in the room.

A girl. Blonde hair. Red lips. She sat opposite, watching Violet with something unreadable in her eyes. It lasted seconds—just a curl of her lip, steel flashing in blue eyes—before it vanished. Then the girl tilted her head, fingers sweeping through her hair, and smiled. Perfect dimples appeared.

Violet wished she'd changed out of her shorts and T-shirt. Her hair was a mess. She looked back at Rochester, heat crawling up her neck.

"Oh," she said. "Sorry—I didn't realise you had someone with you."

"Come in, Violet. I want you to meet my cousin's daughter, Poppy. Poppy, this is my daughter, Violet."

"Hi," Violet managed. Poppy. She knew that name. But no—couldn't be the same one.

Poppy waved lazily, her gaze sliding down to Violet's bare feet. "Hi," she said, cool and smooth. She crossed her legs, showing off black, pencil-slim capri pants and glossy red flats.

"I've been looking forward to meeting you," Poppy added, dimpling. "Uncle Victor's daughter. We've all been dying to see you." She pouted, tilting her head toward Rochester. "But he's kept you hidden away."

"Not quite everyone," Rochester said. That mocking edge again. "She has been out... to a band, wasn't it, Violet?"

Before Violet could answer, he pulled his phone from his pocket. "Important call," he said, already walking out.

Silence. Violet hesitated. She felt hot and sandy, but she couldn't leave Poppy sitting there. Something in the air shifted, prickling the back of her neck.

Poppy fixed her with a stare. "You went with Lewis, didn't you?"

Violet's breath caught. It *was* her. The same Poppy. The one Lewis had told her about.

She didn't answer. Outside, the sun was sinking, the sky burning orange-red.

"He's my boyfriend," Poppy said, her voice sharp with accusation. "We're both students at the Academy." She folded her arms.

"Is he?" Violet forced out, keeping her voice even. *He's told me all about you. You're dangerous.*

"Yes." Poppy tossed her head and gave a short, brittle laugh. Or maybe it wasn't a laugh at all.

She bent, picked up the bag at her feet, and pulled out her phone. "We broke up for a while," she said, scrolling, "but we made up today... this morning, on our run. We're always breaking up."

Then she thrust the phone at Violet. Violet didn't want to look, but Poppy was standing now, the phone inches from her face.

"I thought you should know," Poppy said, almost sweetly. "Uncle Victor was worried you might get hurt. Or... something."

The photo was clear. Lewis's arm around Poppy's shoulders. Poppy looking up at him, smiling. Both in running clothes.

Violet pressed her lips together. "Okay," she said softly, though her stomach dropped. *Trust me, Violet. That's what he said.*

"Sorry," Poppy added, arching one perfect brow. "But… Lewis can be a bit of a… you know." She sighed, as though bored.

Violet felt the air vibrating around her, her chest tight, her fingers trembling at her sides.

Poppy glanced at her face, then quickly looked away. "I've got to go," she said, barely above a whisper. "I'll find Uncle Victor. Say goodbye."

And then she was gone.

Violet stood in the centre of the room, numb. Poppy's words buzzed in her head, sharp and stinging. Her throat burned. The tears were right there, threatening, but she bit her lip hard until the sting distracted her.

Then she bolted, running from the room.

Later, Violet lay on her bed staring at the ceiling. She wanted to trust him. But the photo didn't lie. His arm had been around her. Poppy said they went running.

Violet sat up abruptly, chest tight. She wanted to scream. Throw something. Smash something. The feeling roared through her, raw and jagged.

Anger.

She hated it.

"Hey, who's that?"

Violet turned. Jamie was out on their shared balcony, leaning against the railing, peering down.

She crossed to the French doors and stepped beside him. From there, she could just see the driveway below.

Rochester was talking to Poppy. His driver opened the car door, and Poppy slid inside.

Violet grabbed Jamie's arm, pulling him gently back. She didn't want Rochester to look up and see them watching.

"Who's that?" Jamie asked again.

Violet turned away, wiping at her face quickly. She forced her voice to sound casual. Bored, even.

"Oh… some relative. Cousin or something." She walked back into her room, keeping her back to him. "She's a student with Lewis and Scott. At the Academy."

Her voice was steady. But then, so quietly she almost didn't hear herself, she whispered,

"She's Lewis's girlfriend."

Jamie stopped fiddling with the railing and stared at her.

"What? No, she's not. You're his girlfriend." He said it firmly, like it was obvious, like that settled everything.

Violet paused at the bathroom door but didn't turn around. "I'm not his girlfriend," she said flatly. "I never was."

She shut the door and leaned against it, biting her lip until it hurt. She wasn't going to cry. She wasn't. She pulled the elastic from her hair. He was coming to collect her later. She couldn't avoid him.

Trust me, Violet. Trust me… promise you will.

She closed her eyes. She had to think.

But all she saw was the photo. Lewis's arm around Poppy. Poppy smiling up at him. Him smiling back. Pulling her close.

Violet shook her head hard, as though she could shake it away. But it stayed.

Jamie stood outside the bathroom door, frowning. He didn't understand. He thought Violet was the girlfriend. He thought Lewis was taking her out tonight—he'd *heard* her say that to Veedad.

He liked Lewis. Lewis had given him the best adventure of his life—the hot air balloon, the fall from the sky, the chase—and now they were living in a mansion. That was all Lewis.

Violet turned off the shower and pressed her forehead against the cool marble tiles. She hated herself for believing him. For wanting to. She'd tried not to cry. But now the tears came, hot and quiet.

She wanted Mona. She wanted her old world back, even with all its flaws. She needed a plan. But she didn't know who she could trust.

Dressed now, Violet grabbed her phone. She wasn't going to call him. She couldn't hear the lies.

Her thumbs flew across the screen:

I met your girlfriend today. Don't call me again.

Rochester leaned back in his recliner, pulling his phone from his pocket. He read Violet's message to Lewis.

A small muscle pulsed in his cheek. *That should do it.* He closed his eyes and rested his hands over his chest.

Violet stared at her reflection in the mirror. Her eyes were red and swollen. She forced a smile. She needed to hold it together.

She had to talk to Rochester. She didn't want him asking her questions. She found him in his office, the door open.

"Can I talk to you about Jamie?" Her voice came out smaller than she'd intended.

Rochester's gaze shifted toward the door before he sat up slowly. He would have to lie. He hadn't withdrawn Jamie's enrolment—and he had no intention of doing so. He wanted the boy gone.

"Is there anything more to be said, Violet?"

It wasn't a question. His tone was cold. Icy. It sliced through her composure, making her falter.

"I… I just wanted to thank you. I know it was inconvenient, and I thought you were thinking of the best place to send Jamie."

The look on his face told her she was right. He drew his brows together in an exaggerated show of puzzlement, as if the entire matter confused him.

Then he stood and walked toward her—but he didn't look at her. His eyes were somewhere past her shoulder, like she wasn't there.

His hand brushed her shoulder lightly, a touch cold as ice. Then he was gone.

Violet clenched her fists and pressed her lips into a thin, hard line. Jamie wasn't going anywhere. Not if she had anything to do with it.

CHAPTER THIRTY-FIVE

Lewis couldn't concentrate. The lecture room had gone very still.

"Yes, Carlyle. I'm waiting. We're *all* waiting."

Lewis looked up from his notebook, blinking. Scott leaned close, whispering out of the corner of his mouth. "Asked you to solve the problem on the board."

"Thank you, Streathfield," Professor Smythe said dryly. "Are you with us, Carlyle?"

Lewis frowned faintly, glanced up at the whiteboard. Easy. A simple proof. He scanned it once and rattled off the answer, just as the clock on the wall struck the hour and the lesson ended.

Outside the building, Helen fell into step beside him. "What's with you?" she asked, watching him shove his hands into his pockets.

Lewis didn't answer.

"Lewis. Stop." She grabbed his arm, pulling him to a halt.

He looked at her, irritated. Words crowded behind his teeth but only one rose to the surface.

Violet.

"You're never in class," Helen went on, "and when you *are* in class, you're not really there. I've got notes for you." She sighed. "I emailed them."

"Thanks," he muttered, already reaching for his phone. A message buzzed in his pocket.

He read it once. Then again. "Fuck. Fuck. Fuck." The words hissed out under his breath.

He didn't think. He just called her. But the call didn't ring—straight to voicemail.

Phone switched off.

"What's up?" Scott's voice cut in. He'd seen Lewis's face. It was bad.

Lewis held out his phone silently. Scott read the message. Helen leaned in to see.

"She… met your girlfriend?" Helen said.

Lewis shoved the phone back into his pocket, jaw locked tight.

"Poppy," he said bitterly.

He spun, scanning the campus grounds as though expecting her to be standing there, smiling that smug, triumphant smile. He just knew this had something to do with her.

"This is Rochester," he said through clenched teeth. "It has to be."

"Maybe it's not Poppy," Scott offered quickly. "Maybe it's someone else. Someone Rochester knows. Hell, maybe he *paid* someone to… I don't know… set this up. Wouldn't put it past him."

Scott blew out his cheeks, as frustrated as Lewis. He felt guilty too—like he'd dragged Poppy into their lives.

Lewis's head snapped toward him. "Someone he knows…"

Scott nodded slowly. "Could be."

"He *knows* Poppy." Lewis's voice was flat. Certain.

"Does he?" Helen asked.

"I'd put money on it," Lewis said. "He'd make it his business to know. He knew about our argument," he jerked his chin toward Scott, "he was there, remember? This… explains everything that happened this morning."

"What happened?" Scott and Helen asked together.

Lewis told them quickly—how Poppy had appeared out of nowhere, smiling, leaning in—and then the boy who'd seemed to materialise from behind the trees. And suddenly Poppy, who'd been limping seconds earlier, could run.

It replayed in his mind: his arm around her, the flash of her smile, her phone lifted.

"Fuck!" The word burst from him, sharp and loud. "It was a *set-up*."

Scott stared. "The guy took a photo?"

Lewis ran a hand through his hair, pacing. "I've got to see her."

He looked at Helen, silent question in his eyes.

"Sure," she said, reaching into her bag for the keys. "Car's in the usual spot."

He drove carefully through the city, weaving between slow-moving electric bikes. But once they were clear of the centre, his restraint snapped—he pushed the car hard, tearing down the open road.

Anger burned through him, hot and steady. "Rochester," he muttered, smacking the steering wheel. "Bastard." He forced himself to breathe, gripping the wheel until his knuckles blanched.

And then it hit him—hard and cold. *He told her to trust him.* Now she thought he'd lied.

For one wild moment, Lewis almost turned the car around. Go back. Forget Violet. Focus on graduating top of the Academy, crush his exams, prove himself. But he couldn't.

He pulled up at the wrought-iron gates, Rochester's name curling in black letters. Beyond them, the house stretched at the end of a pale gravel drive, cold and unwelcoming.

He sat there, staring. The gates didn't move. Of course they didn't—he wasn't expected. And then, movement. A figure on the balcony. Jamie.

Lewis jumped out of the car, standing close to the gates. Jamie waved again, then disappeared. Lewis waited, he expected to see Jamie running down the drive. Instead, his phone rang. Jamie didn't wait for him to speak.

"Violet doesn't want to see you," he blurted. "She doesn't know I'm calling—I stole Dom's phone. Your *girlfriend* came to the house," Jamie added accusingly.

"Jamie, listen to me," Lewis said quickly, low and urgent. "I *don't* have a girlfriend. I don't know who Violet saw, but I've never had one. I'm not lying."

Jamie was silent for half a beat. "I thought Violet was your girlfriend." He spoke fast, tumbling over his words. "You act like her boyfriend, you want to see her all the time, and you *look* at her like—"

Lewis couldn't help it—he smiled, just faintly. "Like what?"

Jamie made a gagging sound into the phone. "That *gross* way."

"Yeah," Lewis said softly. "Guess that's what boyfriends do." He hesitated. "Jamie, can you get her to talk to me?"

"She's not here," Jamie said quickly. "She went out with Veedad. Horse riding. He bought her a horse. Didn't get me one though—he was gonna send me away to some boarding school, but Violet made him change his mind." Jamie's voice dropped. "It was over the other side of the country."

Lewis's grip tightened on the phone. *He's trying to isolate her. Bastard.*

"Jamie, listen—give her a message for me. Tell her what I told you. Tell her to trust me. Please."

"Okay," Jamie said. "Gotta go before Dom finds out I stole his phone."

Violet hadn't wanted to go horse riding. She wanted to *talk* to Rochester. But he'd avoided every attempt, riding ahead of her through the long green fields.

She let her horse plod lazily behind, keeping her distance. She wasn't confident enough to trot. Galloping… not after last time. Maybe never again.

She felt hollow. Like something had been carved out of her chest.

It was the same emptiness she'd felt when the man she thought was her father had died. Different—worse, somehow—but the same weight pressing down, draining the colour from the world.

"Stop," she muttered under her breath. "Stop it. Stop."

But it followed her, this heavy ache. She didn't want to be here, alone with her thoughts in endless green. She wanted Jamie, one of his ridiculous games, anything to distract her from the image burned behind her eyelids: Lewis's arm around Poppy.

Rochester slowed his horse, rolling his shoulders back. He felt good. Tomorrow, he'd have the tests done. Dangerous, yes. But science demanded risk—and sacrifice.

He'd delayed Jamie's enrolment by a few days. That was enough. He wanted the boy gone.

Violet was talking to Stewart when Rochester led his horse into the stable. She waited outside by his car, hands shoved deep in her pockets, trying to look composed. But her eyes were swollen, her cheeks blotchy. She hadn't stopped thinking about Lewis. About that photo.

When Rochester joined her, she slid into the passenger seat without a word. As soon as they pulled away, she spoke.

"You *have* pulled Jamie out of Merton, haven't you? You said you would."

Rochester kept his gaze on the road, expression unreadable. "Violet," he said finally, voice calm and soft. "I've had time to think. Yes, I said I would. But it's a wonderful school. One of the best in the world, actually. Jamie's bright. He deserves the best."

Violet stared down at her hands resting in her lap. She glanced sideways at his profile—the hawk-like nose, the sharp jaw, the blank, unmoving face. His green eyes were dull, swamp-water flat.

She squeezed her fingers together tightly. "Not if it means being sent away from me," she said quietly. Then firmer. "No. I won't agree to it."

Rochester ground his teeth and pressed harder on the accelerator. Gravel spat out behind the wheels.

Violet didn't look away from him. She could see the sharp pulse in his cheek, the storm building under his calm façade. She'd made him angry. She didn't care.

He said nothing until he pulled the car into the driveway and cut the engine. He turned slowly toward her. "I can see this matters to you, Violet," he said softly, almost kind. "You're very attached to Jamie, of course. But sometimes…" He smiled faintly. "Sometimes you have to do what's best for him. School term doesn't start for another four days."

He opened his door. Violet didn't move.

"Please." Her voice cracked. She turned her face so he wouldn't see the tears spilling down her cheeks. But she'd promised Jamie. She couldn't leave this hanging. "Please, say he won't have to go."

Rochester exhaled heavily, tilting his head as though weighing patience against control. "Violet, you're being emotional," he said smoothly. "This isn't about Jamie at all, is it? It's that boy—Carlyle. Meeting his girlfriend must have been… upsetting."

Violet's head snapped up. "Why did you invite her?" Her voice was quiet but steady.

He didn't flinch. "It's obvious why I did. Carlyle was trifling with your feelings. I wanted to protect you from being hurt. It seems he's quite a good liar."

He got out of the car, his tone final. "You'll get over it."

Violet glared after him, her chest rising and falling sharply. "Yes," she shouted, her voice breaking, "I'll get over Lewis. But not Jamie."

She ran after him, catching him on the steps. She grabbed his arm, fingers locking around his jacket sleeve. Rochester stopped dead. Slowly, deliberately, he turned. Her hand dropped when she saw his face. A mask of fury.

"Wherever Jamie goes," she said softly, fists clenched tight at her sides, "I'm going too." Her voice trembled on the last word.

Something flickered behind Rochester's eyes. A memory. Anna.

· Her pale face. Her hands spread protectively over her stomach in the library. Her shaking voice, *"You are not going to experiment on my baby!"*

Rochester's jaw tensed. He'd made mistakes before. He wouldn't make them again. Backing down tasted like ash, but he couldn't risk losing control of her. He needed her compliance.

"I see, Violet." His anger slid from his face like water running off glass. His lips curved upward—not warmth, but calculation. "That would be… inconvenient," he said softly. "Having you so far away."

For a long moment, neither moved. A light flicked on above the porch, sensing day shift into night. Then, suddenly, Rochester sighed—a theatrical, exaggerated sound—and tilted his head toward the darkening sky. His eyes closed briefly, as though in prayer.

When he opened them, his expression was transformed. A smile. But his eyes burned cold and sharp. "You win, Violet," he said quietly. And without waiting for a reply, he turned and disappeared into the house.

CHAPTER THIRTY-SIX

"She won't speak to me," Lewis muttered, handing Helen the car keys. "I spoke to Jamie."

Scott nodded toward the library where the lights glowed. "Poppy's in there. You want to talk to her?"

Lewis shook his head. "What's the point?"

Scott smirked faintly. "You could tell her you know she's one of Rochester's little secrets. Cousin's daughter or something. Took some digging—she's got a different surname. Looks like Rochester pulled strings to get her into the Academy. She's not as brilliant as she pretends. Gets plenty of help with her coursework."

"I knew it," Lewis breathed. "Rochester—the bastard."

And suddenly, he didn't feel like giving up anymore.

"How'd you find that out?"

"Genius here," Scott said, squeezing Helen's shoulder. "She hacked into the student records."

Helen's lips twitched into a small, modest smile. "It wasn't hard."

Lewis ran a hand through his hair. "Thanks, Helen. But how do I get that to Violet? She's blocked me. After…"

He stopped himself, jaw tightening. The bitterness slipped in anyway—the ache that Violet had been so ready to believe the worst of him.

Helen watched him, concern flickering across her face. "Do you think Monk knows?"

"I'm going to find out." Lewis's eyes darkened, steel replacing exhaustion. "He's back at the Academy tomorrow. I've got an appointment with him. I'm getting answers."

Scott glanced sideways at Helen. "What if there *aren't* any answers?"

Helen hesitated. "Maybe… maybe Rochester's just being a protective father. There might be an innocent—"

"Innocent?" Lewis barked a laugh, sharp and bitter. "An innocent explanation?"

He spun on them, voice rising. "Are you two serious? Has the damn money scrambled your brains? Have you forgotten?"

He jabbed a finger toward the ground with each word:

"He. Tried. To. Have. Us. Killed."

Scott shifted uncomfortably. "Tried to have us *left behind*," he muttered under his breath.

Lewis swung on him, glare sharp enough to cut. Scott stepped back, palms raised.

"Okay. Okay," he said quickly.

Lewis shoved his hands deep into his pockets and exhaled slowly through his nose. "There *are* answers," he said finally, voice low and cold. Then he turned and walked away.

"Hey," Scott called after him. "We're heading to the club. You should come."

Lewis didn't look back. He lifted a hand in vague dismissal. No chance. Not where he might run into Poppy. He couldn't trust himself not to strangle her.

Exhaustion hit him hard. He hadn't slept more than four hours in the last two nights, and the weight of it dragged at him now. He felt empty, drained. For the first time, he wondered if he'd imagined it all—the urgency, the danger, even Violet's trust.

He tipped his head back, staring at the stars. The lovers' constellation shimmered brighter than he'd ever seen it, haloed in pale gold. He closed his eyes.

When he opened them, he froze. Poppy was walking toward him. Head down. Digging through her bag.

Lewis stepped into the middle of the path and stopped, waiting. Poppy looked up. For the briefest second, fear flashed in her eyes. Wide, startled, hand lifting to her chest.

She didn't speak. She stared up at him—the shadows from the hanging lamps cutting sharp angles across his face, his jaw tight, the pulse in his cheek pounding.

But fear passed quickly. She slid her bag higher on her shoulder and tilted her chin, mouth curling into a crooked half-smile. She knew exactly what this was about.

"What's your problem?" she said casually, voice light, taunting.

Lewis said nothing. He counted silently to ten, holding her gaze the entire time. Finally, he nodded once, as though confirming something to himself.

"You," he said softly, stepping closer. "*You*, Poppy. You're the problem."

Her grin faltered. Lewis lowered his voice, his brows pulling tight. "Why did you do it?"

She opened her mouth, but no answer came. The half-smile collapsed under the weight of his stare. "I don't know what you're talking about," she said finally, shoving past him with her shoulder.

He caught her arm, pulling her around to face him. His voice stayed low, dangerous.

"Why?" he said again. "I *know* it was you. You went to Rochester's house. You told Violet you were my girlfriend. Didn't you?"

Poppy jerked her arm free, rubbing where his fingers had held her. She hesitated, chest rising and falling fast, and then spat the words at him.

"I did it because my uncle asked me to." Her voice trembled with fury. "He didn't want some creep taking advantage of his daughter. Turned out the creep was you. I was *happy* to oblige."

Lewis reeled back as if she'd slapped him. For a second, his brain shorted out—static, blank. Poppy hated him *that much*. Why? Because of that stupid, drunken kiss the night of the dinner? Because he'd pulled back before it went further?

He ran a hand through his hair, exhaling hard. "I don't get it," he said quietly.

Poppy's eyebrows lifted delicately. "There's nothing to get." She shoved past him and kept walking, her heels clicking sharp against the path.

Lewis stood there a long time, staring at the shadows stretching across the ground. It was Rochester. Poppy had admitted it.

When he finally made it back to his room, he kicked off his shoes and collapsed on the bed.

He should have been angry at Violet. Instead, it just... hurt. That she'd believed someone like Poppy. That she hadn't waited. That she hadn't given him the chance to explain.

He reached for his phone. His thumb hovered over the screen, another unsent message forming in his mind. Three failed already. He set the phone on the bedside table, rolled onto his side, and shut his eyes. Sleep took him fast.

***

Violet felt sick. She hadn't wanted to confront her father, and now she'd made him angry.

At dinner, he'd met them both with that sharp, unreadable expression and ignored them through the first course. The room had been silent except for the clink of cutlery on china.

When Rose brought in dessert — a pie with glossy custard — Rochester waited until they were all served. Then, as though it was nothing, he announced:

"Tomorrow, I'll be taking you both to the hospital for vaccinations."

His gaze slid to Jamie. "And we'll get your myopia corrected."

Jamie grinned, a smear of custard on his cheek. "No more glasses!" he said through a mouthful.

Rochester's nose wrinkled. Violet knew what was coming — another lecture about manners, about posture, about keeping one's mouth shut when chewing.

He's only twelve, she wanted to shout. *He'll learn. He doesn't need you crushing him.*

Instead, she picked up her fork and said lightly, "Did you know, in some parts of my world, it's okay to talk with your mouth full?"

Then she stuffed a giant bite of pie into her mouth and spoke through it:

"This," she said thickly, "is a wicked pie." A chunk fell back onto her plate.

Rochester's green eyes flashed. He stared at her, unblinking. Violet met his gaze, swallowed, took a sip of water, and — deliberately — looked away.

Rochester pushed his plate aside, fingertips resting neatly on the white tablecloth. A tight smile pulled at his lips.

Violet kept eating, pretending she didn't notice. The pie was delicious, soft pastry melting against creamy, lemony filling. She smiled across the table at Jamie.

"Tastes like lemon meringue," she said, as if Rochester wasn't there.

Rochester rose from his chair, tossing his napkin onto it. "I'll leave you two to finish the pie. Try not to choke on it. I'll see you in the morning."

They listened to his footsteps fading.

Jamie scraped the last of the custard from his plate. "Where?" he asked suddenly.

"Where what?"

"You know. Where it's okay to talk with your mouth full."

Violet widened her green eyes. "I made it up."

Jamie grinned, but then his expression dropped. "You made him angry." He'd stopped calling Rochester Veedad.

Violet had stopped calling him anything at all. "I know," she said softly. "I just—"

She stopped, glancing around the room as though someone might be listening.

"Nothing." She stood, forcing a smile. "Come on. Let's play one of your games."

Jamie groaned. "You're hopeless at them, Violet."

***

Lewis woke in the middle of the night, still in his clothes. He stripped them off and crawled under the sheets, skin sticky with sleep. He'd been dreaming, but it was gone now, vanished like a ship sliding over the horizon.

He stared into the dark, thinking about Violet. About her green eyes. Her mouth. He groaned softly, turned onto his side. Tomorrow, he was seeing Monk. He was going to get answers.

CHAPTER THIRTY-SEVEN

Violet and Jamie waited on the front steps for Rochester. He was driving them to the hospital himself.

"You scared?" Jamie asked, swinging his legs.

"No," said Violet, touching his shoulder. "Why, are you?"

"Nope." He tilted his head up at her. "Can't wait to get these glasses off." He shoved them higher on his nose, then took them off, squinting toward the metal gates at the end of the long drive. Beyond them, colours blurred into each other, indistinct.

"I'll be able to see *everything*," he said, grinning. "Down the drive, past the gates. Probably better than you."

Then Jamie froze, remembering. "Oh. Forgot to tell you. Lewis came yesterday. You were out riding."

Violet's head jerked up, as if he'd struck her.

Jamie winced. "Sorry. But you said… anyway, he said—"

"You spoke to him?"

"Yeah. I stole Dom's phone and called him." He shrugged, unapologetic. "He said to tell you—"

"I don't care what he said," she snapped.

"Yes, you do. Don't lie." Jamie's voice was stubborn, steady.

He looked over Violet's shoulder. "He said… he's your boyfriend. And you should trust him. Why don't you?"

Violet blinked, stunned. "What? He's *not* my boyfriend." Her cheeks burned hot, anger bleeding into the words. "He's got a girlfriend, Jamie. Her name's Poppy. I met her. *Here.* At the house. He invited her."

She jerked her chin toward the sleek black sports car rolling down the drive.

"She showed me a photo," Violet whispered, voice cracking. She didn't want to remember it.

Jamie frowned, unsettled by the heat in her voice.

The car crunched to a stop. Violet stared at Rochester inside, his hand resting lightly on the radio dial, twirling it lazily. A blast of music burst from the speakers, loud and jarring.

"Wait," Jamie said, grabbing her arm. "I know that name. *Poppy.*"

Violet froze.

Jamie jerked his chin toward the car. "I heard him say it. On the phone. He was in your room. My door was open. He said her name, Violet. He said Poppy. And he said she had to get *evidence.*"

Violet's breath caught, shallow and fast. *Evidence.* Her hand shook as it landed on the cool metal of the car door.

"Y-yeah," Jamie said, nodding. "That's what I heard."

Violet stepped back, forcing her voice calm. "You sit in the front," she told Jamie.

She slid into the back seat, her hands trembling as she pulled the seat belt across her lap. She stared at the back of Rochester's head, biting her lip hard, willing herself not to cry.

Rochester's eyes caught hers in the rear-view mirror. Unblinking. Cold. Reading her thoughts.

She dropped her gaze to her knotted hands, forcing herself to breathe evenly. *Evidence. The photo.*

She hadn't wanted to think about it, but it came rushing back—the insincere curl of Poppy's lips, her polished dimples, and Lewis's blank, puzzled expression beside her.

She brushed her hand quickly across her eyes. She should have trusted him. Now, she might never see him again.

"What vaccinations are we getting?" Jamie asked loudly, shouting above the roar of the music.

Rochester didn't answer.

Jamie leaned forward, reaching for the dial. Rochester's hand shot out, slapping his away. "The usual vaccinations," he said, voice smooth and cold. "For aliens."

Jamie flinched, shrinking into his seat.

Violet leaned forward, squeezing his shoulder. "Jamie, it'll be okay. I'm having the same."

"I *just* wanted to know what they were," Jamie muttered, side-eyeing Rochester.

Violet leaned back, her voice steady but sharp. "I'd like to know, too. Exactly what injections we're having."

Rochester's grip tightened on the wheel, knuckles white. He glanced at her through the rear-view mirror, jaw taut. Then, with one finger, he turned the music off. "Of course you do," he said softly.

Silence filled the car, heavy and tense.

"It depends on your immunity levels," Rochester said finally. "Usually just two injections. Painless." He glanced sideways at Jamie, his lips curling faintly. "I'm sure you'll manage. And you've got Violet here to hold your hand."

Violet caught the edge of sarcasm slicing through his voice.

Jamie straightened. "I wasn't worried about it hurting," he said. "I just wanted to know."

Violet opened her mouth to add something—but then the car turned off the road, pulling into the circular driveway of a white building.

The words above the entrance blazed in deep blue:

VICTOR ROCHESTER HOSPITAL.

Violet stared at the dark glass doors. A shiver ran through her, cold and sharp, as though something had coiled tight in her chest and wouldn't let go.

She *had* to talk to Lewis.

Rochester parked in a space marked **DIRECTOR ONLY** and switched off the engine.

"We're here," he said lightly.

Violet climbed out quickly, circling the car until she was next to Jamie. She took his hand, squeezing it tightly. She knew that look on his face. He was afraid.

And it was Rochester's fault.

Rochester looked across the roof of the car, irritation simmering just beneath the surface. Violet could see it — the slight flare of his nostrils, the clipped way he shut the door. She knew she'd pushed him too far today.

He smiled faintly, the kind of smile that didn't reach his eyes.

"We're here," he said. His voice carried an edge of excitement, like he was taking them to a theme park. "Come."

Violet reached for Jamie's hand, gave it a quick squeeze, and let go.

They followed Rochester as the glass doors whispered apart, sliding back like a curtain of water.

The foyer opened wide around them, mood-lit and hushed. Apricot sofas circled low glass tables; the walls were lined with soft paintings; a towering potted plant stretched toward the ceiling, its glossy leaves catching the light. It looked more like a hotel than a hospital.

Behind a pale reception desk stood a tall man with white-blond hair. He straightened immediately, stepping forward and bowing his head.

"Sir. Everything is ready," he murmured, eyes fixed on the marble tiles beneath his feet.

Rochester didn't answer. He strode toward the wall of smoky glass doors sealing off the rest of the building. They slid open with a soft hiss.

"I need the restroom," Violet said suddenly, scanning for the sign she'd spotted.

Rochester turned sharply. "In here," he ordered, nodding at the sealed doors.

But Violet was already moving, her sneakers squeaking against the polished floor.

She ducked into the door marked **Rest Rooms** and locked it behind her.

Her phone was out of her bag before she even breathed. It was dead — almost. A sliver of red on the battery icon.

She switched it on, fingers shaking, and scrolled to Lewis's name.

The ringing felt endless.

"Please, Lewis, pick up," she whispered. Her voice cracked.

Straight to voicemail. Tears blurred her vision, but she typed anyway.

Sorry. Call me.

Her thumb hovered. She hesitated. If Lewis was right — if her father really was tapping her phone — Rochester would read the message.

There wasn't time to think. She hit send just as the screen went black.

✳✳✳

Lewis checked the time on his phone. Five minutes early.

He waited outside Monk's office, slouched against the wall. He wasn't optimistic — Monk had a way of dodging direct answers — but if he didn't get them now, he was done. He'd leave Violet to whatever life Rochester had carved out for her.

He'd even tried calling his father. No answer. Just a voicemail he doubted would be returned.

He stared at the closed office door, jaw tight. Enough waiting. Lewis raised his hand to knock — but the door swung open first.

Sylvia Saxon, Monk's secretary, blinked up at him as though she'd been caught mid-dream.

"Oh, Lewis," she said, startled. "You're here for your appointment. I'm sorry, you'll have to reschedule — Mr Sampson had to leave." She stepped out, pulling the door closed behind her.

Lewis didn't move. "Where'd he go?"

Sylvia avoided his gaze. "I was… just about to call you." She wasn't.

Lewis took a step closer. He didn't say anything, just looked at her, silver-grey eyes unblinking, steady.

Her hand went to her cheek, flustered. "I—I was going to call. Truly. He only just left, and I needed a coffee first and—"

"Were you," Lewis said softly.

She flushed. It wasn't a question. She swallowed, then turned slightly, lowering her voice. "World Security. He just left. And…" She glanced up, nervous. "You didn't hear it from me."

CHAPTER THIRTY-EIGHT

Lewis broke every speed limit on the way.

The motorbike weaved between cars, slicing through the heavy mid-morning traffic. Every second lost felt like oxygen bleeding out of his lungs.

Ahead, the lights turned amber. He opened the throttle — then cursed and slammed the brakes as they turned red.

He bounced on his seat, waiting. One foot on the ground. Eyes locked on the green ahead.

As soon as it hit, he shot forward, swerving into a narrow side street lined with cafés and tables spilling out onto the pavement. It was packed — office workers grabbing coffees, pedestrians drifting in the weak sunshine, electric bikes parked two deep.

He slowed just enough to avoid hitting anyone, the words of his mother echoing faintly in his head.

Breathe, Lewis. Breathe.

He could almost hear her voice. He'd text her later.

The street opened up ahead. He gunned the throttle and shot forward, helmet low, wind battering against the visor.

The World Security building rose at the end of the road, grey steel and mirrored glass. A knot of cars choked the approach.

Lewis scanned the line — and there. Monk's silver sedan. Academy plates.

He cut sharply between lanes, brakes screeching as a woman in a small car slammed her horn and swore furiously. He raised a hand in apology without slowing.

The security gates were already swinging open.

He wasn't going to make it.

Lewis swerved across the front of Monk's car, yanking off his helmet as he braked hard in the middle of the road.

Security guards poured out from both sides, hands raised, shouting at him to move.

Monk thrust his car door open. "What the hell do you think you're doing, Carlyle?" His face was red, his voice a growl. "Move your bike before you're arrested."

Lewis shook his head. "Not until you hear me."

"You've got ten seconds," Monk snapped.

Lewis leaned forward on the handlebars, meeting his gaze. "The scientist — Callum — he's here, isn't he? He would have been arrested the second Violet came back. You questioned him. He *knows* something."

Monk's jaw tightened. He said nothing.

Lewis smiled coldly. "So that's a yes."

"I'm coming with you."

"Absolutely not," Monk barked.

Lewis steadied his bike, refusing to move. "Then you'll have to drive through me."

The gates behind them rumbled, beginning to close.

Monk cursed under his breath. Options ran through his head like a rapid-fire equation, calculating outcomes. Finally, he jerked his chin toward the passenger door.

"Get your damn bike out of the way and get in."

It took thirty minutes to clear security. Lewis had to wait while his Academy ID was verified. Monk barely spoke, jaw working the entire time.

By the time they reached the secure wing, Monk had confirmed it: Callum and his brother were being held inside.

They followed a guard through a silent corridor until they reached a lift.

Monk frowned, rubbing his temple. "Frontal lobe," he muttered.

Lewis glanced at him. "What?"

"Your frontal lobe. Hasn't finished developing yet. Another five years before you stop being an idiot."

Lewis shrugged. "Guess I'll risk it."

The lift opened onto a holding area. They were led into a small visitor room — four chairs, one table, and a one-way mirror stretching across the far wall.

The guard locked the door behind them.

Dave Callum was already seated, hands folded, his eyes sharp and amused.

"Mr Callum," Monk began, "we haven't met, I'm head of—"

"I know who you are." Callum's gaze shifted, assessing Lewis. "And you are?"

Lewis stepped forward. "Lewis Carlyle."

Callum ignored the outstretched hand and fixed his attention back on Monk. "You here to get me out of this cage? I trust you've seen the video evidence proving I didn't kidnap Anna Rochester. There's no law against helping someone leave a country voluntarily."

Monk's voice was dry. "The *planet*, Callum."

Callum raised an eyebrow. "I've denied that, and I'll keep denying it."

Monk said nothing, but Lewis could see it in his face. The pieces were falling into place.

Callum leaned back, unruffled. "Anna made the video herself. Said she was leaving of her own free will. To protect her unborn child."

Monk glanced down at his hands.

Jenny Callum's phone call hadn't been enough to convict him. "It was a joke," Jenny had laughed when questioned. "Dave and I used to say the only place Mrs Rochester could hide from her husband was in DZ. It was... a joke."

Monk didn't look convinced. "Mmm," he said. "And your brother?"

"Denies it too."

Callum folded his arms, his voice tightening. "So... when are we leaving?"

Lewis leaned forward, ignoring Monk's glare. "I was one of the cadets sent to DZ," he said quietly. "We found Rochester's daughter. We brought her back."

The room went still.

Callum couldn't hide the flicker in his eyes. He knew Violet was back.

Once he'd heard the news, he and his brother had tried to distance themselves — from Perfection, from Rochester, from all of it. But finding Rochester's daughter in DZ had confirmed what World Security already suspected. Someone had helped Anna Rochester escape.

He leaned back, hands trembling in his pockets. Stay calm.

Monk snapped, "Lewis!" A warning. Shut up.

Lewis ignored him. "You know why she left him. His wife. Anna. You know."

Callum's jaw worked. "Where is she... his daughter?"

"She's with Rochester. DNA proved it."

Callum glanced at the one-way mirror. "Can we get some water in here?"

Lewis knew he was right. Callum knew. The thought made him both triumphant and terrified.

A guard brought the water. Callum drained a glass, slow, deliberate. He wasn't talking here. Not with them watching.

"You didn't answer me," Callum said, voice tight. "When are we being released?"

Monk studied him. Fear. He knew it when he saw it. Callum wasn't going to talk under World Security's cameras.

Their release had been cleared hours ago. Monk had just been holding him, squeezing for information — and that flicker in Callum's eyes had told him enough.

"I understand your release is being processed now," Monk said. "Your brother's too."

Relief. Sharp and cold. Callum stood, but fear came with it. Rochester would come after him. He'd have to silence him. Jenny. The girls.

Lewis's words caught him at the door. "I met Violet — that's her name — in DZ. Got to know her. Her mother died when she was young."

Callum turned sharply. "Anna?" His voice cracked. "Her heart?"

Lewis nodded. "Undiagnosed condition, I think. The man she thought was her father died too. I spent time with her, she's… she's alone, Callum. Vulnerable." He hesitated. "She trusted me once, but Rochester's fixed that. I think she's in danger. I think Rochester wants her for—"

He stopped. Saying it out loud sounded insane.

Callum's hand froze on the door handle. "Wants her for what?"

Lewis stepped closer, lowering his voice, glancing at the black glass of the mirror. "Genetics," he whispered.

Callum turned, his face pale. Lewis's hands shook through his hair. "I love her," he said softly.

Callum held his gaze. "I hear you." And then, flat: "I'm getting out."

Lewis turned his back to the mirror, wiping at his face. Callum would talk to him. He knew it.

Monk shot him a look. Not so cool after all, he thought. Too emotional. He wondered if Lewis would even finish the course.

Outside the gates, Lewis waited in Monk's car.

"You're still Bureau," Monk said sharply. "If Callum talks, I want everything. You report back. Understood?"

Lewis nodded. "Understood."

He spotted Callum and another man exiting World Security. "There. That's him — and his brother, I think."

A car pulled up. They were getting in. Lewis slammed the door, bolted from the car, waving his arms. The passenger window slid down.

"Get in, Lewis," Callum said.

Inside the car, a woman with short dark hair turned in the driver's seat, eyes flicking over him.

"This is Jenny," Callum said quickly. "My wife. And Frank, my brother. Meet Lewis Carlyle — one of the cadets who brought back Rochester's daughter."

Jenny nodded once. "Is she alright?"

"She's with Rochester," Lewis said.

Jenny's head snapped toward Callum, then back to the road. Tight-lipped.

Lewis stared between them. "You all know why he wants her, don't you? It's not because she's his daughter, it's—"

"It is," Callum cut in. "She carries his DNA. And something else. Or he hopes she does. You were right — it's her genetic coding. That's what he wants. That's what makes him dangerous."

Frank's voice was low. "It'll make him the most powerful man in the universe."

"For eternity," he added, almost a whisper.

Lewis felt the blood drain from his face. Whatever it meant, it wasn't good. "We have to get her out. Before Rochester—" He couldn't finish.

Callum twisted in his seat, forcing his voice to stay calm. "Listen. He won't harm her. Not yet. Not until the publicity dies down. She's too visible. He'll wait."

But even as he said it, he didn't believe it.

He remembered Anna — young, vulnerable, bullied into silence. He remembered the night Rochester smiled when Callum had questioned him about experimenting on his unborn child.

"Callum," Rochester had said, almost laughing. *The end always justifies the means.*

That was the moment he'd known. Rochester wasn't just ruthless. He was a psychopath.

Lewis rubbed at his forehead. "You think he cares about publicity? He doesn't give a damn. He didn't care about Anna, about Violet's mother. God, what did he do to make her run?"

Callum's chest tightened. He knew exactly what Rochester had done. What *he'd* helped him do. Some things you never forgive yourself for.

"Listen to me," Callum said quietly. "Rochester needs Violet's trust. He won't move until he has it. That buys us time." He prayed he was right.

Frank broke his silence. "I'm not so sure, Dave. Time's what we don't have."

Callum shot him a warning glare. Idiot. Stop panicking the boy.

Lewis dropped his head into his hands. "He's already gained her trust. Got Jamie citizenship. Bought her a horse. And now… she doesn't trust me anymore." His voice cracked. "He's made sure of that."

His phone buzzed. His heart jolted. A message. Violet.

"She wants me to call her," he breathed. Relief flashing across his face.

"Good news?" Frank asked, leaning forward.

Lewis nodded. "I'll call now, but… Rochester's monitoring her phone. I'll be quick."

He called. The voice on the line was cold, mechanical: *The number you have called has been disconnected.*

Lewis froze. "Bastard," he whispered, then louder: "Her phone's gone. He's cutting her off. I need to know where she is—Monk will know."

He called Monk.

"What have you found out?" Monk barked, then stopped himself. "Forget it. This isn't secure."

"Sir, Violet's phone's been disconnected. I need her location. Now."

A beat of silence. Then Monk: "I'll call you back." The line went dead.

Lewis dropped the phone into his lap, rubbing his neck. "Monk's calling me back," he muttered, then swore softly. "Fuck." He glanced at Jenny. "Sorry."

Jenny gave him a small, tight smile. "You okay?"

He shook his head. "No. I'm worried for her. And Jamie." He turned to Callum, desperation raw in his voice. "You *all* know why he wants her. Please. Tell me."

Callum looked at Frank, weighing risk against trust. Jenny touched his arm. "Tell him," she said softly. "He has a right to know."

Frank nodded. "We can trust him."

Callum exhaled slowly, twisting in his seat to face Lewis. Jenny turned away, unable to watch. "It's eugenics," Callum said finally. "The science of altering DNA. We've only used it to eliminate deadly inherited conditions — diseases that used to pass through generations."

Lewis nodded faintly. "Right. That's why people don't die of them anymore."

"Exactly. Life expectancy's over a hundred now. But there was one condition left. One we couldn't crack." Callum met Lewis's eyes.

Lewis's stomach dropped. "You mean… old age."

Callum didn't answer. His silence was enough.

Jenny's hand rested lightly on his arm.

"Dave destroyed the research," she said softly. "He helped Anna escape."

Callum shook his head, throat tight. "I tried. I thought I'd saved her. But now… Violet's back. And she's with him."

The car fell silent.

Lewis didn't want to ask. Didn't want to imagine what Rochester planned. But they all knew.

***

Violet squeezed her eyes shut. She prayed Lewis had seen her message before the phone went dead.

She pushed open the door to the foyer. Rochester was standing by the grey glass doors, waiting for her.

Jamie wasn't there.

She scanned the space as she walked towards him, heartbeat thudding.

"Where's Jamie?" Her voice came out sharper than she intended.

Rochester pressed his hand to the door pad. "He's in here. I've sent him ahead for the eye surgery."

"I should be with him," Violet said, heat rising to her cheeks. "He's only twelve."

She didn't care how she sounded. Rochester should have been more considerate.

"I asked if he wanted you to hold his hand," he said, amused.

"And of course he said no," she snapped. "You—" She cut herself off. *You knew he'd say no.*

"It's done, Violet. Stop worrying. He'll manage five minutes without you." Cold. Clipped. Final.

The floor seemed to shift beneath her. She had tried to make space for him — for the idea of a father — but staring into those green eyes now, lips pressed in a hard line, all she saw was indifference.

"I want to see him." She brushed past him, not even knowing where she was going.

Rochester's jaw tightened. He clenched his fists, then smoothed his face into something resembling patience.

"And so you shall," he said evenly. "After the procedure."

He bent towards her, voice low and controlled, as though speaking to a stubborn child.

"Violet, you are causing a scene. My staff are watching."

She whipped her head around. Two men in white coats were approaching fast from the end of the corridor.

Rochester straightened, turning to meet them, his hand brushing Violet's shoulder as if to steady her.

"Behave yourself," he murmured under his breath — quiet, dangerous.

"I will," she shot back, her throat tight, "if you take me to my brother."

His eyes flashed, hard and cold. He should have admired her defiance — another man might have — but he didn't like being challenged. Not today. Not when everything depended on control.

And then he remembered. The message she'd sent. *Sorry.* To Lewis. He smiled. Thin. Sharp. Deadly.

"Violet," he hissed softly, then straightened, masking it with charm. "Dr Hall," he said smoothly as the man reached them, "this is my daughter, Violet."

Dr Hall extended a hand. "Violet," he said.

She shook it quickly. No smile. "My brother's having his eyes fixed. I want to see him. Please."

Dr Hall glanced at Rochester. A subtle raise of eyebrows. Rochester gave the smallest nod.

"Of course," Hall said, his voice calm, measured. "He's in our day procedure wing. Next floor up."

Violet exhaled, relieved. But Dr Hall was studying her carefully, as though weighing something.

He needed her calm. Rochester was reckless, couldn't he see what he was doing?

Rochester let Hall lead Violet ahead. He followed, his gaze locked on the swing of her red ponytail. His fingers twitched with the urge to grab it, yank it back.

Something was wrong. Violet could feel it in her chest, in her pulse, in the way the corridor lights seemed too bright, too sharp. Her body was telling her to run.

She had to find Jamie first. And then she was going home. Back to DZ.

She didn't trust him anymore. He hadn't kept his word. He'd tried to turn her against Lewis. She would never forgive that.

They reached the lifts. Dr Hall pressed his hand to the keypad, punched in a code, and hit the button.

Violet's chest tightened. "It's a simple procedure," Dr Hall said softly, glancing down at her, trying to sound reassuring. "Only seconds."

"Nothing can go wrong, can it?" she asked. A sudden image of Jamie blind flashed through her mind.

Dr Hall hesitated — too long — then looked up at Rochester. The doctor's eyebrow lifted, questioning. Was she supposed to know?

"No, you'll be fine," he said finally, forcing a smile. "Just a very tiny incision in your stomach."

Violet blinked. Confused.

"She means her brother," Rochester said smoothly, his hand firm on her shoulder as he guided her into the lift. The glare he shot Hall was sharp enough to cut.

Dr Hall recovered quickly. "Yes, of course — your brother. He'll be fine."

But Rochester's fury burned, silent and contained.

An incision. Violet's breath caught. Her pulse roared in her ears. "What do you mean?"

The lift doors slid shut. Moving down.

Down. Not up. "You said the next floor," she whispered, voice breaking. Her chest tightened. Panic clawed at her throat, hot and rising. "Where are you taking me?"

She turned on Rochester, but he didn't answer. His gaze locked with Hall's instead. A silent command.

And then —

A sharp sting against her neck. Like an ant bite.

Violet slapped her hand to the spot, breath catching. Heat bloomed through her chest. The lift tilted, her vision swaying.

"What—what did you do?" Her voice cracked, distorted.

Her hands rubbed at her eyes but the lights blurred, ringing roared in her ears, distant and shrill. She staggered back. "What did you do to me?"

The world folded in on itself. Her knees buckled. Rochester's arms caught her before she hit the floor.

"My father," she breathed, her voice trembling with accusation.

Somewhere, a voice — low, urgent — "Hold her."

And then the ringing stopped. And she was tumbling, weightless, into black water.

***

Jamie opened his eyes. Blinked. Opened them again.

"Whoa."

The world was sharp, colours slicing clean edges into the room.

"You did great," said the young doctor beside him, her hand light on his shoulder. "Just sit still a moment. Let your eyes adjust. Okay?"

Jamie nodded, impatient already.

"Five minutes," she said. "Look around slowly and—"

"—can I borrow your phone?" he cut in. "Gotta call my sister. She worries."

She smiled and handed it to him. "I'll be in my office."

Jamie called. Disconnected. He frowned, tried again. Same thing.

Weird.

He stood, legs light under him and wandered to the window. Outside, a white van sat at the top of the driveway, a stark block against the green grass. As he watched, it rolled slowly to the back of the hospital.

A man climbed out. Opened the back doors. Pulled out a stretcher.

Jamie leaned closer, squinting — and froze.

Rochester.

Now with his new eyes, there was no mistaking him.

Jamie ducked instinctively, heart thumping, then edged back up to peek over the sill.

That's when he saw her. Violet.

In the arms of a man in a white coat. Her head lolling back, her red hair spilling like a scarf towards the ground.

His stomach clenched hard. He wanted to bang on the glass, scream — but he forced himself to move. He had to get help. There was only one person who could.

The platoon leader.

Lewis's phone buzzed. Unknown number. "Carlyle," he answered.

"Lewis, it's Jamie!" His voice was high, ragged. "He's got her — Rochester — he's taken her somewhere in an ambulance. She looked dead, she can't be dead, she was—"

"Slow down. Where are you?" Lewis's grip tightened on the phone, knuckles white.

"At Rochester's hospital but—he's taken her somewhere!"

Lewis's breath came fast. He repeated the message aloud. Jenny swerved the car into a side street, pulling over hard.

"Advanced Laboratories," Callum said grimly. "That's where he'll take her."

"Jenny — we're close," Lewis said sharply. "We pick up Jamie."

"On it."

Jamie bolted from the lift, legs pounding across the foyer. He ditched the doctor's phone on the reception desk, burst out the glass doors and sprinted up the curving drive.

Jenny's car screeched to a stop. Lewis flung the door open. "In. Middle seat."

Jamie scrambled in, wedging between Lewis and Frank.

"Hi, Jamie," Jenny said softly.

He didn't answer. Tears slid hot down his cheeks, silent and constant. He wiped them on his sleeve, sniffing hard. "Just had surgery on my eyes," he muttered, voice small. Jamie's hands shook, knuckles white around the seatbelt.

Lewis kept one arm braced on the headrest in front of him, leaning forward so he could see Jenny's hands tight on the wheel. The engine whined as she pushed the car harder, tyres humming against wet asphalt.

"Tell me again," Lewis said, voice low but sharp.

Jamie swallowed, forcing the words out fast. "She was unconscious, Lewis. A doctor was carrying her. Rochester was there. And —" His throat closed. "There was a van. A stretcher. I thought she was—"

"She's not," Lewis cut in, too quickly. "She's not."

Jamie nodded, eyes darting between Lewis and the blur of lights outside. "I called her. Her number's dead. Disconnected."

Lewis stilled.

A cold weight settled behind his ribs.

Jenny's jaw tightened as she glanced in the rear-view mirror. "I know where he's taking her," she said. "Advanced Laboratories. I've been there."

Callum turned in his seat, voice grim. "It won't matter if we find the place. You can't walk in. High security. Locked systems. You'll need clearance codes just to get through the front doors."

"Then we don't walk in," Lewis said.

Callum frowned. "What are you thinking?"

"That we're not alone."

Lewis punched at his phone, knuckles pale. The call connected after two rings.

"Monk."

He relayed it all in clipped, staccato bursts — Violet, Rochester, the ambulance, Advanced Laboratories.

Monk didn't waste time with questions. "Keep heading there," he said. "World Security's already inbound."

Lewis hung up, but his grip stayed locked around the phone like it was keeping him tethered.

Jamie sniffed beside him, wiping his sleeve across his face. "It's my fault," he whispered.

Lewis twisted, catching his shoulder. "No. Listen to me. You did exactly what you should have. You called. That's why we're going to get her back."

Jamie nodded, but his chest still rose and fell too fast, shallow breaths jerking out of him.

Jenny pushed the car harder, the needle edging into the red. City lights thinned, replaced by long stretches of dark road winding through industrial blocks.

Advanced Laboratories was on the outskirts — isolated, set against scrub and shadows, a concrete fortress built for secrets.

"Two minutes," Jenny said, eyes locked on the road.

Lewis leaned forward, his breath fogging the glass as he stared ahead. He couldn't see it yet, but he could *feel* it — something looming in the dark.

Beside him, Callum muttered under his breath. "You realise he'll be ready for us. Security. Scanners. Everything."

Lewis's voice came out flat, steady. "Then we won't give him time to use them."

The car crested a rise. And there it was. Advanced Laboratories.

A slab of glass and steel rising out of the night, its edges lit by a low ring of white security lights. High fences. A checkpoint booth at the main gate.

Jamie sat forward, breath fogging the window. "That's where she is," he said softly, like saying it out loud might make it real.

Jenny eased the car into the shadows at the side of the road, cutting the headlights. The engine ticked softly as it cooled. For a moment, no one spoke.

Lewis's pulse roared in his ears. He could almost see her. Somewhere behind those walls, Violet lay trapped, and Rochester was waiting.

Jenny turned, her voice tight. "So, what's the plan?"

Lewis didn't answer right away. His gaze stayed fixed on the building, calculating distances, cameras, angles.

Finally, he exhaled, his voice quiet but hard. "We wait for Monk. We wait for World Security."

"And if they're too late?" Jenny asked.

Lewis's hand clenched around the door handle, knuckles white. "Then we don't wait."

Jenny glanced at Lewis in the rear-view mirror. He was pale, jaw clenched, shoulders tight. She didn't ask. She didn't need to. The girl mattered.

***

Violet surfaced slowly, clawing her way through heavy, dragging waves of black.

For a moment she couldn't move. Couldn't breathe. Couldn't think.

Then — voices. Low. Muffled. A room that smelled of antiseptic and cold metal.

Her lashes clumped together as she forced her eyes open. A ceiling swam above her — white, sterile, blinding. A shadow moved across her vision.

Dr Hall. He stood over her, gloved hands steady, but his forehead shone with sweat. He brushed a stray strand of her hair back and tugged a green surgical cap over her head, fastening the ties with fingers that trembled only slightly.

"Don't—" Her throat burned, the word rasping out. She couldn't move her arms. Leather straps bit into her wrists.

"Stay still," Hall murmured softly, his voice measured, soothing. "It'll be over quickly."

Her stomach rolled. *Over quickly.*

From behind a glass wall, Rochester watched. He stood with his hands clasped behind his back, posture straight, face unreadable. Only his eyes moved — sharp, fixed on her like a predator studying prey.

She tried to swallow, but her mouth was dry. Dr Hall turned her arm over gently, exposing the pale underside, a thin blue vein rising beneath the skin. He swabbed it once. Twice. Deliberate. Precise.

Rochester's reflection caught the light — just a flicker — and her gaze snapped to him. He didn't blink. Didn't move. Just… waited.

Violet's chest tightened. Her mind screamed *no no no* but the drug made her body slow, heavy, uncooperative. She flexed her fingers weakly against the straps.

Rochester shifted closer to the glass, a silhouette against the harsh fluorescent light. He tilted his head, the smallest motion, as though measuring her. Calculating.

She hated him in that moment. The certainty of it surged through her like a live wire.

Hall glanced up at him. "Sir… her vitals are dropping slightly. The sedative's strong. I—"

"Proceed." The word cut through the air, cold and absolute.

Dr Hall swallowed hard, nodded once, and reached for the syringe.

Violet's breath came shallow and fast. Her heartbeat skittered, wild. She pulled against the straps with everything she had, but they didn't budge.

"This will sting," Hall whispered, sliding the needle into her vein.

A sharp burn lanced up her arm. Violet gasped, chest heaving, her head rolling against the thin pillow.

The sound made Rochester's lip twitch — not quite a smile. Something smaller. Darker.

Hall drew a vial of deep red blood, his hands steady despite the sweat dripping down his temple.

Violet's vision blurred, edges dissolving. She felt light, untethered, like her body was slipping away from her.

She thought of Jamie. His ridiculous straw boater. His grin. *Please be safe. Please.*

Somewhere, faintly, she heard Hall's voice: "Sample's ready."

Rochester turned slightly, lifting his phone to his ear, his expression carved from stone.

"What is it?" he snapped. He paused, jaw tightening, and then — fury. "Find him." His voice boomed through the glass, sharp enough to cut. "Find the boy and bring him here!"

Violet's stomach dropped. *Jamie. He wants Jamie.*

Dr Hall froze mid-motion, his eyes darting from Rochester to Violet, then back again. He looked pale now.

Rochester lowered the phone slowly, deliberately, and set it on the console beside him. Then he stepped closer to the glass, leaning in, his gaze locking on Violet's.

She couldn't look away. "You won't feel a thing," he said softly, his lips barely moving, the words for her and her alone.

But his eyes — his eyes told another story. She would feel everything.

Hall's gloved hands hovered over the tray of instruments. A scalpel caught the light, its edge sharp enough to split air.

Violet's breathing quickened, ragged.

Rochester steepled his fingers, patient, silent, waiting.

Hall hesitated, his hands trembling now. He was stalling, she could feel it, but not enough to save her.

Her entire body trembled as she forced the words out, her voice raw: "Please. Don't do this."

Hall looked down. Rochester didn't move.

Finally, Rochester spoke, his voice a whisper wrapped in steel. "Begin."

The lights above her blurred, bending. The high-pitched ring in her ears returned, louder now, drowning out thought.

She tried to fight it, claw her way back into her body, but the edges of the world were dissolving, collapsing inward.

The last thing she saw before the blackness surged up was Rochester's reflection in the glass — a faint curve at the corner of his mouth, not triumph, not joy.

Possession.

And then she was gone.

***

Lewis paced between the car and the security gates of Advanced Laboratories, his chest tight with frustration. What was taking Monk so long?

He looked over at the sterile white building, its mirrored windows blank and unfeeling. Violet was in there somewhere. And—no. He didn't want to think about what they were doing to her.

Callum had muttered something earlier about a liver sample before Frank had shut him down. The thought of it made Lewis's stomach turn. He was grateful Jamie hadn't heard.

Back at the car, Jamie's pale face was pressed against the glass, watching him. Jenny had made him sit next to her, her arm around his shoulders.

"He looks frantic," Frank said quietly, nodding towards Lewis.

Callum followed his gaze. "Yeah. He told me he met her in DZ. He likes her." He hesitated, then added softly, "A lot."

The sudden roar of engines snapped Lewis's head around. A convoy of World Security vans tore into view, tyres grinding against the pavement. Lewis ran to the first one, yanking the door open before it stopped moving.

"What took you so long?" he demanded. "She's in there and he's doing something to her—her liver, probably—"

"Calm down, Lewis," Monk said, swinging out of the van, a World Security cap in his hand. "We had to locate someone with clearance to get us inside."

Lewis followed his gaze to where an Advanced Laboratories employee was being hustled towards the gate. The man's face was pale, panicked, his protests spilling over.

"I need to confirm this with Mr Rochester!" he stammered. "My neck will be on the block—"

"It's already on the block," Monk cut in sharply. "You're assisting World Security. Get a move on."

He turned to Callum, thrusting a second cap into his hands. "You're coming too. Better if Rochester doesn't recognise you."

Lewis didn't wait to be asked. He was going in.

***

Inside, the air smelled faintly sterile, sharp with disinfectant.

"It's a labyrinth," Monk muttered as they stepped into the white corridors, faced with a maze of identical doors.

"This is all new," Callum said, scanning the smooth panels as they passed. "But the operating theatre should still be in the same place. Underground." He glanced at Monk. "The fire wouldn't have touched it. North wing. Has anyone got a compass?"

Lewis was already pulling out his phone. "That way," he said, taking off down one of the corridors.

They reached a wall of spotless white tiles.

"It's here," Callum breathed. He pressed a hidden panel — and a faint click answered. "He hasn't changed it. Guess he thought I'd never come back." A shiver ran up his spine.

Far below, Rochester spun around as the lift behind him whirred to life. Someone was in the building.

Above the noise of machinery, Violet moaned faintly. Rochester glanced back at her on the table. Her lashes trembled, her throat working as she tried to swallow.

She thought she was dreaming. Her arms wouldn't move, her chest was heavy, her throat dry. She tried to open her eyes — and saw Hall leaning over her.

"No—keep away from me!" Her voice broke, hoarse, and Hall flinched, the scalpel sliding from his hand, clattering onto steel.

Rochester moved from behind the viewing screen, his expression unreadable. Entrance to his underground laboratory was strictly off limits. But the lift… the timing… Bureau involvement was obvious.

He leaned over Violet, his voice low, measured. "You're alright, Violet. You fainted. Dr Hall just took a blood sample." He slid an arm under her shoulders, helping her upright.

Beyond the sealed glass doors, the lift opened. Rochester saw Lewis first — Monk and two World Security officers hard on his heels. Rochester's lip curled.

"Hall. Help Violet. Get her water," he said, his voice sharp enough to slice glass.

Hall hesitated, frozen.

Before Rochester could reach the doors, Lewis hit them with his shoulder, forcing them open. Rochester staggered back against the viewing screen as Lewis ran past, straight to Violet.

"Violet," he breathed, taking her by the shoulders, pulling her into his arms. "Are you okay? I've got you."

"Lewis… Lewis…" Her voice was weak, cracked with relief. She bit back a sob.

"You're safe," he said softly, holding her tighter.

Rochester straightened his jacket, his voice suddenly sharp. "What the hell do you think you're doing?"

"This is private property, Monk. You'd better have a good explanation."

Monk didn't even glance at him. "Don't need one," he said, nodding at the officers. "World Security."

Rochester's face flushed. "This isn't a police state. You can't just barge in here—there will be consequences."

Monk ignored him, turning instead to Lewis. "The girl alright?"

Lewis pulled back slightly, scanning Violet's pale face, her unfocused green eyes. "Did he do anything to you, Violet?"

"Do anything?" Rochester's voice was cold, incredulous. "If you mean did I arrange for Dr Hall to take a blood sample to ensure my daughter wasn't a danger to Perfection, then yes."

Across the room, Callum's gaze locked on Hall. Guilt radiated off him like heat. He saw the scalpel glint on the floor, saw Hall's shaky hands, and knew.

Moving casually, Callum circled the operating table, keeping his back to the others. Only Hall noticed as he slipped the glass capsule containing Violet's blood into his pocket. Their eyes met — a silent exchange. Hall gave a quick shake of his head. No liver sample. Just blood. Callum's chest eased.

Violet touched the inside of her elbow where the needle had pierced her skin. It stung faintly. She bit her lip, swallowing hard, refusing to cry.

Lewis saw her lip tremble. "Come on, Violet," he murmured, sliding an arm around her shoulders. "Let's get out of here. Jamie's waiting."

Her head felt heavy against his chest, her legs barely holding her up. Without hesitation, Lewis lifted her into his arms. Her arm slid around his neck. She didn't protest. She didn't want to.

Rochester and Monk stood locked in a silent standoff at the glass doors. The World Security officers waited inside the lift. Rochester leaned forward, his voice low and venomous.

"You'll pay for this, Monk."

Monk didn't flinch.

As Lewis passed, Rochester's sharp green eyes met Violet's. He raised his brows, as if to ask what all the fuss was about. Violet turned her face into Lewis's chest.

"Move," Lewis said quietly.

Rochester smiled faintly. "Still trying to be the hero, Carlyle. But this isn't some rescue of the fair maiden." He swept a hand across the room. "I was protecting my daughter."

Then, louder, for everyone to hear: "Violet, you fainted when I told you we needed a blood sample at the lab. Dr Hall sedated you, that's all. I thought it best. The agents from World Security can confirm it was necessary. It's a condition of you and Jamie remaining with me."

Violet's throat burned. *Liar.*

"I didn't faint," she whispered. Her eyes stung. She shook her head. "You said you were my father. Fathers are supposed to…" The rest caught in her throat.

Rochester's expression barely shifted, but his voice cut sharp. "Violet, you're being dramatic. Emotional. So like your mother."

Lewis's jaw clenched, teeth grinding. "Bastard."

Rochester stepped back, calculating, silent. He'd let her go. For now. He'd find her again.

He pulled his phone from his pocket. "I'm calling my lawyer. Then the press. You won't get away with this."

"Take the phone," Monk ordered sharply. The officers moved instantly, one wrenching it from Rochester's hand, the other clamping down on his arm.

"You can't—" Rochester snarled, struggling free. "Damn you, Monk—"

"Yes, yes," Monk said wearily. "I'll pay. Hold him and Hall for an hour. After that, they can make all the calls they want."

Monk turned to Callum, clapping a hand on his shoulder as they stepped into the lift. "Good work," he said.

Lewis wasn't listening, he bent his head close to Violet's ear, whispering something only she could hear.

"I know," she whispered back.

When the lift doors opened, Violet stirred slightly in his arms. "Jamie heard Rochester talking to Poppy," she murmured. "I didn't believe him." Her voice cracked. "You can put me down now, I can stand."

Lewis ignored her. "Better not. I'll put you down at the car."

Outside, Monk stopped by the waiting cars. "Callum. You and your brother are with me. Ask Jenny to follow behind with Jamie… and those two." He nodded at Lewis and Violet.

Lewis lowered her gently to her feet. "You okay?" he asked, scanning her face.

Jamie ran to them immediately, his small hand clutching Violet's. "What's wrong with her?"

Violet crouched slightly, forcing a smile. "I'm okay. Don't worry." She pulled him into her arms, holding him tight until the trembling finally took her over.

Lewis slid in next to her in the back seat, his arm firm around her shoulders. She couldn't stop shaking, no matter how hard she tried. He pressed his lips to her temple, his thumbs rubbing slow circles into the nape of her neck.

Jenny glanced at them in the rear-view mirror. For a moment, her throat caught. They made a beautiful picture, fragile and strong all at once.

Outside, Frank crossed to join Callum and Monk by the other car. Callum handed Monk the World Security cap. "Thanks. Don't think I'll be needing this anymore."

Monk traced the raised WS insignia slowly with his thumb, his gaze drifting back to Violet's pale reflection in the car window.

"She's a problem," he said quietly. "An enormous threat to Perfection. To its very existence."

Callum's jaw tightened. "She can't stay here, Monk. If it gets out that she carries the genetic coding for…"

Monk finished it for him, grim and certain. "Eternal life."

"Where are we going?" Jamie asked, trying to tug his hand free from Violet's grip. She was holding on so tightly his fingers had gone white, and she was crying — the quiet kind, no sound at all, just tears spilling over like a small, steady waterfall.

Lewis had his arm around her. That helped somehow. Jamie decided the platoon leader was her boyfriend again — it looked that way, the way Lewis held her close and brushed her hair back as though she was a kid.

"We're going to follow the car with my husband and the others," Jenny said, "I don't know where we're going either."

"Violet," Jamie said, flexing his hand, "could you may be let go of my fingers? They've gone numb."

"Sorry." She released him slowly, resting her hands on her knees.

Callum walked over to the car, "My brother and I are going with Monk. Things to talk about. Just follow his car."

He glanced at Lewis. Lewis gave the smallest lift of his eyebrows, a question Callum couldn't answer. There were no guarantees here. Violet's very existence could still unravel everything.

CHAPTER THIRTY-NINE

They'd been driving four hours when Monk's car veered off the highway, down a slip road, and then another, before reaching a barrier marked PRIVATE GOVERNMENT PROPERTY. Tall metal gates blocked the entrance, a wall behind them hiding whatever lay beyond was barred with solid metal gates.

The sky had dulled to a steel grey as the sun dipped away.

Monk got out and spoke to the soldiers guarding the gate. Jamie had climbed into the front seat when he saw Jenny's husband and Frank get into Monk's car.

"This is great," said Jamie eyes wide at the armed guards. "Are we on the run?"

Violet almost smiled. She wished she was more like Jamie, he never got bored, he always saw the positive in everything.

"Yes," said Lewis, "we're the good guys outwitting the bad guys with cunning."

"And stealth," Jamie added, grinning, but his voice wavered. He turned to look at Lewis. "Then you need to tell me everything. What's going on?"

Lewis caught Jenny's eyes in the mirror, then looked at Violet. He hadn't told her everything yet.

"Yes," Violet said quietly. "What's going on?"

The flare of anger in Lewis's chest surprised even him. "We're all on the run," he said, voice sharp, "because your father is a callous indifferent bastard."

Violet blinked, stung by the heat in his words. She wished she felt angry too, instead of hollow and sad.

"I guess I know that," she said softly. "I just… don't know why, Lewis. Jamie and me – we're the only ones who don't know why he did what he did."

"You'll know," Lewis said after a pause. But you need to hear it from someone who can explain it."

"Yes," said Jenny quietly. "Let Dave tell her." He owes Violet that much."

The gates swung open, and Jenny followed Monk's car up a narrow road winding into dense forest. The branches overhead, knitting together into a dark, mottled tunnel.

Violet swallowed, fighting waves of nausea as Jenny swung the car hard around a tight bend. She loosened her seatbelt and lay down, closing her eyes. Lewis eased her head onto his knee and brushed his fingers against her cheek "Motion sickness?"

She nodded.

Jenny turned the radio on low, the music trickling softly into the silence.

"Do you know where we are?" Jamie asked.

Jenny gave a small, nervous laugh. She would never forget this road, she had driven it once more than eighteen years ago. "I know the general area, it's private, belongs to World Security." She didn't add *and Frank, works here.*

"We're climbing," said Jamie peering out into the darkness. "It's a mountain."

"How you doing Violet?" Jenny asked gently.

"Okay," Violet whispered, though her voice didn't sound like hers. She closed her eyes. She just wanted this over.

"Can I change the music?" Jamie asked suddenly. "This dreamy tinkling rubbish is putting me to sleep.

"Sure," Jenny said. "Find something to keep us awake."

Lewis knew where they were going. He'd known the moment Monk's car turned off the highway and his chest had felt crushed ever since.

Violet reached across and found his hand, holding it to her lips.

***

Callum finally broke the silence, "I suppose there is no other…" Monk cut him off sharply, "No, there isn't it. We've had the conversation already."

Callum clenched his jaw. It had been his idea but now closing in on it, he hated himself for it.

"It's the only solution," Monk said softer now. "If she stays, we keep her and her brother in isolation. Under lock and key. Or.." He stopped; he couldn't finish.

"She's more dangerous than…than…whatever her world made."

"Tetraethyl?" said Frank, "The stuff they put in petrol that destroyed their ozone layer."

"No. Worse. The bomb. Nuclear something." Monk waved a hand, impatient. "Point is -she's dangerous."

Callum pressed his palms to his eyes. Back when he helped Anna escape, he'd thought he was saving her and her baby from Rochester. But here they were, following behind him – that baby, now grown, carrying the gene he'd helped put there. He didn't want to know if it had worked. He prayed it hadn't.

Frank broke the moment. "Look!" he said, holding out his phone. "It's out. On the news. Rochester's spoken to the press."

"Radio." Monk spat the words out.

Callum jabbed the buttons until Rochester's name filled the car.

'…her father Rochester has told reporters it was with a heavy heart he alerted the press to the danger his daughter Violet and her half-brother present to the country. Tests conducted by Rochester's Hospital revealed they're both carriers of previously unknown viruses. Their capture and segregation is critical…'

Monk reached over and switched it off. "Frank. Time frame?"

"Fifty-five-minutes, twenty seconds."

Callum exhaled, long and shaky. Monk's eyes stayed forward, jaw tight. *Please let this be the last place they look.*

***

"What?" Violet struggled to sit up. Through the fog of sleep, she'd caught her name.

Jenny tensed. Lewis's stomach clenched. Rochester had done this – turned his daughter into Perfection's most wanted.

"Change the station." Jenny said quickly, her voice too light.

"It's about us!" Jamie said ignoring her and cranking up the volume.

They listened in silence as the shadows of the trees slid across the car like smoke.

When the news flash ended, Lewis spoke first, "You don't have a virus. Either of you. That's Rochester's lie. He wants everyone scared of you so they'll stay away. Then your quarantined, he gets you back, and they'll test you – prove him wrong."

"And I have to go back to him?" Violet whispered, clutching her stomach.

Lewis lowered his head to hers, voice rough. "You won't. That's a promise."

Jamie grinned faintly. "Here that, Violet? The platoon leader says we're safe. So, what's the plan?"

Lewis hesitated. He'd already figured out the plan. Hated it. But all he said was, "Not sure yet, Jamie. My boss decides."

The car ahead slowed to a stop. The headlights lit up a squat timber building. Soldiers standing on guard. And somewhere above them, snow waited in the dark.

The convoy stopped Frank and Monk got out of the car. Thin mist curled along the road, lifting in pale threads of smoke.

Lewis held his breath as Frank and Monk held out their credentials. Two soldiers walked over to Jenny's car. She opened the window.

"Do you need us to get out?" Jenny said. The soldier looked across at Jamie. Jamie grinned at him.

"Pop the boot please." He had his orders. Safety checks. No one got past this point without it. He turned the contents over with his rifle. Clothes, fishing gear, life jackets.

"Can you explain the contents of the boot ma'am." His voice was full of suspicion.

Jenny frowned.

"The life jackets ma'am…clothes?" He snapped.

"Oh…that… yes, that's our fishing equipment. We've been on holiday. No time to unpack."

He turned and walked away speaking into his earpiece.

"He's making a call," said Lewis, "Checking the details." Lewis got out of the car, scanning the station, his hand flexing at his side. Violet recognised it instantly – the way he did that when he was nervous, like a reflex he couldn't control.

Violet stepped out into the sharp air. Her breath misted and disappeared into the fading light. The forest below was already dark, shadows spilling across the ridges. Somewhere beyond the peaks, hidden by cloud, was wherever they were taking her.

She glanced at the cables stretching into the fog. Thin black threads vanishing into white nothingness.

Her stomach twisted.

Jamie darted past her, chasing a soldier's stride with a thousand questions, his energy sparking against the heavy silence. Violet wanted to hold onto that – his lightness, his disbelief – but it slipped through her fingers like mist.

Lewis came to stand beside her. Close, but not close enough. "It's going to be okay," he said. Violet turned and looked at him. His face looked so pale in the dim light of the car. He smiled; it made her chest hurt. The saddest smile she'd ever seen. His grey eyes looked like ice, they glittered and then he turned his head away.

"They'll explain when we get there," he said quietly, not looking at her.

"I don't want explanations," she said, her voice catching despite her effort to keep it even. "I just want…this to stop."

For a moment neither of them spoke. The wind carried voices up from the lower station, scraps of orders, the whirring hum of machinery.

His jaw tightened. "You'll be safe, Violet."

"You can't promise that."

"I can," he said, steady this time. "And I will."

She wanted to ask him if she'd ever see him again, but her voice wouldn't form the words.

She thought he might say something more, might reach for her, but he just stood there, fists shoved into his pockets, gaze somewhere beyond the clouds."

Dave had retrieved blankets from the car and gave them to Violet and Jamie. He helped Jamie put it around his shoulders. "You okay Jamie?" He could see that beneath his sunny exterior his eyes looked worried.

"Yeh, I'm okay. I want to know what the plan is." Said Jamie.

"Let's get out of the cold first. We've got a short walk and then a cable car ride up the mountain and a blazing fire and hot chocolate at the Lodge.

"Lodge?" said Jamie.

"Yeh, like a ski Lodge." He gave Jamie a little push, "Okay follow Frank."

Jamie pulled the blanket up to his nose. Jenny took hold of his hand. He was going to tell her he didn't need his hand held but Jenny said, "Don't let me fall, the ground's a bit frosty."

"Okay," Jamie was glad she needed his help. Something was very wrong. They weren't going skiing. He knew that much.

"You still feeling sick?" Lewis said, his arm around Violet's shoulder.

"No, it always stops when my feet are on dry land…or frosty ground." She rubbed at the glittering earth with her shoe. She could feel Lewis's muscles bunch in his arm as he went to take a step forward. Violet didn't move, she anchored her heels to the ground.

"What's wrong?" said Lewis. Violet was staring at the ground, her hair had fallen over her shoulder, her neck looked so white. He wanted to lean down and drag his lips along the creamy skin, take her ear between his teeth. He closed his eyes. *She knows.*

Violet kept her head down. Lewis pulled Violet against his chest, he saw the others had entered the cable car station. He wrapped the blanket around them both.

"How long before…" he didn't let her finish the sentence, he covered her mouth with his. This was all they were going to get. The last kiss goodbye. He wanted to lock the memory of it in his mind forever.

Violet pulled away, she couldn't see him for the tears that were filling her eyes. Lewis brushed his wet eyes against her cheek, "Not long enough." He said.

She pressed her hands against his chest, he kissed her again, his lips soft against hers, he cupped her face in his hands, "Violet, Violet, Violet.." His voice cracked, he was breaking apart bit by bit.

The thud of the cable car docking at the little wooden station made them both look up, "The cable car," said Lewis. Violet turned her head, she saw the doors open.

Lewis dropped his hand from hers when they reached the cable car. Everyone except Monk was already inside sitting on the two benches that ran down either side of the car. Monk stood at the door blocking the way.

Lewis placed his hand gently on Violet back and guided her forward. "I'll be just a minute," he murmured, "I want to talk to my boss."

Monk raised his bushy eyebrows. His expression said *not now*. "Time?" He barked, not at anyone in particular.

"Forty minutes, thirteen seconds. Ride to the top takes ten, that leaves…"

"I can count Callum," Monk looked at Lewis, "Make it quick Carlyle,"

"Outside," Lewis said.

Monk hunched his shoulders against the dropping temperature. The cold bit through his coat. He wanted this over. The girl, the boy - gone. And with them, the threat to the existence of Perfection.

"Sir, Lewis began, "I was wondering if we could…provide Violet and her brother with some money. I've still got the credit card we used in DZ-"

"You have?" Monk's voice cracked sharp. "And what else haven't you handed back to the Academy?"

"I forgot. And -" Lewis hesitated. "I've still got that money from Rochester. It's in my account. We could transfer it to Violet. It's hers, really. I never wanted it."

"Very noble of you," Monk said dryly. "Yes, we could do that. And then you wouldn't worry. Is that it?" He turned his back.

"No, one other thing." His voice thinned, almost lost in the cold air. Snowflakes drifted between them, settling on Monk's shoulder, dissolving instantly into nothing. Violent would disappear. Like that too. Here one minute then gone.

'Sir." Lewis said. "do we know where the portal's located in DZ?" *Please somewhere safe. Not a desert. Not the ocean.*

Monk didn't answer. He held his palm open, catching a flake, staring at it as if he'd never seen one melt before.

Lewis's chest constricted. Pain pressed against his sternum. He tried to slow his breathing. *She's not going to make it.*

Monk saw it- the colour draining from Lewis's face, the pulse pounding at his neck, his pupils wide with dread. The unshakable Carlyle, close to cracking.

"I take it… it's not good," Lewis managed, forcing his shoulders straight. He couldn't let Monk see him unravel.

Monk tilted his head, considered lying. But no. Carlyle needed to face it. Life didn't give you what you wanted. Sometimes, it ripped people away.

"Transfer is approximately twenty kilometres off the west coast of DZ," Monk said flatly. A drop of one to two metres. It's called the Indian Ocean."

Lewis felt the air punch out of him, "The… Indian Ocean," his voice broke, anguish raw in the sound.

"Sir, couldn't we hide them? Keep them here. Or – another country. Do the transfer later."

He knew he sounded frantic, but the vision of Violet and Jamie in open water played like a horror movie behind his eyes.

Monk shook his head, "World Security want them both dead." He shrugged, almost casual. "I got them to agree to this." He jerked his head behind him at the cable car. "The risk to Perfection is too great. Work it out. An elite that lives forever. An expanding population that never dies. His eyebrows lifted. "This way they have a chance," A pause. "And we get rid of them."

"A chance?" Lewis's voice rose, jagged with fury They've no chance. They'll drown!"

"Keep your voice down Carlyle." Monk's tone sharpened. "I think it's best if you wait in the car. You've said your goodbye.

"No way, I'm coming," Lewis's voice was iron. His mind was a storm, racing through possibilities. Thirty-five minutes. There had to be something.

"They have to go Carlyle," Monk warned. "I don't want a scene. Keep your mouth shut."

Lewis wasn't listening. His thoughts scrambled, colliding, reaching – then one caught. Sailing. Boats.

"Life Jackets." He breathed. And then he was running for Callum's car.

"Life Jackets?" Monk repeated. Baffled.

Lewis yanked open the boot. The light blinked on. His hands tore through the pile of waterproof jackets until he found the orange vests beneath. He grabbed two, stuffing clothes into a spare jacket, tying it with fishing line. Dry clothes. They'd need them.

"Carlyle!" Monk barked. "What the hell do you think you're doing?"

Lewis ignored him, sprinting back with the bundle and two life jackets clutched tight.

"They can wear these," he said breathless.

In his mind, the image had changed" Violet and Jamie in the water, alive, orange vests bright against the grey ocean. Could Violet swim" She'd said....she could, hadn't she? She had to. They both had to.

"NO" Monk snapped the word at Lewis. He lunged to grab them.

Lewis stepped back, holding the jackets to his chest. ""It might save their lives." His eyes burned silver in the moonlight. He didn't care if Monk saw the tears.

Monk saw them and froze. "Are you mad Carlyle."

Lewis dragged his forearm across his face, "Yes," he said roughly. "Mad as hell at my part in all this. The mission …" His voice caught, raw "…It wasn't noble, wasn't heroic…" He nodded toward the cable car. "She meant nothing to Rochester. He never cared. Never loved her…" He took a breath.

He didn't want Violet to see him like this. He brushed past Monk, "I'll tell them what to expect."

***

Violet sat with her arm wrapped around Jamie, his head resting against Jenny's arm, already asleep. Her own skin was pale, almost translucent against the soft fall of snow at the windows. She stared at the glass, watching flakes cling, melt, vanish. Her mind floated with them, each thought dissolving before she could catch it.

Her heart had stopped pounding. That terrified her more than the panic. Maybe she was in shock. Maybe she was already gone.

Frank sat opposite, his face grave, hands clasped like a mourner at a funeral. When Lewis entered carrying the bundle and two life jackets, Frank glanced up sharply, then to Monk. Monk's slight shrug said everything. *He knows it's the ocean.*

Lewis dropped the jackets by the door and sat beside Violet. She didn't look at him.

He reached for her hand. Warm. Small.

"Your hand's so cold," she whispered.

"Hot Chocolate!" Callum announced suddenly, breaking the silence as he reached into the cupboard above the small sink. He turned holding the tin out to Jamie – who rubbed at his eyes and started flicking through the screen on his Sixty-Six watch.

"Want some?" Callum tried again.

"I'll make it, "Jenny said softly, taking the tin. She touched her husband's chest. "You should talk to Violet."

Callum nodded touching Lewis on the shoulder, "I need to talk to her," he said.

Lewis hesitated but moved away, glancing once at Violet's face before walking toward Monk. He had to get the money transferred now. If they made it. When they made it.

Jamie looked up, he saw Callum on the bench next to Violet, speaking in a low voice. Violet's hands flew to her mouth. Her head shook. *No. Not true. Couldn't be true.*

"There's something else you should know," said Callum. No time to soften it. No time for gentleness.

Violet rubbed her hands along her arms. She couldn't think what living forever meant. She just hoped she could live through the next 24 hours and keep Jamie safe.

Callum took her hand carefully, "It's about your mother. She came from your world, DZ. She was found near here when she was just a toddler. Two, maybe three. She must have wandered from her parents. The timing was right, she dropped into this world. They traced her to a region called Scotland."

Violet blinked. "Scotland," she repeated.

"Yes, she was sent to quarantine. One of Rochester's doctors was working at the hospital -he saw her, adopted her. No one knew. They told me years later, when we began the experiments. I told your mother before she left. I thought she might find someone."

"I was born there," Violet whispered, distant, almost to herself.

"What's up with Violet?" Said Jamie. She had her hands over her face. He didn't want her to cry. He took a step toward her; Lewis caught him by the arm. "Just wait Jamie. Give her a minute. She'll tell you later."

Callum's eyes softened. "I'm so sorry Violet."

She stood abruptly, shaking her head, searching for air. For Jamie. But Lewis was already there, his arm sliding around her shoulders, steering her into the small back room. He had to prepare her. Somehow.

"What is it?" Violet turned to him, wide -eyed. Her voice cracked. She could see it in his face — more sky falling.

"You knew," she whispered, choking on the words. "All along. You said he...he didn't care about me..." Her throat caught. "I hope he's wrong. I don't want to." She couldn't finish.

Lewis shook his head. Violet, listen. It's not that. It's the transfer." He spoke quickly, forcing steadiness into his voice. "It'll put you and Jamie in the ocean. Twenty kilometres off the coast of Western Australia, near your city. You'll need these." He nodded at the life jacket on the floor.

Her breath hitched. "Life Jackets? The Ocean?" The words barely formed. *The ocean. The dark.* "Will it be dark...like here?"

He hesitated. "I don't know. But if it is... the lights from the coast will guide you to shore." He placed his hands on her shoulders; she looked so calm too calm. A trance, maybe. "You can swim Violet?"

She nodded, "Yes. Not well, I never liked the beach...the sun it gave me freckles. But Jamie can. He's really good. We'll be okay" She reached up and brushed his damp hair back from his forehead and smiled faintly. "You need a haircut,"

He caught her fingers, pressing them briefly to his lips. "I know," he murmured.

"Byron," she whispered.

The name stabbed through him. He swallowed hard, forcing the tears back, forcing composure. He couldn't break. Not now.

He grabbed one of the life jackets forcing himself into motion. "Here," he held it out to her. "Listen carefully. When you hit the water – it's no more than two metres, maybe less – pull this. It'll inflate automatically. See this?" he touched the small light on the shoulder strap. "It'll flash on and off.

Violet brushed her fingers over it, as if testing reality, as if any second she might wake up.

Take this," he held out the credit card. "Monk is activating it now. It'll have everything Rochester gave me."

She took the card tracing the raised letters. Lewis Green, not his name. But something she could keep. She slipped it inside her sweater, under her bra.

"My pin number is my birthday 1404. Remember that?"

She nodded, "It's in two days," she whispered. "You'll be twenty."

Lewis frowned, "Is it?" He'd lost track Another life, another time. He wished he could share all of it.

"Violet." He said softly, "I don't know how, but I'll find you. I will. That's a promise."

Her hand trembled as she touched his lips, silencing him. She didn't want promises. Not ones he might die trying to keep.

She rose onto her toes and kissed him. Soft. Fragile. The kind of kiss that ached – because it carried the weight of everything unsaid. She wound her arms around his neck, clinging like she might fall without him.

Lewis groaned into her mouth, pulling her against him, arms wrapping around her as though she was already slipping away. His kiss was tender, reverent desperate. As if holding her here could keep the world from shattering. But he was the one breaking.

She pressed her forehead to his, whispering into the breath between them, "Best get Jamie ready."

He searched her eyes, memorising her face like a map he'd never see again.

She gave him crooked, brave little smile. "He'll think it's an adventure." She was glad of that.

Lewis ducked his head around the door, scanning the lounge room – no Jamie. Frank stood by the window, phone pressed to his ear, the glass already blurred by gathering snow. Monk hovered near him, listening intently. Dave leaned against the bathroom door, shoulders set, watchful.

Lewis caught Dave's eye, "Tell Jamie I need him when he's out," he said quietly letting the door swing half-closed.

Inside, Violet was bent over the jacket, fingers fumbling with the straps, checking the inflator, lips pressed thin. *Remember. Focus. You can do this.*

A soft knock. Frank slipped in, Jenny crouched on the tiles with the first aid kit open, syringe ready. Dave had given her the phial of Violet's blood. They didn't know if it would work – but the thought of Violet trapped, forever, watching Jamie grow old without her, was unbearable.

"Tell the kid," Dave whispered pulling the door shut. "He's smart."

Jamie rolled up his sleeve, wide-eyed. "Cool," he said. "You done this before?"

"Plenty," Jenny smiled faintly, swabbing his arm. "Met Dave at the hospital, - broke his nose playing basketball." The needle slid in, smooth and precise, the red rising through the tube. "Half a phial," she murmured, withdrawing it quickly.

Jamie barely winced. "Didn't hurt a bit. If this means I live forever? I've got plans."

Jenny pressed gauze to his arm and taped it. Jamie tugged his sleeve down, gaze flicking to the syringe.

"What about the rest?"

"Disposing of it," she said, holding it over the sink.

"Wait." Jamies's voice sharpened. "Give it to Lewis."

Jenny hesitated.

"I heard him." Jamie insisted. "He promised Violet he'd find her. If she's scared – and she will be – it could take him a long time. He'll want the option."

Lewis was already at the door, reading Dave's expression.

"In," Dave said. "Jenny will explain."

CHAPTER FORTY

Snow whispered beneath their shoes as Frank led them to the transfer portal. The track narrow, winding up through the trees. Lewis stayed beside Violet and Jamie, his fingers laced with hers, squeezing like he could anchor her to him. Neither of them spoke.

Jamie glanced up from his Sixty-Six watch, catching Lewis's expression as he stared at Violet's profile. The softness in his eyes – Jamie decided then no one would ever see him look like that.

"Think this'll be as fun as last time?" Jamie muttered.

Frank snorted under his breath.

Lewis didn't answer. His chest burned with the urge to take Violet and Jamie, run down this mountain, find some hidden cave, never come back.

"We're here," Frank said, stopping before a squat, pale concrete block – barely bigger than a bathroom. "Two minutes." he said checking his watch.

Jamie swiped his watch. "Roger that."

Frank keyed in the sequence.

Lewis brushed a strand of hair from Violet's face, drinking in the green of her eyes – the impossible depth of them. She raised her hand, placed her palm against his chest, feeling his heartbeat beneath her fingers, then pressed it briefly to her own heart as if trying to match the rhythm.

"Lewis…" Her voice trembled, lashes wet, one tear breaking free and trailing down her cheek.

He leaned closer, aching to kiss her, but Frank's voice cut through.

"Time. "Now!"

Jamie grabbed Violet's hand, pulling her into the portal. She turned at the threshold, light shifting around her.

"I'll love you forever," she said, smiling through tears – a smile bright and fierce enough to blind him.

And then she was gone.

The floor dropped. Violet's stomach lurched; Jamies arm locked around her waist as the walls compressed, folding her into the moment, breath shallow, eyes screwed shut. She thought she heard a voice - *I've got you.* -and then they hit the water hard, plunging deep into blackness.

She surfaced, gasping, inflating the jacket, night air sharp on her lips. The moon carved silver across oil-dark waves.

"Lewis!" she screamed – but the sound dissolved into wind and salt spray.

Somewhere behind her, he ripped off his shoes. scanning the chaotic water. Jamie was already pulling his cord; the life jacket inflated. Violet spun, wide-eyed, and saw lights -boats – the jagged shape of land.

"Jamie. This way!" she called, striking out hard. "Rottnest – I can see it. "Get going," said Violet. They were so close.

He swam behind them, slowly slicing into the water, keeping pace behind them, guarding their back. Only when their feet touched sand did Lewis climb ashore, breath ragged he called her name.

CHAPTER FORTY-ONE

3 years later somewhere on the West coast of Australia

She leant her arms on the wall of the balcony overlooking the ocean. The sky was a brilliant sapphire blue, the sun burned low in the sky, a light breeze off the water feathered her hair. It was a perfect day.

"Hey you," he said slipping the silk robe of her shoulders and kissing her neck. She turned into his arms, pulling the robe around her naked body. He stopped her and pulled her against his bare chest.

"The neighbours," she laughed licking her tongue across his nipple.

He shuddered, "They can't see. I designed the house so I could do this," he cupped her breast in his hand. She pushed his hand away and led him back to the bedroom.

He lay back on the bed and held out his arms, "Here," he said. She smiled and knelt on one knee beside him. "We don't have time," she stroked her fingers over his chest. He looked into her eyes; they looked like the green of the ocean.

"We don't?" He arched an eyebrow catching her behind her neck he brought his lips to meet hers. She collapsed against him and rested her head against his chest. She could hear his heart beating in her ear.

"I can hear your heart," she murmured.

"That's good news," he said, turning slowly on one elbow, her body sliding onto the bed beneath him.

"Let me check yours," he pressed his ear against her breast. "Mm can't hear a thing," he turned his face and caught her nipple between his lips, working his mouth around it until he heard her gasp.

"Good, that got it started," he whispered staring into her eyes. He shook his head, "Keep looking at me like that I think my heart will burst out of my chest."

"Can't have that," she closed her eyes laughing as she arched up towards him.

Twenty minutes later they were both under the shower, "Don't let my hair get wet," she said as he played the shower hose over her soapy body.

"You're done," he said, turning the hose on himself. "Go get ready, the guests are arriving in…"

"…less than an hour," she shrieked wrapping the towel around her.

"Hey, you two decent, I've got something to show you," someone called from outside the bedroom door.

"No, out in a minute," Lewis answered.

Jamie leant against the marble bench top; he studied his appearance in the glass doors of the cabinet over the sink. He was wearing the suit Violet had picked out for him. He had the tie in his pocket. He glanced at his Sixty-Six; everything was going to plan.

He picked up the two envelopes from the bench where he had placed them. He turned them over in his hands, he couldn't keep the grin off his face.

Lewis paused as he stepped into the kitchen. "Wow, looking good Jamie." He said as he rubbed the towel across his head and then combed back his hair with his fingers.

Jamie straightened up. He was nearly sixteen and as tall as Lewis.

"What have you got to show us?" Lewis saw the envelopes in Jamie's hand. He had a good idea what was in it. "Hey Violet get out here fast," he shouted.

"I'm here," she said shaking back her long red hair. "Lewis," she held out a coronet of flowers of purple lavender and white jasmine for her hair, "Can you pin this in my hair for me, just one here and…" Jamie held his arms out as he turned slowly around. "Oh Jamie… you look so handsome."

"I'd prefer hot," said Jamie, "that's more important than good looks. The Platoon Leader here has good looks but…"

"…he's hot," Violet said firmly holding her head still and looking up into Lewis's eyes as he placed the flower crown on her head, "and sexy," she mouthed silently. He shook his head at her as he pushed a pin carefully into her hair.

"That's it, perfect," Lewis held her at arms' length, and then stepped back. She wore the dress he had seen hanging in the walk-in robe. It was new, bought for the day. He had wondered if it might be too simple for the occasion but what would he know.

It was plain, a pale teal, the colour of the ocean when the sky was turquoise. It hugged her figure and then swung out around her bare feet like a cascading waterfall. Two shoestring straps held the dress in place. The colour rose in her cheeks as Lewis stared at her, she turned away to hide the fact, the dress shimmered like moving water.

"You look beautiful," he said, *those lips, kissable lips.* He touched his lips to hers.

"You look alright," said Jamie. Violet flared her eyes at him, "Brat," she said. "Come here, let me put your tie on for you."

He lifted his chin as Violet folded the collar of his shirt up. He grinned at her, "Can you reach?" He had overtaken Violet more than two years ago and was a good head taller than her now. She yanked at his tie, "Hold still you."

"Okay, now spill the news in the envelopes you're holding," said Lewis.

"Oh Jamie, your results," Violet cried.

He held out the envelopes to Violet and stood watching as she read first one letter then the other. "Jamie, Jamie, you're so clever," she pressed her hand to her lips, "Harvard…and… Cambridge, have both accepted you to do a PhD."

"What's it going to be?" said Lewis, "Genetics or Astrophysics"

"Both! I'm going to do a joint doctorate – get two." He touched his watch; he'd downloaded everything he could from Rochester's laptop and the published research archives. He could probably do another two doctorates but he knew what he wanted to do. "I want to help save this planet, help everyone live longer… just not forever." He raised his eyebrows.

Violet blinked back the tears.

"And one day I want to explore other parallel universes. There has to be more. We know it's not sci-fi, don't we?" He grinned, there shared secret. He would never forget it, the blinding light, and then the icy cold water, and Lewis, the platoon leader stepping out of the water with a bundle of dry clothes for them.

"Almost three years to the day," whispered Violet. She reached for Lewis, he put his arm around her and threw his arm around Jamie's shoulders, "Fantastic Jamie,"

"Thanks," said Jamie. "Wouldn't have happened if you hadn't come with us, would it Violet?"

"I'll never forget it," said Violet.

How could she forget that night when Lewis gave up everything in that split second to follow her into the blinding light. It wasn't the walls of the portal pressing in, it was Lewis with his arms around them both as they fell to earth and then she pulled herself out of the water and stepped onto a moonlit beach and heard him say her name, and he was there, the water dripping from his hair saying those words, 'Said I'd find you.'

Lewis kissed the top of Violet's head. He guessed what she was thinking; those first moments on the beach when she looked too shocked and too panicked to ask him why he had followed her…followed both of them. He had not given her the opportunity to ask anything, he started barking orders at them. It wasn't until they were all off the Island and spent their first night in a hotel making plans that she found the moment to ask him.

It was late, he had gone out and bought a laptop and was setting it up, they needed to make plans and he wanted to find out if Violet and Jamie were listed as missing persons. He remembered how quiet she had gone, sitting cross legged on the bed watching. He could feel her eyes on him, she was looking for something some sign that he had made a colossal mistake. He had smiled to himself; he was waiting for the question. He had left everyone to be with her, and she was worried what that meant. Was he going to be a dead weight of emotional responsibility around her neck? Fair question he thought.

"Why did you follow us, Lewis?"

The critical question had come at the wrong moment. "Hang on Violet, I'm just setting this up, in the middle of an important operation." He had tapped in the responses to set up the laptop. He needed to answer her, to reassure her. He looked up from the laptop and gave her a crooked smile, "Well a couple of reasons, one you're not a good swimmer and it would be on my conscience if… you know, the sharks. Two I was going to have to share the money with Scott and Helen… mm maybe that's number one and of course this girl," He threw her a blinding smile, "told me at the last possible moment that she was going to love me forever and I didn't want to miss out for one second."

Jamie sighed, would those two ever stop looking at each other like that. He rolled his eyes at them, "Fish and chips," he said suddenly, "that's what I remember, and the platoon leader marching us off to the toilet block to change into those terrible clothes."

"Ha, we looked a mess," said Violet.

Lewis smiled, he remembered Violet in the baggy shorts, no shoes and the jacket down to her knees.

"But not a mess for long," said Lewis, "Monk kept his word, we got the money."

When Lewis left them at the toilet block and walked into the Island's supermarket and pushed the credit card into the only ATM on the island, he shouted with relief. It was there, more than twenty million Australian dollars. It saved them that night and they had used the money carefully. It had built the house they lived in and started their renewable energy business.

"Okay, let's get this show happening," said Lewis. "That sounds like the caterers. Jamie show them where to set up."

"I'm glad we're having it here," said Violet sliding the doors back to the veranda; the sun was an hour away from touching the ocean. "Just us and our friends."

They had invited twenty people they had met through their work; people who shared the same vision for the future. They had been cautious at first, kept a low profile, moved far up the coast. When they found out that Mona had sold the house and disappeared, they knew they were safe.

"Okay, all sorted," said Jamie, "Can't wait to get the mushy bit over and start eating,"

"Nothing we do is mushy," said Lewis, "It's serious stuff."

"Okay take your word for it Captain," said Jamie looking at his watch, "but talking of serious stuff I need a word with both of you now. In the study."

"What?" Violet frowned.

"Come on," He walked down the hall towards the front of the house. He looked at his watch again, the timing was critical.

He shut the door behind them, "Sit there Lewis, he pointed to a chair in front of his laptop. Violet, you stand here, need you both in the camera."

Violet rested her hand on Lewis's shoulders. She smiled at his reflection in the screen and raised her eyebrows. Jamie studied his watch, and the screen suddenly lit up, it looked like a hailstorm.

"Getting something!" said Jamie. "Okay, Jamie calling, ready to receive you over."

The screen seemed to wobble, the hailstorm became snow, the snow cleared a face appeared.

"Dad! Oh god, is that you dad?" Lewis leant forward in his seat, "Dad, I can see you, can…"

John waved at him, his smile a mile wide, "See you son and lovely Violet, you look beautiful Violet. Lewis you've grown and Jamie"

"Hi," said Jamie.

"I've got someone else here to say hello," said John, he looked off screen somewhere and Scott's head appeared.

"Hey man, looking good you two, congratulations. Helen, get here and say hello." Helen's head appeared she waved at them.

"Man, oh man," said Lewis. "How have you done this?"

"Rochester's Sixty-six, Jamie worked out the last nineteen." Scott held up his watch to the screen.

"We've been working on it for the last six months, wanted to wish you all the best. Now we're both first class officers, never know when you might see us. I'll let you talk to your dad." Scott gave a thumbs up.

"Dad I can't believe this, I never thought…" he shook his head. "So good to see you dad. I've missed you…I'm sorry."

"No, you're where you should be son and today proves it. I've told your mum…she's good, she's travelling somewhere…but would be good if we could do this again with your mum."

"Yeh can do," said Jamie, "going to lose transmission any moment."

"Ok, love you dad."

"Look after each other you two, we'll do this again."

The screen went blank. Violet squeezed Lewis's shoulder, he had his head down, his hand over his eyes. "Man, oh man, Jamie," he choked back a sob, "You're a fucking Einstein."

***

"It was a wonderful wedding Lewis, can we do it again?" Violet fell back on the bed. She rolled over to face the bathroom door, Lewis was in the shower, she rested her cheek on her elbow. He was good to look at. He had a swimmer's shoulders and a runner's legs. "Just perfect," she said.

Lewis pulled the shower screen back, "You looking at me again?"

"Cat can look at the King," she smiled and stretched her arms above her head.

"What does that even mean?" he said, stretching his damp body alongside hers and pulling down the straps of her dress.

She sat up, "Wait, you'll make it wet. I'll want to wear it again for my next wedding."

"Such a tease Violet Mack...whatever your name is."

She threw her dress onto the floor and turned to face him. "I suppose it could be Green." She lay on top of him.

"You packed for tomorrow?" he said.

"Yes, I'm packed," Violet groaned, "the Uber is picking us up at 5.30am. It's too early.'

"I'll make you breakfast," he said sliding his fingers down to her hips and hooking his fingers in her silk pants. She put her hands over his and pushed them down.

"Have you packed?" she said reaching her hand down to touch him.

"Uh huh, mmm,"

"Warm clothes like I told you. It's winter in Scotland snow, ice, really cold." She flicked her tongue across his lips.

"Jamie's still working out the itinerary. I can't wait to see my grandparents again." She kissed him hard and threaded her fingers through his hair. "Oh," she groaned into his mouth. She pulled away holding herself up on one elbow. "What do you think" she said her green eyes sparkling in the light of the lamp.

He closed his eyes and pulled her close. He didn't answer.

"Lewis?"

"What do I think about what?" He said pressing his lips into her neck.

"My surname, Green or Mackenzie."

He didn't have to think about that. "Mackenzie, you're a Mackenzie. We can both be Mackenzie."

"You'd change your name?"

"Yeh sure, Green's not my name. Changed universes for you, change a name. Hey, got a better idea." He placed his hands under her shoulders and lifted her head so he could see her eyes.

"How about we change our name to Darcy and you can call me...what was his name..?" he closed his eyes as he fought to remember the name of one of his nemesis, "Fitzwilliam," he said almost triumphantly. "Fitzwilliam Darcy," he nodded his head and looked thoughtful as though he was trying on the name for size. "Yeh you could call me…Fitz I'd like that."

Violet couldn't read the steady look he was giving her. "You're not serious, are you?"

"But one word from you," he said rolling her onto her back and stopping any more discussion on the topic.

Acknowledgements

To my first readers, Leah, Jo B, Julie, Lea, Lois and Sophie— thank you for stepping into this story when it was still finding its voice. Your quiet encouragement has been invaluable.

To my sister Susan, my number one fan and fiercest cheerleader — your unwavering support and enthusiasm have meant more than I can say. You reminded me why I started, and why I kept going.

About The Author

Joy Taylor was born in the UK and now lives in Perth, WA.

She's been a high school teacher, teaching English and Maths, and is now a lawyer representing children in the Western Australian Family Court. When she's not writing YA novels she likes to paint, hang out with her family and walk her dog.